THE KINSHIP
OF SECRETS

Center Point
Large Print

**This Large Print Book carries the
Seal of Approval of N.A.V.H.**

THE
Kinship *of* Secrets

A Novel

EUGENIA KIM

CENTER POINT LARGE PRINT
THORNDIKE, MAINE

This Center Point Large Print edition
is published in the year 2019 by arrangement with
Houghton Mifflin Harcourt Publishing Company.

The text of this Large Print edition is unabridged.
In other aspects, this book may vary
from the original edition.
Printed in the United States of America
on permanent paper.
Set in 16-point Times New Roman type.

ISBN: 978-1-64358-229-0

Library of Congress Cataloging-in-Publication Data

Names: Kim, Eugenia (Eugenia SunHee), author.
Title: The kinship of secrets / Eugenia Kim.
Description: Center Point Large Print edition. | Thorndike, Maine :
    Center Point Large Print, 2018.
Identifiers: LCCN 2019014557 | ISBN 9781643582290 (hardcover :
    alk. paper)
Subjects: LCSH: Sisters—Fiction. | Families—Korea (South)—Fiction. |
    Families—United States—Fiction. | Large type books.
Classification: LCC PS3611.I453 K56 2018b | DDC 813/.6—dc23
LC record available at https://lccn.loc.gov/2019014557

For Sun Kim

THE KINSHIP
OF SECRETS

PART I

WAR

1950–1953

1

Invasion

On a chilly summer night, a newsmonger trudged uphill to a residential enclave of Seoul, the last neighborhood on his route. By the dim light of his lantern swinging atop a bamboo pole, he checked his watch, clacked his wooden clappers three times, and, with the crystalline tones of his nighttime newscast, sang, "Attention, please, attention. Tuesday, twenty-seven June, three-thirty a.m. The North Korean People's Army retreats after our heroic counter-offensive in Uijongbu. Enemy tanks were destroyed, and our forces have mobilized to repulse the enemy all the way to the Yalu River. President Rhee urges the people of Korea to trust our military without being unsettled in the least, to carry on with their daily work and support military operations. Attention, please, attention."

His call echoed against the bulky profile of a Western-style house, where Inja, nearly four years old, lived with her maternal uncle, aunt, grandparents, as well as a cook and her teenaged daughter. Though it was the hour of dreams, Inja slept hard and still, her steady breaths matching

11

those of her grandmother snuggled in the bedding beside her. The day before, Inja had accompanied Uncle downtown to read posted news bulletins, and his strained and rapid stride elevated her fear of things she didn't understand—*communists, invasion*—and had exhausted her.

Inja's dreams, both waking and sleeping, were often fanciful visions of her parents and her year-older sister in America. Having been left behind in Korea when she was a baby, Inja had no concrete memory of her family. They appeared to her as shadow people, their smiles as still as the few photographs they sent. To animate their grainy black-and-white features into an idea of *mother, father,* and *sister,* her imagination blurred them into amorphous shapes—loving, said Uncle, and generous, as proven by the monthly packages they sent—ghost people to whom she was bound.

Yesterday, Uncle and Aunt argued fiercely about the merits or foolhardiness of leaving their home and fleeing south. Inja had thought the mystifying and controversial *invasion* could be an exciting change of routine, and though she had no say in the decision to stay or go, she longed for adventure. Already her shadow sister had journeyed halfway across the world, while she herself had gone nowhere.

A dry wind carried the newsmonger's song into their yard on his return trip down the hill,

and Inja woke. She heard a pop of electricity—
Uncle turning on the lightbulb dangling from the
ceiling in his sitting room. Its blue glare streamed
down the hallway, and his feet padded out to the
porch. Her uncle was a calligrapher who created
newspaper mastheads and banner headlines,
so he had many contacts in the news business.
Whirring crickets muffled Uncle's queries to
the man on the street. Inja opened her eyes wide
as if it would help her to hear better. No strand
of morning light yet touched the shutters. She
slid out of the bedding, careful to not disturb
Grandmother, crept into the long side room that
was the hub of the house, and peeked out the
front door.

In the darkness, Uncle ran straight into her.
"Umph! *Yah,* why are you up? Are you okay?
Let's see that nose."

Startled tears sprang from her eyes, but she
smiled and rubbed her nose to say she was
unhurt. "What did the man say? Are we going on
a trip?"

"Heedless ears make heedless thoughts," said
Uncle. He crouched to meet her eyes in the
shadows cast by the bedroom light.

She stepped into his open arms and his ready
hug. With such protection, *invasion* couldn't possibly harm her. "Will we all go together?"

"I'll talk it over with *Harabeoji.*" Since Uncle
didn't say no and discussions with Grandfather

usually meant he'd made up his mind, she was certain they would go. A sliver of glee shivered down her back, and she hopped out of his hug. "I can pack all by myself. I can help with *Halmeoni.*" Inja could keep her tiny Grandmother's cane ready when she wanted to stand, or fetch her Bible, a clean pair of socks—whatever she needed.

"Don't disturb her. You go back to sleep, and I'll wake you if we decide to go. And if we do, it's only for a short while."

"Okay." She returned to her room. Uncle was lax with discipline, but Inja had grown dutiful under the rough watch of her strict aunt and a stern command or two from her grandparents. Back in bed, with the pulse of Grandmother's breath in her ear, she lay wide awake and listened to unintelligible talk between the men, and soon a rising volume of complaints from Aunt. With such fights frequent in their house, Inja had learned to muffle the bitter tones and ugly words by diverting her attention to making lists, some-times of what came in the last package from America, what clothes had been distributed, what candy had been devoured, what new words she'd learned from reading newspapers with Uncle, or the quirky things Yun—her nanny, who was Cook's thirteen-year-old daughter—did that made her laugh. She created an imaginary list of what she would pack.

14

Bible picture book from Mother, my
  favorite of everything
Blue KEDS sneakers from Mother (I
  copied those letters from the blue rubber
  label at the heel)
Socks and clothes

She ran her hand over the pressed linen surface of her Bible storybook, always nearby, and
fingered its borders tooled with gold swashes.
As high and wide as her chest and as thick as
three fingers, it required both arms to carry it.
If she took the book, little else would fit into a
small bundle for their journey, so she sat against
the wall and thought about all the things from
the American packages she'd have to leave
behind, all the gifts from her mother and father
and sister. These items lay on a corner shelf
nearby, and as the room grayed with dawn,
their silhouettes made it easier for her to inventory.

Pink rubber ball
Small doll with yellow hair and moving
  arms and legs
American flag on a chopstick-sized stick
A miniature spoon with words etched in
  its bowl
Bamboo flute
Shiny wrappers from candy and gum

A brooch made of pompoms, shaped like
a poodle (a strange American dog)
Card of hairpins with a picture of a pretty
girl with brown curls
Coloring book, all done, and six crayons
(Yun was better at staying inside the
lines)
Woolen scarf with mittens knitted onto
the ends (no one liked it because it was
red)

Cross-legged on the floor, she opened the Bible
book to feel the glossy leaves of its illustrations.
It was too dark to see, but she'd studied them for
so many hours, she could guess what image was
beneath her fingers by the bulk of pages in each
hand. They were vivid and unforgettable, and
from memorizing what her uncle said about the
captions, she had learned what *Fear* looked like,
and *Greed, Sin, Pride,* and *Envy.* It did not have
a picture of *Communist Invasion,* but she thought
their forthcoming journey might mirror how the
Chosen People had crossed the sea floor while
God held the raging waters back.

Inja leaned against the wall and fell asleep to
sounds of activity in the kitchen and in an outside
shed, where an oxcart had been stored since the
war with Japan before she was born.

And on the other side of the city, the newsmonger snuffed his lantern in the dim gray

before sunrise, noting a strange red glow beneath darkening clouds on the horizon. He pocketed his clackers and frowned at the teletype saying that the gains he'd just reported were lost. He conferred with his editor, who relayed the rumor that President Rhee had fled Seoul by train overnight to Suwon. But the editor also said they would not alarm the populace with confusing news of battles—or presidential flight. The newsmonger rubbed his eyes and went home to soak his feet.

2

Red-Letter Day

That Tuesday morning in Washington, DC, the muggy summer sun rose in a clear sky, geraniums emitted their bitter fragrance, and bluets beckoned under bushes lining the lawns of quaint houses in the suburb of Takoma Park. Miran, age four and a half, and her mother pushed an old perambulator uphill, containing a package bound for relatives in Korea. Miran had been lucky with this package. Her mother doubted if their relatives would like the licorice in Good & Plenty (two for a nickel on sale at Safeway), and she'd given one of the boxes of candy to Miran. The child was jealous of the bright-colored gifts and even the old toys packed inside the cartons going to Korea. Once a month she helped her mother send another box or two overseas. Miran flattened grocery bags to wrap the cartons and ran strips of gummed tape over a wet sponge in a saucer. Her mother wrapped the packages with the bags, tape, and twine, using Miran's finger to help tie the knot.

Miran steadied the package angled in the stroller, and the candy box rattled pleasantly inside the pocket of her twill skirt. She sucked the pink-and-white sugar coating off each piece, and when her mother wasn't paying attention, she spit out the pungent chewy center onto the grass median.

Miran accompanied her mother, Najin, to the post office to act as go-between at the mailman's window. They had come to America two years ago and had planned to return last summer—so Najin hadn't studied English quite as diligently as she might have—but Miran had contracted scarlet fever and was quarantined in the hospital for weeks. Then, last fall Najin had lost a baby. Miran didn't understand what that meant, except an ambulance came for her mother. Miran had spent the night with the next-door neighbor and was babysat there a week of afternoons following nursery school and also evenings while her father visited the hospital.

She liked the neighbor, Mrs. Bushong, who talked with a twang: "a Virginia countrywoman," her father had said. Mrs. Bushong fed Miran hot dogs and fried bologna sandwiches, and showed her how to make Jell-O. She was allowed to play with Mrs. Bushong's collection of salt and pepper shakers. Miran's favorite was the black-and-white plastic toast in a silver toaster with a spring lever that really worked.

The other thing she knew about losing a baby was that her father had taken the sofa cushions outside to hose them down, and after they'd dried, he covered the blotchy stains with a purple-and-green crocheted afghan.

She'd been allowed a single visit to her mother at the hospital, and its arid hallways of polished linoleum and nurses in squeaky shoes brought back memories of being sick herself, and of waking at odd hours to always find her mother on the chair beside her bed in the isolation ward. When Miran had visited her mother at the hospital, Najin looked pale and smelled funny, but she'd given her a lollipop. Leaving the hospital, Miran asked her father what did it mean to lose a baby; was it like leaving her sister in Korea? He said nothing and took her to the water fountain to wash her sticky fingers with his handkerchief, and she wondered if he was sick, too, since he coughed and his eyes were wet.

Miran didn't remember Korea, but she did remember getting lost on the ship crossing over. She had wandered the gray metal passageways for hours, looking for her father, who had berthed with the men. She'd heard her mother often tell that story to dinner guests about how worried they were and their joy at finding her. Najin was an animated and passionate storyteller, and prone to tears when talking about Miran's sister and the relatives to whom they sent packages. To push around remains of uneaten food—kimchi stew or mushrooms—meant her mother would invoke this sister's name: *Finish eating—Inja would love every bite of this*. When she spent the night at her friend Sarah Kim's house, she heard a different refrain from Mrs. Kim if she abandoned her peas—that children were starving in China—which made equal sense to implying her leftovers could save people so far away; the only way you could reach them was to dig a hole straight through the earth.

Miran held the heavy post office door open for her mother, and they rolled inside with scrapes and squeaks. Relieved there were no other customers who would coo over the "adorable Chinese girl" and pat her hair, she stepped with confidence to their favorite mailman. He knew their routine and wouldn't need her help to explain what kind of service her mother wanted and how much insurance to buy.

"Good morning, Mrs. Cho and little Miss Cho. One for sea mail?" He weighed the package, accepted the customs declarations and insurance forms Najin had filled out in advance, and he pushed a bowl filled with peppermints closer to the edge of the counter for Miran. Their task was completed with no undue attention drawn to them, no incident of language or writing misunderstood, no need to explain they were from Korea, a peninsula between China and Japan, or that she was almost five years old and would attend kindergarten in September.

On their walk home, Najin admired the irises and blooming dogwoods in people's gardens. "There are no flower gardens like this at home," she said, "just vegetables and beans—things to eat." She spoke to her daughter in Korean, and Miran answered in English.

The Good & Plenty box scraped against the cellophane-wrapped peppermint in Miran's pocket. To please her mother and gain permission to eat the second candy, she said, "Look, *Umma*, dandelions. Should we pick some for *Appa*'s dinner?"

Najin smiled. "It's too late now—they're too tough, but we have squash flowers blooming in the backyard, and I'll show you how to make soup. And yes, you may open the peppermint."

Awed at her mother's ability to read her mind, Miran worked her tongue around the sweet-sharp treat and swallowed happily. "Umma, that's two candies today—it's a red-letter day!"

"All that sugar means you'll be skipping around the yard like a rabbit," she said. "And what does it mean, *a red-letter day?* Like a *valentine?* Did you learn that at school?"

"From Mrs. Bushong. She said it's for a holiday or birthday you write in your calendar in red ink to make it special. Will you put it in your notebook?" The only things her mom collected were American sayings—"colloquialisms," said her father—in her diary, translating their funny

23

literal meaning along with their implied meaning. Most were heard from their family friend Miss Edna Lone, an expressive woman whom they'd met on the Pacific crossing. A former missionary, she was fluent in Korean. She attended their church occasionally, came to dinner often, and uttered such outlandish things as *Katy, bar the door; dollars to donuts; happy as a clam; over my dead body; kit and caboodle; easy as pie; it's a piece of cake;* and many horse idioms: *don't look a gift horse in the mouth; straight from the horse's mouth; hold your horses; if wishes were horses, beggars would ride.*

Miran felt smart with her mom's colloquialism collection, since she could explain the sayings she'd heard in school and at the grocery store. "It's like when Miss Lone comes to dinner, it's a red-letter day," she said.

"I see. It's a good saying but has an opposite meaning at home. To write someone's name in red ink in the family register means they've died."

They turned the corner toward home, quiet, and neared their small front yard edged with hedges. Najin said, "You mustn't forget your language; we'll go home soon—perhaps later this year."

Miran ignored her; she'd heard this so often it had lost its meaning. It meant her mother was missing her family, primarily the baby—her little sister—left behind, but Miran was thinking about the baby they'd lost at the hospital and how the water had run as red as a valentine when her father had hosed off the brown stains on the sofa cushions.

On this companionable walk home in the bright morning, even while planning squash soup for Miran's father, they couldn't have known that at that moment at the Voice of America he was poring over the AP, UP, and BCC teletypes. Calvin Cho worked as a translator and broadcaster at the VOA Korean Service during the week, in addition to his pastoral duties at the Korean church. As the teletypes ticked, Calvin juggled the shifting reports of attacks, counteroffensives, retreats, impasses—and worse, his own fears about his daughter living in Seoul with his in-laws. He hadn't told Najin about the North Korean invasion earlier because he assumed the action would end up being another inconsequential skirmish. But now he feared the worst, God forbid, a communist aggression that could slide into a devastating nuclear world war. This news was too important and fraught with miscommunication for a telephone call; he would tell Najin about the invasion when he got home at dawn. She would be frantic with worry about Inja and her family in Seoul, and he would have to give her assurances that—except for his enduring faith in God's mercy—he didn't have.

3

Southbound Journey

Tuesday morning in Seoul, the sun rose to light the way for a trickle of people leaving their homes, soon to join like-minded travelers on the main road to the train station and other points farther south. Smoke fringed the northern skyline above the hills, deceptively graceful tendrils billowing from missiles and fires lit by the invading Red Army. Worry creased the brows of those who saw the dark clouds, and rumors swirled as the day progressed. Soon, hundreds upon hundreds of Seoul's citizens mobbed the roadway, all fleeing south to perceived safety. A wave of confusion marked by shouts surged from the left, and hysteria seemed to balloon until a man bellowed, "Calm down! Panic won't move you any faster!" The refugees settled down and trudged one foot before the other, men's backs and women's heads laden with bundles, suitcases, urns—all manner of valued possessions.

Amidst the thickening crowd, a two-wheeled oxcart piled high with the Han family belongings juddered on the dirt road. Inja perched on its front ledge, and her pant legs snagged splinters on the rough pine. Her uncle held the position of the ox, the cart shaft tethered with a rope harness around his chest, his shoulders and legs the primary source of locomotion. Aunt and Grandfather each carried a basket of provisions strapped to their backs and pushed from behind. Grandmother sat atop. To see the scores of refugees allowed Uncle his righteous harrumph to Aunt that the decision to leave was well supported, but their sluggish pace allowed Aunt her righteous argument for staying home.

They neared the main paved road, and Uncle strained against the ropes into the turn. The cart slid into a rut and jostled its cargo. Something thudded into Inja's back and shot her face down in the dirt. A wheel spun out of its rut and gained speed inches from her head. She screamed. The wheel groaned over clods of dirt a finger's width from her hair, and she tasted dust, a millstone crushing bone. Her own cries, mixed with Uncle's shouts, sounded far away. He grabbed her and drew her to his chest, his body wedged against the cart. Grandfather tugged from the rear and Aunt snatched wooden blocks and chocked the wheels. The crowd parted around their rickety wood island with its mountain of bundles. Grandmother hung on to a rope with one hand, the other covering the fear she held in her mouth.

Inja's arms clamped around Uncle's neck, and her legs strangled his waist as her tears soaked his shirt. He hugged her hard and squeezed between the cart and the sea of refugees to deposit her next to Grandfather. She leaned against her grandfather's thighs and was moored by his newspaper-and-tobacco smell, his long artist's fingers firm on her shoulders. Uncle climbed on the cart, untied its crisscrossed rope, and handed a domed iron pot to Aunt. "Not that," Aunt said. "That's the best one."

"The other one's buried. She'll sit up here with Halmeoni. Carry the pot or leave it behind."

"Inja can sit on it—she's small enough to sit inside. She should've held on tighter. We shouldn't have left home— this awful crowd!"

"Yah, do you want to carry the pot or your niece?"

Inja hid her face in her grandfather's *hanbok*, his Korean gentlemen's clothes, and he patted her shoulder.

"I'm already loaded like a mule," said Aunt, snatching the cook pot. "We can't leave it—she can carry it in her lap."

"Woman! Then tie it to the shaft, but leave me enough rope."

At the front of the cart, Aunt threaded rope through the pot handles, griping. "We've already been walking an hour. Who can keep up with all these people shoving and pushing? We'll never make it to Suwon like this. Didn't I say we should've stayed home? The hardship! Traveling

29

with two old folks and a child who isn't even ours. And what about the servants—a woman and her skinny brat at home—so who's going to protect our house, and who can trust the president, and why should we trust that you know where you're going . . ."

"Enough!" said Grandfather, a scolding so rare it stopped her rant.

Uncle hefted Inja high next to Grandmother, who tucked her hand with Inja's under the rope. "Thank God, you're safe. Hold tight and you'll be fine," she said, hard consonants hissing through lips weakened from last year's stroke. "We ride like royalty, eh? Usually an all-day walk to Suwon."

Inja welcomed the warmth of Grandmother's hand. "Why are we going to Suwon?"

"There are rumors that President Rhee moved the government to that city, so we will all be safe there."

"Where will we sleep?" Inja said.

Grandmother's smile deepened the intricate web of wrinkles around her eyes. "Your mother once worked at an orphanage near there. The *jeon* you give at church feeds those poor little orphans. The man in charge is an old family friend."

"Will we meet the orphans?" Inja had never met an orphan. Were they dirty and scrawny like the kids on the roadside who begged and scratched their lice-filled hair—or did they look a little like her? Earlier in the spring, a teenage boy in her Sunday school had called her an orphan as if it were a dirty word. The children were playing team tag during the grownups' fellowship hour. Inja's teammates trapped this boy in a circle and she tagged him, but he said it didn't count to be tagged by a mongrel orphan. Everyone laughed, and Inja said that she *did too* have parents—but her throat burned. Their teacher also heard him and forced him to apologize, but Inja had heard the sneer in his "sorry."

"Yes, we'll visit the children," said Grandmother, "and though we aren't at all rich, you'll see how much poorer they are. They may crowd around you and stare, so be polite and treat them nicely."

Inja blurted, "Will they know we've gone to Suwon?"

"Your mother and father?" said Grandmother in her usual considered way.

Inja nodded. She knew the question made little sense, but she worried about the thread between her parents and herself and how easily it frayed to nothing. Days, even weeks would pass before she thought about her family in America until a letter or a package came. She was just a baby when her parents had taken her older sister, Miran, to America with them. They were supposed to come back soon but never did.

"I'll write to your mother when we get to

Suwon," said Grandmother. "We'll stay a week, two at most." All her wrinkles curled in her smile. "Even if your mother doesn't know where you are at this moment, God always knows."

Inja hid a frown. Grandmother said this often enough to make her uncomfortable, like God was a mosquito bite one forgot about until it itched again. When adults asked her if she missed her mother and father, she readily said, "Yes," but surely God knew she didn't have an answer. Would he think she was lying? Perhaps he understood that she didn't know what it meant to miss one's parents.

Grandmother tucked Inja's hair around her ear. "Your mother may not know exactly where you are or what you're doing, but she has you in her heart always. She prays for you and knows you're safe with family."

This oft-repeated sentiment soothed Inja deeper now than when Grandmother expressed it after a package from America was delivered. She curled her hand into her grandmother's dry and scratchy palm.

The cart creaked and lumbered to the rhythm of Uncle's stalwart shoulders and able legs making way through the crowd. Inja relaxed at her higher vantage point and counted the princess trees rising above roadside walls, the sweet perfume of their bell-shaped flowers wafting amongst the smells of sweaty people, tobacco, and sewage.

Though a few vendors hawked cigarettes and whatnot, most shops were shuttered and gates padlocked, unusual for a weekday morning. She shifted her bottom and admired her blue KEDS sneakers in the sunlight. They brought to mind her pre-dawn inventory of the things her mother had sent her and what she'd left behind, and she remembered whom they'd left behind as well.

"I miss Cook and Yun. I wish we didn't have to leave them," she said.

Her grandmother sighed in answer. The warm air whirled with noise—shuffles, snatches of words, babies crying, complaints, hums, the creaking cart. "Your mother didn't want to leave you, either," said Grandmother.

Inja's eyes opened wide. Perhaps because we choose to be ignorant about things we most fear, she had never before considered to ask why she hadn't gone to America, too.

"You should know this." Grandmother's eyes shifted to an unknowable distance, as if to gather words from the past. "It would have been a difficult overseas journey with two babies, your sister just out of diapers and you just weaned. They promised to return in a year or two, but I had a premonition before they left that I would never again see your mother or you two girls. Your sister was a sickly baby and had almost died—"

Inja's ears grew as alert as a rabbit's. "Is that when she had the scarlet fever?" She remembered that story because she'd imagined her sister as a little red girl.

"No." Her lips softened. "This is a story about you. I had a dream."

Inja's family attended to their dreams. In the letter that came with the Bible storybook, her mother had described a dream she had when pregnant with Inja, foretelling that she would be a girl. Her mother had learned to be alert to her dreams during her fourth month of pregnancy because Grandmother's own fourth-month pregnancy dreams had accurately predicted her children's gender.

Among the sea of heads, baskets, and bundles surrounding them on the road, Grandmother said, "The dream was troublesome and I prayed for guidance. I was in a factory filled with broken looms and spindles. There were no workers, and though the machines' arms were split in pieces, the looms clacked and the spindles spun on their own—so noisy I couldn't hear my footsteps. But I could hear a baby crying and knew it was you. The racket grew louder, as did your cries, and I was in a panic to know which way to turn. I woke up then and thought little of it. But when I fell back asleep, and for the next two nights, I dreamed the same thing, and each time my panic grew until I woke to find tears on my cheeks."

Inja sat still, her round eyes wide.

"Yes, dreams are sometimes more real than life. If something worries you for days, you must free it from your heart before it becomes the splinter that festers into a wound. Do you understand?"

She nodded. She'd seen the crown of thorns piercing Jesus's bleeding heart in her Bible story-book.

"I told your mother and we prayed together for many days, and she decided Miran should go, but you should stay with us."

The cart jolted and Grandmother grabbed Inja's knee, but both sat securely. The crowd surged around them.

"So don't blame your parents," said Grandmother. "It was as much my doing as theirs."

The many questions this story raised only increased Inja's confusion. How did the decision rise from the dream? She also hadn't known that blame was deserved, or even how to blame parents who were ghost people. Perhaps if she'd been older than the child she was atop that cart, she could've vocalized what lay inside her unformed heart: what did this half-told story mean? Why her sister, Miran, rather than herself? Everybody wanted to go to America. *Mountains of gold, streets strewn with coins, heaven on earth* were the sayings, though her mother wrote that it wasn't at all true.

Grandmother closed her eyes, and Inja held her

hand to ensure she wouldn't topple over as she dozed. With her grandmother's warmth beside her, her confusion subsided. She had everything she needed.

4

Duck and Cover

In the kitchen Miran and her mother ate lunch by themselves after Calvin called to say he'd be working a double shift. Miran was glad because they would save the awful-colored squash-blossom soup for when he came home that night. He usually worked the night shift at the Voice of America, coming home early in the morning to sleep until after lunch. But he hadn't come home at all that morning, and phone calls were exchanged between her parents. This in itself was unusual—her father rarely called home because of the cost—and though the calls were short, her mother's initial shout, then her terse Korean alerted Miran to unknown tensions.

So when Najin brought her sewing to the sofa beside the big shortwave radio, Miran asked if she needed help threading needles. "Yah, good girl." Her mom gave her the pincushion and a spool of green thread. "This is for you and your sister." She displayed two cotton dresses.

Miran hated green, Najin's favorite color, but she said, "They're pretty. We'll be like twins." She would appreciate having a sister at home, and a twin would be a bonus. Would it be like talking to oneself in the mirror? Miran never talked to her mirror image—too shy even to talk to herself out loud.

On the couch she rearranged the pinheads on the tomato-shaped pincushion to make pleasing concentric circles, but her mother didn't notice.

Najin said, "Your sister is so far away, we worry. There's trouble in Korea."

She didn't know how to ask about her father's phone calls, or why they'd worry—her sister had always been far away. She knew what it meant to be in trouble—playing too loudly or straying too far to hear being called. But she couldn't imagine what kind of trouble Korea could be in, so she squinted her eyes and licked the end of the thread. The radio was tuned to her father's VOA station, and when her mother turned up the volume, she heard his melodious formal Korean, tinny through the speaker. "Is that Daddy?"

"Yes, but this is a rebroadcast. It's nighttime in Korea, and he's not on air right now. I wanted to hear the news; I missed hearing about the invasion, or I heard it and thought it was nothing—though it's nothing for you to worry about." But her mother sounded jittery, almost angry.

Miran's uneven comprehension of her mother's sentences, plus what meaning she discerned from tone, combined with the building strain of

38

the day to yield a pervasive sense of dread. She wished her fluent-in-English father was home so she could ask if the Russians were going to attack with atomic bombs. Every morning in nursery school before milk-and-cookies and recess, a siren blared from a flagpole on the playground for the atomic air-raid drill. The teacher would yell, "Drop!" and all the children would crawl under their desks, fold up their bodies, hands behind necks, until minutes passed and the siren sputtered to silence. At first she thought it was a game, but by winter she'd seen the Bert the Turtle filmstrip called "Duck and Cover," and she grew afraid. Flying glass, rampant fire, walls collapsing—she hustled under the desk, her mind filled with images of mayhem like in the paintings of Hell found in the art books on the shelf below the shortwave.

Calvin came home midafternoon and had a short but intense talk with Najin, his tones soothing though officious. Najin turned and said to Miran in an angry voice, "Your father and I will get the laundry. You stay inside." Miran was certain she hadn't done anything to make her mother so angry as to be red in the face, so she sneaked into her parents' bedroom to peek out the window into the backyard, wondering if her father would get a scolding. They were taking shirts and towels from the clothesline, and her mother's voice rose and fell, impassioned and questioning, against his steady, placating tones. Then her mother snatched a washcloth from the clothesline so suddenly the clothespins popped off. She covered her face with it, and her shoulders shook. Witnessing this strange behavior made Miran both afraid and guilty, and she hurried back to the living room to tidy up the sewing notions.

Calvin went to bed until suppertime. Later at the dinner table, he asked Miran what she did that day but wasn't focused on her answer. He launched into a prolonged conversation with her mother, and Miran grasped that their relatives were in trouble, not because they'd done any-thing wrong, but because Korea was fighting with itself. Sometimes her father lapsed into English, as he often did when repeating himself, and she heard, "Your brother knows better. He's lived through war, and he'll stay put," and, "I'm sure she's safe. He would've telegraphed if there was need." Her mother's tone in response was scornful and impatient.

She wondered if it meant more packages would be sent, checks in airmail envelopes, telegrams, or the most costly means of communication—an overseas telephone call that took hours, some-times a day, to execute. Her mother ate little, not even the ugly soup she'd reheated, nor did she chastise Miran for not touching hers. Miran would wait until she had her father alone doing the dishes together as they always did. But he went back to bed after dinner, and she and her mother put away the food and cleaned the kitchen without talking.

Najin pulled down the ironing board from its kitchen cubby and ironed Calvin's shirts, while Miran matched and bundled socks beside the laundry baskets in the living room. She wanted to sneak into her parents' bedroom to ask him what was happening, but a mantle of silence had permeated the house, a silence only penetrable by a language she didn't have.

5

Flowers

The sun at midafternoon cast short shadows among the people heading south. The crowd grew thicker than before, and its earlier mood of panic had dulled, as if the air itself were tired. Inja woke from her nap, her neck complaining, saliva pooled beneath her tongue. She was hungry and noticed Grandmother shifting in a way that indicated she might need the bedpan. Inja's mother had sent this stellar example of American ingenuity after learning about Grandmother's stroke.

Uncle's back was bent and sweaty with exertion from an uphill climb. When they reached a level crossing, he unwound the ropes, stretched his arms and shoulders, and stood on the cart shaft to scan the vista ahead. Inja sat tall to see what he saw. People and their bundles filled the down-hill road far ahead to a turn toward the railroad station and the bridges that crossed the Han River. Whirling dust and fumes of heavy vehicles clouded the distance, and the canvas tops of army trucks showed them attempting to maneuver upstream through the mass exodus. More people joined the main artery from side streets, the women balancing huge bundles on their heads, the men carrying the most surprising things lashed to the A-frames on their backs: a chest of drawers, a bag of grain twice the size of the carrier, a frail elder.

Grandmother gave Aunt a jug and gourd to dole out drinking water, and Uncle edged around the cart. "We should reconsider Suwon," he said to Grandfather. His firm stance was directed at Aunt, who would challenge him.

Inja settled closer to Grandmother to have a lap to hide in should they begin fighting, but Grandfather said, "What's your thinking, son?" and thus closed the possibility of criticism. The old man, a vigorous seventy, commanded the respect his age required. A few wisps of gray circled the back of Grandfather's head like a victor's laurel, and his goatee was as stiff and white as the traditional clothes he wore. He had fewer wrinkles than Grandmother though he was ten years older, and no liver spots on his cheeks like other elders at church. Inja had once heard Aunt whispering to Cook that Grandfather wasn't wrinkled because he was a lazy man who had never worked a day in his life. Inja was so shocked and ashamed to have heard such a declaration about a revered elder that she couldn't even weigh its truth.

"Let's avoid Suwon altogether and cross at the ferry." Uncle tapped the cart. "That chaos ahead looks impossible for this beast. We'll go through the alleys to the fire station and take the hills behind Itaewon to the river." Itaewon housed the army hospital and garrison.

"Lose the cow, then fix the stable, eh?" said Aunt, taunting with a proverb.

"The cart will be worse at the bridge with these crowds," said Grandfather, silencing Aunt. "The ferry's a good idea, and we can get news at Itaewon."

Though Inja regretted not getting to meet the orphans, she hoped to see the handsome uniformed soldiers performing their military exercises when they passed the base.

"I'm thinking Gwangju by way of Seongnam."

Grandfather nodded and the decision was made.

With much shouting and pleas of forbearance, they pushed and dragged the cart to the nearest alley. The narrow lanes, broken cobbles, and rugged dried mud made the cart sway and buck, but they soon turned a corner where the only crowds were dogs rooting in trash heaps and gullies. After a maze of backyard walls, they stopped near a patch of bamboo, and Inja scrambled down to help Aunt carry Grandmother piggyback to the shade, then found the white enamel bedpan and the old blanket they'd use as a curtain.

Uncle changed his shirt and said he'd see how far they were from the ferry.

Aunt waved him off. "You'll get us lost again." She turned to Inja, her voice rising. "Did you sit on this?" She held a basket wrapped in cloth, the rice-and-barley balls Cook had prepared for their journey, now concave with the indentation of someone having sat on them.

Though it was Grandmother who'd sat on the food, Inja stiffened for the tongue-lashing, but Uncle said, "What does it matter? Leave her be." He smiled. "She only made it sweeter for us."

Adoration for her uncle flooded Inja's chest, and she wanted to run and hug his legs, but he turned and strode toward the river ferry. The family rested and ate, and Inja climbed on the cart to find her book. A streak of black screamed across the sky and crashed in a distant burst of thunder and smoke. Two others followed, farther away. Grandfather helped Inja clamber from the cart and sat her next to Aunt. "Stay close!" He skirted the walls to see better but came back shaking his head. Aunt tidied their belongings and readied a gourd of water and food for Uncle.

Uncle soon returned, his face grim. "The ferry's impossible." He ate the rice ball in a few bites and described the army's attempts to commandeer the ferry amid thousands of refugees thronging the dock. "They're bludgeoning their way to the river!" he said. "We were right to avoid the train station—that explosion means the city is breached."

Aunt gasped and Grandmother sighed, and a dart of fear pierced Inja's sense of adventure.

Uncle turned to her, his face changed by a smile. "But I saw Khang at the ferry. We'll go through the hills behind Itaewon, and he'll meet us there."

Inja's heart knocked to hear this name. Khang was the porter who toted the heavy American packages from the ferry to their house, with two, sometimes three cartons roped together on his A-frame. He spent his days at the Sobinggo ferry dock, waiting to be called for jobs that would earn him a few *jeon* a day. Once Uncle saw how Khang favored his niece, he designated him as their porter, an enormous privilege for a simple laborer, the likes of whom numbered hundreds at the dock, railroad station, and in the alleys of factories and back doors of businesses, all vying to transport any sort of load. Though his mouth stank from rotted teeth, Khang always carried a small flower tucked behind his ear—in winter, a feather or sprig of pine—which he would solemnly present to Inja after he'd plunked the cardboard packages on their porch. A giant man, his thighs were as thick as her waist, and his head as bald and brown as a chestnut. When she shook his hand to thank him for the honeysuckle sprig or dandelion, her entire hand, fingers wide, fit with room to spare within his calloused palm. His gnarled hands were rough, but his touch was gentle, and when he bent to speak to her, he always turned his mouth aside.

So to hear her uncle mention Khang filled her stomach with special warmth. Uncle was saying, "—and he knows a man with a raft behind the temple at Daehangang-ni, upriver two kilometers, for the right fee." Aunt patted her waistline where she'd tied a cloth belt thick with bills beneath her blouse, but Uncle said he had enough on hand, and they should leave.

Rested and with renewed urgency, the Han family made good time through the alleys until they came upon a dirt path that cut through the hilly woods behind Itaewon's army base. No one was about, and a foreboding quiet swept through a grassy meadow. They kept going until Inja saw a familiar form sauntering between the trees ahead.

"It's Khang!" She hopped down from the cart and ran. She hadn't realized how puny she'd felt until Goliath had joined their party. How could his massive size and strength not protect them from the Reds? When she neared, he bent to offer her a flowering quince branch he'd tucked in the back of his rope belt. Its fragrance, tangy and sweet, erased her apprehension, and she was grateful. He lifted her beside Grandmother, who reached to smell the persimmon-colored flowers. The men conferred in hushed tones. Khang shouldered the ropes beside Uncle, and the two pulled the cart at a brisk pace for the remainder of their journey to the river. No one spoke except for Grandfather, who walked beside the cart and pointed out to Inja certain things along the way—the waning sun streaming in slanted beams through a young grove of birches, a tiny rhododendron bush with a single violet-hued flower, the scent of must and loamy pine when they wheeled through an old part of the woods, a chipmunk's striped back flashing on the forest floor.

The moon, almost full, shimmered through the tall reeds behind the riverside temple at Daehangang-ni. Cattails rustled with murmurs of many people hidden within. Inja sat beside Grandmother on the bank by the maiden grass, while Uncle greeted the raft's owner with an American-style handshake to pass a wad of notes. "Well met," said the man, putting Uncle first in line.

The raft slid up, a broad flat craft reeking of tar and dead fish. Its two occupants, pole men, changed sides. Khang rolled the cart to the center of the raft, chocked its wheels, and the family clustered around it. Inja stood on the cart shaft beside Uncle, who wrapped his arms around her. The raft owner told everyone to sit on their bundles or hold them aloft to allow space for others. He cautioned them to remain quiet and still, as the cross-current pulled fast and he feared the enemy had reached the riverbanks. Fifteen more people boarded and the river sloshed over the raft, soaking those sitting on the outside. Khang stood on the wet wood nearby, and nearest the edge in front of him was a young mother, balancing a big round basket on her head, and her son, a boy about Inja's age, who sat on a bundle.

The raft lurched and the current swept it down-river. The dank rot of the marshy riverbank faded, and the craft's foul odor dissipated in the night's cool breeze. The crossing was slow, hand-poled efforts to tack against the current, and someone whispered, "It might drag us as far down as the ferry." Debris and unknown floating things tapped the edges of the raft, and Inja feared they were bodies.

Something big crashed into the edge that plowed the current, and the woman with the basket lost her hold. The basket fell and hit her son, and the boy and the basket tumbled with a quiet splash into the river. She screamed, "My baby!" and jumped in. Uncle cried out and reached for her. She floundered and slipped below the dark water. A man struck Uncle, and others wrestled him to the wet wood. Grandfather was beside Inja in an instant and held on to her as the raft swayed. Khang kicked the mother's bundle aside and leaped into the water. Uncle shouted, "No!" and someone muffled him.

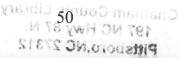

Inja strained to see in the moonlight. Her eyes couldn't open wide enough. Far downriver, Khang's big head bobbed once and disappeared beneath the surface. Uncle went lax and silent, and Grandfather touched Inja's cheek to turn her eyes from the river.

6

Night

The rising moon, one night from full, illuminated the Takoma Park neighborhood with silver, and in the dark woods next to the Cho house, crickets pulsed their night song. Najin, fearing for her daughter in Korea, had allowed Miran into bed with her, but she herself couldn't sleep. When she heard Miran's gentle snores, she got up. Her nightly habit of writing a letter to her mother made her wonder if the mail could still be delivered to Seoul. She loved the American post office—so reliable it could find ways to get through war, as it had when she'd lived through war.

Calvin's confidence that the invasion would soon be pushed back gave her enough encouragement to gather her writing things at the kitchen table, and she sat, legs curled up on the chair. She addressed her letter to her mother with *Halmeoni*, Grandmother, in the Korean way, and decided she would write nothing but good news, in case the family was truly embattled. But her fears poured out instead.

27 June 1950
Halmeoni,

Inja's father says the news from Korea is not good. I am heartbroken not to see my baby Inja—not a baby anymore and does not know her own mother. I do not mean to burden you with all that is in my heart, but at times, when I am alone in the kitchen and everyone is sleeping, I know I have failed two daughters and I have failed my husband. What use is it to regret leaving a baby? What use is it for this evil mother? Thinking of an innocent child, I hear her calling us, "Umma, Appa," and see her running around the room as if she is looking for us, afraid. She had just begun to crawl when we left . . .

She wept for the child she'd left behind to suffer whatever might befall her, and she wept for the baby boy she'd miscarried. She tore up the letter, tied her hair into a bun, and made a cup of Sanka. Filled with helplessness, she paced, the wind creaking in the woods. When bird calls signaled pre-dawn, she checked on Miran and found she had fallen off the bed, still fast asleep. How had she not heard the thump of her fall? She was a terrible mother, abandoning one child and ignoring another. She tried to write in her diary—

My heart is full of worry. And what about Halmeoni, unable to walk in the midst of a battlefield? I cannot think of it . . .

—but her fears were so great words could not contain them.

At six-thirty when Calvin hung his hat in the mud porch, she got up from the table to make him breakfast. "What news?" The very thought of Inja's safety made her heart pound to send out signals of love and concern.

"I'm sure she's safe at home with the family." Calvin ran his hands through his thinning hair and unknotted his tie.

She studied him. He looked weary and tense, but his skin still gleamed with the same sheen she had admired in the first photograph she'd ever seen of him, his jawline squared and strong. "Miran's sleeping in our bed—I hope you don't mind."

"Of course not." He went to hang up his suit jacket and tie.

She leaned into the hallway. "What news?" she asked again. And when he came back, frowning, unbuttoning his cuffs, she uttered an endearment, "*Yeobo* . . . ," knowing he was as worried as she. Nothing they said to each other could relieve this unyielding anxiety they shared. What point was there talking about such helpless fear?

"I don't think he'd make a move without

contacting us," Calvin said, referring to her brother.

"But what if the battles should reach them?" How foolish they were to have left her. Only a year or two, they'd said, but starting a church took longer than expected, and even though Calvin had a great job, they were never able to raise enough money to return home.

"They're far enough from downtown. I've sent him a telegram—it'll be tomorrow before he receives it."

She wondered if the telegraph was still operational.

He gave her a grave look. "The Americans have evacuated their embassy staff and families."

Her stomach caved—it was worse than she thought. "They aren't going to fight with us?"

"It's sensitive. Entering war with North Korea would be akin to declaring war with Russia. At least it could be taken that way."

"I heard your broadcast—"

"I'm sorry. That's already old news. Their attack had multiple prongs. One of the reasons I think your brother will stay in place is because the citizens have panicked and people are fleeing. He's much more sensible than that, especially considering he's got two elderly parents . . ."

He didn't need to finish. Her brother had shown himself through his letters to be a devoted and loving father figure. Throughout their youth,

Najin had regarded him as lazy and selfish, but he'd had a daughter whom he lost to pneumonia, and Najin had witnessed his love and dedication to that child, especially during her illness. That experience was among the reasons she had believed her daughter would be well cared for while they were away. But with this kind of external stress, would he make the right choices for her daughter and his family's sake? She was also assured for Inja's well-being because of her own mother, who for the few years of their being away would raise Inja as Najin herself had been raised. But Grandmother had had a stroke last year, and they should have found a way to go home then.

"We can push them back. The president is safe in Suwon."

"So he fled before the people could." She stood to boil water.

"I'm not very hungry. Rice and water is enough." Calvin sat. "It's his duty, but I heard he learned about the invasion while he was fishing in Biwon."

"I can see why you call him wannabe king." Biwon was the famed luxurious garden on the grounds of the Yi dynasty palace, with rich plantings, stately pavilions, and several well-stocked ponds.

"He took the train to Suwon at night." Though Calvin was a conservative and wanted unification as much as anyone did, he was no fan of President Syngman Rhee, whom he called a megalomaniac.

In a flash of irritation, Najin said, "How is it you know more about the whereabouts of the president than about our own child?" She turned to face him, stricken. "Oh! I'm sorry."

"You don't have to apologize, Yeobo. I understand."

"Is there nothing we can do?"

"We can pray."

"Yes." She turned to the stove with tears for Inja and prayers for her family's safety.

They talked little while he ate, both knowing talk was pointless in assuaging their fears. She washed his dishes and he went to bed, tucking Miran in beside him.

When he left the kitchen, her helplessness swept through her body and left her frustrated and angry. Best to do something productive, so she sat at her sewing station in the dining room and hemmed the matching green dresses until she found herself nodding over her stitches.

7

The Warehouse of Christian Living

The farther the Hans got from Seoul, the more the crowds thinned. The going was slow on hilly terrain, the way sometimes paved, though mostly not. As night progressed, clouds blackened the stars and veiled the moon. Inja's uncle pulled the cart all night, two shirts wrapped around his shoulders, blistered hands and feet bound with strips of cloth. Aunt and Grandfather had also padded their shoes with rags.

From Seongnam to Gwangju, there were no rooms at any price, and though many refugees made camp by the roadside, Uncle said it was too risky. Not only did they have many obvious possessions to tempt thieves, but the rumors of Seoul's fall to the North Korean People's Army made the main roads the logical choice for enemy advancement.

Bundled in blankets, Grandmother sat atop the cart with Inja half-prone in her lap, but the child could not sleep. When she closed her eyes, she saw the boy and his mother tumble into darkness. If she opened her eyes, she seemed to see through the dark with unusual intensity, the air too loud with locusts, the wheels' groans like bears prowling. She cradled the quince twig, its flowers wilted, and pinched a few petals to bring to her nose—the sharpness of citrus and green.

Grandmother stroked her hair and sang hymns about the kingdom of heaven, making Inja recall the garden in her Bible book. A group of fair-haired children, bathed in light, gathered around a gently glowing Jesus, who had both hands raised as if telling them a story about the holes in his palms. In the background were statues of lambs and cherubs, and Uncle had told her it was a children's graveyard. Perhaps the boy would go to that heavenly garden, but where would his mother go? Inja cried a little for the boy, separated from his mother, and understood then what it might mean to miss one's mother.

At midday, they stumbled upon a roadside inn in Chowol township. The owner had no room for even one more refugee, but told them about a warehouse four kilometers south in a village called Ssangdong. Owned by a churchgoing man—a supplier of gravel and sand for highways and bridges—he had opened his yards for refugees who could profess honesty and Christian brotherhood. As the sun touched distant hills, her uncle found the gravel trail that led to the ware-house, and at last they came upon hundreds of people gathered in small clusters around a huge factory building and several sandlot sheds. Inja smelled the appetizing smoke of cooking fires, then as they neared the warehouse itself, the stink of the open latrine dug behind the structure.

Those crowded inside the warehouse gave them baleful stares. In a last surge of effort, the three Han grownups pushed on and found an outside spot where several families had made camp around the fat trunk of a plane tree. Its broad limbs and wide leaves shaded a narrow-roofed open shed, where they found a corner to settle. Before he collapsed from exhaustion, Uncle unloaded a few bundles and positioned the cart to create a boundary for a square that Aunt spread with mats. Later, after Inja had investigated the grounds, she saw her family was well stocked compared to others who'd fled with what little they could carry on their backs.

She found a small gourd among the kitchen things and asked Aunt for water for her quince twig. "You'll be wanting that water to drink, so don't ask for more later—"

"Is there no pump?" said Grandmother on the mat, massaging her legs. "Maybe a brook?"

"We'll look for one," said Grandfather. "You'd best eat first," he said to Uncle, who had crawled on top of the unpacked bundles and was asleep.

Aunt gave Inja a water bucket, saying, "—and see what fuel you can find."

Grandfather got a hand axe and looped lengths of hemp rope on his shoulder. The two walked beyond the camp to a field where the setting sun lit the tops of tall grasses with gold. Children's heads bobbed above the grass, and their laughter rang loud. Grandfather said she could play tomorrow, but she shrugged. He bent and peered into her eyes. "I can see why you wouldn't want to play, but tomorrow I promise you'll feel differently. Life continues, and so must we."

This made Inja feel worse. She did want to play and felt badly about it. She bowed her head. He squeezed her shoulder, and it was as if he'd made her heart pump new blood that reached the tips of her fingers and warmed her cheeks.

"And help Halmeoni with her feet tonight; Aunt is exhausted. Halmeoni can show you what to do." Even before Grandmother had had her stroke, she faltered when she walked. Uncle insisted she see a doctor, but she said it was pointless. Cook had taken care of her feet every night. Since they shared a room, Inja had seen Grandmother soaking her feet in a steaming basin, then Cook would wrap them in strips of cloth. She wondered what kind of malady would require such nightly care.

Others had already cut down the few trees edging the meadow. The best Grandfather could do in the dark was to bundle twigs and grasses. He asked a woman who was also gathering kindling where water could be found, and they followed her directions to a pump on the far side of the warehouse, where a dozen women and girls were queued. Grandfather set down his sheaves nearby, said he'd wait for her, and began conversing with men who leaned against the entrance, smoking.

The muddy ground by the pump made Inja's blue sneakers squish, her steps spongy. A girl who might've been twice Inja's age lined up behind her, a tin kettle in hand. "Nice bucket," she said, her tongue rolling the inside of her cheek as if worrying a canker sore. She bent her narrow face close and whispered, "You have to be careful around here. People steal things." Her sour breath felt damp on Inja's cheek, and she wrinkled her nose, clutching the bucket. "You came at the right time," said the girl, too close. "Don't come in the morning, everybody wants water then, or in the middle of the day when it's hot. You're little so I'll pump for you. You can't wear shoes on the platform. Just watch me and you'll know what to do when it's your turn."

The line moved and Inja took a big step forward, but the girl stayed close. "Did you just get here? From Seoul?"

Her dislike of this talkative nosy girl with her crudely patched skirt kept her lips sealed, but when the girl pouted with hurt, Inja said, "Yes, today."

"Us too, from Seoul, but we've been here since last night and got the best spot inside, until the farmers came. They had nothing, and my mother said to hide our food so they won't steal from us. They're from Munsan village and tell terrible stories with lots of crying and wailing. Did you hear about the fires? The Commies killed everybody in sight. They lined them up and shot them. They spoiled the women and threw the bodies in the fields. That's what they said. Babies too. Speared them straight through."

Inja was sure she was exaggerating if not outright lying, but the words blew hot in her ears, an assault on her memories from the river. She moved with the queue.

"You're just a baby yourself, aren't you? You don't even go to school yet, do you?"

"Soon," said Inja.

The girl swung her kettle and leaned in so close, Inja felt her cropped hair tickle the back of her ear. "Everybody will be dead by then. All the teachers and principals. There won't be any more school ever. You wait and see." She tossed her hair back and laughed. "Hah! Listen to me. You'll be dead, too. No one left to wait and see!"

Inja grasped the bucket to her belly and looked for Grandfather. His conversation with the men seemed far more amiable than hers. The girl reached the platform, kicked off her straw sandals, and pushed ahead. "Watch me now." She pumped vigorously until water trickled into her kettle. She told Inja to put her bucket beneath the faucet. Inja stepped out of her shoes and complied, then the girl pumped twice and said she had to go.

The heavy pump handle made Inja stretch her arm high at its upper position, and she held on with both hands when her socks skidded on the slick wooden platform. An old woman next in line hurried to help, and the bucket was full at last. The horrid girl was gone—and so were Inja's blue sneakers. She left the bucket and ran to the warehouse in muddy socks, but it was impossible to see into the dark interior. She erupted in tears, and that made her even angrier because she was acting like a baby just as the girl had insinuated. And then it felt good to cry, and she squatted right there and wept for Khang, the boy in the heavenly garden, and his mother, elsewhere in the kingdom, separated from her child.

Grandfather crouched beside her, and she sputtered out that her sneakers were stolen. His peaceful features knit into a frown. "There's nothing to be done for it, *meong-keong*," he said, using a familiar endearment. "We'll see about this in the morning. Come, your aunt is waiting." She retrieved the bucket, and he carried it, the bundled rushes tied to his shoulder. "If you didn't

65

bring another pair of shoes, I'll make you sandals with these grasses. Yah, you didn't know your grandfather used to make everybody's shoes, eh? My sandals are so strong, they'll last the whole summer long. Tomorrow you'll be running and playing as if nothing happened."

She wanted to please him, but only faltering breaths came out.

They found their way back by the flicker of others' fires. A cool wind threatened rain, and she felt chilled and hungry. Aunt must have been feeling the same, for she didn't scold Inja when she saw the shoeless muddy socks. They ate a simple supper of dried fish and boiled leeks, and used the hot leek water to soften the last of the rice balls Cook had packed. Grandfather woke Uncle to eat, and they talked about Uijongbu, Munsan-ri, Seoul invaded, bridges exploded with hundreds of people on them, a threat of rain. The men rearranged the bundles, spread a blanket beneath the empty cart, lay side by side, and were soon asleep.

Aunt cleaned the pots, and Inja took the bucket with the last of the hot water to Grandmother, who sat on the mat near the fire, its grass-fed flames sparking in the night breeze. She held a handful of withered twigs.

"What's that?" said Inja, yawning.

"Cover your mouth. It's willow bark. It helps with the swelling and prevents infection. Let it steep and help me take off these wrappings."

Inja tossed the herbs into the bucket and unrolled Grandmother's bandages. The firelight revealed swollen ankles and reddened and shrunken toes, and Inja saw she had no toenails. She dropped the foot and drew back.

Grandmother winced and Inja said, "Sorry!" She dipped Grandmother's feet into the bucket, and the willow infusion smelled like wet dog. Inja tightened her lips against revulsion and to silence the questions clamoring inside.

"I know they're ugly," said Grandmother. "An old woman's arthritic feet."

"Is that what happens?" Inja tried to think if she'd ever seen Grandfather's naked feet. She hadn't. "Harabeoji, too?"

"Silly child. Of course not." Grandmother cupped handfuls of herbed water and wet her ankles. "Another long story for some other time."

That made three stories Grandmother owed her, the two from yesterday—a long time ago— the one about her sister's near death and the story about why her mother decided to leave Inja behind, and now this one, about what happened to her toenails.

Aunt unrolled the women's bedding close to the wall. "Stop pestering her and wrap her feet. Then wash yours in that water and rinse out your socks, and don't throw it out yet."

Inja knew better than to toss out water that

could still be used, but the herbal mix repulsed her. With her back to Aunt she made a face, but Grandmother saw and frowned. When she showed Inja how to wrap her feet, she murmured, "Your toenails won't fall off if you use that water. I had frostbite a long time ago, before you were born. It took years for them to come out, and they still bleed at times." She dried Inja's hands, and though the child could barely see her features, she hoped Grandmother saw hers as humbled.

Aunt had made a private area with the blanket draped around the bedpan. The last to use it, Inja went to empty it in the latrine ditch. She looked for the girl with her blue sneakers, but few people were about. After she rinsed the bedpan with the herb water, she leaned it against the cart to dry and arranged the quince twig by her bedding, its few tawdry petals shut for the night. The moment she closed her eyes, she felt the heavy hand of sleep, but remembering the girl's all-too-true warning about thieves, she dragged herself up to rummage around for her book. In her bundle she also found a pair of rubber shoes that Uncle had packed for her, and she hugged them, grateful for his foresight. The book wrapped in her jacket became her pillow, and she hoped the memory of its pictures would lull her into a kinder world of dreams. She woke once to a downpour, and Uncle and Aunt rushing about, leaning mats to shelter them as they slept.

Inja's eyes opened to a bright morning, someone shaking her shoulder. Aunt hissed, "Where's the bedpan?"

Inja waved toward the cart.

"It's not there. Halmeoni needs it. Go find it!" She swept off Inja's quilt.

Inja hugged her elbows and looked around. Everything shone from the rain, and though the ground was wet, the mats had kept them dry. Grandfather sipped hot water, the lines on his face carved deep, his eyes hooded, and he crouched in that particular way that meant his back pained him. Many nights Inja heard him cry out for Uncle to rub his back. Uncle had told her that Grandfather still suffered injuries from police beatings after he'd demonstrated for Korean independence early in the Japanese occupation years—the year Uncle was born. He also told her that story when they celebrated Sam-il, March First Independence Declaration Day, using respectful high language when he described Grandfather as a great patriot, a hero who saved Korean history books doomed for destruction by the Japanese.

The cart was upended. "I put it against that wheel," Inja said to Aunt.

"*Aigu*, someone stole it! You should've hidden it."

"Where's *Ajeossi?*" Perhaps Uncle had moved

69

it when he'd turned the cart. Though he was her *weh-samchon*, maternal uncle, Inja familiarly called him Ajeossi, using the same habit with Aunt.

"He's gone to get the servants and to find us an inn." So much had happened that it didn't surprise Inja to learn he would attempt to help Cook and Yun get out of Seoul, where now there was war. Inja wanted Cook and Yun, but she wanted Uncle back, too. She shut her eyes and said a prayer, and Aunt flapped the quilts and yelled at her to find out who stole the bedpan.

Inja tugged on dry socks and her rubber shoes, her face sour. Aunt shoved her hip and said, "Do as you're told! What kind of child acts like that? It's no wonder your mother left you behind"— her usual rant, and one impossible to ignore.

Inja plowed through the bundles piled beneath the overturned cart, resentful and certain Aunt wouldn't have said that if Uncle were around. She skirted people's camps and sloshed through puddles. Fat raindrops splashed her neck as she looked for gleaming white enamel or a flash of blue sneaker. She tripped on a root, and pain surged through her toe. She seethed at her thin rubber shoes, that thief of a girl, and swore to stray all day to avoid Aunt, though her stomach rumbled. After she used the latrine, she dawdled at the warehouse's cavernous opening, addled enough by anger to want to beat up the bad-breath girl. Then, far beyond the pump, she glimpsed a familiar white oblong and she strode toward it with purpose. There was the bedpan, balanced on stones over a small fire, a woman stirring something in it. Inja neared and smelled onions and soy sauce in its smoke.

She ran back to Aunt. "I found it! Come and see."

Aunt followed her, fingers curled like a hawk's talons, but when she saw the woman cooking with the bedpan, she stopped and clutched Inja's shoulder. "Hush! Let's go back."

At their camp, Grandmother fanned embers beneath the old iron cook pot, boiling water. In the other pot, fresh barley rice had been shaped into balls. Aunt told her about the bedpan. "That poor woman didn't know better. We can't say anything now." Grandmother agreed they'd make do without it. Then they snickered, heads lowered. "She'll wonder why her soup tastes so delicious," said Aunt.

"Wait until Cook hears about that special seasoning!" said Grandmother, and they laughed aloud, mouths covered in modesty. In this desperate place where people stole things, certain manners such as saving face, even for strangers and thieves, still mattered. Inja had wearable shoes and the family had two cook pots. They could forgo a prized bedpan and a coveted pair of sneakers.

Later that morning Inja spread blankets out to dry, pumped buckets of water, and Grandmother showed her how to lay hot compresses on Grandfather's back. Then Aunt told her to do what she wished as long as she stayed out of trouble. She ran in the steamy fields all afternoon with other children, playing war, and looked in vain for the horrid girl.

Uncle stumbled back to their camp after midnight, and Inja crawled from bed to give him a relieved hug. Covered in soot, his clothes smelling of metal and smoke, Uncle's eyes were empty circles of black in the firelight. Aunt shooed Inja back to bed, and the long shadows cast by the fire and their quiet talk drew her into a sleep layered with sadness that neither Cook nor Yun had been rescued from Seoul.

8

Telegrams

A week after the invasion and still with no news from her family, Najin was like a spitting tiger in a cage of helplessness. The bits of news Calvin reported seemed unreliable and always unconfirmed. She knew she should pray, but mostly she was silently cursing the ways of this world. Everyone from church was shocked that the communists had captured Seoul, but how could they have not known about the invasion? All the might of this great country she lived in and the supposed power of the United Nations were pointless against the greed of men.

After Calvin woke, he said—as she paced the dining room dusting needlessly—"The house is in a remote neighborhood of no military interest. They're safe there. The People's Army may be communist, but they're still Korean brethren."

"Stop pandering to me," said Najin. "It feels like the propaganda that turned brother against brother in a mere five years."

The phone rang—another church member, calling Calvin to hear any news. Everyone had relatives in Korea. The Korean embassy knew nothing, could do nothing. At least Calvin had the latest news and offered prayers. Najin asked the Lord's forgiveness for thinking that her husband was a better ambassador of Korea than the embassy staff themselves. He'd sent telegrams to her *dongsaeng*, younger sibling, every day, without answer or even confirmation of delivery. Neither of them could eat or sleep well. She heard him rustling around in the kitchen and went in. "Here, I'll pack your dinner." She filled his Thermos with coffee.

"I meant to tell you," said Calvin, "that American soldiers stationed in Japan are moving toward Suwon, and navy gunships have joined the battle."

"That doesn't make me feel better. The idea of gunfire and bombs in the streets of Seoul is horrifying. Where is my family? Where is our child? Why hasn't he telegraphed?"

"We'll hear something soon, I'm sure of it, and you should rest," said Calvin. "You've exhausted yourself with worry. You must pray."

"It only brings it to the fore," said Najin. "I'd rather be distracted, though even then I feel bad for not being focused on this one thing."

Calvin donned his jacket and opened the mud porch door to retrieve his hat. "I'll telephone you if there's anything big that changes, and if you get a telegram today—"

"I'll call right away. Do you have a dime for the bus? Okay, goodbye."

Najin hugged her arms and scanned the back-yard where Miran played near the woods. The garden beckoned her. The irises needed last year's dead foliage cleared around new shoots, the arrow-like buds ready to burst in purple-bearded glory. Beside a low patio wall near the porch steps, the orange tiger lilies were in bloom, filling the rectangular patch edged with phlox. The slate patio reminded her of her childhood courtyard, and it touched her with nostalgia. Her stomach gripped with thoughts of Korea, and she turned to the house. The best remedy for worry was work—she could not follow her husband's admonition to rest.

Najin went to the basement and took the laundry outside to hang. Mrs. Bushong was gardening in the adjacent backyard, and she stopped to lean over the chain-link fence. "Mrs. Cho, I heard about Korea," she said, tugging off her gardening gloves. "My boys were in the Philippines in the war."

She didn't feel like chatting but had to be polite to this lady who had been so kind to Miran when Najin had been hospitalized. She put down the basket of clothes and waved, but didn't approach the fence. She understood the Asia connection Mrs. Bushong had attempted, though it was somewhat off. "They too young," she said of Mrs. Bushong's two veteran sons who were ambulance drivers.

"They signed up soon as they could. That's how those boys were. You'll have a boy one day and you'll see what I mean."

Najin knew she meant well, but she felt a stab in her womb for her lost baby boy.

"Why don't you and Miran come for dinner tonight? My boys are out, and it's just me and the mister. We got sparklers for the little one."

Najin put down the clothespins and neared the fence, hand extended to shake. "Is very kind, but I need near the telephone. Miran alone, okay?"

"Sure, send her over."

Later when Mrs. Bushong brought the child home, she reported that they'd grilled hamburgers and had potato chips and Pepsi, and Miran was all smiles. Mrs. Bushong also carried a saucepan of chicken broth with rice for Najin, who forced herself to eat some of it while Mrs. Bushong was admiring Miran's books, since she'd gone to so much trouble. The rice tasted like the cardboard box it came in, and Najin had trouble swallowing it. She prayed Mrs. Bushong would leave soon.

After sunset when Mrs. Bushong finally left, Najin made rice without turning on the kitchen lights so the neighbor wouldn't see her cooking. She told Calvin about the evening when he came home the next morning, and they laughed a little, but then felt guilty. Najin said, "We can't know if

Inja has rice or anything to eat. Such heartache."

She was worried sick, but nothing could be done. She cursed the world. Then she prayed.

A telegram came Monday afternoon, and Najin was overcome. She shut the front door at once and tore the blue envelope open, forgetting to tip the delivery boy. Miran spied the young man pacing the porch before he left.

Calvin, who was working a double shift again, came home at five o'clock with a rolled-up map that he spread on the dining room table. Miran kneeled on a chair and studied it with her parents. "The red dots are where battles have been reported," her father said.

"So many near Seoul," said Najin. They talked about the other dots on the map, including green for American bombings. There were several mentions of Russia.

Miran wanted to ask if the maps meant the atomic war was coming, but her mother told her to bring the magnifying glass from her father's bureau in their bedroom. When she handed it over, her father was drawing a wavy line in yellow grease pencil down the peninsula to a green dot he called "Daegu," and her mom bent close with the glass, saying, "Chowol, Chowol-ri."

The telegram fell from the table, and Miran nabbed it. She found a piece of blue construction paper from her room and worked hard to copy the telegram's heading, EAST WST GLOBL SERVICE TO CALVIN CHO TAKOMA PK MD FR KNG TEGU, in green crayon, and the strange message in brown letters: FAMLY SAFE CHOWOL RI WLL WIRE END. She showed her facsimile to her father, who taped it to the kitchen door and held her up to see it. "This means your sister is fine. They got out of Seoul before the invasion and somehow ended up in a tiny village somewhere north of Daegu, where we know the UN forces have gathered. We have no idea how it happened or who sent the telegram, but it's good news." He squeezed her and set her down, and the loss of his herbal smell, his strong arms and solid chest struck her with the surprise of an unknown need inadequately met. A tear sprang from her eye, and she grabbed his pant leg.

He patted her head. "I have to go back to the office to bring home a more detailed map for your mother to find that village. But I have tomorrow off after lunch, so we'll see the fireworks at night like always, okay?"

"What about the parade?" she said, and regretted it when he frowned. She had been such a good girl lately, so invisible, and should have remained that way. "Maybe your mother will go, but if she can't, I'll ask Mrs. Bushong if she's going and can take you."

On the muggy morning of July fourth, Najin

78

said she needed to stay at home to wait for a telegram—the telegraph office never closed. Miran thought about the delivery boy pacing the porch and how her mother was now pacing similarly. Telegrams did that.

Mrs. Bushong took Miran up the street to sit on the curb and watch the colorful floats, marching bands, cars with local dignitaries throwing candies, convertibles with lodge princesses, and the concluding fire engines. She came home in high spirits, gave her mother a pocketful of candy, and demonstrated bubble-gum blowing, her teeth stained blue, her fingers and cheeks sticky sweet, thanks to an indulgent Mrs. Bushong.

She played outside with neighborhood kids all afternoon and was so sweaty that Najin gave her a bath before sundown and the fireworks. When Najin poured bathwater over her head and shoulders, she seemed unaware of the soap getting into Miran's eyes and was absentminded with the rough washcloth. Though Miran knew she had no right to call for her busy mother's attention, she had to ask, "Did the messenger boy come?"

Najin smiled, surprised. "He didn't come today. Maybe tomorrow. He brought good news yesterday, and we hope he will bring more."

"A red-letter day," said Miran, and was gratified to have made her mother laugh.

Calvin made popcorn, and they took the bus to

the school field for the fireworks display. Things seemed like normal then, lying together on a blanket *ooh*ing and *aah*ing over the fireworks. With fingers over her ears against the booms, Miran claimed the blue ones, then the red ones as her favorites. Her mother liked the green bursts, and her father laughed that only white was left for him. On impulse she asked, "What would be my sister's favorite?"

Neither of her parents answered or spoke for a while, and all the fun left their little family island on that blanket. If Miran's ears hurt with these explosions, what was it like for her little sister where real bombs with real explosions were going off? She feigned a big yawn and said she was tired. They left before the grand finale, and no one spoke the whole way home. She knew it was her fault.

5 July 1950. I long for more news of my daughter. What use is it to write letters? My heart does not know what to do. How big a resentment and bitterness Inja must have toward a world where her mother and father left her to suffer. There is no way I can help her, or make her understand, to ease her pain for the fate I put her in. A few nights ago, many scenes from the past of her infant face, of her growing, passed before my eyes. In the

afternoon I had a fever since I did not sleep. Poor pitiful child, there is no way to bring her here. My heart burns knowing I made a lifelong wrong decision. Is this our destiny for years to come?

It made me so sad to see a photo of some mother and daughter in Korea who had drowned together in the river. What guarantee is there that my Inja, my parents, and my brother are not in the same predicament? Who knows the void in my heart?

Only when I think of how good Miran has been behaving does my mind ease and I can have some comfort.

The wind has turned and the curtains billow with the smell of summer rain, wetting the floor. I must close the window, but I give this last prayer: Forgive me, Lord, if in the darkest places hidden deep in my heart—hidden even from my own sincerity—there should reside the thought that I have brought the wrong daughter to America.

A week later on Monday the tenth, when Miran returned home from sneaking out to the park, Najin told her they'd gotten a good telegram and asked if she wanted to go to the library. "We haven't done many things together this summer, and I think you need books to keep you near so I know where to find you." But she wasn't at all angry at Miran and showed her the telegram. "I will read it to you."

ALL WELL INJA FINE STOP ONE WEEK AT REFUGEE CAMP TOO CROWDED STOP SEOUL EMBATTLED FLED SOUTH STOP COOK MISSING STOP NEED MONEY NABI INN AT CHUNGBOOKDO UMSUNMYON GUM-WANGLI ADVISE NEXT END

Miran understood the first few words, but the rest made no sense. She gave her mother a questioning look, and Najin said it was impossible to write Korean in English. "You're such a good English speller that when you're older, you can turn it into the same spellings for the whole world." Miran beamed, though she knew it meant she'd have to learn Korean, and this was another reminder that she didn't speak it.

"This says"—Najin folded the telegram—"that your sister is safe at an inn in a little village, as are all your relatives from Seoul. It's a miracle they got that far on foot, and you should pray thanks for their safety in the middle of wartime." She gave a quick spontaneous prayer, and they walked to the library, eight blocks away.

Miran checked out ten children's picture books, five on her card, five on her mother's card, and did stay home reading for several days. But as the week progressed, the relief and ease of that library-going Monday slipped into a renewed kind of tension, with much talk of President Truman, something called "a police action," money, kimchi-making for money, sewing for money, discussions that touched on edges of anger, which quieted everyone for a time, many mentions of her sister's name and her mother blowing her nose, then her own name mentioned for unknown reasons—until it all stopped. She never found out why.

By Friday, Calvin said the war still had not advanced to Geumwang village. How long could they live at an inn? The longer the war went on, the more impossible it would be to pay for an inn. What would stop the communists from taking the entire peninsula? Calvin reported that the UN forces in Busan had built a stronghold in Daegu and would soon travel north for certain victory. Then Najin's family could go home— everyone could go home, the nation united. But Najin trusted nothing when it came to war. She had known its desperation, its deprivation, its shifting disposition. Something must be done.

She grabbed the Yellow Pages from the telephone table and sat to pore through the restaurant listings. Surely there would be a Chinese or even a Japanese restaurant who might want to buy Korea's famed kimchi. She wrote out a list of a half-dozen Chinese and one Japanese establishment. Calvin could later make the sales calls. He could also find a wholesale market to buy cabbages and spices in bulk, though it would cost extra to have them delivered.

Satisfied with the earning potential of gallons of kimchi (aware that she was *counting her chickens before the eggs hatched*), Najin went downstairs and cleaned up the utility sink area, where she would fashion a work station for her kimchi-making business. Then she went around the house watering her many plants: philodendron, African violets, purple coleus, and ferns. Mrs. Victoria Kim had started her with a few cuttings when they moved to DC, and now she had pots full of lush plants. What a luxury to have greenery in the house! She emptied the watering can in the ferns and thought, *I've fed Miran, her father, and now these plants, yet I can do nothing to help my family in danger.* The fears she'd swallowed made the porch floor spin, and she knew, because she felt helpless and fragile, that she must lie down.

Prone on the couch, Miran playing nearby cutting pictures out of a Sears catalog, Najin searched her memory for people she knew from Chungcheongbuk Province or even the neighboring provinces. She thought back to the time during the depression, soon after her family's move to Seoul, when she'd left to work at the orphanage in Suwon. Perhaps the director was still there. His name popped into her memory at the same time she recalled she'd been forced to leave the orphanage when he professed his love. Stupid man! He was married, too, and with her husband absent—in America—she was too vulnerable for this unwanted attention. Those beloved orphan boys were lost to her because of his weakness.

She went to the kitchen sink to put dishes away and looked outside to the cloudless sky, a brief prayer on her lips for the boys, now men if they'd survived the Pacific War, and now this invasion. Thinking of the orphans and Suwon brought back the eager eyes of other children from her first teaching job after Ewha College— in Yeoju County near Icheon—and in that instant she found the solution for her family. According to Calvin's description and the map he had drawn for her, her family would have passed through Icheon on their journey south.

In the remote mountain village of Wolsong in Yeoju County, she had been principal, teacher, and hunger-staver for a one-room classroom of eight girls and five boys, aged seven to fifteen. She taught them grammar, arithmetic, history, and geography, and showed the older girls how to find and prepare edible plants in the forest and meadows. After sending money home to her father for her brother's college tuition, she spent her remaining spare wages to buy barley and dabs of miso for soup to feed the children. In her first winter in that tiny village, a fallen tree had shattered a window. She lamented the loss of glass but created a sturdy shutter by refashioning the wooden drawer from her desk.

A fifteen-year-old student, a boy named Longi, was so impressed with her ingenuity, he described it to his father, who owned a lumber mill in the neighboring town, *Icheon*. The next day Longi brought a few boards and hand tools to make shutters to protect the other windows, and the added insulation kept her classroom warmer for the remainder of the season. As principal, she was required to report to the Japanese when youths turned sixteen, the age for military conscription, but in her two years there, until her post ended from lack of funding, somehow none of the students, including Longi, grew older than fifteen. Longi's father came to see her before she left, told her his name and how to find him should she ever need to fix more shutters or any other sort of assistance a grateful mill owner could provide.

Icheon might be less than forty kilometers from Geumwang village—and the inn. She couldn't remember the father's name, but wrote down

Chae Longi in her diary, underlining it twice. She calculated he'd be about twenty-four years old now, and as the only son was undoubtedly running the mill with his father. With Calvin's help, she could find him . . .

9

Busan

Between the Nakdong River delta and the busy ports in Busan lay Ami-dong, the small Ami neighborhood. Only the poor had lived on its precipitous hill, but now, with this southern city congested by refugees, all available living space was crammed with ramshackle dwellings occupied by rich and poor alike. Still, in the sheer inclines toward the summit, pockets of meadow remained, and Inja's family made plans to build a small house there. Its undesirable location was further underscored by the odorous and ashy emissions of a tall smokestack just over the crest—a tannery, Inja was told.

Sufficient wood, brick, and mortar were acquired from the man who'd rescued them from the inn at Geumwang village, where they'd lived for several worrisome weeks, waiting for some kind of answer, and money, from Inja's parents to whom Uncle had sent a telegram. The inn's inflated fees had drained most of their cash, and Uncle wanted to continue journeying south, but ahead lay the Sobaek Mountain range, and, besides, the cart axle had snapped.

Then seemingly out of providence itself came an old truck, its bed half-filled with building materials and a cheerful driver at the wheel. "Inja's mother sent me to take you all the way to Busan!" he cried at their perplexed expressions. For the first half of the ride, Inja's grandparents and aunt rode in the back of the truck along with their belongings and the dismantled cart, and Inja sat up front with Uncle and the driver, Mr. Chae. His father was the millwright in Icheon, about fifty kilometers from the inn. Inja sat on her hands to soften the bumpy ride. They passed rock walls with determined bushes sprouting from crags, an old pine forest, and after the road flattened she saw villages in the distance, rice fields, occasional groups of refugees walking south, a bloated dead mule covered with flies.

Mr. Chae explained everything with many toothy smiles and outright laughter at his pleasure in repaying a debt to Inja's mother. "I was the only son so I was sent to school." He turned to Inja and said, "So you're the daughter, eh? You should know what an enterprising woman she is."

Inja asked Uncle what *enterprising* meant. He explained its meaning and said that Mr. Chae's very appearance proved her resourcefulness.

"The winters in those hills were freezing, and the straw-and-coal-dust fuel we had was so feeble that none of us could hold a pencil for the cold." He described how Inja's mother cleverly fashioned the broken shutter, and that his father came to meet this teacher who was also a carpenter. "We repaired all the shutters, and from then on until the next year when they closed the school, I brought scraps of lumber and sawdust bricks to feed the stove."

"What year was this?" said Uncle, looking thoughtful.

"I know it well—1942 to 1944—because in December 1942 I was supposed to be drafted, but for two years I never turned older than fifteen!" He laughed.

"*Yaaah,*" said Uncle. Inja gave him a questioning look, and he said, "Your mother was as much of a patriot as Grandfather at that time, and she created her own form of rebellion at great risk." Inja pondered this for a while, and concluded that she, too, would like to form a rebellion someday.

When they reached Busan the following morning, Mr. Chae helped them situate and build their simple house. After that he made regular visits to the city, his lumber now in demand and selling at wartime prices. He asked Uncle to thank his sister for this bonus of work he wouldn't have considered had he not driven them to Busan, and for adding to his growing list of things for which he felt gratitude.

Mail service in Busan was active and letters

were exchanged. Packages from America began to arrive to their new home about once a week. Grandmother's eyes were failing, and eyeglasses were impossible to acquire, both because of cost and availability. She asked Inja to read a letter received in early December during the first winter of the Korean War.

24 November 1950

Halmeoni, thank you for sending her artwork and writing. She draws quite well, better than most kindergartners, a true artist, as does Miran, both natural talents like their grandfather and uncle. I am sending you a ten-dollar bill. Please tell Dongsaeng to give it to Chae Longi. We can never repay him for all he has done for us. Though I worry every hour about your well-being, at least I am secure in knowing you have a sturdy home, small though it may be, and are far from conflict. The knowledge of your safety is my answered prayer. I mailed a package today. Perhaps Dongsaeng's wife can sell a few things at the market to buy food and medicine.

Are you well? Is the house warm? Is there enough to eat? What kinds of things do you need? Is there no word from Cook? Is Inja taking care of you?

Yesterday was the American holiday of Thanksgiving and our missionary friend, Miss Lone, came to dinner along with a few Korean parishioners who have no family here. Miss Lone now works for a congressman—it was she who told Inja's father many years ago about the job he now has, and she herself is an important worker in the government. The talk turned to home. You and Inja are always in my heart, and throughout the week my hopes were high that the war would end soon. With Seoul liberated and Pyeongyang captured, MacArthur said the troops would be home by Christmas, but Inja's father says no one in his office can support that belief.

My greed for hope made me hasty in expecting war's end. I will temper that now. But I do not want to worry you. You need to take care of yourself and eat well to get stronger to walk. I am so pleased to hear that you can stand up a little.

More tomorrow, but do tell me when you received this letter so I can know how long it takes to get there.

Grandmother smiled at Inja. "My blessings are great. No one else could take better care of me than you, my child." She told her to fetch brush and ink, and she'd dictate a response on the empty backs of the letter just received—paper was scarce—turning the envelope inside out to use it again as well.

In those war years, Inja attended girls' school in Busan and celebrated three of her birthdays and as many annual holidays with gifts from her mother's packages. Among her favorite things were the surprising variety of sweets her sister, Miran, had collected on the odd American holiday of Halloween, including the Chuckles jelly candies her Sunday school teacher cut into bits so all the kids could have a taste. Everyone was certain each color tasted different. She got lots of clothes old and new, fresh pencils, white KEDS, and a can of Spam—the second most unforgettable present in her entire life, the first being the Bible storybook. Years later, even the memory of that tangy pink meat made her tongue tingle, its soft yet firm texture bursting savory meatiness with every chew. Aunt thinned the jelly juice with hot water, and they had it on their rice. For weeks afterward, Inja cut her finger-tips playing with the sharp-edged tin and its little metal key wound tight inside the spiral left from stripping the can open.

Most of the clothes were distributed at their makeshift church, but the better items and special goods were bartered at the port markets a half-hour walk from Ami-dong. Inja often accompanied Aunt on these tasks to help carry bundles of clothes, bars of soap, toothbrushes and combs, the occasional luxury of a tin of talcum or bottle of cologne that could buy them a week's worth of fish. For one of Inja's birthdays, they received a pound of wheat flour, a tin of sugar, and instructions to make a birthday cake, but it failed because they had no fat and Aunt could only find one egg at market—and it cost them an entire bar of Camay soap. They ate the sweet biscuit thing anyway.

In the industrial section south of Ami-dong, ports bustled with towering ships delivering military vehicles and monstrous guns, and Inja would get glimpses of the big-nosed soldiers with hair of different colors and in all kinds of uniforms. She was most impressed with the Korean Navy Guard, their white gloves and helmets gleaming in the sun. The beloved MacArthur, who had liberated Korea from the Japanese, was often mentioned, but she wasn't attentive to the details of war. The UN forces and the Americans had saved Seoul that autumn—then lost it to the Reds by winter, proving Uncle right in judging it unsafe to return home. Battles raged back and forth across and above the thirty-eighth parallel, and the Han men cheered at victories or glowered at defeats. Then came the grim reports about numberless Chinese troops crossing the Yalu River to further spread their communist dogma. When President Truman fired MacArthur, the entire city lamented, fearing that his replacement, Ridgway, wouldn't command the same respect from his troops. Ultimately the opposite was true, and rumors spread about MacArthur's *delusions of grandeur* in threatening the Chinese with the atomic bomb. Her uncle and grandfather agreed that fighting North Korea was one thing; entering war with China was something else altogether. This confused Inja, since the Chinese troops were already fighting alongside the North Korean People's Army, but Uncle said it was politics, a term that always ended their conversations like an obstinate blockade.

Busan's climate was milder than Seoul's, though it did snow once toward the end of the first winter of the war. Uncle said the battlefields up north were the coldest ever—below zero—and as such, the communists weren't the only thing killing the marines, civilians, or the enemy alike. At home in Seoul, if a blizzard rattled the doors or freezing temperatures iced the river and the streets, people would stay inside for days, but now up north, war would not wait. Icy winds howled through the hills of battlefields denuded by artillery and left a trail of deadly cold in its wake.

For Inja, the most frigid place she sat that winter was halfway down the hill, in a big brown tent holding the bare bones of a church her uncle and grandparents had formed with help from her family in America.

Days passed as before, but rougher, as if they lived the same life but on a lower, darker register. All of her classmates were equally occupied with family problems, lack of rice, today's lessons, and who was friends with whom, so while the children knew there was war, its movements and meaning meant little except hunger and hard times. Inja remembered the porter, Khang, and though his presence faded with time, on occasion she would smell roasted chestnuts or a citrus flower and the moment would grow heavy with yearning for Cook and Yun, for sweet slabs of remembered childhood in Seoul.

What began to matter was her absent mother, even if the packages she sent made Inja the best-dressed girl in Ami-dong. Uncle said her schoolmates teased her out of jealousy because of her connection to America. She did have that advantage, but she hated being known for it. She had clothes but little else. Textbooks were shared, white rice rare, and fresh fruit a thing of memory. Their diet was red and green mung beans and barley supplemented with vegetables from their garden, and Aunt was so dreadful at the fire-pit stove that the half-cooked beans made Inja's belly swell.

All the girls walked to school with their

mothers, sometimes an aunt or grandmother, and in the afternoons, the women waited outside the school to accompany their children home, to ask about their day and coo and praise artwork and checkmarks on papers. Outside that circle of women—in rain, snow, or shine, during field trips, on picnic days, and at school functions—there was Grandfather, silent and stately in his hanbok, and in inclement weather a gray fedora, his arms at rest behind his back or tucked inside his sleeves. When school let out, he would greet Inja with a solemn nod and they'd walk home. She wondered if he dreaded that moment as much as she did, all eyes turned to them. She could almost hear the tongues of the mothers clucking in their throats, the children smirking behind their hands. But she grew to love her grandfather's quiet dignity, a refuge from the critical stares that continued throughout those Busan years.

Life in the close quarters of their two-room house often erupted. The biggest fight happened when Uncle received fifty dollars from Najin and gave it wholly to the church. "All that money!" said Aunt. "A rock instead of rice or a hired girl." The church laid a granite cornerstone inscribed 1952 with the pen names of Inja's uncle and mother, which became the name of the EunCheon church, meaning "hidden brook." Nothing was hidden in that little wooden house. Every shout rattled the walls and shook Inja's bones. But afterward, days would be filled with a veneer of calm, all the sharp edges in the house softened in the way that the ash from the crematorium's chimney covered the hill.

Inja had at first believed the smokestack just beyond the ridge belonged to a leather factory, hence the odors, but it didn't take long to learn what it really was and why so few others lived nearby. Every day, army trucks trundled up the rocky dirt road to the "factory," gears whining. During the monsoons their first year in Busan, a nine-year-old boy had hopped on the back of a truck, slipped off the ramp, landed headfirst, and drowned in a flooded gulley. The newspaper reported he'd wanted a ride, but the neighborhood kids said someone had dared him to slap a body bag to prove he could survive such proximity to death. The boy's death confirmed everyone's innermost fear of the dead. Most of the children had seen and smelled corpses somewhere on the journey south, but revulsion of dead bodies went deeper, a long-held traditional fear of disease and decay that unnerved even the most Christian of them, like Inja's family, who never talked about the white powder coating the cabbages and peppers in their kitchen garden, the flakes they combed from their hair, the mounds of gray cut through by their footpaths, the particles that seeped into the house and dusted their floors and cook pots, which they wiped clean every morning.

10

Dog-and-Pony Show

A cold snap in early October 1952 made the leafy canopy of Takoma Park brilliant with magenta and gold, the perfect backdrop for the Halloween parade on the elementary school grounds. Miran wanted to go as a war refugee, but Najin said, though it was an original idea, it wasn't something fun and shouldn't be chosen as a costume. "Go as a Korean princess instead—it's prettier and we have lots of hanbok. They're so colorful, no one will know it's not how princesses dress." But Miran knew, and in answering the questions about her costume, she said, "I'm a Korean girl." The irony was missed by everyone, including herself. She didn't win the first-grader's prize—a robot child did—but she went trick-or-treating with the neighbor kids until nine-thirty that night, and Najin didn't notice until she got home with toffee stuck between her teeth and a pillowcase half-full of candy and popcorn balls. Seeing her mother's alarmed expression that was turning dark, Miran offered the pillowcase and said, "I got it for my sister." She had so much candy, she really didn't mind giving away most of it for the packages going to Korea, whose frequency had increased to once a week, sometimes two at a time.

Though Miran disliked having company for dinner since it meant she had to sit, quiet and still, while her parents had long conversations at the table in Korean, she enjoyed Thanksgivings both because Calvin cooked most of the feast and it was easier to be his helper than her mother's helper. Plus their number-one guest, the bilingual former missionary Miss Edna Lone, made an effort to include her. She worked on Capitol Hill for a congressman from Maine, her original home. Whenever she visited, it was Miran's joyful task to print Miss Lone's outlandish utterances in her mother's notebook, and this time she went on a riff of animal idioms for the child's benefit, and they both laughed over:

> Don't have a cow
> Kill two birds with one stone
> Blind as a bat
> Busy as a beaver
> Mad as a wet hen
> There's more than one way to skin a cat
> Dog-eat-dog world
> Dog-and-pony show

The radio predicted a blizzard of epic proportions for Thanksgiving weekend, and a powdery

snow was falling when the other guests arrived—
two exchange students from Adventist College,
and the Kims and their daughter, Sarah. When
Miss Lone dug into her mashed potatoes, she
said, "My mother would go to hell and back to
make gravy like this!" Miran dropped her fork at
the bad word and everyone laughed, even Najin.

The talk at the table grew serious, as it always
did, and the language shifted to Korean as if only
that language could contain the complexities
of war and politics. Miran and Sarah cleared
the dishes and made faces at each other. Then
they threw snowballs outside until it got too
wet and cold. Miran didn't own a collection of
Madame Alexander dolls like Sarah did, but they
had almost as much fun with her Sears catalog
cutouts.

Two weekends later, Najin dressed her up in
Korean clothes almost as if it were Halloween,
except she herself dressed in her best winter
hanbok. Calvin said they'd be giving a presentation about Korea and the war for Miss Lone's Red
Cross Volunteers' club, and her mother smiled
and said in English, "A dog-and-pony show."
John, one of the exchange students, came with
his car, and they packed his trunk with a roll map
Calvin had brought from work, Korean display
dolls in glass boxes taken right off the mantle,
baskets emptied of their sewing notions, and
lacquer and mother-of-pearl boxes. Miss Lone

introduced them, and Najin gave her daughter a tiny prompt to start the program. Miran stood and sang the children's songs "Mountain Rabbit" and "White Butterfly," thoroughly charming the audience. While her father spoke, Miran sat still on a chair up front, her gloved hands folded in her lap, and sensed the approving eyes of her mother. She heard her sister's name mentioned and listened.

". . . our youngest daughter, Inja, who just turned six, is one of those Korean refugees forced to flee the communist invasion. For more than two weeks, my wife's family went a hundred miles on foot with two elderly people and our daughter, from Seoul to a UN-protected village, while the capital city became a battleground for democracy. They are fortunate to be alive. And we recently learned that my wife's cousin also fled Seoul days after the June invasion with her six-year-old daughter, but in the crowds of refugees she lost hold of her child's hand, and to this day has not found her. These are the daily tragedies of the beleaguered Korean people . . ."

This last story captured Miran's imagination, and she visualized that poor girl of her same age wandering a desecrated Korean countryside in her hanbok, crying for her mother.

Calvin asked for donations of clothing and dried goods to send to the refugees, and they stood with

John and Miss Lone to sing the Korean national anthem. Miran didn't understand the words, but she knew the song well enough to sound out the syllables, and she saw that the soaring drama of its melody made her mother's eyes fill with tears. Her own heart surged with a strange kind of pride and a complexity of emotions she was too young to untangle.

Thus began a series of presentations at civic clubs, churches, and community centers, and boxes and bags of donations soon filled the living room and spilled onto the front porch. The work to sort, clean, mend, pack, and ship was endless, and Miran began to dread the meetings for the constant coordinating of transportation— John, Miss Lone, a volunteer from the hosting organization, or the bus—and the tons of stuff they yielded. Then, that Christmas, Dr. Kim gave her father his old Plymouth Road King, saying he needed a legitimate excuse to buy himself a Cadillac Coupe de Ville with power windows, and this was the least he could do for the refugees. After several polite back-and-forths, Calvin accepted, and Miran became queen of the back seat, starlet of song and stage, never mind that her repertoire was nursery songs, her venue a church basement.

On Sunday, December 14, 1952, in the third winter of the Korean War, Najin hosted a few families to celebrate Miran's birthday, two days late. Four girls—Miran, her friend Sarah, and Gloria Park and Susan Lee from church—sat at the kitchen table with special birthday food while their parents ate rice and Korean side dishes in the dining room. Najin had seen a picture in a donated *Ladies' Home Journal* of hot dogs made to look like sailors in their bun jackets, banana slices for their hats, mustard faces and buttons, and dollops of ketchup for the sailor knot. The kitchen was decorated with balloons and crepe-paper streamers, and Miran couldn't have been more pleased. Everyone gathered when she blew out her seven candles, and the child was so happy with her present of a fur-collared winter coat—new, from the store—that she refused to take it off, even though she was sweating, making Najin laugh.

The talk at the adults' table was of Korea. Eventually Najin cleared dishes and went to check on the children, and Mrs. Kim followed with dirty plates in hand. The kitchen ambiance was bright and warm. The kids ate cake and ice cream, and Miran sang "Happy Birthday" quietly to herself. They were playing the game Chutes and Ladders that Gloria had given her.

"Yes," said Mrs. Kim, stacking dishes on the sideboard, "I prefer to be in this world of children, too."

"It's simple and innocent, still so full of hope."

"Sticky, too." And they laughed to see the messy faces and hands of the girls.

"You mustn't give up hope," said Mrs. Kim, handing Najin dessert dishes from the dining room.

Her words pierced Najin. It opened her heart to her other daughter, who had never tasted ice cream. In that instant, with Inja's face floating before her eyes, she happened to glance at Miran, whose features unsettled her—so different were they from what she was envisioning. The moment passed but left her breathless and ashamed. She loved each child equally, but in such moments when Inja's absence surfaced, it created so strong a yearning that Miran's presence felt irrational and inexplicable in comparison.

"Are you all right?" said Mrs. Kim, concerned eyes on Najin.

"Yes—sometimes I forget about hope."

"Please don't despair. Look at these little ones and how natural it is for them to look forward to each day without question. Their attitudes are exactly what your daughter Inja is feeling, war or no war. That alone should make it more bearable."

Najin grasped her friend's arm. "You're right. Thank you. I mustn't forget that each child is a mirror of another in some way."

"And Christmas is coming—the perfect time to be delighting in our children."

Najin sighed. "I know it isn't useful, but all I can think of is how many Christmases we've missed with her. Poor child! Will she even know us as her parents?" She felt she was saying too much to Mrs. Kim, but no words could relieve her guilt at being a terrible mother. She supposed this was the reason her mind lost thoughts of Inja at times—a just punishment for having left her behind.

The counting of spaces in the game erupted as the board was toppled by Gloria. "I should win, I brought the game, it's not fair!"

"You would've been second if you didn't ruin the board, stupid," said Susan.

"You're stupid," and Gloria threw the spinner at Susan, hitting her in the face. Susan cried out, and her mother, hearing her daughter, took her to the bathroom to put a cold-water compress on her cheek.

"Gloria Park!" said Najin. "You know better than to throw things. Clean up the game, and I think it's time for everyone to go home."

"I'm sorry I won," said Miran in a small voice.

"It's not your fault," said Sarah, putting the pieces away. "Besides, it's your birthday—you're supposed to win."

Najin and Mrs. Kim looked at each other, pleased with Sarah's display of maturity.

Gloria's mother came into the kitchen, learned what happened from the very mature Sarah, and made Gloria go apologize to Susan in the bath-room. Susan had been hit on her jaw, and Dr. Kim examined it with a jokey exaggerated pro-fessionalism, which soothed the child and made everyone laugh. With the mishap smoothed over, the guests departed. Miran helped clean up the kitchen table, still humming "Happy Birthday" to herself, making Najin and Calvin smile.

"I wish all battles could find peace that easily," said Najin, her hands soapy in the sink.

"This war is bound to end," said Calvin, drying dishes. "The UN is pressuring everyone to find a truce, and the losses are only multiplying with little gain."

"When it ends, do you think we can go home?" As soon as she asked, she understood they had somehow gotten themselves into a position of not returning. To date they hadn't been able to save a single penny for the journey home, and even without the complications of family ill-nesses, Calvin's job and his ministry had become permanent. "Or bring her home here?"

Calvin said, "Yeobo, I'll give Miran a bath, then let's talk."

After Miran was in bed, Calvin came into the kitchen and sat. He'd need to nap at least a couple of hours before leaving for work, so she was aware they had little time.

"The table's all sticky," he said, and she smiled and got a washrag. He put the balloons in Miran's room so she'd see them in the morning, and pulled down the streamers, careful with the tape on the kitchen wallpaper.

"Why haven't we talked about this before?" said Najin.

"It's a funny thing about assumptions—they have a life of their own until they're called upon. We've been busy and our minds are more on today's needs than tomorrow's."

"*K'rae*," she agreed. She had been so pre-occupied with Inja's and her family's immediate safety, she'd thought little of the next steps. She put the washrag down and sat across from him.

Calvin said, "I'm thinking back to my own assumptions, and I see they shifted according to what was on the agenda at that moment: we'd go back for Inja and your family, or so that Miran wouldn't lose her Korean; we'd stay because of work and church."

"That's true for me as well, but I always assumed we'd go back someday, if not soon. I don't know how, though. We can barely send a few dollars to Dongsaeng."

"And now?" said Calvin.

Her heart surged with pain, and she used the washrag to wipe her tears. "I want our child in my arms."

He reached across the table and held her hand. She squeezed it and released.

"I do, too," he said. "Ultimately, after this war,

it may be less complicated to bring her here than for us to attempt moving to a war-torn country without prospects of work, though I could probably get a job with the American military."

"We always meant to go back with funds to start a school. Who knew it would be so hard to save money? Instead, we started a church right here."

"We still have the house in Seoul."

"With the war . . ."

"We don't have to decide anything at the moment," Calvin said. "Let's pray on it and see what happens."

"Okay. You should go to bed, you'll be exhausted."

He kissed her forehead and left.

She got up and put away the dishes, hung Miran's new coat in the closet, and piled the few birthday presents on the kitchen table. She tried to gauge how she felt: Disappointed? Relieved? All she felt was the ache of wanting Inja at home, it didn't matter which home. But she also saw they'd made a life here, in America, that would be hard if not impossible to leave.

23 Jan 1953, Friday. Earlier in the month when the house was quiet, I heard Halmeoni humming hymns as she always did when working, and when had she ever not been working? It was unseasonably

111

warm, so I thought the radiators were buzzing, but I heard her sing all week. I got Dongsaeng's letter today after asking him if something had happened, but he said all was well and my asking about it made him realize she rarely sang or hummed at all these days, except at church. I cannot know why her lifetime habit is silenced, but I have decided I must have music in the house not only to compensate for this small loss, but because hearing her sing made me long for her and for music. I will tell Miran's father the child should have piano lessons, though I'm the one wanting to play once again. He won't care about the cost, probably his biggest folly. Dongsaeng says to send them things they can sell. He has no thought about what it costs here.

18 Feb 1953, Weds. We cut back on the frequency of our dog-and-pony shows. Calvin is exhausted with pre-diabetes. People still leave things on our porch. Postage went up, but I can still send packages filled from the bounty of America's gold mountain. How sweet that Inja shared her candy at Sunday school—I suppose I should thank Dongsaeng for raising her with good Christian spirit.

And I do thank him for bringing her to safety during the invasion. He surprised me with his persistence and strength. Perhaps my child has changed him, too. My mind grows cluttered with absent buttons, missing keys to anchovy tins, broken zippers, mothballs, and crumbling soap bars. But she is always in my heart.

The Cho family continued to make presentations about Korea, though not as often. Najin had to let out the sleeves and hem of Miran's hanbok, until she cut down one of her own Korean skirts and blouses for her growing daughter. Najin's kimchi business brought in thirty-eight dollars every two weeks, and she sent goods and money to her brother. The civil defense drills continued at school, and Miran still helped with the packages, though now Calvin delivered them to the post office in his car. Miran kept a detailed inventory of each carton at her mother's request, recorded in leather-bound diaries.

97th package to Han Ilsun, 25 March 1953
    7 polo shirts
    5 nightgowns
    10 slips and underwear
    6 pair men's socks
    9 dresses, 7 made and 2 purchased
    5 yards of material

5 cards of hairpins
10 air fresheners
toothpaste, toothbrushes
2 bottles cologne
1 can DDT
1 doz. chewing gum in box

16 lbs. $2.24

Miran's printing grew smaller, developed into cursive and got even smaller, a maturity demonstrated in the progression of those lists intermixed with Najin's entries in Korean. And her arithmetic improved when Najin began listing prices of purchased items and asked her to total them up per package, per week, per month. She sat on the floor for countless hours with her mother to tape and tie up boxes, and never once revealed her longing for the chocolate bars, chewing gum, the trendy sneakers, the pink toothbrush, the pencil sharpener shaped like a globe that got sent overseas. She thought her Korean sister was lucky, luckier than she was, but it was risky to be jealous of this sole sibling whom she might actually like, so, instead, she resented Korea and everything Korean.

PART II

ARMISTICE
1953–1956

11

Return to Seoul

Ami-dong locals proclaimed the summer of 1953 as the hottest ever recorded, with frequent cloud cover that elevated the humidity to nonstop sweltering. Some blamed it on a surge of aggression by Chinese troops, or a Russian atomic bomb at an undisclosed location to commemorate the death of Stalin, or alchemy performed by Chairman Mao to disrupt the forces of nature. All such talk ended when a cease-fire was declared on July 27, its requirements finally negotiated to satisfaction by both sides. Inja learned in class how to spell *armistice, Eisenhower, Panmunjom, Demilitarized Zone.* When she showed Uncle the A+ on her spelling test, he praised her work, then said that with the exception of a few kilometers at the DMZ, their divided country ended up being exactly like it was before the war, so nothing had changed—and everything had changed.

Schools closed for the August summer break. Despite the stifling heat, Busan witnessed an exodus of its northern refugees, some on trains but most on foot as they had arrived. Uncle

declared it was time to go home. The crematorium's stack still belched its dreadful smoke,
making their sorry real estate unsalable, but
he sold its raw materials to a man who wanted
to build an addition to his house. The family
parted from the EunCheon church that he and
Inja's mother had helped establish. Though sad
to leave her teachers, Inja was eager to go home,
hoping Uncle and Aunt would fight less in their
bigger house in Seoul, or at least she could avoid
hearing them in a different part of the house. She
remembered little of Seoul, though she recalled
the crowds at departure, falling under the cart,
the nighttime river crossing, and that she'd
received the Bible storybook soon before they'd
left. She still treasured it and had copied most of
the English letterforms of the captions, though
she didn't know how to pronounce the words. At
bedtime certain pictures from the book came alive
in her imagination—the women ogling Moses at
the well, Lot's daughters eyeing him with lust,
the half-naked idolaters at Mount Sinai—and
warmth would blossom in her gut. She'd sigh
with pleasure and fall asleep, dreaming of books
filled with glossy color plates.

The family of one of Uncle's acquaintances,
a fellow he'd known from grade school in
Kaesong, shared a boxcar with them and other
Seoul-bound folk, who sat with their bundles and
suitcases. There were seven members of the Jeon

family, all adults except a boy Inja's age, named Hyo. Before boarding, he bumped into her and feigned a broken rib with such conviction that she almost called for Uncle, until he started laughing. Inja had saved a stick of Juicy Fruit gum from her mother's last package and gave him half. The Han family settled inside, sitting on bundles knee to knee with others, and she showed Hyo how to wrap his tiny lump in his half of the gum's foil for the next time. Hyo's father, Mr. Jeon, told Uncle in a loud voice that now was the time to invest in industry—automobiles, electricity, construction, steel, that sort of thing. He boasted how well he'd done with bricks and said that the way to overcome the communist threat was to bolster industry. Uncle agreed, amiable, and Aunt said he wasted all his money on church.

The train grew more crowded as it continued north. At Daegu, Inja and her uncle peeked outside to see many people sitting on the roofs of the railcars and hanging off its ladders, and she was glad they were inside and not in danger of falling off the train, even if it was stuffy and hot. Though Busan had been her primary home in her memory, she wouldn't miss the ramshackle school where she'd been the brunt of much teasing because of her mother who wasn't a mother. They sat in the dark closed car, coughing in wafts of coal smoke when the train took a corner, and dozed as the light broke through the cracks in the wood.

The keening wind and clamorous train prevented conversation. She and Hyo chewed their gum twice more, then tucked the wads of foil into their pockets for later. Nothing but a hint of that delicious sweet fruitiness remained in those wads, but they chewed them with gusto anyway.

Both grandparents had aged during the war years in Busan, and Grandmother had grown forgetful and repeated herself, which drove Aunt mad. Though still interested in politics, Grandfather had shrunk, his face drawn with many unmentioned aches.

At Yongsan, the Seoul terminus, they parted from the Jeons, who hired a man with a cart and several porters to haul their many bags and bundles to a downtown hotel. Inja's family found a nearby inn to rest for one night, while Uncle went to investigate the condition of their house. He returned long after dark, sweaty but pleased. "It's vacant now," he said, "but someone was living there. There are bullet holes in the walls and dirt is everywhere—broken crockery. Nothing of ours remains, though I can't recall what we left—some chests and tables."

"Any sign of Cook and her daughter?" said Grandmother, lucid.

Inja had almost forgotten them, and at this mention a sharp memory rose of Cook laughing with Grandmother on her back, of Yun's thin wrists and timid smile.

"Perhaps they'll find their way back to us," Uncle said, more placating than optimistic.

Inja understood they had been lost in the war, like so many others she'd heard about in church and school, and they would never know what happened to them. She said a prayer, asking God to see them to their home village, safe and with plenty to eat. Even it if wasn't true, that tiny bit of hope embedded in those few words gave her an image of Cook and Yun that made it bearable. Cook was an uneducated widow with a thirteen-year-old daughter, now sixteen, who had been her nanny and friend, and they had left them behind. There was so much to feel bad about in the war. A few words of prayer helped shift those feelings into the recesses of a busy mind.

Uncle said, "The city is empty. Everyone is hiding or—who's to say where they've gone? There's a new American base a few streets from our house, and downtown is all bombed-out buildings blackened by fire. Lots of soldiers, both ours and GIs, checking papers—mine were checked dozens of times."

The next day they packed quickly and left the inn. Uncle carried Grandmother, and Inja stayed in step with Grandfather, burdened by her own small bundle, with three porters trailing behind. She almost turned to examine these laborers to see if any were big or friendly, but instinct told her such a gesture was pointless—and sad.

When the sun peaked and they neared their road, smoke still rose from the black rubble of the decimated house across the way. Though Inja was eager to be inside their gate, she hung back until Grandfather said, "Don't worry, there are no bodies."

Their property appeared small, the two houses covered in grime. She didn't remember the front house, which had always been leased out, but the rear house had a strange familiarity, dreamlike yet sturdy, and she felt older to have a memory of those rooms. She and Aunt opened the windows wide and scoured the sills, shelves, and floor. Grandfather went to bed with a stomachache. The few markets open were those edging the city, so Uncle and Aunt took salt to trade for rice, cabbage, what other food they could find, and medicine for Grandfather. Uncle said to clean well so he could fill the bullet holes with straw and mud.

With a bucket of water and a rag, Inja washed the walls and remembered having heard that her father had built this house with his own hands. What did his hands look like, and would she ever know them? Now they were home, and a new life would begin. Now the war was over, and perhaps her American family would return. She stopped scrubbing, and water dripped from the rags and puddled on the floor. She hadn't ever before wondered what it would be like when—or if—her parents returned, nor had Uncle ever mentioned such a thing. Her mother's letters spoke of "our reunion" and "after the war," a time that had now arrived. Unable and unwilling to imagine it, she sopped up the spill and edged the idea out of her thoughts as easily as she wrung out the rags.

12

Professions

Traces of sunrise tinted the dawn sky pink on Easter Sunday, 1954. Though the temperature was predicted to reach eighty by midday, the morning was cool. Miran donned a beige sweater over a peach-colored Easter dress that Najin had sewn, identical to the dress she'd sent to her sister in Seoul. Miran wondered if it was as scratchy around the neck for her sister as it was for her. She tugged on donated white gloves that looked almost new. Her mother wore a pale green hanbok—traditional dress because they would be in the company of wounded Korean War veterans at the Walter Reed Army Hospital for Easter sunrise service. Her father wore a black suit, his clerical collar and vest, and had laid his minister's robe and shawl on the back seat of the Plymouth. He had been invited to give the sermon and had spent long hours writing his talk on sacrifice and resurrection that would end with a special note of gratitude to these American young men and their fallen brethren.

In previous years at this sunrise service, they'd stood on the ridge of a broad valley of lawn behind the hospital. As before, potted Easter lilies' heavy sweetness lined the pathways, and hyacinths bobbed in the flower beds below azaleas of many colors. Today Miran and Najin sat on the reserved folding chairs in front of the platform, upon which Calvin sat with other clergy behind the pulpit for the Christian but nondenominational service. The seating area was set aside for military dignitaries, veterans' family members, and soldiers who could walk with or without crutches, and a wider area of the yard was reserved for the wounded, who were escorted out in wheelchairs and on gurneys. Miran couldn't help but stare at the stark white bandages visible on some of the men, scars that marred facial features, gazes that looked nowhere, gaps where limbs should be. She admired the men in white pushing those wheelchairs and gurneys, the women in navy blue capes and crisp nurses' caps standing nearby, and wanted to know what had happened to these young men who'd gone to war in her parents' country.

Her father, the shortest man on the platform, seemed to be regarded with respect by the others, and she was impressed by his command of the pulpit, his cadence in delivering the sermon. On occasion she had heard him give sermons in English as guest minister at the Takoma Park Presbyterian Church, but this dawning day seemed to bestow on him a majesty she hadn't known he possessed. She did not rustle in her seat, suck on Life Savers, or doodle on the program as she did at Korean church; she sat rapt to be able to understand all the words he spoke, if not the depth of their meaning. His message recognized these heroic men who suffered not for material gain and perhaps not for any purpose they could easily discern in such a distant and foreign nation, but for duty, for an idea of freedom. His passionate gratitude for their service gave her determination to be of service to the men in return. She would be a nurse.

Later that morning at home, while Calvin dressed a ham with pineapple and cloves, Najin and Miran sat at the table dyeing hard-boiled eggs, a first for the family. Calvin had bought the egg dye on a whim while grocery shopping for their big Easter dinner. Miran wore the one pair of rubber gloves in the house, and it wasn't long before Najin's fingers were multicolored from fishing the eggs out of their hot dye baths. Miran slipped a pale pink egg into the crate to dry, and Najin's wet fingers accidentally dripped a little blue on its top. She laughed. "It looks like you, Yeobo! See, Miran, how it looks like Dad's hair? Let's get crayons and pens and make them people."

They spent the remainder of the morning laughing and making a mess of things, the kitchen ripe with the smells of dye vinegar and baking ham. The gloves were too awkward for fine handiwork, and soon Miran's fingers were as stained and colorful as her mother's. Najin discovered how the wax crayons resisted the dye, and used this decorating technique to make likenesses of each of their guests for place cards. Such fun they had that morning, and all the guests laughed at their egg images and at Najin's and Miran's mutually colored fingertips. "She's a true artist," said Najin, smiling at her daughter.

Days later at the public library, Miran read about Florence Nightingale and Clara Barton. Throughout that year, reading two steps above her grade level, she read books about student nurses. Those stories were filled with problems with head nurses and attractive doctors, crabby patients and friends who were mean to each other to get ahead. She decided to be a librarian.

That autumn they celebrated her Korean sister's birthday, September 24, with hot dogs, cake, Pepsi-Cola, and balloons taped to the walls, just as they celebrated hers every December 12. Her mother gave her a hug, a deliberate act of affection so rare she wiggled out of it right away. Najin turned with tears in her eyes that Miran didn't understand weren't about her, and Calvin made a fuss of cutting the cake. "It's a special time," said Najin. "You're both the same age until December. Like twins."

Miran, disoriented, said, "No, it's her birthday,

not mine." She didn't even know this Korean sister who was supposed to be her twin and could barely recall seeing her in photographs. There were framed portraits of Miran's grandparents in their bedroom, but none of her sister. And where were pictures of her father's Korean family? The earliest photos she'd seen of herself were as a toddler on the ship traveling to America. She would be a photographer, like Margaret Bourke-White from *LIFE* magazine. She'd make a record of herself and her parents, and maybe the relatives to whom they continued to send packages would send pictures, so she could see if she and her sister of the same age for the winter months looked as closely alike as twins.

A few days later when she taped shut the next package going overseas and saw a Brownie camera and several rolls of film tucked inside, she understood it was one more thing war-torn Korea didn't have. She would be a missionary and then she could also be a nurse, librarian, and photographer—and see for herself how near a twin she was to her foreign sister.

24 September 1954, Friday. Inja's eighth birthday. Now the girls are the same age again. Sometimes I imagine out of the corner of my eye it is Inja at home, and such longing fills my arms that I go over and give Miran a hug. She squirms away

in surprise. It is quiet with Miran back in school this fall.

134th package to Han Ilsun
    6 yds. cotton flannel
    2 women's suit (Victoria's)
    3 heavy pants given by some club
    2 hand towels
    1 Pond's cream
    2 fluffy slippers for Aunt and housegirl
    2 school dresses—twins with Miran
    1 Brownie camera, 6 rolls film
    2 painting colors and brush—birthday
      presents
    art paper
    kids' scissors
    2 picture books
    4 Lux soap

    22 lbs. $3.28

13

Postwar Story

The autumn after Armistice Day hardened into winter. What vegetation was left in Seoul's mountainous forests—already stripped of trees during the war—was denuded to mud by the hundreds of thousands of returning denizens seeking to heat their homes or shacks, while Americans worked with the Rhee government to rebuild the demolished city. The cold north winds roared unhindered down the stark mountain slopes and rattled through the house. Aunt's cousin Ara, ten years older than Inja, had come from the country to be housekeeper and cook. Their rice was no longer burnt or watery, and Ara addressed Grandmother's needs—she had become incontinent and the diapers were a terrible chore. Ara had the same pretty oval-shaped face as Aunt, with narrow straight eyes like two lively lines on fine creamy paper. At first she was quiet and unsure, but soon her singing rang through the house as she washed floors. Plans for Christmas 1953 did little to brighten the dreary winter, until shortly before the holiday Uncle announced to the family that at last Aunt was pregnant. The ensuing jubilation was tempered by the lack of nutritious food for Aunt and other hardships of postwar restoration.

By the following springtime in 1954, the city of Seoul remained in disorder. Inflation ran high and reconstruction slowed, but main roadways were clear, and vendors crowded the markets. Many new shops—mere shacks—cropped up in Itaewon by the central American military garrison at Yongsan, as did the inevitable drinking establishments and shantytowns of prostitutes. Except in the vicinities of military bases, electricity was rare, streetlights nonexistent, and nearly all of the few vehicles on the streets belonged to the army.

Education was made a priority during restoration, and though Inja had attended school soon after returning to Seoul, she was now enrolled in a new elementary school for girls a thirty-minute walk from home. Uncle convinced Mr. Jeon, with whom they'd shared the boxcar, to buy the land of the burned-down house across the road, and workmen were building a Western-style brick house. Grandfather told Inja such a modern structure would chase away the communist ghosts, and she was relieved. She played with Hyo for hours in those piles of bricks, constructing forts, buildings, and soon an entire town, until the workmen needed the bricks to finish the house. Still, many were left in the yard, and they played and became friends, despite his family being rich and hers poor. Hyo told her he'd kept the chewing gum for a week, beating her record of six days.

On May 17, Buddha's birthday and a school holiday, Uncle and Inja walked to church to drop off a bundle of clothes. She wore gray cotton trousers and a white blouse from the last set of packages, and as she slipped her hand under Uncle's elbow, she smelled the mothballs her mother always tucked among the garments. Though her mother often wrote "when we are together" in her letters, no one mentioned specifics about a reunion. It had always been something to hope for, which was fine because it seemed impossible, but how and when would it happen? Would it be here at home or there in America? If it were to be the latter, how would she travel to America, and would all the family go? Aunt's pregnancy and her grandparents' frailty, as well as the unimaginable cost, would prevent them from leaving Seoul. And what would happen to Ara? Surely after losing Cook and Yun, they wouldn't leave her behind. Inja's footsteps crackled beside Uncle's on the pebbly road, and they passed a temple bedecked with paper lanterns. She wasn't supposed to pray to Buddha, and she was afraid to pray to God, not knowing what to pray for. Why would anyone pray for there to be *no* hope for something as exciting as an American reunion?

"Will they come to Seoul now?" she said, head bowed.

"What? Your family? Of course not!" Uncle gazed at her and shifted the bundle under one arm to hold her hand. "It's darkest beneath the lamp," he muttered, meaning one does not often see what is closest at hand. Inja breathed the mothball smell from her collar. "Things have changed," said Uncle, and she knew he meant "since the war."

"Your mom and dad can't come back now. Your father is a big man on the radio that broadcasts democratic ideas to North Korea, anti-communist ideas, you understand?"

She nodded, impressed with her important father—on the radio! They didn't own a radio, though one was often blaring in the square. "Is that him on the radio downtown?"

"Wouldn't that be amazing? But no, those are all Seoul stations." He stopped walking and turned to her. "Also, around the time you were born, he worked for the American military. The communists would target him as an American spy, a wanted man. With so many North Korean kidnappings these days, all kinds of people are disappearing, like that film star and her director husband, taken right off the street. It would be dangerous for him to return."

It thrilled Inja to know he would be considered a spy, but she wasn't sure how she felt about them never coming back. They resumed walking.

"Your parents are now trying to bring you to America, but it's costly and complicated."

They reached the church, and she paused on the steps and touched his elbow. "Does it mean I won't have to go?"

"Not for a while. It could be a long time. Your mother is heartsick with missing you, and your father is trying to find a way." Uncle dropped his bundle and held her shoulders. "Do you mind very much?"

To show that she was actually quite relieved, she wrapped her arms around him. When they disengaged, his eyes, wet with love, shone. He said something prayerful about the great measure of his sister's love, such that she'd leave her firstborn with him. Inja examined him, her eyebrows raised in question, but he wiped his eyes and drew her into the church.

After they dropped off the bundle of clothes in the narthex, they entered the sanctuary and slid into a back pew halfway illuminated by colored light from an intact stained-glass window, dust particles wafting in its rainbow hues. Uncle patted the warm wood, inviting her to sit closer. "There's something else you should know because you're older now. You've lived through war, so I think you can understand how such a thing can happen."

She was eight, but she knew he meant she was

old enough to know why their church had most of its windows broken and covered with canvas, the Sunday school wing a jumble of crumbling walls and broken roof tiles, most of the congregation scattered.

"I will tell you a story about a baby who came before you were born."

"Your baby girl? My cousin who died?" She'd heard about Uncle's daughter on occasion, a fact from before she was born about a little girl named Sun-ok who'd gotten pneumonia. She figured it made Aunt's pregnancy all the more precious to them. What a joy it would be to have a cute baby in the house!

He squeezed her knee, smiling, but with sad eyes. "It's good of you to remember the cousin you never met. No, this is about a different baby girl."

Inja settled in beside him, legs crossed on the seat, chin in her palms, the sun warm on her hair. Uncle's voice echoed dully in the empty sanctuary like a bell with a muted clapper. "Did you know that during the war your mother was a midwife?"

He meant the war with the Japanese, not the war they had just lived through. "She helped women deliver their babies," said Inja, "mostly poor women who couldn't pay."

"Who told you that?" he said, pleased.

"Halmeoni."

136

"Yes, she helped many mothers like that. And this story is about such a mother. It was a cold winter, and everyone was hungry those days . . ." He explained that Inja's father's job with the American military government took him all around the country. He'd been named Minister of Education and was tasked with examining all the high schools and universities to see which should stay open, merge, or close. He traveled for weeks at a time and was away that night.

"A woman came to our gate and shouted for the midwife. She was already in labor, and it was strange that she hadn't gone to the hospital. In the years under the Japanese, many women wanted to avoid their hospitals, but now it was all Korean doctors and American missionary doctors, and your mother hadn't delivered babies for some time, so we were surprised. I went to see who was shouting, and the woman stumbled through the gate like an apparition. She was very distressed." Long pause.

"Your grandfather and I were in the sitting room on the other side of the house, but we heard the piteous cries of the woman being helped by your mom, grandmother, and aunt. The baby was a porcelain-hued girl, but then she turned blue. Your mother told Aunt to take care of the woman, who was dazed, crying, saying crazy things. They worried she might have an infection or was bleeding inside, but your mother was occupied with the baby. She held the infant, chest down, and rubbed her back, and she started breathing. I saw her in the kitchen where they'd prepared warm water and clean cloths. *Yah,* she was a beautiful baby! Skin like raw silk, small ears and a bud of a nose, thick hair—and everyone cooed to see such perfect features. Aunt came in to say that the woman had delivered the afterbirth and was calm now and resting, and we admired the newborn who mewed like a kitten and wiggled just as she was supposed to.

"Your mother wrapped up the baby and went in to give her to the woman, but she was gone."

"Without her baby?"

"Yes." Uncle seemed to have words teetering on the edge of his lips, but he remained thoughtful. "She ran away in the minute or two Aunt had left her alone. She took her clothes, even the wet and bloody things, stole a quilt, and disappeared. I ran outside in the cold, and even though there was curfew, I went everywhere trying to find her. I searched for many days and learned from some people in the neighborhood that she was a widow who had moved away some months ago. I never found her." He shifted in his seat and gazed at the altar far ahead.

In that silence, Inja remembered the mother and her son from the river, separated in the kingdom of heaven. She had seen the picture of the children's graveyard in her Bible book many times since, and it always struck her with a longing for something she couldn't name.

"We asked at the hospital and among church people if someone could take the baby, but food was scarce and nobody could take her. Your mother registered the baby as abandoned and kept her. We were worried that your father wouldn't approve, but he accepted her like that." He clapped once, and the sound reverberated in the lofty damaged ceiling of the sanctuary.

Inja sat up straight.

Uncle sighed and pulled out his handkerchief to dab his brow. "This happened just one month after my little girl died, so I thought God had given us a great gift, and I devoted myself to helping the baby survive. Those first months she was very weak and couldn't eat. The doctor thought her digestive system wasn't fully developed, but there was no fixed reason, just as there was no reason for my Sun-ok to die. I stayed up countless nights dripping rice water into her mouth, praying. Then by late spring she was fine, a sweet and loving baby with milky skin, her personality watchful and calm."

Inja had an internal sense of descending quiet, like going into a dark cavern where a door would open. She untangled a memory of a story Grandmother had once told about a sick baby who almost died. This baby in Uncle's story was an orphan. Kids teased Inja by calling her an orphan, but the baby in Uncle's story had it worse—her mother didn't want her. Then she remembered those stories were told when they were fleeing Seoul and heading to some orphanage where her mother had once worked. Were they going there to visit this girl? The orphan girl would have been a little older than herself . . . An image of broken looms and spindles from Grandmother's dream flashed behind her eyes. Inja looked at Uncle and knew what he would say next.

"Yes, little one, that was—that *is* your *unnee*, your older sister." He turned and clasped her hands. "Your father embraced the child as his and named her Miran, which means beautiful orchid, because her delivery to us was rare and foreign, and therefore all the more precious. I wanted to adopt the child myself, but your mother was already attached to her from having delivered her. None of us were surprised that your father was gentle and loving with his surprise daughter. And then your mother was pregnant with her own first child, and they named you *Inja,* which means revered and benevolent daughter." He paused and gave her space on the pew. "Do you understand?"

She took time to think. Each thought and memory opened the door wider, and windows flew open in her mind. It made complete sense. From what she could remember of the few photographs from America, Miran didn't resemble her, and she now wondered how much her sister resembled their parents. Miran's eyebrows were straight, her nose cute and little, her face a pleasing heart-shape unlike her own rounded cheeks. Grandmother had said that her sister was a sickly baby, which was why—and because she was the eldest—they had taken her to America. She said to Uncle, "Ajeossi, is she still sick?"

"No longer. But more than once we thought we'd lose her."

A little explosion of memory connected this to Grandmother's unfinished story about her sister almost dying. And now she didn't know what to think. She loved her uncle and her grandparents, but even if Miran was a sick baby, why, if she wasn't a real sister, a real daughter—why had she been the one to go to America with her parents?

Uncle must have read her thoughts. "It shows something about your mother's love for us, for her family, for me."

Her mind swirled with questions and something dark she didn't like feeling.

"They meant to stay in America for two, three years at the most, but the war . . ."

Always it was *the war.* This war, the war before, the one before that. It seemed everyone used it as an excuse for all ills. And perhaps it was.

Uncle touched her arm to make her look at him. "Though you were a baby of an age that would have made overseas travel difficult, the truth is your mother loved us—Halmeoni and all of

141

us—your mother loved us so much that she left behind her blood child for us to love. Had she left the adopted one, we would have doubted that she would return. Neither of your parents could have predicted this war, but I want you to understand the measure of the sacrifice your mother made for our sake. I consider it a special gift of love that she gave us her favored, her blood daughter."

He drew his finger down Inja's cheek, and she tried to smile beyond her confusion.

"She's always taken care of me in more ways than an older sister should," said Uncle. "And to me, your being with us is a testament of that great love, a love greater than human limitation—that she would give her most loved child to me to raise until she could be reunited with you."

Inja's uncertainty melted in the intimacy that shone from his eyes. He made her feel special to have been the one chosen to be left behind, and she felt grateful for Miran, for Miran's being an orphan, for Miran's infant sicknesses that had made it possible for her—Inja, her mother's true firstborn—to be with this most beloved of uncles, this most beloved of men, who clearly loved her more than any living thing on this earth. All she could do was meet his eyes, those depths of acceptance and joy, and clutch both arms around his neck to show that she did understand—and that she was grateful, too.

14

Fallout

Since first grade Miran walked the six blocks to and from school by herself. Though the war in Korea had ended, the Cold War escalated and the civil defense drills continued. By third grade, keen on spotting the signs with the three yellow triangles in a black circle, she'd identified every fallout shelter in her neighborhood and around the downtown church they rented for afternoon Korean service. She hoped when the bombs dropped she'd be near the library's designated shelter—the reference room encased in the basement's thick cinder-block walls. Not only did it have a bathroom and a water fountain, but she could also read the encyclopedias from A to Z and learn about the world.

When Miran began fourth grade in September 1955, Najin had a job on Mondays, Wednesdays, and Fridays teaching the Korean language to intelligence officers at Fort Holabird—work procured by an American military man her parents had met before Miran was born. On weekends, Najin continued to make kimchi for a few restaurants as well. By the basement utility sink, she washed and salted cabbage in a big galvanized tub, added garlic and radishes, paprika and hot pepper, then stuffed the kimchi into gallon jars and let it ferment beside the cool concrete walls until it could be sold at four dollars a gallon.

Calvin had been promoted to translation editor at the VOA and now worked regular nine-to-five hours, so Miran came home to an empty house three days a week. On the afternoons Mrs. Bushong caught her going around to the mud porch, she'd invite her over for cinnamon toast, but Miran tried to avoid the chatty neighbor, no longer interested in her salt and pepper shakers, and all the more uncomfortable with adults. She'd been told to practice an hour on the old upright piano Najin had bought earlier that spring, and do the laundry or other housework and homework, but as the weeks passed, she discovered she could do what she liked as long as the visible chores were done and she was home by five to make rice.

To expand her personal domain, Miran explored different routes home and discovered a corner store frequented by the sixth-grade safety-patrol kids. If she saved her milk money, she could buy a 3 Musketeers. The crosswalk before the store was monitored by a tall girl with wiry brown hair. One afternoon in October, Miran lingered half a block from the store and learned the girl's name from two boys who defiantly walked through her stop-and-wait signal. One said, "Janet, Janet, alien from a retard planet," the other said, "Planet Moron," and they laughed. At least someone else was being called that, a label attached to Miran because her unfamiliar name slipped so easily into "moron." She felt a strange mix of disdain and sympathy for Janet.

"I'm going to report you," Janet shouted, red-faced. She turned, saw Miran, and glared. Though Miran felt bad for her, that look made her afraid, and she went home. She played fingering exercises on the piano and swept the front steps and sidewalk.

On Monday the week before Halloween, Miran's saved pennies burned in her palm, and she ventured to the corner. She stopped behind Janet's correctly spread arms blocking her from crossing the street. A long time passed and Janet didn't put her arms down, though not a single car was in sight. The girl stood stiff as an arrow, eyes front.

Miran said, "Hi," and stepped next to Janet on the curb.

"I'll report you if you cross," Janet said.

Miran turned and left, and by the time she got home, she was hot and frustrated. She fumed at her cowardice of Janet. Had she always been so weak? Teachers who remarked on how quiet she was made it sound like praise, but they couldn't see the vast room of silence inside, its walls as thick as a fallout shelter, smothering her words.

On Wednesday she trudged down Maple Avenue, telling herself to go ahead and cross over to the store no matter what, as a test of her courage. She saw Janet's back—and also the cute boy who was the captain of the safety patrol on the opposite corner. With such monitoring, Janet would be forced to allow her to cross, and Miran approached with bravado. Janet didn't move her head, but her eyes slid down to meet hers. The patrol captain waved all-clear, and Janet turned sideways to swing one ushering arm.

Victorious, Miran stepped off the curb.

Janet sing-songed below her breath, "Ching-chong Chinaman."

Miran's neck flushed, and she whirled and threw the pennies at the patrol girl's face. Janet's eyes opened wide and she round-housed both hands, striking Miran on the head and shoulder. The patrol captain shouted, ran across the street, and grabbed one of Janet's wrists. Another blow landed on Miran's neck, and she fell, more stunned than in pain—furious to be crying like a child. She caught her breath and wiped her tears with a sleeve. Her knee stung from scraping the asphalt, her skirt was torn, and a dull pain throbbed on her collarbone. Another safety patrol boy had appeared and was picking up her pennies.

The captain crouched by Miran. "Are you hurt? Can you get on the sidewalk?"

Miran scrambled to her feet and suppressed the twinge from her scraped knee. "I'm fine."

He said to Janet, "She's just a kid. You're twice her size!"

"She started it! Dumb Chink hit me with that money." Janet rubbed her arms.

"Did she call you names like that?" the boy asked Miran. "You can tell me. My name is Daniel Walczak, and I'm the captain of the safety patrol."

His attention almost made her cry again. Now she was more afraid of her parents finding out than anything else. The other boy gave her the pennies, and she slipped them into her pocket.

Daniel leaned in. "She's a troublemaker. Did she start it? That's demerits for Janet."

Something recognizable flicked across Janet's features, and it unleashed in Miran an unplanned barrage. "It's my fault, not hers. We were pretending to fight. I tripped. It's not fair to get her in trouble. We're friends! I have to go home. Bye, Janet!" She tried to smile as if they were longtime buddies and turned to go, careful to not limp.

"Wait, what's your name?" called Daniel to her retreating back.

"Sarah. My name is Sarah Kim." She waved, ran, and hurried left at the corner, where she cried a little more to calm the wordless jumble inside.

At home she applied mercurochrome and a bandage, changed out of her school clothes, and washed her face. The mirror revealed a bruise forming on her collarbone. Miran practiced scales on the piano and prepared a story. She had run home, not paying attention, and tripped on a fire hydrant at Philadelphia and Grant—the need for specificity while lying was instinctive. She'd scraped her knee on the concrete and bruised her neck on the fireplug. She was fine, but it still hurt a little—could she stay home from school tomorrow?

Later, she basked in her parents' concern, but felt guilty and didn't ask for the day off.

Over the weekend she and her mother worked on her Halloween costume, sewing dozens of brown-paper-bag "feathers"—simple oblongs—in layers onto a long jacket and a boy's cap from the donations. Miran pasted round reptile eyes on the cap, yellow construction paper on its visor for a beak, and skinny yellow triangles on her shoes for claws. When she tucked her head down and flapped her feathered arms, she did look like a big brown owl or at least some kind of bird, and it made Najin laugh the whole time they worked on it together. "You'll win first prize this year, I'm sure of it," said her mother.

At the annual Halloween parade in the schoolyard, Miran won the blue ribbon but was embarrassed because the school principal kept asking for her mother to join them on the platform. Of course Miran had brought the mimeographed flyer home, but she hadn't shown it to her parents, knowing they'd be working. When she stepped down and rejoined her class, only the teacher said, "Congratulations." She bowed her cap to hide her sad eyes.

"Sarah Kim? Where'd you come up with that name? Great costume!" Rescued by Daniel Walczak, the captain of the safety patrol once more! But he wasn't alone—a tall witch with green goo smeared on her cheeks was behind him. "Once I saw it was you, I got your pal Janet to come over, too."

"Um, hi—" Miran said. She couldn't tell if he was sincere, accusing, or teasing. A hank of dark hair fell over his forehead, and her stomach did a turn, a sensation utterly new to her. She liked it and was afraid of it at the same time.

Janet narrowed her eyes but dug into her trick-or-treat bag and stuck out a full-size Milky Way bar. "Here, take this."

Miran stood still, wings at rest, owl eyes wide.

"Come on, I got it for you. It's from outer space, from Planet Janet." She blushed crimson under that green goo, dropped the candy in Miran's bag, and sauntered off.

"Neato," said Miran, trying out the trendy phrase.

"Right, cool, whatever-your-name-is," Daniel said with a wide smile, saluting her.

She walked home, wearing her costume and a goofy smile, the blue ribbon pinned to her owl chest. But no one was home to see how happy she was until suppertime, by which time the curtain of silence had already dropped. Still, Najin was thrilled that she'd won, and her father taped the blue ribbon to the kitchen door.

15

Medicines

On Seollal, New Year's Day, everyone wore new, though used, clothes from America. A celebratory feast was supposed to be prepared to set the precedent for the coming year, but even chicken feet couldn't be found for the special soup, vegetables impossible to locate, rice cakes a mere dream. Uncle's worry multiplied about the family's need for protein. The rare times they had fish, it was served to Aunt. Inja was small for eight, Grandmother was shrinking, and even Grandfather was diminished. He ate little, yet his stomach rounded. He attributed it to their diet of beans, but Uncle worried about malnutrition. Grandfather's solution was to sit on the porch with a slingshot in hand, waiting. When robins, grackles, or even sparrows skittered across the courtyard—*twang!*—he'd fire and land one. Inja admired his accuracy but didn't have his patience and wandered off. After he shot two or three, he called Inja to bring a bowl of water. They dipped and cleaned the birds, speared them on a stick, and she turned the tiny birds over a small fire. No one but Inja and Grandfather would eat the scrawny birds—more bones than meat. The two sat side by side by the smoldering fire and chewed the charred shreds that tasted of smoke, sucked on the hollow toothpick bones, and licked their fingers.

Winter blossomed into spring, and the clang of hammers, children playing, and mixed smells of city life filled the road, as did the constant popping sounds of practice gunfire from the military base nearby. Uncle entered contests to design logos for newspapers, magazines, and new businesses. He won every time and said he made a good living off the prize money, though Aunt's expression suggested otherwise. He paid for night school for Ara, who was excited to learn to read and write. Because of Ara's night school and Aunt's pregnancy, the bedtime job of soaking Grandmother's feet fell to Inja.

Most days Grandmother sat complacent, a fly-swatter in her hand. She often had her Bible open, but it lay unread while she studied the daylight slanting through the window as it crawled across the floor, on the alert for insect intruders. She had been the guardian of Inja and her mother for so many years, and she remained a sentinel in their shared room. Inja no longer minded tending to her feet, though she wondered if it was neces-sary. Her nail-less toes were always dry beneath their wrappings and, though odd-looking, were scrupulously clean. She seemed to have no pain.

Every night, Inja threw shards of willow bark to steep in a basin of hot water. Though the willow tree that Inja's father had planted in the backyard had gone the way of most of the trees around Seoul for wartime fuel, it had yielded a half-dozen baby willows that they nurtured behind the protection of their walls. Until the trees grew bigger, they bought the inexpensive bark from the herbalist.

One night Inja wondered about the cause of Grandmother's ailment. "Halmeoni, do you remember how you got frostbite?"

"Did I have frostbite? Maybe a long time ago." Something changed in her voice, and her eyes filled with old sorrows.

Inja said, "Don't worry. It doesn't matter," and dried and wrapped her water-wrinkled feet. She read aloud a chapter from the open pages of her Bible, Psalms, and helped her settle in bed, more curious than ever about how she had gotten frostbite. But Inja had homework to do and forgot about it until Saturday, when Uncle said he was going downtown.

Every weekend they went together to read the banner headlines flapping in the square, pick up a newspaper, see if any new contests were posted, and browse the open markets to "evaluate the reconstruction," said Uncle. Sometimes they witnessed protests by university students waving placards against the president's repressive laws that filled prisons with regular citizens accused of being communists.

On that glorious spring day, Aunt had curled Inja's hair in an unusual display of kindness, and she wore a white puffed-sleeved blouse from America tucked into loose brown trousers, and a sky-blue sweater buttoned at the neck. Uncle, handsome and hatless in a soft gray suit and vest with a bold green-patterned tie, turned heads as they held hands and walked the Seoul streets. They entered the square, Uncle saying hello to acquaintances, and stopped at the apothecary for pregnancy medicine for Aunt. He bought Inja nutritional medicine, too, which she detested. They'd boil the root for hours, and then she'd have to drink the nasty brown-black liquid, floating with root hairs and alien specks. She held her nose against gagging for "the sake of her growing bones." When she was done, she could hear as well as see the grit slide back to the bottom of the bowl. Inja was certain her bones would grow better without the vile slop, but, as Uncle said, she was her mother's special gift to him, and he was determined to have her healthy and strong.

Inja refused to let the thought of that awful medicine ruin their afternoon. The warm breeze blew her sweater open and her trousers flapped as they walked through crowds of people enjoying spring, even the giant American soldiers in clumsy boots and ugly hats. She and her friend Hyo often played around the gates of the military base. Lots of children gathered at the gatehouse, vigilant to vehicles trundling by, hoping a friendly soldier would toss candy or gum. "Chee-ai! Chee-ai!" they'd all yell when a soldier neared. Inja thought they were hollering for American candies, and it was months before she understood it meant "GI." She and Hyo had a pact to split any treasure they caught, and so far they had tasted butterscotch, Tootsie Roll, Mary Jane, and their beloved Juicy Fruit gum. They often did better than the others because they were nicely dressed with scrubbed faces.

Uncle and Inja stopped at a park, and he read the paper while she squatted by the crocuses and poked a beetle lumbering through the turned earth. "Yah," he said, "come look. Another contest."

She leaned over his knee and read the tiny ad. "First prize, forty thousand hwan! Ajeossi, what will you buy?" The government had tried to curtail inflation by issuing *hwan* instead of the severely devalued *won*, and she, along with most of the populace, was perennially confused about its value.

"Even a monkey falls from the tree." With this cautionary proverb, he tweaked her nose. "Especially a favorite monkey." He folded the newspaper under his arm. "It would've bought twice as much last year, but it's still a fine sum. I'll buy fish or meat for your *ajumeoni*, aunt, to fatten that growing baby boy—"

"Is it a boy?" she cried.

"—or girl," he said, laughing. "Now that I know what a grown daughter is, I'd be delighted to have another." He took her hand, and she felt happy to the core, though of course everyone wanted a boy.

They walked all over town that day, and on the way home, he asked if her feet were hurting. She said, "No, but, Ajeossi, what happened to Halmeoni's feet? How did she get frostbite?"

He sobered. "She told you that?"

"Not the whole story. Is it a secret?"

"No. Sort of." A group of GIs passed by, joking with each other in their throaty English, and the dust swirled. "It was hard times," said Uncle. "Your mother was a young woman, married then but living at home with us, and your father was in America going to seminary."

"When they were separated because of the Japanese."

"Yes, smart girl. You remember that story." Their shadows melded behind them, and the bushes beside the military base walls wavered in a breeze, seeming to sparkle in the canted sunlight. "It was winter and I can't say for sure, but it seemed like the coldest winter we'd had in a long time, probably because fuel was scarce.

Everything was scarce, much worse than in Busan."

She was going to say, "That wasn't so bad," but remembered Aunt and Uncle's fights and kept her mouth shut.

They took several paces, and Uncle said, "Your mother was imprisoned by the Japanese."

She dropped his hand and stopped, eyes wide. "Why?" She knew so little about her mother, and then it occurred to her that she didn't know her at all. Who was this woman who would take her adopted daughter to America instead of her real firstborn? But— in prison! "Did she do something wrong?"

"Of course not." He walked on and she caught up. "It doesn't matter why. The Japanese were in charge, and they arrested people for their own reasons. Like your harabeoji."

Inja remembered the story about Grandfather demonstrating for independence. "Did she march with him on Sam-il?"

"No, she was a child then. This was more than twenty years later. Japan was at war with China. Or was it Pearl Harbor? I was in school in Seoul, I think. No, I was home. Where was I?" He grew silent as the sun slid deeper behind walls and buildings. "I remember now. It was his letters—" He frowned. "Never mind about that. The fact is, they arrested people at whim. They only fed the prisoners thin soup, so Halmeoni carried rice to your mother every day. The prison was on the other side of town, two hours' walk each way. Like I said, it was the coldest winter . . ."

Their steps slowed and he remained quiet. On snowy days if Inja played outside in rubber shoes, her toes felt the cold first, and when she came inside, Uncle would rub her feet with vigor until they were pink. Poor Halmeoni, walking with frozen feet day in and day out—and Inja thought of her poor mother, in prison, freezing. "How long was she there?"

After a protracted silence, he said, "Three months."

She couldn't fathom this length, or an era when they would put her mother in jail for no reason and make her grandmother crippled because she brought her food.

"Praise God, your mother came out unharmed," said Uncle, his voice firming, "and if I remember correctly I think she led the prison warden to Christ—a Japanese major who thought his emperor was god. It was a bad time, but there was that glimmer of good."

Inja walked sideways beside him, her eyes on his features, seeking an explanation. He stooped and took her hands. "Inja, child, your mother doesn't know about Halmeoni's feet. Don't ever tell her. It would kill her."

"But how could she not know?"

"Those were hard times, and we moved to

Seoul soon after that. Harabeoji was ill, your mother was weak from prison, and Halmeoni hid her affliction because everyone was suffering. Your mother would feel terrible about it—guilty, as if she had caused the frostbite herself. No need to add to her troubles. She's got her hands full in America. Agreed?"

"Yes, Ajeossi." She squeezed his hands, and he hugged her hard. She felt privileged, serious, and adult in accepting the responsibility that secrets required.

They reached their gate. "Let's give Ajumeoni that medicine, shall we?"

She had lots of thinking to do about this conversation, including the intriguing notion of knowing something important in her family that her own mother didn't know. It reminded her of what Grandmother had said when she was younger and wanted to know if her mother could feel what she was feeling—that God always knew. If her mother didn't know about Grandmother's toes, maybe God didn't always know either. She suspected this might be blasphemous, but she was certain of one thing—she would be forever gentle with Grandmother's feet and would never again complain, even inside, about taking care of them.

Inja's baby cousin, Seonil, was born August 12, 1955, on a moonless night that made the midwife complain about their exceedingly dark house. The only electric light was a single bare bulb, hung from a wire strung across the ceiling of the sitting room, and the midwife insisted that Aunt give birth there.

After many hours, Aunt yelled, the midwife commanded her to *breathe and push, breathe, big push now!* and then came a squishy plopping sound. The midwife shouted, "A boy!" followed by a walloping baby cry. Aunt groaned, and Ara praised her and snapped a clean cloth open. Inja smelled the fresh linen against the scent of something dark and pungent. The light swung to reveal a wet hairy globe cradled in the midwife's spindly fingers. After making sure Aunt had delivered the placenta and was fine, the midwife cradled the baby, swaddled loosely to show the men its sex, which they called his pepper.

Inja had to tell Grandmother several times about the baby. *"Omana!* A boy," said Grandmother. Then, "Whose boy? A baby boy? Omana! A boy." What didn't need to be said by anyone was that their family line was now secured with this boy, and the joy of that security was inherent in each *Omana!* she uttered.

By the time Inja left Grandmother still musing about a baby boy, Grandfather had strung peppers across their gateposts to announce and celebrate his grandson, and Uncle was in with Aunt, cooing to his son in tones of reverence.

• • •

Aunt grew more amiable, especially while nursing Seonil. After the baby's hundredth day celebration, Inja often had to watch him, at first a somewhat fussy baby with a fat round head and merry eyes. But when he grew heavy, the novelty of caring for him wore off. Weekends he spent most of the day wrapped to her back, and sometimes when he wouldn't stop wailing, she'd pinch his fat elbow. Aunt would yell, "Go walk that child! What are you doing to him?"

"He's cranky, that's all." But he was also easy to play with, and his jolly laughter made them all laugh.

The autumn after baby Seonil's first birthday, Inja came home from her new fifth-grade class to find everyone circled in the sitting room, even Grandmother, marveling at something on the floor. She peeked in and saw a brown-and-green-shelled turtle sliding down the sides of a big basin. Bigger than her wide-open hand, its splayed legs floundered on the slick tin surface, the nubbin head tottered to and fro, and its bean eyes rolled, making Seonil laugh.

She crouched by the basin with the others. "Wow. Where'd that come from?"

"I bought it for Seonil." Uncle pushed away Seonil's eager hands. "Don't touch, it'll bite."

"Where'd you get it?" Inja wondered if the refurbished zoo was selling surplus animals.

161

"Apothecary. Be quiet, you'll scare it."

Apothecary! The creature's presence took on a sinister meaning—but Uncle had said it was for Seonil. They watched the pitiful antics of the turtle trying to escape the basin, and the adults argued whenever it moved if it was clever or stupid. Seonil reached to pet it, and the turtle withdrew into its shell. He clapped and Inja laughed with him—the turtle was cuter inside its house—but the others sighed with dismay. "Aigu," said Aunt. "It took hours to coax him out." Inja watched the turtle doing nothing for a while, then went off to play with Seonil.

Sometime later they were still there, crouched around the closed turtle now perched on a board laid across the top of the basin, a few leafy greens piled enticingly by its head end. Uncle held a twig and Ara held a cleaver. Grandfather said they were waiting for the turtle to come out to eat the lettuce, then Uncle would make it bite the twig defensively and he'd pull so Ara could chop its head off. Inja shuddered—poor turtle!—and watched until she got bored again.

She made newspaper hats and boats with Seonil in the next room, occasionally hearing the knife slam the board, followed by groans, and she'd score one more point for the turtle's clever side. Thus far, the turtle had two points for stupid—getting caught and leaving its house at all—and eight points for clever.

Slam! then cheers! She ran to the kitchen, leaving Seonil happily tearing up paper boats. Uncle was washing his finger where the turtle had bit him, and Ara stood by with a cloth to tie it up. Grandfather held the poor headless turtle upside down, its legs and tail limp, while Aunt held a small bowl beneath Grandfather's every shake and squeeze to catch the turtle's blood, which was intended to strengthen Seonil's male vigor. Grandmother kept asking how the turtle got in the house. Thoroughly repulsed and fascinated, Inja stood half outside the doorway until the turtle dripped no more. She was surprised how little blood the turtle had—two small spoonfuls—and was glad it was scant for Seonil's sake.

The grownups descended on him, and when they decided to hold him down to pour it down his throat, Inja ran outside. To the sound of his wretched cries, she crept around the front yard hidden from the house, relieved that she wasn't a boy.

16

Twins

Inja, my child, here is a letter from your sister. Her writing is worse than her Korean speech, but she wanted to write to you herself, so she asked Appa to translate it for you. When we are reunited, I know you will help her with her language, and perhaps she will help you to learn English. The very thought makes my heart yearn for you girls to be together, and I pray it will be soon. Mother

December 12, 1955

Dear Little Sister,

Today is my birthday and I am ten years old. I learned today we are both in the fourth grade although I am older than you. That is funny! Dad says it is because school is different in Korea, and also it is different how you count your age over there. He says Koreans are one year old from the day you are born, but we are counting your age like we do here. That is good because I got an A in arithmetic, but it is confusing, and you would be older than me! Isn't that funny? For three months we are the same age! Yes, strange! When it is your birthday, Mother calls us twins. But since you are still nine, we are not twins until your next birthday. I will make you a card to go in the package for your birthday. I got mittens, saddle shoes, underwear, construction paper, and a box of 64 Crayolas. I did not get a Barbie doll. Do you have a Barbie doll? I will ask Mom to send you the same presents so we can be twins. Maybe she will buy you a Barbie doll.

Yours truly,
Your almost twin sister,
Miran

PART III

RECONSTRUCTION
1956–1962

17

Friends

After the letter from Miran on her birthday, Inja thought about her sister more often, and when her own birthday came the following September, she wondered if, when she got to America—it was always a *when,* she assumed she'd go there someday, somehow—she'd have a party like those shown in their photographs with cake, candles, balloons, hot dogs decorated to look like sailors, streamers strung from the ceiling light fixture, funny cone hats, and presents in bright papers with ribbons and bows. Instead, she invited three classmates for birthday soup.

On her tenth birthday morning, she woke and found two handmade cards from her sister—"인자, 생일 축하합니다 Happy Birthday, Inja," wrote Miran in crooked childish Hangul, and "Happy Birthday, Anna," in beautiful English cursive with little flowers all around.

Anna was the American name her parents had chosen for Inja. They used it when they gave talks about Korea and received donations. Assimilation required having an American name, even if it was never used, like the name *Alice* for Najin, or *Miriam* for Miran. They didn't do the presentations any longer, but the enemy was still very present at a mere sixty kilometers north of Seoul, and infiltrators and dissidents were always getting imprisoned by President Rhee. Protesters were saying that the president himself was a communist, so Inja was confused, and Uncle explained, "It's politics." Her father had also written to tell her about her American name, and to challenge her to find the three passages about the prophet Anna in the Gospel According to Luke, an easy enough task.

Along with the birthday cards Miran made were presents Uncle and Aunt had saved from her mother's packages. Inja was so pleased, she didn't mind that they lacked wrapping paper or bows. Spread out beside her bedding was a pale green dress trimmed in white lace with a flounced skirt that had two front pockets, a matching hair ribbon, a box of chocolate-covered raisins—raisins and chocolate were precious market commodities she was never allowed to keep—a sky-blue coin purse that snapped open and shut, and tucked inside was an American silver Mercury dime for her ten years.

Inja showed everything to Grandmother, who admired her gifts with enthusiasm, then wanted to be shown again and again until Uncle said he'd walk her downtown to have a birthday portrait taken in the new dress to send to her parents. She scrubbed her face, combed her hair—still curly from earlier that week after her bath when Ara had twisted it up in rags—knotted the ribbon into a smart bow beside her ear, dressed carefully, and bounced out with Uncle for a lively walk downtown to the photographer's studio. In front of the camera, Inja curtseyed American-style, and the loud flash and praise from the photographer and Uncle had her feeling queenly.

At home Inja stepped regally into the kitchen. Aunt washed vegetables, and Ara *soaked and sliced dried seaweed,* while a pot of broth, floating with beef bones, bubbled on the stove and sent its steamy deliciousness throughout the house. At the market, the seaweed had cost one tube of Ipana toothpaste, and the beef bones cost three yards of corduroy.

"Very fancy!" said Ara. "You look beautiful."

"It's a pretty dress, so don't get it dirty when you set the table," said Aunt. "We'll eat first, then you can have lunch with your friends."

Wearing a big cloth over her crinkling skirt, Inja was proud to serve her birthday soup to her family, and just as happy to clean up and set the tables again. She made sure the sills were dusted and the room neatened of its usual haphazard newspapers, clothes, and books. Then she sat and waited, her stomach growling for soup. Every ten minutes, then every ten seconds, Inja checked the window, the gate, and then outside to peer down the road.

At half-past twelve, Aunt came in carrying Seonil. "Where is everybody? Ara says the soup is getting too cold and thick."

"I guess they're late." Her legs seemed stuck to the floor.

"You're sure you asked them properly? I have to take the soup off the heat."

She remembered precisely when and how she had asked each invitee. *Will you come over for my birthday lunch next Saturday at noon?* Maybe she hadn't been firm enough. Maybe she should've given them an invitation card, like the rich girl, Myeonghi, had given to every girl in their classroom for her birthday party. Inja hadn't attended that party since she hadn't had a decent gift to give her—all she had was an old book that she loved, its covers torn, and used clothes. Myeonghi came to school with new books and new clothes every month. Inja heard later they had eaten American-style cake and every girl was given a banana. She regretted missing Myeonghi's party most because she'd never tasted a banana. She hadn't thought to write out invitations for the three girls she'd asked, including Myeonghi.

"I'm sure I did. They each said yes," she said, melting inside. Aunt's look dared her not to cry. Inja picked at her skirt.

172

"You can wait a little longer, but I can't let that soup go to waste. I'll feed some to the baby." She went to the kitchen, grumbling to Seonil about waste.

Inja did not check the windows, the gate, the road, or the clock. She sat beside the tray tables she had charmingly arranged with four place settings of lidded bronze bowls in which she'd serve the soup. The light shifted as the minutes of humiliation compounded. She heard movement in the house—Grandfather lying down, asking Uncle to rub his back. Grandmother's flyswatter slapped the floor now and then, Ara changed and washed diapers, then Uncle went out, and later Aunt returned from an errand with Seonil.

"What's this?" she said from the kitchen. "*Yae-yah!* Bring me those bowls!"

Inja crept to the kitchen, bowls in hand. Aunt doled out three portions of congealed soup, and slammed the lids on each. "I won't have good food wasted in this house. Do you think I cooked all this for nothing? Take these to your friends."

Inja's face must have shown her incredulity because Aunt struck her cheek. "Don't come back until they've eaten every bit."

Aunt had never hit her before. Inja wrapped the bowls in cloths, pulled the ribbon from her hair, and went down the road. She loitered across from Myeonghi's big house, all its many

173

windows glowing with electric lights. Myeonghi was practicing piano, and Inja wished she were Myeonghi—or anyone but herself. She waited a long time by the gate. The piano keys plunked, then someone else played something short and melodic, and Myeonghi plunked again, but all Inja heard was the smack of Aunt's hand on her burning cheek and an inner clock ticking despair.

The setting sun touched the rooflines on the hilltop and cast long shadows. She walked down the street to the second girl's house, the bowls heavy as boulders, and crossed to the back door where the girl usually went in after school. Inja could see her through the kitchen window doing something with her mother, both of them smiling. She thought of Aunt waiting with arms crossed in their kitchen. She gripped the bundles and called, "Hello." They didn't hear, so she turned, relieved, but then the girl saw her through the window and came to the door.

"Inja, hi! What are you doing here?"

"I—"

"What've you got?" She pointed to the bundles. "Wow, that's a pretty dress."

Before the girl could say anything to make it worse, Inja blurted, "My aunt says you should have this soup," and held out a bowl.

The girl's face changed. She remembered. They both flushed purple. The girl opened the soup bowl and recoiled at the sight of the tangled, gelatinous mess.

"Never mind!" Inja grabbed the bowl and spun.

Soup slopped on her skirt as she ran from the yard, but not fast enough, for she heard the girl yell, "I'm sorry, I forgot!"

She slipped into an alley and had a long cry. She would never be able to face that girl again. She dumped one soup right there, then wondered if Aunt, with all her strange behaviors, would somehow find it. She scraped out the other bowls in a different alley near a tied-up yellow dog that gobbled it up. He wagged at her expectantly, and his curly tail and eager tongue were so comical she smiled and said, "Happy birthday." Then she cried again. She wandered the alleys that smelled of rotting trash, waiting for moonrise when Aunt would be settled in her bedroom.

Ara was cleaning the kitchen from supper. Without a word, she washed the brass bowls and fed Inja rice topped with bits of seaweed arranged like a flower, a dollop of bone marrow and red pepper paste in the center sprinkled with sesame. At bedtime, Ara took her dress and removed from its pocket the blue coin purse with the silver dime and put it by her pillow. Inja did not dream of hot dogs made to look like sailors or triangle hats or streamers. But when she woke the next morning, her laundered and ironed dress was laid out beside her bed like new.

• • •

For school lunchtime, all the girls brought rectangular tins with two lidded compartments, one for rice and one for *banchan,* a side dish. Girls like Myeonghi who daily brought a different and delicious banchan—varieties of vegetables, an egg, anchovies, or strips of pollock—compared what they had that day, opening both lids of their lunch containers wide. Ara packed rice for Inja daily, but there was nothing to put in the banchan side except sesame salt. It was tasty but embarrassing, and she dipped her spoon into the rice first, then the sesame salt, and took care to open the tin only wide enough for the spoon so no one could see the paucity of her lunch. Then she'd snap the lid shut. A number of other girls snapped their tin lids, too, and punctuated lunchtime with percussive evidence of poor meals. One day in late winter, Inja happened to see a classmate named Yuna snap her lid shut at the same time as she did, and their eyes met. They smiled at each other a little ashamedly, and that's when they became best friends.

Because Yuna lived with her paternal grandmother, she was somewhat like Inja—with parents but without them. Her mother had died during the war, and her father had remarried a woman who didn't want the first wife's child. Yuna's father visited every other weekend, and when Inja saw her on the following Monday, she was always sad. Even her two braids drooped. She would walk Yuna home in silence and hold hands. They understood each other. On those days they did their homework at Yuna's house.

Inja excelled in art, and her pictures often dressed the walls of the classroom. Mathematics also gave her satisfaction, and she was a particular ace in geometry. Math logic brought order, reason, and balance to shifting complexities that seemed to be propelling her toward the unknown and constant abstract of "reunion" and America. No matter how many variables one posited in math, a correct outcome could be achieved.

Some weeks later Myeonghi brought a banana with her lunch. Inja and Yuna sat at their desks on the other side of the room, but it was impossible to ignore the banana with everyone admiring it. Though Inja had only seen pictures of a banana, she wasn't envious enough to go and inspect it with all those girls attending to Myeonghi. She cracked her lunch tin open and asked Yuna, "Have you ever tasted a banana?"

"Yes! At her birthday party. Mmmm. But why didn't you go?"

Since they were friends, Inja could tell her honestly that she hadn't had a decent gift to give to the richest girl in school. "What did you give her?"

"A white patent leather belt from my father. I didn't want to wear it because he gave one just like it to his wife. It made me sad every time I saw it." She ducked her head, and one of her braids slipped around her neck.

"That was a good gift," Inja said to make her feel better. "But tell me about the banana!"

Yuna blushed and made a big show of snapping her lid.

"What? What happened? You said you tasted banana."

"It's embarrassing."

"It's only me." She snapped her lid in response.

"Okay. Promise you won't tell anybody."

"I promise or put a needle in my eye," Inja said, stabbing at her eye. Yuna had taught her this American saying, which didn't make a whit of sense but was a witticism just between them.

"She had a whole bowl of bananas cut open like flowers. One for each girl." Yuna gestured toward Myeonghi and her disciples. "Like she's peeling it right now."

Between the bodies of her entourage, Inja caught glimpses of Myeonghi dramatically peeling each strip of banana skin halfway down until it looked like a fat yellow-and-white lily in her hand. "Wow." Her tongue curled imagining the taste. Maybe it would be like honeysuckle.

"It was the best thing I ever tasted," said Yuna, almost purring. "Sweet but not too sweet, a mellow fruity taste, not as tangy as Juicy Fruit gum. And the texture matched the flavor exactly."

"Gosh, you're making it into a poem," Inja said, and they giggled. "But what's so embarrassing about that?"

"I wanted to eat it slow to enjoy every bite. That's why I can describe it to you like a poem." She smiled. "But the other girls ate theirs fast to hurry to the dining room for cake. I didn't know what I was supposed to do with it when I was done, so I left it on the front room table."

"Is that all? Did somebody get mad?"

She lowered her voice. "After cake, we all went back to the front room to watch Myeonghi open her presents. She found my banana and said, 'Who didn't eat the rest of their banana? Oh well,' and then she peeled the petals down to the base and ate the bottom half of my banana!"

Inja couldn't help it and burst out laughing, drawing attention from the smug girls.

"Don't laugh! I was so stupid." But Yuna was laughing too.

"I probably would've done the same thing. Who knew?"

"I mourned not having that second half of my banana for a long time."

"So it's only a half-poem."

They giggled at everything through the rest of the lunch break, and Inja was so happy to have her friendship, even though Yuna had tasted banana and she hadn't.

Later in the spring on an unseasonably hot

day, Inja and Yuna decided to visit the army base after school. Everything seemed accented with yellow from the sun's warmth, especially a yellow kerchief wrapped around the forehead of an ice-pop man hawking cold treats in a circle of sunlight. He had positioned his straw-lined box in the courtyard just beyond the checkpoint and before the main gate, where Korean vendors and shoeshine boys were allowed to ply their trade. "Ice cakee," he called. "Ba-na-na i-ce cakee!"

Inja still had the Mercury dime in her coin purse at home, more than enough for two ice-pops, and enough to lure the vendor outside the courtyard, which was off-limits to children. "Let's go home and get my money," she said to Yuna.

Her friend shifted her books from one hand to the other.

"You wouldn't have to pay me back," Inja said. They dawdled, but the idea of tasting the poetic banana, and especially in the form of a cooling ice-cake, made Inja grab her elbow. "It'll only take a minute."

When they turned to go, a red-faced soldier who sat on a broken section of wall gave them a cupped-hand wave meaning *come here*—a gesture Americans didn't know was obscene. Yuna stepped back, but the GI's fat yellow eyebrows made Inja think it was a good omen, so she tugged Yuna to approach. He rummaged in his pocket. Maybe he'd give them gum, and Inja

180

could save her dime for another time. The GI was so big and craggy, she thought there might be troll in his ancestry, but he had an enormous smile that made his eyes crinkle into fans at the corners. He said in broken English, as if they were idiots, "Girls, come look-see?"

They hid nervous smiles behind their books.

"I buy you ice-cakee, you likee?"

Inja and Yuna looked at each other and nodded.

The soldier made an exaggerated display of buying two ice-cakes. He returned to the broken wall in the sunshine and pointed to the narrow space beside him for one of them to sit. Inja pushed Yuna forward, and she squeezed in next to his big thigh. He gave her an ice-cake on a stick and held the other one out to Inja, patting his knee.

She took a step and reached for the ice, its tip thawing white to yellow. The soldier said something friendly, closed his knees, and patted them as if enticing a toddler. Yuna was fully absorbed in biting down on her ice, not offering any assistance. Inja knew she wouldn't tell, and as a bead of banana-yellow formed and slid down the ice-cake, temptation overrode taboo. She had already broken several rules: don't beg, don't go to the American base, don't talk to soldiers, don't take gifts from strangers, don't dawdle after school, and show the utmost respect to your elders—especially men. Faced with the melting ice on a hard paper stick, Inja rationalized that no one had ever said, "Don't sit on a soldier's lap," and with that thought, she scooted onto his knees, her back stiff and as far away from his chest as she could manage. Yuna still refused to look at her and gobbled her ice, braids swinging.

Inja licked the drop that cut a slow path through the frosty surface, and all her taste buds turned to gold. It was as coolly flavorful as she had dreamed, as rich as the color yellow. She stuck the ice entirely in her mouth, eyes closed to absorb its delicious round sweetness.

"I'm done!" said Yuna, jarring her reverie. "Let's go." She jumped up and tugged Inja's hem.

The soldier said something, put his hands on Inja's hips, and jiggled his knees. Her insides turned and grew very still. He said things in a strange tone, as if his teeth were clenched. Inja twisted to release his grasp and glance at him, both dreading and drawn to see his expression. He blinked, eyes so pale as to look empty, his nose enormous and mottled with tiny red veins.

"Come on!" Yuna tossed her paper stick and ran without looking back.

The GI said something wheedling and bounced his knees, his hands firm on Inja's hips, making her bite the ice and slide deeper into his lap. She threw the ice-cake in the dirt and pushed at his unmoving hands, then kicked her legs against his shins as hard as she could. He let go, laughing, saying something lewd, she was sure, and she ran and spit out the melting shard in her mouth that now tasted like metal.

Inja and Yuna avoided each other for a day until a game of rubber-band jump rope reunited them. Neither said anything about the soldier, nor did they ever return to the military base. Inja lost her desire for ice-cake or other treats from "chee-ais," and she forever disliked the color yellow.

18

Illegal Aliens

Miran spent ten days of a two-week school vacation in April at Sarah Kim's house, which meant a pine-paneled recreation room all to themselves with television and Barbie dolls. Mrs. Kim was either busy with her bridge club or shopping downtown, and the girls had the run of the house. Since they were, at age eleven, borderline too old to be playing with dolls, they compensated by making up elaborate stories inspired by Sarah's discovery of dirty magazines and paperbacks with shocking covers in Dr. Kim's closet. Using three Kens and a half-dozen Barbies, they cut black electrical tape into strips they positioned over the Barbies' eyes, breasts, and crotch, like in the magazines, and Sarah tittered when Miran tied the otherwise nude pointy-toed ladies up against chair legs and had the Kens beat them. Miran couldn't say where she got such ideas, which weren't depicted in Dr. Kim's pulp books, but the play was exciting and both their cheeks would be rosy after hours of planning and staging stripteases by the Barbies that devolved into beatings by the Kens. By the third night, Miran felt bold enough to sneak the dark-haired Ken doll into the guest room and pretend he was Daniel Walczak. Her imagination took over, and she'd find herself sweaty with wet underpants even though she hadn't peed the bed.

All kinds of treats and snacks were readily available, and explained why Sarah was chubby—something kids at church made fun of. This made Miran attach to Sarah the underdog all the more, like she had earlier with Janet. Potato chips were delivered weekly in tins bigger than her head; a porcelain container shaped like a cat was always filled with store-bought cookies; Hershey bars stacked in the freezer sat next to three quarts of ice cream; and piles of fruit went rotten on the living room coffee table.

While visiting Sarah, Miran got to skip church and watched so much television her glasses fogged. They dressed up in Sunday clothes, and Sarah's dad took them to the movie theater, with popcorn, Coca-Colas, and Milk Duds, on Friday and Saturday night. They went out for dinner almost every night, and she experienced Hot Shoppes, White Castle, Kresge's soda fountain, and Ledo's Pizza, plus Chinese food delivery, and on Sunday night turkey TV dinners on folding trays in front of *The Ed Sullivan Show*. Sarah's parents had cocktails and made Shirley Temples for the girls, garnished with cherries from a jar and little paper umbrellas saved from restaurants.

Miran was utterly spoiled by the time Calvin came to drive her home, and she sulked in the front seat, a position she rarely sat in and would normally have been thrilled to occupy.

"It seems you had a good time," said Dad.

"Um-hmm."

"What was your favorite part? Dr. Kim told me about all the many things you did."

"I liked everything."

"Learn anything?" This was his usual question about her activities, and at the moment it irritated her and prompted a thoughtless response. "Yes— that it's dumb to be poor and have no television. Mom would like *The Ed Sullivan Show*. And since she read that *LIFE* magazine over and over again about Grace Kelly's wedding in Monaco, she would've loved watching it on TV, like *every*body else in the *entire* world did but us."

A cold silence emanated from her father's side of the car. "Not everyone," he said, quiet. "Not your sister in Korea; have you considered that?"

If Miran could've thrown something she would have, but Dad had put her things in the trunk, even the hand-me-down leather purse Sarah had given her—her first purse ever. A girl should not be separated from her purse. She said nothing to prevent an outburst of frustrated tears. The threat of childish tears made her reassess her attitude, and she took a few surreptitious big breaths, lips tight. She felt stubborn, ugly, and closed-up—far

187

from the feelings of freedom from the previous week, which she'd mistakenly attributed to the Kims' being rich. It wasn't that their generosity of things had opened up her heart to Sarah and her parents—and thus to herself. It was the generous attention she'd received in that house, from outings to being asked questions at the dinner table, to witnessing Sarah and her mother talk about clothes and shoes—in English—like girlfriends, her own opinion sought after, and an unprecedented privacy in her guest room that would never be invaded by an inquisitive mother who was too busy to keep track of her daughter except by snooping through her things.

Miran sighed and did the right thing. "I'm sorry, Dad. I had so much fun, and they're so different from us." She noticed he was taking a circuitous route home.

"I know. It *is* your first extended visit outside the house, so some adjustment is to be expected. They do live quite extravagantly, but they've been generous with us, too." He patted the steering wheel, and she remembered Dr. Kim had given them the car years ago when they were thick into the dog-and-pony shows. It was rusted in places on the chrome bumpers but without a single dent, and her dad had learned how to maintain the motor to keep it running reliably. "We just don't have that kind of money, and even if we did, much of it would still go to support your sister and your uncle's family in Seoul."

Her dad was so measured in his speech, always thoughtful and distant—and so unlike Dr. Kim, who joked and hugged Sarah with ease. Calvin turned the Plymouth onto Thirteenth Street, which led farther away from their house. "We missed you," he said.

"I missed you guys too," she lied. Their daily calls to check in had made her crabby and mono-syllabic on the telephone. "How's Mom?" she said dutifully.

"Making kimchi. Your mother was always a hard worker, and she's much happier these days having that teaching job."

"I wish I were old enough to have a job. I could earn my own money and buy Mom a television." Miran had planned to ask him for a weekly allowance beyond the milk money, but her outburst had squandered that opportunity. She hoped he'd get the hint with this approach.

"Ask, and ye shall receive," said minister Dad. "I'll buy you anything you need, within reason." He had gotten the hint, as this was his usual response to her occasional—and denied—request for a weekly stipend.

"A television."

"Can't afford it."

"Fifty cents a week?"

"I have an idea for you to consider that's better than that, and I've been meaning to discuss it with you. Miss Lone wants help with her finances."

Miran frowned. "You mean she needs money and that's why I can't have an allowance?"

He laughed. "Not at all. She has a job for you, if you're—"

"—yes, I'll do it," she said. Miss Lone had been a frequent visitor to their house lately, bringing documents and having long talks with both her parents in Korean. Miran felt less shy with her now, as Miss Lone always took time to have a word or two in English with Miran—the usual stuff about school or her piano lessons, but it was something.

"Before knowing what it is?"

"Yes. What does it pay?"

"Goodness gracious. Don't put the wagon before the horse," he said, smiling.

"Don't put the *cart* before the horse. Mom's got that already," she said, referring to her mother's idiom collection.

"Just testing you."

"No, Dad, you weren't!" said Miran, and they laughed.

Thus it was repaired between them, and Calvin told her that Miss Lone, being a spinster, wanted to invest in her future. She needed help charting daily rates for certain companies. It meant that Miran would learn how to read the stock market pages. The number of companies she'd chart could vary from five to fifteen, and the pay was a dollar a week. They were heading there now, something he would've told her earlier if he'd had an opportunity. She took this mild rebuke easily and apologized for her earlier crabbiness.

"Thanks, Dad."

"You're welcome. Get ready for your first job interview."

She straightened her blouse, tucked it into the matching capri pants, and wondered how much it cost to buy a television. At Miss Lone's apartment she aced the "interview," got a lesson on how to read the New York Stock Exchange listings, and received graph paper, a colored pencil with red on one end for when the prices went down, and blue on the other for up, a ruler, and a list of twelve companies and their abbreviations.

While Miss Lone and Calvin had coffee in the living room, Miran sipped a Pepsi at the dining room table and charted the first stock on the list: IBM, which stood for International Business Machines. She heard the grownups mention "immigration," "congressional bill," "laws," and "resident" several times and with such intensity that on the way home Miran put stock prices and even the price of a television out of her mind.

"Is it okay if I ask what you and Miss Lone were talking about?" Miran had learned "polite" was the best way to be nosy. "And why she's been coming over so much?"

"It's complicated, but you know we've been trying to bring Inja here for years." He turned onto Military Road. "Soon after the war, we began to ask government officials how we could reunite our family, and it was discovered that our visas had long expired. We hadn't paid any attention to that business because of the war, and we had become what they called 'illegal aliens,' like creatures from Mars." He smiled but grew quickly serious. "That very day I was issued a procedural arrest, meaning I had broken the law, but did not have to go to jail like a common criminal."

"Wow."

"Yes, indeed. For years now, Miss Lone's congressman has helped us gain the correct legal status to live and work here. I needed to have a green card, which meant we could be 'permanent legal residents.' Then, two private laws were passed last year that helped make us legal. That was the first step."

"Me, too?"

"Yes," said Calvin. "Your name was on that law with ours. Whatever happens to me and your mother happens to you, though it doesn't apply to Inja since she doesn't live with us. Miss Lone has advised us to pursue a different legal path to allow her to rejoin us, and part of that step is for us to become American citizens. New changes in the immigration laws have made it more complex, but you and I will study to become citizens soon."

"Cool." She saw familiar buildings and houses go by as they crossed town toward home. And she wondered about Inja actually coming to live with them. Would she even *like* her? Something about that thought felt wrong, as if having a sister meant they'd automatically like—and even love—each other. But what if they didn't?

19

Collect Call

A quiet Christmas and New Year's 1958 came and went. The packages from Inja's mother grew scarce, though her letters remained frequent. Najin's job teaching Korean to intelligence officers had been increased to five days a week, and she still made kimchi for restaurants. Now she sent checks to Uncle rather than packages.

Seonil, two and a half years old and curious about everything, had Aunt veering from laughter to wrath. One cold day in early March, Yuna came over to see Inja's Bible storybook. They sat against the wall of the sitting room, and Inja explained the pictures, since Yuna was Buddhist. Grandfather hobbled in with a bowl of that awful nutritional medicine. The smell—something between mushroom and sewer—pervaded the room, and Yuna made an "ugh" face.

"I'll take it later, Harabeoji," said Inja.

"Your family suffers so you can have this!" He leaped across the room with sudden agility, and the medicine sloshed on her legs. He yanked her arm to stand, and she drank the potion, amazed at his burst of strength, and worse—that he'd thoroughly shamed her in front of Yuna. He took the bowl and left. Yuna closed the book and went home. What had happened to her beloved Grandfather? Everything was different now. With Uncle always looking for work and Seonil taking the rest of his time, Inja had no one. She put her head on her book and the tears ran.

The next day Grandfather stayed in bed. Inja thought it was her fault. After school she lingered by his door while Uncle rubbed his stomach. "Bury me in a high dry place, in the sun," he said. "A high dry place."

"Don't talk like that," said Uncle. "Your stomach always gives you trouble and you always get better." But he promised he would.

He couldn't eat for four days. Ara fed him clear soup that dribbled down his beard. "Remember the slingshot and the birds?" Inja said to him. "Remember the little hollow bones?" Then she felt bad, since he himself was mostly bones.

That night he kept everyone awake groaning in pain. Uncle took him to the hospital, and Grandfather lay in bed there nine days. During that period Uncle visited Mr. Jeon across the street to ask for a loan for the doctor bills. Mr. Jeon paid for the entire hospitalization and also bought a funeral plot for Inja's grandparents on the mountain cemetery in Osan. Uncle remembered Grandfather's request and chose a plot three-fourths up the mountain, and three-fourths more expensive. The cemetery director guaranteed it was dry.

"How can we ever pay him back?" said Aunt.

"He insists it's not a loan. The price of his land and house has grown ten times, and he says he owes me for the good advice to build there when we came back from Busan. He's been investing in real estate since then. Inja's mother will help me pay him back." Across the road the Jeons' house lay on a sprawling lot that dropped to a breathtaking overlook of the valley downtown. All those childhood days Inja had played with Hyo in the yard, she had never noticed the view. Hyo went to a boys' school, and she saw him now and then in the neighborhood, but his rich life made her shy, and she always turned her head as if she hadn't seen him so he wouldn't feel obliged to say hello. Tall office and apartment buildings rose throughout the city, and land with spectacular views like those from his yard had become precious commodities. "We should save to buy the adjoining burial plot for us," said Uncle.

"As if we can save," said Aunt, ending the conversation.

Grandfather came home without a diagnosis or treatment, though Uncle was certain he had stomach cancer. During his time in the hospital, Grandfather's cheeks had hollowed and his stomach had grown distended, rocklike. He lay on his quilts, too weak to sit, and cried out for Uncle to massage his belly. Though earlier that winter Aunt's complaints had escalated about the two senile old people whose demands overtook the house, she now treated him gently, dripping water between his lips.

Inja loved her grandparents still—how could she not—but they were greatly altered, unwell and aged. Inja spent hours keeping Grandmother company, doing what she asked, again and again, telling her about school, over and over, and caring for her feet. Though cheerful and complacent, when confused Grandmother grew anxious and needed constant explanation until Inja had to go out, no matter the weather, so as not to repeat the same thing once more. "Why's that man hollering?" she'd say. "Can't you make him stop that moaning?"

Grandfather's biggest comfort was Uncle, rubbing his stomach. Inja knew he was dying. She thought about the crematorium in Busan, the bodies lurching in shrouds on the back of the trucks going up the hill. But her grandfather wouldn't be incinerated like those dreadful dead dragged out of battlefields and ditches, their ash falling like snow over all of Ami-dong. Uncle had repeatedly promised him a high mountain grave—dry, calm, and close to the stars.

He died two days after coming home, the

evening before Good Friday. Inja was woken by Aunt's funereal wailing, and the unusual subsequent silence confirmed what she'd guessed. In the moonlight Grandmother lay bathed in muted silver beside her in their blankets, sleeping peacefully, her face relaxed. Inja decided not to wake her. April winds rattled through the window crevices, and she donned a sweater and went to Grandfather's sickroom, her bare feet grateful for the heated *ondol* floor.

Ara and Seonil clung to the door frame, both crying soundlessly, which made Inja cry, too. Poor Harabeoji, to die in such pain. The blankets had been pulled away, and his thin chest and legs lay twisted and wrinkled in his clothes. Aunt and Uncle were doing something around his head. Even before she saw his face, she saw that his body was different, lax. They had tied a cloth under Grandfather's chin to keep his mouth closed, and it shocked her to see how lifeless he was. He was not at all in that body, and this absence saddened and frightened her. She clung to the doorway with Ara and Seonil. But then she heard Uncle praying, giving thanks that Grandfather was freed from his agony. She thought of Grandmother, calm in her sleep, and it made her think of him that way, too.

Uncle saw her, his eyes reddened and his nose running. Aunt, who also had teary eyes, gave him a handkerchief, her gesture tender. Uncle said a prayer, faltering, and told everyone to go to bed. He straightened the blankets, turned down the oil lamp, and sat on his knees near Grandfather's body, where he would keep vigil all night until the undertaker came in the morning to perform the rituals of burial.

When Inja crawled back into bed, Grandmother stirred, said something unintelligible in her sleep, a sigh coming deep from her lungs. Inja prayed for Grandfather, hoping he would visit Grandmother's dreams to say goodbye. They had always been old to her. She prayed he would have the young man's body he'd had before his back was ruined by the Japanese policemen on Sam-il. She prayed he'd leave this earth at peace knowing that with Seonil, the august 400-year line of Hans would continue.

Uncle shook Inja awake, and her eyes opened to the night-dark room. "Put something warm on," he whispered.

"What time is it?" She crawled out of the quilts.

"About six o'clock. Ajumeoni is keeping vigil for Harabeoji for now. I shouldn't leave, but we've got to telephone your mother."

Inja remembered, found socks and a jacket, and hurried outside for her shoes. Their pre-dawn neighborhood felt completely foreign, a town of shadows and vacancy. The moon had faded low on the horizon, and their footsteps on the dirt road were accompanied only by crickets. Her eyes fixed on each of the occasional streetlights until they reached its dim circle, where familiar corners and edges of buildings were visible. They walked on, and the familiar faded into the black beyond the light.

Uncle said the telephone and telegraph office would open its doors at this hour. Even during the war, he had never called America because of the exorbitant cost. And since then there had been no news dire enough to send a telegram. Though she had passed this international communications office numerous times on their strolls to the square, there had never been a reason to go inside.

"I'm going to tell them about Harabeoji," said Uncle, "then you can talk to your parents for a minute."

Inja's fingertips tingled, then every part of her shivered. She had never before used a telephone. As far as she could remember, she had never before talked to her parents.

Uncle greeted the man at the counter. "We'll make a collect call to America, Washington, DC. Can you tell me what time it is there?"

The man scribbled some numbers and said it was five-thirty in the evening, yesterday. Inja had learned that in the southern hemisphere of the world the seasons were opposite from Korea, and time changed as the earth rotated. She understood this mathematically, but it never made figurative sense that *now* was *yesterday* in America. It only made sense when she thought of America as a place so distant that the very nature of time was altered.

Uncle wrote down Inja's parents' names, the name of their district, and their telephone number, then he ushered her into one of six wooden booths with shutter doors lining the side wall. He sat beside her on its half bench and lifted the receiver to his ear. She put her ear to it, too, but no sound came out. She stood and swung the door open and shut to bring fresh air into the little booth, which smelled sour with tobacco, until he said to leave it alone. He told her how to talk on the telephone and to not talk long. He spoke quietly, in a monotone.

The telephone man put on a headset and did something behind a machine. He conveyed their information, then waited, then spoke in Japanese, then waited a long time, then spoke loudly and carefully in English, waited again, did this one more time, then told Uncle to stay silent on the line while the American operator confirmed that her parents would accept the collect call.

Uncle held the receiver loosely to his ear and told Inja to lean in. She heard buzzing and a tiny tinny voice. A pause, then a man answered in English, the tinny voice again, then a click, pause, and the man again, his voice deep, sounding like it was coming from underwater. "Is everything all right? How is Inja?"

Her mouth dropped open, and she covered it when Uncle gestured to make no sound. It made sense that her father sounded underwater when she thought about how far away he was. Uncle told her later they used radio to convey the call.

"*Maehyeong-nim*," Uncle said, using respectful address, "she's fine. She's right here with me. It's Harabeoji. He died at ten fifty last night."

A long pause filled with crackling, then her father's response, which Inja began to understand was delayed by distance. "Oh no! Yeobo, come to the phone. What happened?"

Uncle told him about the hospital and the last few days after Grandfather came home. He mentioned the burial site. In the middle of this conversation, she heard her mother say, "It's me. Inja is with you?"

"She's here. You can talk to her, but tell me if that burial site is acceptable."

He talked to Najin about the cemetery and money, then he lied, saying Grandfather did not suffer—Inja understood why he'd do this—and reassured them Grandmother was fine. He gave her the receiver.

"*Yeobosayo*? Hello?" she said as instructed. The line clicked and hummed, the heavy device warm against her ear.

"It's wonderful to hear you, my daughter. You

sound so grown up. Are you very sad about Harabeoji?"

"A little." Disoriented by the reality of her mother's voice, she didn't know what else to say, so she added what she thought her mother would like to hear. "He'll be happy in heaven."

"Yes, he is. Sadly, I cannot come for his funeral, but please write and tell me about it, will you?"

"Yes, Mother."

"Pray for your harabeoji, and I pray for the day when we can be together."

"I will, Mother. Thank you."

"Here is your father. Goodbye, my daughter. Be good and help Grandmother." The connection got very messy then, or Inja's mother needed to blow her nose.

"Inja, how are you my child?" said her father. He sounded commanding but gentle.

"I am well." Again she couldn't think of what to say, so she repeated, "A little sad."

"We are all praying for Harabeoji, and you and the family. Are you studying hard?"

"Yes, Father."

"I know you are. We miss you. We miss you very much."

"I miss you, too."

"God bless you and the family."

Uncle gave her the signal to hang up. "Thank you, Father. Goodbye."

"Goodbye." She heard her mother chime "goodbye," too.

Uncle hung up and they looked at each other. "You did very well. I'm proud of you." He gave her a hug, which brought her back to this world, the world she belonged in, though it was a sad world without Grandfather. Uncle paid and signed a receipt. On their walk home, dawn broke and spread a violet hue over the buildings. A swallow swooped from its nest in the eaves. Uncle took her hand. "What did you think of the call?"

"It was strange."

"I know. Amazing, isn't it?"

That wasn't the kind of strange she meant, but she couldn't define her feeling until much later—after Grandfather's funeral and the next quiet weeks in the house without him. Returning to school gave Inja time to think about her first telephone call. Hearing her parents talk despite the static had made them more real than their letters, photographs, or packages ever had. The physical presence of their voices was like a shadow echo that followed her for days, and it made the concept of a reunion real, too. By now, since she was old enough, they all knew she'd be the one going to America once they figured out the red tape. If a telephone call cost that much, what impossible cost would get her to America? This gave her a sense of guilty assurance. The few times her father wrote, he explained the different things they were trying, including something special with the government, and her mother had also tried to explain it. Because of that telephone call, what had always been a benign idea now felt like a threat. She knew that sentiment was bad and wrong of her, and she would never mention it, but there it was.

20

Grandfather's Burial

The night after Easter Sunday, April 6, 1958, Miran woke to terrifying moans from her parents' bedroom. She'd heard her mother's dreaming screams before, but this time they seemed to escalate until her father said, "Yeobo, wake up, you're dreaming."

"A terrible nightmare," Najin said.

Every night from that night forward, Najin's dreams made her shout out loud, a sound more like groans, her mouth sluggish with sleep. Fortunately, Miran had Easter vacation from school and spent the remainder of the week at Sarah's house, but when her father picked her up, he said Mom hadn't been sleeping well and to be quiet when they went in as she was napping on the sofa.

Miran and her father tiptoed around the house the following week, for as soon as Najin came home from work, she'd lie down and be asleep in seconds. But the nightmares kept her awake after dark; then she would get out of bed as if running from her dreams and stay up sewing, planning lessons, correcting papers, writing in her diary.

On the third Monday in April, when Miran came home from school, she went into her mother's sewing cabinet drawer to resew a loose button on her blouse. She found an opened thick envelope from Korea tossed atop the notions. Usually letters from Seoul came in thin blue mailers, so she examined the many stamps and compared the Korean writing to the pile of letters from Seoul stashed in the buffet table drawer. The envelope contained photographs from Uncle.

She took the envelope out of the house to a little secret alcove beneath a pokeberry bush in the woods. She sat on a cinder block beneath the umbrella of vines, and a wad of black-and-white photographs fell to her feet. To avoid the stain of the poisonous berries scattered on the ground, she grasped each crinkle-edged photo by the edges. They were grainy pictures of a funeral in Korea—her grandfather's burial. She'd been told he'd died on the evening before Good Friday earlier that month. Many images were of lines of people—men in black suits, women in white Korean dress—threading up a mountain path. One man, seen from the back near the robed minister, stood at the head of the line carrying a woman piggyback. Having heard before how her uncle carried her grandmother everywhere after her stroke, she deduced this was them. She didn't remember her grandfather at all but knew his elderly face from a photographic portrait hung in an oval frame in her parents' bedroom. He had a stern demeanor, his mouth mostly hidden by a white mustache and goatee, but Miran had noted the smile lines around his eyes.

She shuffled through images that showed the coffin—its rectangle wrapped in cloth—being lowered by men's dusty hands straining against ropes into the open grave. She fanned the photos in her hands like a flip book, and the staccato movement sent shafts of feeling into her gut that both excited and made her afraid, as if she were looking at the *LIFE* magazine photographs of survivors in concentration camps or the shocking burns on the bodies of victims from Hiroshima.

She'd never known someone who died, and now she thought about her own father in that box and felt something singular for her mother, a sensation beyond the usual distance and alienation. She also felt bad that she had no sadness. People were supposed to be sad and cry when a grandparent died. Janet, the patrol girl, had taken a week off when her grandmother had died, and all the teachers had been super nice to her for the rest of the year. Miran's mother had gone back to work the following day.

She tried to reorder the photographs in sequence, glanced at the letter written in dense Korean with brush and ink on tissue, and slid it all back into the envelope. At home she slipped it back into the drawer and hoped her mother wouldn't notice it had been disturbed.

In a cavernous hall, dank, cold, Najin shivers. Far ahead are dim outlines of a long wooden box, ropes coiled beneath, the smell of decay. She approaches, fearful. The light grows as she nears the coffin's open top, its surface murky and gleaming. Out of that blackness her father sits up slowly. Water drips from his hair, streams from his plaintive eyes, and pours down his beard to his soaked hemp gown. He raises both arms, and water pours from his sleeves. She screams.

22 May 1958, Thursday. I cannot sleep for the nightmare. It comes every night no matter how hard I pray or how tired I am. Last weekend I dropped a gallon of kimchi, and yesterday I was short-tempered in class. It's the same dream of Harabeoji every night, but it still frightens me with the intensity of the first time. C says I moan and thrash. For his sake I tried sleeping on the couch, in Miran's room, a cot in the basement, but still it comes. Tonight I will make ginseng tea and go back to our bed.

2 June 1958, Monday. I looked in the mirror this morning and did not recognize

my eyes. They are like an old woman's eyes and circled in shadows.

14 June 1958, Saturday. I slept the whole night through with nothing! Thank you, Lord. The letter to Dongsaeng must have helped. I told him about the dream, so he can go up and check on Harabeoji's grave. Miran is on school vacation, and yesterday we went to the post office together to mail my letter to Dongsaeng. I was happy to spend a little time with her, and we stopped at the library on the way home. I dozed while she looked for books.

14 June 1958, Friday

Noona,

Older Sister, I do not want to worry you but something strange has been occurring for some time now. We are all fine and Inja is fine, so do not worry about that. She is a treasure to me, and I honor my noona for trusting her to my care. This is a testament of your love, and I weep with the joy it gives me, with the joy she brings to me and to this family. Halmeoni is also fine, the same, and not getting worse. She is quieter now with Harabeoji gone, but she still wields her flyswatter like she is attacking the communists.

I am writing because of Harabeoji. I am having a terrible nightmare. It is the same dream every night for the past 7–8 weeks. I am afraid to sleep. I get up and copy the Bible all night so I will not have this dream again, then I end up napping during the day, which makes Seonil's mother angry. The dream is this: it is very dark but I see Harabeoji's coffin at the far end of the room. I always feel afraid, but I am compelled to go to him. When I get closer, all around the floor are the ropes they used to carry him up the mountain. Then Harabeoji sits up from inside the coffin. Every time it is horrible and I shout with terror! He is wet through and through, and water pours from his head and falls from his beard. His eyes are holes but he seems to be crying and all this water could be his tears! Then he raises his arms, as if he wants to grab me, and the water runs out from his sleeves and makes waterfalls down his fingers. I am so frightened I shout. That is when I wake up.

I went to the minister to ask him what I should do. What could it mean? He said I should pray and ask forgiveness for the sins I have committed against my father. Well, I have had my whole life to think about that, and that is nothing different from the suffering of my daily life. This is why I copy the Bible now, hoping it will bring me closer to God and away from this fear, to redeem my many wrongdoings. Finally Seonil's mother grew tired of my napping and being irritable from lack of sleep, and she insisted I go to visit Harabeoji and pray. It was time to see his grave anyway and see how the grass is growing. So I went there, a long bus ride and a longer walk, and I knew it would be a long day so I didn't bring Inja or anyone.

I asked the cemetery director to go up with me to see the grave. He was happy enough to go with me. He remembers Harabeoji because there were many people at his funeral and the path was very steep, especially for the old people. Almost the entire congregation was there. I sent you the pictures. It was a great honor! The director and I went up, and the grave looks peaceful and calm. The grass is growing on the mound, soft and sparse like on a baby's head. I asked him, when it rains, does the water pool anywhere nearby? He pointed out the hilly land all around, and the stone-lined gullies they installed to control how rainfall streams down the mountain. Even so, those gullies are far from Harabeoji's site and it has been a dry summer. The farmers complain. There was no groundwater nearby.

I stayed with Harabeoji a long time after the director left, to pray and ask him to forgive me. I left many tears there. Perhaps his spirit is angry because I did not sleep by his grave for a month. Nobody does that anymore, at least no one I know. All of us still honor him with mourning clothes and his altar at home.

You are wiser than I am, and the night is the realm of women. Also, your husband is a great man of God and educated in these matters. Maybe he can explain what this means, and give me guidance on what I should do.

Your loving Dongsaeng

Najin received this letter ten days after he wrote it. Her mind churned. Then she saw her brother had written to her on the same day she had written to him about the dream, and her heart dropped to her feet. Ice crawled down her back and set the inside of her skin on fire. She thought better of dashing off an incoherent response and telephoned Calvin to read him the letter. Her thoughts were wild with fear and dread, but the sound of his voice calmed her.

"The dreams are symbolic, not a mirror of reality," he said with his minister's authority. "Perhaps it's a kind of grieving between brother and sister who have long been apart."

Najin didn't say anything to that. She felt only relief to be apart from her brother, though she had come to trust him with Inja. Still, he was a dreamer who wept too easily, a man who was slipshod about practical matters such as work and money, just like their father. Perhaps this was the reason Grandfather came to her, weeping. She still held bitterness toward him for her mother's hard life, especially since her mother had never complained about the menial work she did to earn money to send her children to school, while her father did nothing.

"What should we do?" she said to Calvin.

"It would be unwise to disturb his grave, if that's what you're thinking—a worse act than to suffer the unknown of this dream."

"You're right. I suppose there's nothing to be done, then." She sighed.

"I'll be home at the usual time," he said.

She sat a long while by the telephone, then wrote to her brother explaining what Calvin had said, though she didn't mention the "grieving brother and sister" part.

Najin set the letter to her brother on the sideboard for Calvin to mail tomorrow at work. There was no urgency with this letter. If nothing could be done, she supposed she must live with not understanding the meaning of the dream, and maybe it would cease now that it had been exposed through letters. She thought of her life and saw that she had always lived yearning in the realm of the unknowable—a young girl seeking her father's love, desiring education, good work, a full belly; longing to find her husband again, to survive the war, to have had a son, to have birthed more than the one surviving child; praying to freely give up everything in her will to God. Now she prayed for the unknown day when she might again see her mother, the unknown moment when she could hold her daughter close to her heart. These uncertainties had become a permanent state of her being. She had long lived with this paradox, and what did her days hold for her if not that? The terrible dream troubled her deeply, but she would learn to live with that, too.

21

Hyo

It seemed the moment Inja turned fifteen in September 1961, her thin body took on curves and her thoughts turned to boys, especially Jeon Hyo, her childhood friend across the road. Until high school, Hyo had taken the tram to prestigious schools in Seoul's Sinchon district, and she doubted they'd shared two words since their childhood of playing together with the bricks in his yard and begging for candy at the U.S. Army base. Their neighborhood, crowded with old homes, had few high-rises, but since land for apartments was dear, the U.S. Army base closed and the GIs moved to Yongsan Garrison. Hyo attended a private high school for business education, while she attended the equalized or public high school nearby. All of their schools were segregated by gender. If South Korean youth were going to be adults and married one day, Inja often wondered about the wisdom of the Ministry of Education until she remembered it was her own father who had helped establish the current system.

After classes teens gathered at a small park

between the two schools, a rare opportunity to have fifteen stolen minutes of freedom from adult supervision. Hyo, being rich, wore neatly pressed shirts, lined jackets, twill trousers, and shined leather loafers. School uniforms had been abandoned by necessity after the war—few could afford to make them. And though the clothes Inja's mother sent might have been outdated by a year or two in America, they were the rage of fashion among her peers. She had saddle shoes, sweaters with pearlized buttons, shirtwaist dresses, and plaid skirts, some so brightly colored Uncle said they were unfit to wear in public. Instead they were used to patch their quilts and make floor pillows.

Inja and her friend Yuna, whose father bought her new clothes when he visited—out of guilt, she said, gleeful to show off a new blouse—would hurry to the park after school, strolling arm in arm as if it were nothing but a lovely day, even if they were crowded under a shared umbrella in the rain. Girls would cluster on one end, the boys on the other, and now and then the bold would walk in between. She and Yuna were regular "walkers," giggling at each other, feeling grand in their finery, pretending they weren't looking at the boys, who pretended they weren't looking at them. Then one day when Yuna was sick, Inja promenaded alone, hugging her books, feeling foolish, wishing she had more than one girlfriend.

Hyo detached himself from his group and said, "Want some Juicy Fruit?" His hands were empty, but his eyes were filled with merriment. And such eyes! Round and rimmed with thick lashes, the smooth planes of his cheeks pink with embarrassment.

"You remembered," Inja said, so startled—and thrilled—she stopped.

"I never forgot." He shuffled. "Sorry, I don't really have any, but I will the next time."

Next time? A ripple ran from her scalp to her toes, and a silence that seemed to go on for hours fell between them. They were halfway between the two groups and in danger of merciless teasing by the girls. "Well, I guess I should go home now," she said.

"I may as well go with you since you're right across the street." He hoisted his book bag over a shoulder and waved to the boys, who made faces and called him a kissy-sissy. "Never mind them," he said, "they can be idiots."

"Girls can be that way, too." This simple exchange united them and muted her skittering nerves.

"How's it been since leaving Busan?" he said.

No one had ever asked her that before, not even Yuna. She'd seen Hyo many times since Busan, but it was the type of question neither of them would have considered as children. "It's okay," she said, conscious of how easily his footsteps fell in with hers. "I have a six-year-old cousin who hates school, though he's smarter than he pretends to be. But I barely remember what Busan was like." How else could she answer? Everyone knew how it was: scarce food, scarcer fuel, families unable to communicate across the demilitarized zone, relatives missing or dead. Few people, except politicians, talked about wartime; its commonality of suffering had made the subject cliché.

"I remember the Juicy Fruit."

That smile! "You could buy a case of it now," she said, then wished she hadn't—it exposed her thinking about his wealth.

"Yes, madam, and how would you like that delivered?" He made a little bow, and she laughed and kept her smile on him, appreciating how he covered her blunder. Their steps slowed in effortless unison. Though much was roiling inside, she also felt relaxed—an odd but pleasurable paradox.

"How is your uncle?" he said. "The last time I saw him was more than a year ago, arguing with my father about *Dictator* Rhee before he was ousted."

She came to a halt, surprised—and intrigued—by his boldness. "Surely he didn't call him that."

"He didn't, but that's what they were arguing about. It's how I learned my father had grown rich with his regime."

Inja's mind opened with the possibility of talking politics with Hyo, who clearly shared her uncle's viewpoints, and she was intrigued that his tone hinted at conflicts with his father. Yuna had never been interested in the frequent student protests or what they meant. Inja only had Uncle with whom to discuss the news. He did talk to her about it more after Grandfather had died, but he preferred to tell her what to think. She wanted to talk to someone her age to know more about what *she* thought.

Hyo stopped and kicked at the dirt road. She turned to say, her voice more fierce with envy than she had intended, "Were you downtown for Four-Nineteen last year?"

"I was."

"You must tell me everything!" She side-stepped into the shade of a maple and hugged her schoolbooks. Last spring's protests were exciting, tragic and historic, and students—like them—had changed the world. It became known as the 4.19 Student Uprising, a series of unforgettable public demonstrations that had ousted President Rhee.

In the eight years since armistice, Rhee Syngman of the Liberal Party managed to retain his four-time presidency by altering the constitution, fixing elections, and arresting opposition party members as communists. Uncle, once a Liberal and now a Democrat, was angered by these maneuverings, as were the hundreds of students who protested regularly outside the National Assembly Building. "It can't last forever," Uncle had said, "like the Japanese rule didn't last forever."

He was right. The death of a seventeen-year-old boy, Kim Ju-yeol, sparked an accelerating foment against Rhee. This southern villager was killed in March the previous year, and when Inja had learned about it along with the rest of the country, she couldn't stop thinking about him. He and his older brother had gone to Masan City, not far from Busan, to take the Commercial High School entrance examination—two country boys hoping to advance their position and improve their family's lives. They stayed in Masan five days to await the results of the examination, and one afternoon joined a protest denouncing Rhee's most recent rigged election. Ju-yeol disappeared that night. Twenty-seven days later, his body surfaced in the waters near the Masan docks with a tear gas shell lodged in his face and protruding from the back of his skull. A photograph of his floating body was published in newspapers, and people thought he'd been tortured by the police with pegs to his eyes. Uncle had hidden this newspaper, but Inja had heard him shouting and Aunt exclaiming he was right, and so rarely did they agree on anything she wanted to find out why. She wished she hadn't seen it. That poor boy!

Ju-yeol's terrible death filled the Masan streets

with demonstrators getting angrier as they grew in numbers, until night fell and they were met by a barrage of police weapons. Many were shot outright, youth leaders were arrested, and Rhee installed yet another new law to cancel school throughout South Korea. Uncle said it was a stupid attempt to quell unrest; now the students had no reason to be anywhere but in the streets. With schools closed, Inja stayed home and studied her history books to understand more about what was happening. The only relatable event was Sam-il in 1919, so eerily similar it made her wonder if they were stuck in a loop, a Möbius strip of history destined to repeat again and again until—she couldn't imagine an ending, and that was the point. It would never end. She played with Seonil, sat with Grandmother, and together she and Uncle read the newspapers he brought home twice a day. She was aware how easily she'd slipped into Grandfather's role, and how much pleasure it gave them both.

In response to the massacre in Masan, university students staged a peaceful demonstration at the National Assembly Building and were attacked and beaten by thugs everyone knew had been hired by Rhee's people. Word spread and by the end of the next day, one hundred thousand people rallied for an end to the dictatorship. Rhee called the militia, police, and even the Palace Guard to put down the demonstration.

Hundreds were killed and thousands wounded. When Inja sneaked outside and climbed the hill, she saw smoke in the distance from fires burning downtown. It unearthed a forgotten childhood memory of distant smoke and falling under the cart, and Inja had to go inside to ask Uncle to confirm the memory. He filled in details of spotty memories she had about that time, and she was awed by what he had done to take them out of danger. She gave him a tight hug of thanks, and he told her, again, how she was his sister's precious charge, and he would give his life to save her.

On the sixth day of intense and widespread protests, hundreds of university professors formally joined the demonstration and marched together with kindergarten children to the National Assembly Building, an act that drew cheers and fostered hope. Uncle said it was purely Confucian to revere our scholars and bestow a wisdom on them they might not actually deserve. This, April 19th, was the 4.19 Student Uprising.

Inja said to Hyo, "What was it like? When were you there?" She didn't try to hide the admiration in her voice.

"I joined the second wave with the university professors. I shouted until I was hoarse." His eyes gleamed with passion, his grin tight with determination. "The sense of unity and purpose was unforgettable—and the power it had!"

Rhee's concessions that were meant to appease the demonstrators failed, and with foreign pressure and both the police and military beginning to defect, he stepped down. South Korea had a true parliamentary government for a short while, though neither the new president nor the prime minister could muster enough loyalty to truly lead the nation.

"I'm jealous, but you should be proud. My uncle would be proud of you."

"And my father would be appalled, so please don't mention it to your uncle. They disagree politically, but I think they're still friends."

"They are, and I won't." It seemed she grew closer to people through having secrets.

"Ultimately I don't think it made a difference," said Hyo, sighing. A month later the vulnerable presidency had been overtaken by military coup by General Park Chung Hee.

They stepped back onto the road. "How about you?" she said. "How's it been since Busan?"

"It's okay, too," said Hyo. "No more siblings though. Still just me."

There was something he wasn't saying, but she thought they might get to that *next time*. She changed the subject. "My uncle says your house has the best view in Seoul."

"I suppose." They turned the corner to their street, and though they were both silent, it felt

225

comfortable and natural. "You should come over to see it and judge for yourself."

"Okay." Inja had never been curious before about the inside of that prominent brick house, but found she had a sudden keen interest in it. What was Hyo's life like?

"Tomorrow after school?" he said. "I'll have gum by then."

"That doesn't matter," she said, laughing. "It'll be good to say hello to your mother. I haven't seen her in years."

He made a sound, almost a snort. "They're never home. It's me, the cook, the gardener, and the housemaid. My mother has a job now. She said she got restless after I started middle school, so she's working at Father's company. 'To look out for him,' she says. And he says he allowed it so he can look out for her."

His tone made her turn to check his expression. Bitter, angry. She stopped and impulsively grasped his arm, forgetting that he wasn't Yuna, forgetting that he was a boy. "What's wrong?"

"Never mind me. I've been in a bad mood today, that's all." Hyo held her fingers on his arm a brief moment, and she snatched them away. He laughed. "But I'm in a much better mood now."

He made it so easy to not be embarrassed. "Me, too, though I wasn't even in a bad mood."

"And what about your mother?" he said.

Inja was surprised he didn't know, but why

would he? As children they wouldn't have talked about such things; they just played war and built cities with those bricks. She explained about her parents being in America and how they couldn't come back considering the threat of North Korean infiltrators kidnapping her father, and how U.S. immigration laws made it impossible for even a daughter to be reunited with her family. It had become a practiced speech by now—to school entrance examination proctors, to teachers, to new church members. Once a year on her parents' joint birthday, she and Uncle would look through the Cho family album, where they'd glued every photograph that came in her mother's letters. Miran's shy smile filled the frame of her photos. She was a straight-A student, played piano well, and read many books. Mother wrote that she loved bike riding and Campfire Girls—a group that did things together like visit old people and spend weekends in the woods learning how to cook over open fires, as if those were oddities one should learn how to do. Inja wondered what it felt like to ride a bike, to know the touch of piano keys while making music, and occasionally she wondered what her mother told her sister about herself.

"Does that mean you'll be going to America one day? Or will they come back?" said Hyo.

She hadn't thought about it for some time. "They're trying to find a way for me to join them, but it's been like this for so long, I don't think about it much. I'm happy here," she said, avoiding his eyes.

"I'm glad." He paused at his gate. "See you tomorrow afternoon."

She smiled and went through the front yard around the rental house to home. What had troubled him when she'd mentioned his mother? Hyo's father had visited Uncle a few times, so she knew him better—a florid man with a square face who wore patterned ties, a huge gold watch, and who smelled like pungent sweetness. Uncle told her it was Old Spice, the most popular American aftershave lotion, and she kept the thought to herself that it did indeed smell like old spices. At least she had busy rooms full of relatives, while Hyo went home to that big house with only servants waiting for him.

The next morning Inja dressed carefully in a white blouse, a blue-and-gray plaid skirt, and tied a turquoise scarf around her neck. She combed her hair into a ponytail and knotted a white ribbon over the rubber band. When she found Hyo waiting by their front gate, she turned scarlet. He looked much taller than the day before. He took off his cap and bowed to her, and the sunrise glowed on his parted shiny hair. Though the day was brisk and leaves flew wildly in the wind, she felt warm the entire way to school. They talked about their various teachers and favorite subjects—his, chemistry and history, hers, geometry and art. He said he hated piano lessons most of all, but his parents continued to hire the teachers, who, in his parents' presence, often praised his talent, though he was certain he had none.

"What I wouldn't do to have piano lessons!" she said as their toes stepped in unison. "I used to hide outside of Myeonghi's house in her hedges, listening to her play the same song over and over, and making the same mistake each time."

"She's actually very good," said Hyo, making Inja instantly jealous, an uncomely sensation. "I've been in recitals with her."

"Do you play duets?" she tried to make it sound nonchalant, but the way he laughed told her she'd failed.

"No, we don't." He looked at her and kindly didn't mention the vivid color in her face and neck. The humiliation lodged in her stomach, and she was surprised it wasn't an unpleasant sensation.

"When you come over after school today, I can teach you a little piano, okay?"

"I learned the keys and scales at church," she said, "but I've never learned a song."

"How about 'Twinkle, Twinkle'?"

Perfect because that's what your eyes are doing. "Wonderful, thank you." With that, she felt ashamed to have lied to her uncle about saying she was going to Yuna's house that afternoon. She wouldn't do that again. He'd completely understand that she wanted to learn piano.

They neared the park before their paths would split to their respective schools, and Inja held back, wary of the other students. "They'll tease you to death."

"I don't care. We're old friends. Do you care?"

I do. About you. "Not one bit."

They entered the park together and suffered several widened eyes, titters behind hands, and whistles and catcalls from the boys. She didn't mind at all.

With permission from Uncle, Inja went to Hyo's house three afternoons a week for informal piano lessons. His house was much as she imagined it would be: polished pale wood floors, American-style sofas in gold brocades, lacquer cabinets and shelves, modern kitchen and bathrooms, soft electric lighting in every room; and he had his own bedroom with shelves full of books, which she saw only by peeking in through the door-way. Those books garnered many talks between them, and he shared with her *The Stranger* by Camus, Turgenev's *Fathers and Sons*, books by Dostoevsky and George Eliot—whose name confused Inja, though her novels won her over—along with masters Yom Sang-seop and Hwang Sun-won. These writings expanded Inja's view of the world, even of her own national history in the way that only books can—by seeing through the eyes of the people who lived through those times, and others from foreign lands whose history and culture marked men so differently, their minds went to darker and deeper places than she had ever considered. She thought she wasn't smart then, though she knew she had talent in art and found comfort in math.

She came to admire Hyo as an intellectual whose passion for thinking about their purpose in life inspired her, and also made her believe he would, one day, be a great leader. Inja did not yet know the purpose of her life, and she felt that her quest was stunted by the looming possibility of going to America, always a concept that lay before her, and one she more easily pushed aside the more she spent time with Hyo.

The Jeons had a special room for the piano with thick carpet on the floor and leafy-patterned drapes covering the window to dampen sound. She met Hyo's mother, a heavily made-up woman who fawned over her to please her son. Mrs. Jeon gave Inja a half-hour of his piano teacher's instruction on Saturdays. By Harvest Moon, Inja could play "Twinkle, Twinkle" and "Silent Night," the melody with her right hand and one or two chords with her left hand, while Hyo played richer harmonies on the scales below. They spent many hours together like this, and soon their shoulders and thighs would touch on the piano bench and neither would move apart. Over time, on that piano bench where it was easy to converse with their eyes on the keyboard, she learned that his father had had several affairs, and now his mother was having an affair as well—one she flaunted in front of Hyo and his father. It was scandalous and unsettling to hear how they intentionally broke the sacred trust of family loyalty and love because of selfish needs and petty revenge.

"I'm sorry" was all Inja could say when he told her, and "I can't imagine what it must be like for you." She dared to touch his knee.

He grasped her hand. "It's why I admire your family so much. You say they fight and complain, but they're still faithful to each other. Maybe it has something to do with being Christians. But yours is still a complete and traditional Korean family—something we're losing with Park's urgency for industrialization. There's a reason why the Russians are so powerful—it has to do with their national character and traditions, and though they may be five hundred times bigger, it's not that different from ours."

Inja squeezed his hand to soften her words. "You have to be careful about mentioning the president—or the Russians, Hyo. They'll mark you as a socialist, or worse."

"I know, I know. But I admire how your uncle

cared for your grandparents—your grandmother still. I told you that my father sent my aunts to live with my grandparents in Daegu, but he bribed them to go so he wouldn't have to take care of his own parents. He was embarrassed by their country ways. There's beauty in our traditions, and though it's something I'm destined to do, I can't imagine it. I can't imagine being the man of a house where they still hate each other so. I suppose I am my father's son then, because I'd rather run away than live with them for the rest of my life."

Inja had nothing to say, though she wished it were different for him. Aunt and Uncle still yelled at each other, but she had also seen moments of tenderness between them, especially after Seonil was born. She thought of Yuna's broken family and remembered how Grandfather often spouted the Confucian tenet that the family unit was the core of the nation, and without solid families, no nation could maintain its strength. "Even if I were a boy," she blurted, already knowing her attempt to console was selfish—and as such doomed to failure, "I wouldn't know what to think of a future with parents I've never met in a country I've never been to."

He smiled. "Let's trade places."

In an instant, his relaxed humor startled her into the understanding that sometimes being selfish was more honest—and successful—than trying to think of what the other person would like. But at his suggestion, she cried, "Oh no—you'd hate living in our tiny house! You couldn't possibly do Halmeoni's feet," which led to a discussion about her duties at home, Inja careful to not reveal the secret of Grandmother's frostbitten toes. The mood had lightened, and he tinkered on the keyboard to sound out a top song he said he'd heard almost hourly on the radio, "Stand by Me" by Ben E. King.

That autumn Grandmother grew tinier in body and spirit, and talked clearly about the old days as if they were yesterday. Uncle said this was not uncommon with the elderly; he'd seen it happen with the old-timers at church. Inja heard new stories about Grandmother's brothers and her own family before she married, including how she had learned to read and write by eavesdropping on her brothers' lessons with such cleverness that her father relented and hired a tutor for her as well. If Inja asked Grandmother something, her focus would shift and she'd tell Inja about how much, as a child, she had loved listening to stories. Then she'd tell them to Inja: Old Testament stories about children, like Joseph and his brothers, or folk legends about filial love and duty—how a princess sacrificed herself to the sea god to spare her father, or those princesses in the Middle Ages who threw themselves over a cliff into a waterfall to avoid being spoiled by the Hideyoshi marauders. When Inja was a child, these stories were meant to demonstrate how to be a good daughter, and though no one expected her to jump into a waterfall, it was easy to be an obedient daughter of faraway parents who couldn't make real demands of her. Grandmother would say, "You were such a good baby, the best of any baby I'd ever known," which is precisely what she said about Inja's mother and Uncle as infants, and about Seonil, too, so it always made Inja laugh.

Soon after New Year's Day 1962, Inja received a letter from her mother, including a color photograph of their Christmas tree from Miran's new Kodak Starflash camera. When the Christmas package arrived from America, Inja received the same camera as well, plus boxes of flashbulbs and six rolls of film. Uncle couldn't find a place to develop the color film, but Hyo told them about a shop in Yongsan by the American military garrison. It was so much trouble and so expensive to develop the film that Inja rarely used the camera.

Icy winds rattled their window sashes and doorjambs, and Inja soaked Halmeoni's feet and described the Cho American Christmas: "—many presents with bright wrapping paper, and a tree covered in silver. Mother says it's 'tinsel,' as if it were made of 'tin.' " She babbled on, letting her imagination go in thinking about their Christmas and the kinds of presents they opened. Her imagination only went as far as the kinds of presents she'd received over the years in her mother's packages, but she listed them all, and Grandmother seemed happy, the flyswatter forgotten in her hand.

That night as Inja crawled in next to her in bed, Grandmother told her stories about Miran, including the one Uncle had described about Miran's birth and her runaway mother. Though Inja remembered about Miran's childhood illnesses from Uncle's stories, Grandmother was a better storyteller, and her vivid descriptions of a weak and thin baby, crying piteously, brought new understanding about her brush with death. Grandmother also told her something she hadn't known—that her father partly blamed himself for Miran's illnesses since he had been traveling so much during her early years. The child hadn't been officially registered as being adopted until many months later, and therefore her mother couldn't take Miran to the U.S. Army hospital, which had better surgeons and medicine.

Grandmother said, "She threw up everything she ate, and finally when she grew feverish, your mom took her to the missionary hospital. Her fever persisted for a week at that poor hospital. Your mother was already carrying you in her belly and was so exhausted, the missionaries wouldn't allow her to spend every night with Miran like she wanted to. Uncle went instead, but they wouldn't let a man stay overnight in the women's wing."

Now the stories coalesced. "So she almost died then?"

"Yes, and your father blamed himself, like he blamed himself for being in America, which was the reason the Japanese put your mother in prison . . ." She sighed, and Inja remembered it was that imprisonment that damaged Grand-mother's feet, walking hours in the ice to bring her mother food and hope. But she had known nothing about her father's role. What had Uncle said? That the Japanese put people in prison willy-nilly, like President Rhee did.

Grandmother wasn't sleeping, though she had quieted. Inja murmured, "Halmeoni, why did they put Mother in prison?"

"They were in charge of everything, including the mail. And of course a separated husband and wife would write to each other. Since he was in America, they believed he was a spy, and if he was, then his wife was surely a spy as well. Those were hard times."

Inja recalled those exact four last words from Uncle's telling of this story. She had lived through a war of three years, but was too young to remember its brutality. But her parents, and Uncle, too, had until the atomic bombs lived all their lives under Japanese rule; her grandparents for more than half their lives. She couldn't imagine it.

"Remorseful. That's what your father was most of all. And Miran being so sick while he was away only made him more so. It's one of the reasons he didn't pursue another posting with the army when his job ended—he wanted to be close to home from then on. And that's when they decided to go to America so he could raise money to start a church or Christian school in Seoul."

The irony struck her. She felt compassion for her father's sense of remorse and responsibility, despite which there continued to be distance and separation from some part of his family. And more than a decade later, he was all the more distant from home than ever. But now, after all this time, home for them was America, and it was she who was far from them.

Grandmother sighed again and rustled in the quilts. "Don't tell your sister this, though—she'll feel as bad as your father if she knew, and though surely your mother would remember, these are the sorts of things one doesn't talk about. But you're fifteen now . . ."

Inja lay down and snuggled in. "Thank you, Halmeoni," she said. "Without you I wouldn't know my parents at all."

"You just wouldn't know the stories," she

said, voice fading into sleep. "Your heart would always know them . . ."

Inja studied the rafters and the faint light refracting inside from the icy outdoors. Of course they had to take Miran with them to America—not only was she weak and had almost died, her father blamed himself for it and for her mother's hardships. She thought about all the family secrets they held on this side of the world and wondered what secrets her family in America kept from her, and if she'd ever learn about them. She was aware of a strange kind of power one gained from holding secrets, and how confidences begat a kind of self-confidence—how the power of secrets required an inner strength and the maturity of discernment to keep them hidden. But she was also aware that Grandmother had instilled in her too much integrity with her own example of hiding hurtful secrets, and that she would never abuse that power.

The next afternoon, a cold Saturday blanketed with heavy gray skies, a familiar whistle sounded outside the Han gate. Inja slipped on her coat and shoes and went to meet Hyo. His jacket collar was turned up and he stamped his feet, and she smiled because it was so pleasing to have such a handsome friend. He held out a bundle wrapped Japanese style in a pale green silk. "Merry

Christmas," he said. "Or should I just say Happy New Year?"

"You don't celebrate Christmas, so Happy New Year to you, too." She stuck her hands in her pockets. "I'm so sorry that I didn't think to get you a present."

"Don't be silly." He held it out so she couldn't refuse it. "This is very small, and you know that I have everything I could want, plus more. My parents are always buying things. Why do you think we have a house crowded with junk?"

"I wouldn't call that junk." Lately Hyo's mother had been on a shopping spree for art, and she'd commissioned Inja's uncle to create a calligraphic scroll with a four-line poem on the arrival of spring by Midang, Korea's foremost poet.

He stuck his hands in his armpits. "Just open it, would you, so you can get out of the cold. So I can get out of the cold."

She unknotted the silk, itself a lovely gift. A narrow box lay on top of a black leather book with nothing written on the cover or spine. She tucked the silk and little box under her elbow to open the book, a bound sketchbook of quality blank paper.

"It's for your art," said Hyo, looking pleased at her expression of wonder.

"It's too beautiful. How can I ever use it?"

"Of course you'll use it. Now your drawings

won't have those lines underneath." She had sketched him at his piano once, but the only pad she had was primary school paper gridded in red for practicing one's letters. "Quick, I'm freezing. Open the little box."

She snapped open the padded box to reveal an obsidian-colored fountain pen with gold accents. She had never owned anything so equally exquisite and practical. "Omana," she whispered.

"Gu-roovy, yes?" he said, using their newest English slang from the radio.

"Very *gu-roovy*," she answered. "It's so kind of you, so thoughtful. Saying 'thank you' doesn't seem to be enough."

"I have the ink at home. Next time you come over, I'll show you how to fill it, then you can do a proper drawing. You'll like how it feels, see? It's like mine but black." He retrieved his own silver-cased pen from inside his coat, and she couldn't tell if his teeth were chattering for the cold or to catch up with his nervous patter. She caught his eyes, and her own spilled with surprised tears, for in that moment she felt closer to him than she had to anyone in her life other than Uncle—not because of the gifts he'd given, but because he was so full of wanting to please her.

"What's wrong?"

"Nothing—really nothing's wrong. I'm overcome. You're so thoughtful. Thank you . . ." She bowed.

He bowed back. "I'm glad you like them. I'm freezing. Happy New Year, Inja."

"Happy New Year." All she had to offer was her hand, slightly damp from wiping her tears, and he took it, squeezed it, and dashed back home.

When she went inside, Ara and Aunt were busy in the kitchen, Uncle was at his desk working on Hyo's mother's scroll, and Seonil lolled on newspapers Uncle had spread out for him to play with, so only Grandmother saw Inja sneak in with presents under her coat. Inja showed them to her once, then several times, nearly fifteen happy repetitions, until Grandmother lost interest and went back to her flyswatter.

Spring came, giving Grandmother more purpose in her vigil for flies, though she mostly napped in the soft warmth of the spring sunlight beaming through the sitting room window. Seonil, in first grade, grumbled frequently about how mean his teachers were, but he had many new friends his age. He clamored for Uncle to walk him to this boy's house or that one's, and Uncle always complied.

Yuna, whose opinion mattered, approved of Hyo, and though he was often on Inja's mind, she tried to refrain from talking about him too much. One day in April in the after-school park, Hyo introduced them to his schoolmate Junghi. Fortunately for them all, he took an immediate liking to Yuna, who was flattered and pleased to not be the "third wheel," which she'd read about in American magazines her father gave her— *Teen* and *Ingenue*. These magazines also kept them relatively current with rock-and-roll music and "teen idols." They all knew Elvis, of course. Yuna had a phonograph and a 45 rpm record of "Are You Lonesome Tonight?" When she played that song and it was just the two girlfriends, they danced around the turntable waving scarves, singing in terrible English with fake vibrato, until Yuna's grandmother complained about tigers fighting in the room.

Junghi sealed his friendship with Yuna when he brought her records. He wouldn't say how or where he got them, but Hyo said Junghi's father worked in Yongsan and had connections. At the park Junghi would show them a corner of a 45 sleeve poking out of a math book, and they'd beg to know what it was. The four spent many afternoons at Yuna's replaying the same record, since they had so few, and memorizing the English lyrics. They figured out how to do the Twist, thanks to Chubby Checker, until that record was so worn, it was more scratchy rhythm than tune. Luckily the flip side had "Let's Twist Again."

Inja wrote home dutifully to her mother every week, not mentioning Hyo—though once, in a rare revelation beyond what she usually wrote about school and how everyone was at home, she did tell her about Yuna and her phonograph, hoping her mother would get the hint and send her some 45s. Once she tried writing to Miran, suspecting she'd have a record player and lots of rock-and-roll music, but Mother wrote back saying she was a good sister, but Miran couldn't read or write Korean. She also wrote, what is "Mar-ba-rhettes" and who were the "Oeb-buh-rhee" Brothers?

22

The Fury

The Plymouth Fury that Calvin bought in the fall of 1961 was the source of the first fight Miran could remember between her parents. Without warning one Saturday in October, her father drove up in a brand-new, turquoise-green, two-door hard-top, a long and lean car, home from his usual errand of buying Napa cabbage for kimchi at the Florida Market on Capitol Hill.

"Omana!" Najin said, looking out the dining room window. They ran outside as Calvin got out with a huge grin—a grin that lost some of its brilliance when he saw Najin's crossed arms and furrowed brow.

"It's beautiful—a spaceship!" said Miran. She remembered the conversation she'd had with her father about them all being illegal aliens together. "Is it ours?"

"It is," said Calvin, eyes firm on Najin. "On sale. The color is 'twilight blue metallic.' "

Miran opened the passenger door and tipped the seat forward to climb into the back. Her parents circled the car on opposite ends as he pointed out features. His hand dusted the straight lines of the back apron, its center fin, the protruding circles of taillights on each side. "It's easy to handle." He slid into the driver's seat. "It has an automatic transmission, so I can teach you to drive."

"Groovy radio, Dad," said Miran. "Looks almost like a piano with dials."

Najin said nothing, though she did sit inside for a moment, and her hand skimmed the striped bench seat.

"Come see the trunk."

They got out, and to cover her mother's silence, Miran admired how neatly everything fit inside: the splintering crate of cabbage, a big carton with a gross of eggs and a bushel of apples, the bulk of which they'd sell or give away at church, plus a spare tire tucked in the side.

"Help your father unload," said Najin.

"What do you think?" said Calvin.

"Very clean." Still hugging her arms, Najin went inside through the mud porch.

Her father remained silent as they toted the produce and eggs into the cool basement.

On her way to the library that afternoon, Miran saw him washing the car and offered to help, but he said no, the burden was his.

Later that night, from her bedroom she heard them talking. Her mother said stuff in Korean with a scattering of English, *foolish, gullible,* as if English were the only way those words could be spoken.

Her father said *on sale, trade-in, monthly payment,* then silence. The front door closed and, soon after, the car doors shut.

Miran slid out of bed and kneeled backward on the living room couch to peer between the Venetian blinds. She vaguely remembered peering out at her parents in the backyard when she was small, but couldn't remember for what reason. They were sitting in the car, and she thought it was all okay then, and maybe he was showing her the push-button radio. But as her eyes adjusted to the streetlight, she saw his unmoving silhouette, while her mother's hands chopped the air until whatever she was saying fogged up the windshield. Miran went to bed having learned three things that night: her parents did have big fights and had taken care to hide them from her; her mother thought her father a gullible fool; and though he was a revered minister and radio broadcaster who spoke perfect English, it was her mother who had the upper hand in the family. She supposed they hid their fights to appear the perfect, harmonious Korean minister's family. Her father didn't seem to care that much about what others thought, but her mother did—a trait she'd passed down to Miran.

Miran had saved money from her job with Miss Lone, and later that fall, following her father's precedent of not asking permission, she bought a fancy hi-fi portable stereo for $69.95.

Inspired by the swelling civil rights movement, she discovered R & B, soul, and folk music. She laughed when her mother asked about the "Marbarettes" and the "Eburry Brothers" for Inja, and she sacrificed a precious 45 of the Marvelettes' "Please Mr. Postman" to a package going to her sister. She taught herself piano chords to play along with Dylan and Seeger, and checked out from the library a piano songbook of American folk music. If words wouldn't so easily come from her mouth, perhaps music could provide the expression she needed, even if her mother complained about the caterwauling.

Distance had grown between herself and Sarah Kim, who was in a different school, which had never been a problem before but now mattered. Miran's favorite haunts at Blair High School were the art and music rooms, and both teachers, who appreciated her talents, welcomed her presence and made her stand out in class, building her confidence and helping her make new friends. She still had her Campfire Girl Troop—they were all kooky together—and now a few friends who were oddballs like herself: a black guy who was passionate about modern dance, a half-Japanese and half-American girl who waited tables at her mother's Japanese restaurant, and a fellow artist guy who'd grown up in Bangkok with his Foreign Service parents. Miran found a home with these friends, began smoking cigarettes with them, tried beer, wine, then marijuana, and had passionate discussions about Mao's *Little Red Book*, the *Tao Te Ching*, Hesse's *Siddhartha*, music, astrology, ecology, and civil rights.

Russia unleashed the largest-ever nuclear bomb test in October 1961, and soon after, her friends said their parents had been complaining with other parents about Chairman Mao's book being available in the school, as well as their readings of Stalin and Lenin in social studies. One Wednesday afternoon, Miran left a flyer from school in the pile of that week's junk mail. Neither of her parents went to school meetings, so she hadn't expected them to notice. The mimeographed announcement read: *Emergency PTA meeting! Parents concerned about the proliferation of communist propaganda in our school, please join in efforts to eliminate radical leftist influences from our children's education,* with the date—that very evening, at seven o'clock. It listed a half-dozen "radical leftist" books they hoped to ban. Miran's mother was home at five-thirty, her father at six, and dinner was usually six-thirty, but when Calvin saw the flyer, he asked if she'd like to go with him—she said yes, hoping to see her friends—and told Najin to hold dinner for a couple of hours.

They climbed into the Fury and scooted smoothly down the driveway for the twenty-minute ride to Blair High School. When he parked, some loitering boys, greasers, whistled at his car. He pretended to ignore them, but Miran saw hints of his prideful smile. Inside the gymnasium, they both got coffee, and, seeing she was the only student there, except for the PTA student representative, she detached from her father and climbed the bleachers toward the shadows of the scoreboard. The school was strange at night, even with a room full of a hundred or so parents. She spied her two favorite teachers and wondered if kids weren't allowed at PTA meetings. Her father sat on a bottom bleacher row, looking small and formal in his black suit.

The principal stood, introduced the PTA president and other PTA officers at the front table, and a fiery discussion ensued about the need to ban those books. Miran doodled for half an hour, bored, sure that these square but very vocal parents would get their way.

Her father raised his hand like a little kid and was recognized. "Dr. Cho," said the principal, and Miran's eyes widened, not only because the principal clearly knew her father, but he'd addressed him thus. Her eyes only grew wider as her minister father stood and in his sermonizing voice addressed the entire room.

"My wife and I are Korean immigrants," he said. "Many of you remember how Korea was a battleground for democracy, with North Korea under Russian and Chinese communist control and South Korea supported by the United States. Many of your fathers or brothers or you yourselves may have fought in the Korean War."

Some murmurs of assent rose from the attendees in the bleachers.

"Both my wife and I were raised and educated in the northern part of the peninsula of Korea when we were one country before there was a North or a South, before communism and democracy were at loggerheads. My wife's family has all managed to move to South Korea, where they live in a tenuous peace less than forty miles from the border of North Korea. But my family"—he paused and cleared his throat, and Miran wasn't sure if it was theatrics or sincere emotion—"my family are lost in the communist North. I have not been in contact with them since 1950. My father was an outspoken opponent of communism, so if he is still alive, surely he is imprisoned."

Miran's eyes opened wide. She had never known this about her father's family. It wasn't the kind of confidence her father would've shared with her, but perhaps it was one of the stories her mother told that she hadn't understood.

Her father said, "I believe I can safely assume that I, more than anyone else in this room, should have a say about whether these books that outline the tenets of communism should be allowed in school."

People clapped in agreement, the most vigorous applause coming from the supporters of banning the books.

"When I was a young man," he said, and Miran groaned inwardly. He would tell another story before announcing his position, "—and sought an education in religious studies, I asked my father, a minister, what books he would recommended for me to read. Naturally there was the Bible, the Gospel of Matthew to be exact, then the Greeks, but he included in my long reading list Friedrich Engels and Karl Marx, the fathers of communist ideology. I continued my studies of communism, which was gaining a following in my country because we needed new ideas. But it was an ideology of repression, not freedom and the celebration of individual thought and open discourse. So now I am a die-hard supporter of democracy and will soon become a proud American citizen"—smattering of applause— "and if you ban these books, I will ensure that my daughter, who is somewhere around here—"

He looked but failed to pinpoint her since she'd made a point of receding even farther into the shadows. "I will ensure my daughter reads every one of the banned books and shares them with her friends." Surprised responses buzzed through the rows of parents, and, after a moment, a few faculty members applauded loudly. He con- cluded, "I don't think any person here can deny that education trumps ignorance in any kind of war."

The principal and some teachers clapped, then more teachers, then parents joined in, then those at the front table stood up clapping, and soon Miran's short father received a standing ovation. After that, the meeting was adjourned with no further discussion.

Driving home, Miran felt she ought to say something, so she said something safe. "That was interesting."

Calvin turned and smiled. "I hoped you'd think so."

She wanted to say how proud she was to be his daughter, how sorry she was about his lost family in North Korea, but these simple words were too difficult to express.

The next day in school, though she'd had nothing to do with it, Miran became a hero among the teachers—"Cool Dad," they said, and the word spread throughout her tenth grade. The problem for Miran was now she would have to read those books, and while she was interested enough in Mao's story, those other heavy philosophers were going to be a challenge.

23

Halmeoni

On a Monday morning in mid-April 1962, Inja woke early for school, looking forward to another afternoon with Hyo at his piano. She climbed out of bed, and when Grandmother didn't stir, she knew. A glance showed the outline of Grandmother's body, tinier in its stillness, and the dawn glossed her features with the colors of the moon. Inja ran down the hall yelling for Uncle, horrified by the thought of having slept soundly beside her grandmother while she'd taken her last breath, that no one had witnessed it, which was the last act of supreme respect to give an elder, and that she had possibly slept beside her dead body for hours.

Uncle hurried to their room, took one look, and collapsed to his knees. Then Inja really understood she was gone, and this pure finality plunged her into tears. She crouched beside him, and though they both wept, she felt very alone until Aunt and Ara came and cried out, and Uncle put his arm around her.

She dressed in a plain white blouse and black skirt and went outside to tell Hyo, who was waiting to walk to school with her. He touched her elbow, and when she asked if he'd tell Yuna to tell the principal, he said he'd tell her but would stop by the school himself.

In the main sitting room, after the undertaker left, Uncle prepared a low table in front of a screen that mostly hid Grandmother's sealed coffin covered with hemp cloth. Inja brought in three branches of blooming forsythia, which reminded her of something similarly laden with sadness she couldn't quite remember from her childhood. Uncle lit candles and opened Grandmother's Bible to Psalm 23. On the back of the makeshift altar, he set up a colored portrait he'd painted that matched the one he'd made of Grandfather. Tomorrow he would drape the portrait with black ribbons. Then, leaving Aunt and Seonil to keep vigil over her body, Inja and Uncle went out to alert the minister and to telephone the family in America.

Unlike the night Grandfather had died, their walk to the telephone office seemed too bright and clear, as if a kind of lens had fallen on her eyes that made the colors more saturated, the edges of shapes sharper. She couldn't understand how people on the street could go about as usual, how the trams could rattle in their tracks, their wires crackling as if nothing had happened.

The telephone process was the same as when Grandfather had died. Calvin answered and

Uncle told him the news, then he repeated it when Najin came on the line. He discussed the plan for the funeral with her and said many tearful times that he, too, felt sorry she couldn't be here, but it couldn't be helped, and that Inja would gladly stand in for her. When it was Inja's turn at last, her handkerchief was sodden and the tears wouldn't stop.

"*Umma-nim*," she said, bursting upon saying, "Mother."

Through the static Inja could hear her grief. "Inja, my child, are you well?"

"I am. I'm sad for you, mother."

"Yes, my child, I'm sad for you, too. Even sadder that I cannot be with you now. But Halmeoni is at peace now, where she always knew she'd find it."

"She told me you used to sleep with her in the way that she and I sleep together. Slept together. I will miss her most at bedtime." *I will miss her all the time.*

"You were a great comfort to her. She wrote so often how clever and funny you were." She said something quickly to the side, then, "I'm going to give you to your father now, but I am praying for you, and you must pray for Halmeoni and Harabeoji, and your sister who never had the chance to know them. Will you?"

"I will. Thank you, Mother. I will pray for you and Father, too."

"Goodbye. It's so good to hear your voice, so mature—here's Appa."

The conversation with her father went similarly, except he asked Inja to write to them as frequently as she could during the coming week, and to describe as plainly as she could the services for Grandmother. He also said that she had been especially blessed, that God had been waiting for Grandmother for many years but wanted to be sure her granddaughter knew her before he allowed her to receive the great gift of heaven. "I do feel blessed, Father." And she did feel calmer with his assurance that the clarity and beauty of Grandmother's faith had rewarded her with spiritual peace.

She and Uncle wiped the tear-dampened telephone receiver as best they could, he signed papers, and they went home arm in arm.

24

Grandmother's Burial

The telephone sat on a little table connected to a bench in the hallway between the two bedrooms. Miran dozed during the late evening call, but then she heard her mother say, "No, we can tell her tomorrow. No need to wake her. Go back to bed—I can't sleep."

"Of course. I'm sorry, Yeobo," said Calvin.

Miran heard him deliver a prayer, and her mother sniffling as she said, "Amen."

After her father went back to bed, Miran crept into the dining room. Najin sat, feet tucked up on the chair, writing in her diary in red ink, words in Korean and Chinese characters. "Can I make you a Sanka?" Miran said.

Najin glanced at her, and Miran was startled by how drawn she looked, yet also how beautiful, as if light were shining from her eyes and skin. "Yes," she said. "Halmeoni passed away this morning. Died in her sleep, you understand?" Miran nodded, and her mother's eyes narrowed. "Or was it yesterday morning? The time confuses me. Is it tomorrow morning? I could still talk to her—" Tears. Miran brought her a box of tissues.

"Did the telephone wake you?" Najin said.

"Yes. I'm sorry about Halmeoni, Mom."

"Yes, it's sad, thank you," she said in English. "Sanka is good."

Miran made her a cup, then left her, knowing she'd be up writing all night.

Najin had penned in red ink: *Song Haegyeong, Monday, 16 April 1962, 6:30 a.m.*

She wrote a last letter to her mother, using her diary since it would never be sent. It had been years since she'd written to her with any real intimacy—in Grandmother's diminished condition Dongsaeng or Inja read Najin's letters to her. Her heart opened with love and gratitude for all they had suffered together, for the protection and encouragement she'd received, and the joy they'd shared even during hard times.

Mother, I remember we were gardening late one summer toward the end of the war. We both used slanted pieces of bamboo to unearth those feeble potatoes since all of our tools were "donated" to the weekly metal drive. Do you remember how we laughed at how easy it was to find potatoes this way? You whispered, like you were saying something bad, it didn't matter that the Japanese took everything—look how fine we were

260

doing. Always you found goodness in hardship.

Even then you sang as you worked. It saddened me to know your songs had been silenced in these last years. I heard your voice clearly that day years ago that spurred me to buy the piano, and it will always be your piano, its notes your spirit. I weep for Inja, your granddaughter, her grief we can only share in heart.

I thank you with every ounce of my body, with every beat of my heart, for raising my daughter in the way you raised me. I pray that she gave you comfort in my absence. You were her beacon as you were for me. I think of my childhood with such a loving and strong mother, and I am humbled by this blessing. How many hundreds of times did you guide me to modesty, to compassion, to prayer, to grace. How much you taught me about how to work and live! I thank you in prayer.

I think of the rice you brought me for ninety days that terrible winter, and the message at the bottom of each rice bowl that gave me hope, precious hope when so little was to be found. I could not see your face nor hear your voice for all those days, but you were with me then. Your courage became my courage, your faith, my faith, your sacrifice, my survival.

How I regret not being with you these last years!

She stayed up all that night writing to her mother, grieving. When she heard Calvin's alarm clock buzz, she washed her face at the sink and started a pot of coffee. Miran came into the kitchen, said again how sorry she was about Halmeoni, and leaned in for a hug. Najin held her close, comforted by the rare intimacy.

Over breakfast, Calvin made Najin, who'd taken the day off of work, promise to rest, then he'd come home and make dinner. So when Miran came home, her mother was prone on the couch, though awake by the time she came into the living room.

"*Aigu*!" Najin said. "It's late."

"You were supposed to sleep," said Miran.

"I couldn't. That dream of water . . ."

A chill cascaded down Miran's back. "The one about Harabeoji in his grave? The same one?"

"Yes, awful. Did Appa tell you about it?"

"A while ago." Miran had an image of her grandfather, like in his portrait, but with water pouring from empty eyes, from his sleeves. She shook it off and wondered what people were supposed to do when there was no funeral to go to. Even after Grandfather had died, there was no discussion about returning to Korea. And if it was impossible to bring her sister to America, surely it was equally impossible to go to Korea even once for Najin to have seen her mother. "Wow. I haven't heard you having nightmares for a while."

"Not this one, not for years now. Terrible."

"Do you want to try to sleep in my room?"

"Good idea. You change clothes first."

Najin slept soundly in Miran's bed until Calvin came home, and after a few days, when it grew apparent that it was the only place Najin could sleep without that dream, Miran moved downstairs to a cot in the basement, where her dad had put up studs and drywall for a third bedroom he hadn't quite finished— no doors, in need of paint, and only a few sticks of donated furniture. On the weekend Dad took her downtown to Lansburghs, and they bought a double-decker bed, a tall chest of drawers, and a bureau with six lateral drawers and a mirror. She already had a bookshelf, lamps, some odd side tables, and a rocking chair, so finally she had space and privacy she hadn't known she was craving.

Najin converted Miran's former bedroom into a sewing room, and the existing bed doubled as a surface to lay out patterns and fabrics as needed, or as a place where she could rest undisturbed by the nightmare that clawed into her nights.

25 April 1962
Mother and Father,

It is two days after Halmeoni's funeral. We are all at home, feeling sad and missing her. I am missing you and Father also. And my sister. There are still visitors to the house, but not so many now. Ajumeoni said there was lots of money given, and Ajeossi said it will pay for her funeral. I will go back to school tomorrow. Ajeossi says I do not have to go back until next week, but it is too quiet around here, and I see her shadow everywhere. I hear her flyswatter, and it makes me jump. I do not want to make you too sad, but Father had asked me on the telephone to describe the funeral to you. Ajeossi is writing to tell you about that part and is sending you photographs as well, and he said I should instead tell you everything that led up to her service.

Last week, Ajeossi got a telegram from the cemetery director in Osan late Wednesday morning, the day before Halmeoni was supposed to have her funeral, saying there was a problem and to come right away with the minister. We went to see Reverend Shin and asked him to take us to the cemetery. He has a car and a driver so we didn't have to take the tram, train, and long bus rides to the twin cemetery mountains there. They are beautiful, these mountains, especially in this season, because they are cultivated and landscaped. There are still cherry blossom trees blooming, bright yellow forsythia scattered among the gravesites, and flowering plums and pear trees as well, though their flowers are mostly gone now. Still, it is very pretty and peaceful. Halmeoni would have enjoyed it. The paths are steep and narrow, mostly just dirt, but by the graves of rich people, there are white pebbles spread on the pathways. You can tell who is rich from as far away as the opposite mountainside. But not rich in the way Halmeoni was.

Harabeoji's grave was very high up the mountain, so we walked a long way up, even after the cemetery director drove us most of the way in his car. Before that, though, Ajeossi and Reverend Shin had a long talk with the cemetery director in his office. I waited outside the door since his office is so small and dark, and it was a sunny day. Voices were raised for a while, but when they came out, everything seemed settled. We went up the mountain and were out of breath by the time we got there, especially poor Reverend

Shin. There were many workmen waiting for us with shovels and ropes, smoking cigarettes. I am sorry to tell you that Harabeoji's gravesite was a mess of mud and dirt. They had deconstructed his mound, and though I remember how much grass had grown on his grave last fall, all of it was now covered by orange mud. Inside his grave I could see his coffin, still looking sturdy, but mostly it was a muddy hole, with muddy water puddled in the footprints left behind by the workers.

Mother, Ajeossi fell to his knees when he saw this, and Reverend Shin helped him stand. Reverend Shin gave a short service and we prayed, then we stood aside while the men put ropes beneath Harabeoji's coffin to lift it out from the mud. There were four men: two on each side, but they could not lift it. The ropes slipped from their hands, though they had wrapped their palms with rags for a better grip. The director went down to his office to get more men. We waited a long time, and the sun was warm on our backs. We prayed. Poor Harabeoji! The sun started to cast long shadows, and I think it was around five o'clock when four more men came back with the director. So with four men on each side, they were able to lift the coffin out. It made a loud sucking noise when it was freed from the mud.

Mother, I am sorry to tell you this next part. Since it was so messy all around the gravesite, the men had laid planks nearby and they set his coffin on those planks above the mud. Then they drilled and made about eight holes around the base of the coffin. Especially the first time they drilled, water spurted out. Soon, all the holes had arcs of water, and we waited until it was drained. Ajeossi and I looked in the grave hole and the water level had risen. An underground stream, he said. Who could have known, I asked him, but he did not answer. Mother, tears were raining down his cheeks. I think he blames himself, but that is not fair. It is not his fault. It is nobody's fault.

The men brought buckets of clean water and washed off Harabeoji's coffin. They said they'd wrap it anew after it dried. They shoveled the mud back into the hole as best they could, and we cleaned our shoes in one of their buckets. Ajeossi wanted the coffin to dry completely, and he wanted to stay with Harabeoji until he could be buried again. But the cemetery director thought it wasn't a good idea, it being so muddy. I worried that Ajeossi might get sick if he were to stay on that mountain through the night. I am certain Ajumeoni would be upset. Reverend Shin reminded Ajeossi that we still had Halmeoni's funeral, which we had postponed a few days, and he himself would be busy every night with Holy week leading up to Easter Sunday. The director said the weather report was clear all through Easter and Monday, which would give plenty of time for drying. While we talked beside the grave, the sun touched the tops of the mountains, and Ajeossi agreed to wait through the weekend for Harabeoji to dry. Then they would bury him again with Halmeoni in a new spot on Monday, having a double funeral of sorts.

Ajeossi made the director promise that a man would stand watch over the coffin at all hours, and he promised. I do think he fulfilled this promise. Mother, the director was so upset when he saw the water and when he had to get all those men, that it seems to me he would do anything to make up for this mistake. Though it was not his fault either.

It was a long day yesterday, and even today I am feeling sad and tired. Can there possibly be more tears inside? And then I think of Halmeoni and her wrinkly smile, her eyes half-crescents, and I am crying again. The new gravesite is not very far from the old one, but even higher on the mountain, in a more beautiful spot near a grove of dogwoods, which Ajeossi says is Halmeoni's favorite flower—the Easter flower because of its scarlet four points. I did not know this. Mother, what is your favorite flower? I will have to think about what is my favorite flower, and then I will write again and tell you.

I only tell you about being sad and crying because Ajeossi says it is better to be sad together. I think he is right about this. So I am sad with you, Mother, as is all your family here.

Your daughter, Inja

P.S. My favorite flower is quince blossom.

25

Special Allowance

Inja was glad for certain traditions, such as taking note of one hundred days after Grandmother's death to honor her and spend time at the graves. On July 25, a hot dry day, Inja and Seonil were excused from school, and the family went to the cemetery with a picnic made by Ara. Aunt was pregnant again, but only newly pregnant, so she climbed the mountain with careful steps on those narrow paths with the family. As with her previous pregnancy, Aunt's spirits were jovial and she was especially frivolous with Seonil, who would be seven years old in a few weeks. Though Inja thought the day might be sad, it was soothing to mark a beloved's death, and they spent the entire day remembering Grandmother. Inja and Aunt laughed together when they recalled how the bedpan was used as a cook pot at the refugee camp during the war. Uncle scattered grass seed on the grave mounds and planted a white azalea at the head, and many prayers were delivered. Inja left that mountaintop comforted to be with her family, though it was hugely diminished without her grandparents. She knew her parents and Miran would've been pleased to have been there that day, and it was probably the only time she truly longed for the presence of her American family.

But when Inja turned sixteen in September, her life changed forever. She had sent her parents birthday cards she'd designed and printed herself in graphic arts class and was expecting a package for her birthday on the twenty-fourth, a week after theirs. It came with a dozen Life Savers rolls packaged like a book and brand-new clothes: a fuzzy white sweater—"angora," wrote Mother—sewn with seed pearls in a flower pattern around the neckline, her first pair of high heels—black leather "kitten heels" with pointy toes—and a blue-gray knife-pleated skirt that never needed ironing. Included in that package were cute cards from her sister and a thick letter. Miran also sent Inja a drawing of herself from art class, and Inja was struck by her sister's pensive look, her features so unlike her own. She thought Miran's long, untied-up hair was a disaster.

Inja missed sharing all her presents with Grandmother so she went to Yuna's house. She showed off her new clothes and Miran's drawing. Yuna said that's how the girls were wearing their hair now: long, loose and straight. She'd read in *Ingenue* how to roll your hair in curlers made of orange juice cans to straighten it. "I don't know," said Inja, examining the photos of girls with long blond tresses. "It looks okay if your hair is that color, but otherwise it looks like a funeral."

"Don't say that!"

"I'm teasing." Inja undid her ponytail, spread her hair over her face and shoulders, clawed her hands and howled like a wolf. Yuna screamed and they fell apart laughing. But Inja sobered, for she had come over to talk to Yuna about the fat letter, which she hadn't yet shown to Uncle. She tugged it out from her skirt pocket and displayed a sheaf of tri-folded documents. "I wanted to show this to you."

"They look official. Do you know what they say?"

"I don't know exactly, but my mother writes here that since I'm sixteen I need to sign in all the places marked with an X, have a non-family member witness it, and send them back to her. It's something about immigration."

Yuna took the papers and studied them one by one. "There are lots of places to sign. What does it mean?"

"I don't know. She wrote to Ajeossi about it, so I have to find out what he knows. My mother says all this is thanks to an American woman, someone they met on the ship when they went to America. She works for the government, for a minister in parliament or something."

"But why is that lady meddling in your

273

family's affairs?" Yuna handed her back the sheaf.

Inja appreciated Yuna's loyalty, but for all the years they'd been friends, Yuna also knew about an imminent reunion—except it had never happened, and here she was, on the verge of her adult life with friends of her own, successes she was proud of, college to plan for, family she loved. It couldn't be happening now! "She's helping. She's helping my parents bring me to America. I think that's what these papers are for." She folded them back into the envelope.

"Don't sign them!" Yuna made to grab them.

"I don't think I have a choice."

"You do. You could pretend they were lost in the mail. You could say they blew away when you opened the envelope, that it was a sign— you're not supposed to go where you don't know anybody and you don't have any friends. You can't go to America! You can barely speak English. What about Hyo?" Tears were in her eyes, and Inja tried to ignore them. She had cried buckets for Grandmother and it had helped, but for this there was no point in crying. Nothing would help.

"Don't make me cry. Maybe it's nothing. Maybe it's paperwork for them to come and visit here. If they came, they'd see my whole life is here already. They'd have to see—"

Yuna turned to wipe her eyes and said, too

brightly, "You're right! What was the American saying your mother wrote about roosters crossing the road?"

Inja smiled. "Chickens. You mean, 'Don't catch your chickens before they cross the road.' She says it means not to expect things that haven't happened yet, though I don't know how to make sense of it."

"Doesn't matter," said Yuna, and she folded Inja's fingertips over the envelope. "Let's wait and see what those papers say before I get any more upset." She shoved Inja, and Inja shoved her back. Then they listened to music and read magazines as usual, though both felt an ominous tug each time "America" was mentioned.

That evening Ara made a fuss over Inja's dinner and gave her a small birthday cake made of *ddeok*, rice cake with a candle stub in it left over from Seonil's birthday, which went out in a tiny puff of smoke when it reached the table. Inja pretended to blow it out anyway and thanked her. She handed out Life Savers rolls as if she were Father Christmas, and Aunt excused her from cleaning up after dinner. Usually Uncle would use that time to play with Seonil or catch up on the newspapers or work on his self-imposed task of copying the entire Bible in his elegant calligraphy, but tonight he agreed when Inja asked if they could go for a walk on such a beautiful night.

In the clear cool dark, a strand of moon shone among the bountiful stars, and she wondered if they would look different from America. But she remembered about the hemispheres and the earth's rotation, and found tiny consolation in knowing the same ceiling of splendor would be above her as long as she remained above the equator.

They walked without speaking for long stretches of road, and because Uncle was unusually quiet, she knew he was aware of her need for this time with him. The tops of the trees swayed in a night wind, sounding like the ocean waves she first saw and heard in Busan, and it made her feel like a child. "Ajeossi, Mother sent me papers to sign, and I don't know what they mean."

He sighed and opened his elbow for Inja to take his arm. Their footsteps crunched along the packed dirt road, and they walked awhile before he cleared his throat. "She wrote to me, too, as did your father. It appears you may soon be going home to live with your family."

Of course she had suspected this, but to hear it filled her heart with dread. Tears fell. She pulled a handkerchief from her pocket and dabbed her cheeks. "My home is here." She tried to sound calm and adult.

"Yes, and there is always a home for you here, but your real home is with your parents. You've always known this. I've always known this. Now it seems it will actually happen."

Inja heard the grief in his voice but was too full of her own sadness to take his in. They walked farther, out of their neighborhood and beyond the park and her school. The road wound around, unfamiliar, and broad open spaces made them vulnerable to cooler winds. A storm brewed inside her, and anger, resentment, injustice, and loss broke into sobs, but they didn't stop walking.

"When will it happen?" she said when she knew her voice was steady.

"She couldn't say. It could be next month, three months. But it's certainly going to happen, so you must be prepared."

Inja focused on the sounds of their darkened footsteps, the waves swaying through the treetops. "We should go home now," she said, her throat catching on "home."

He pivoted and offered his other arm, then hugged her hand to his ribs. "Your mother's letter explained the plan, which is why they don't know exactly when it might happen. Do you want to hear about it?"

"Yes please." She hoped, with failing desperation, there could be a breakdown in some part of that plan.

"The woman helping them—you'll meet her I'm sure—is Miss Edna Lone."

"Miss Edna Lone," she repeated, tempted to curse the name.

"Before the war she was a missionary in Anseong and Seoul, but now she's an aide for an American politician from her home province, and it was he who took up your parents' case. I don't know why he did, though. I suppose politics works the same there as it does everywhere. Who you know is who you do favors for. Miss Lone has been his aide for a long time, and perhaps this is a reward for her loyalty."

They neared the park, and the silhouettes of trees and structures grew familiar—a familiarity both comforting and sad.

"Your mother says they're trying to get around the immigration law by creating an exception to that law. It's called a 'special allowance,' and the plan is to add the special allowance to another law they think can be passed."

"What law?"

"I'm not sure, but your father says it's a small bill that should get voted on with no problem."

"They haven't voted on it yet?" There *was* hope.

"Don't get your hopes up." Uncle knew her too well. "Your father says it's bound to happen; they just don't know when."

"What are all those papers for, then?"

"We'll take them to a lawyer and have you sign

them with an official witness. It's to certify your birth, since your birth record went up in smoke, and your citizenship, education, health and health history, genealogy, that sort of thing. They want to be sure you're not a communist spy," he said, a weak smile in his voice.

"What about the cost?" If her parents hadn't ever been able to afford it, how could they now afford to bring her?

"They took out a loan for your plane ticket."

"Oh."

"Your parents love you very much, and they've been waiting for you a long, long time." Uncle folded her in his arms. "It doesn't matter where you live," he said. "I'll always love you best." He held her for several minutes in the shadow of their battered and beloved wooden gate, while she mourned the inevitable loss of her uncle, the heart of her Korean family.

Passage of the bill failed in November. Inja breathed relief, and the bill underwent revision. Holidays and anniversaries came and went. Samjinnal, the spring festival that annually occurred on the third day of the third lunar month, fell on March 27 in 1963. They were supposed to have azalea ddeok, but the blooms were late, though the flowering trees at her grandparents' graves were in glorious color. Uncle, Seonil, and Inja visited the cemetery with a modest picnic lunch. Aunt stayed home, complacent during her pregnancy, nearing full term.

Inja talked to Grandfather and thanked him for his care when they fled Seoul during the war, the little birds he brought down with a slingshot and roasted for her, walking to and from school in Busan though it had embarrassed them both, and even for the horrible medicine because he believed it would make her stronger. But it was he himself and Grandmother who had made her strong. She thanked Grandmother for teaching her about her family, faith, and a mother's love, and she bowed goodbye to them both in case she wouldn't be back. That very thought sent shivers down her legs, and she bowed fully to the ground three times more, gripped by that premonition.

By then, all of her papers had been verified and she had procured a passport and visa, but her desire made it easy to believe that the bill would never pass. Life went on as before, her sixteen-year-old life filled with school, American music, an occasional cinema, and her friends, Hyo, Yuna, and Junghi.

On Tuesday, April 2, the telegram came:

BILL APPROVED STOP PLANE TICKET VIA SPECIAL DELIVERY 9 APR TUES-DAY STOP DEPARTURE 12 APR GIMPO STOP BRING SCHOOL TRANSCRIPTS END

Inja had ten days to prepare. How could a slip of blue paper so dramatically change her life? The next day, to order her transcripts and officially withdraw, Uncle accompanied her to school with Hyo. Hyo had paled to learn how soon she would be leaving and asked her uncle many questions about what her life would be like in America. Inja appreciated this, as they were questions she could not ask without tears, questions she hadn't even thought to ask for the grief that heavied her heart.

"She'll go to school soon," said Uncle. Inja walked on the opposite side of Uncle and kept her head bowed. "Except for English and history, I think she'll do very well. Her father says Korean schools are more rigorous than those in America, and she'll have help, attending the same school and same grade as her sister, Miran."

"Yes, sir," said Hyo. "It's good that her favorites, math and art, don't require too much language."

Uncle clapped Hyo's shoulder, and the young man blinked in surprise. "Very astute," said Uncle. This normally would have embarrassed Inja, but she was too absorbed in misery.

"Is the school far? Is it coeducational? Will she have one teacher or teachers for each subject?"

"Yah," said Uncle. "You're going to have to write and ask her."

"I think it's very exciting, sir, and a wonderful

opportunity." He was a good friend, so positive. He added, "I believe all her classmates will be quite jealous of her going to America."

"You see?" Uncle said to Inja, and she attempted a smile that came out as a scowl.

"Here's where I turn off," said Hyo. "Will she have time to come over this afternoon for another piano lesson? May we spend next Saturday together downtown?" How polite he was, and how kind.

"Of course. Her last day of school will be Friday, so everything will be normal until then." But Inja knew nothing would ever be normal again. She bowed goodbye as Hyo walked backward to wave before he turned and strode off toward his school.

"A cultured young man," said Uncle, his eyes teasing. Inja couldn't bear the thought of leaving Hyo, too. Their friendship had rescued her from ridicule, and their regular little club of four had elevated her status to "sophisticated" within the girls' school. Who now would save her from the petty meanness of girls, which she was sure existed in America as much as it did here. At least she would have parents and even a sister in the same grade. But what about her mother? Though Inja knew something of her through her letters, in reality she knew nothing about her. What did she smell like? Did she wear perfume? How did her hands move? What kind of shadow did she cast? Was she a happy person? Did she like to laugh and sing like Grandmother had? Inja knew she was industrious—always her letters described one job or another, a sewing project or preparations for a dinner or church event. She prayed her mother wasn't crabby like Aunt.

Inja couldn't say why she feared meeting her mother more than she did her father and sister. Perhaps it was because her mother had expressed her yearning for a reunion so often through her letters that Inja feared she would never be able to meet her expectations. What about her own expectations? All she felt now was resentment at having to leave. And anger.

The principal of Inja's school wanted to have an assembly to celebrate her unique opportunity, but she asked if she could leave as usual on Friday without a fuss. The principal studied her for a few seconds and said, "We'll miss the most artistically talented student in this school. I wish you well. Don't forget us and write often." Inja and Uncle bowed, he went home, and she went to class, aware now of her unwanted special status of being bound for America. She felt like she was on a runaway bus with barred windows.

That Saturday Hyo planned an outing at Jongmyo Shrine in central Seoul. The four friends took the tram to the shrine—which Inja had toured with her elementary school long ago—and strolled through the open gates down the main path. No one walked on the raised middle pathways, crumbing in many places but still intact, reserved for royalty. They teased each other and talked about what each of them might do their first day in America. Going to a record store was high on the list, under the assumption that being in America meant they would be rich. But soon the austerity of the budding trees and still ponds made them pay attention to their sacred surroundings. Jongmyo Shrine was the only historic site left fully intact throughout Japanese colonization and the Korean War. Its buildings needed paint, the grounds needed cultivation and tidying, but the structures and plazas were much as they had been for hundreds of years—broad cobblestoned expanses in front of elongated buildings, all their many identical doors shuttered and bolted, which contained the memorial tablets of five centuries of Yi Dynasty kings and queens. In hushed tones, Hyo explained how the plazas and certain side buildings were used for Confucian rites and offerings.

Yuna and Junghi wandered to the secondary plaza while Inja and Hyo contemplated the faded expanse of the shrine against a backdrop of gray sky. "I wish I had my sketchbook," Inja said.

"I can see why."

"It would be three lines of different grays," she said. "You know so much about this; I'm surprised I know so little." She kicked at a tuft of weeds poking between the stones at the edge of the plaza.

"You're Christian and probably they didn't teach you about Confucian rites on purpose." He bent to tug at the weeds.

" 'For I am a jealous God, and thou shalt not have any other gods before me.' First commandment, I think," Inja said. "Exodus. I have to practice how to be a minister's daughter." A wan smile to cover an inner quake.

He rose and crushed the grassy weeds between his fingers. She smelled their rough and wild green.

"And those very commandments say to 'honor thy father and mother,' right? Who came first," he asked, eyes teasing, "Confucius or the Bible? They didn't know the Christian god until Western missionaries came to the Far East, and that was only a century ago. The Buddhists and Taoists were tolerated, but Confucianism was the religion of the state long before the Christians came."

Because of Inja's grandparents—both educated aristocrats—Confucian thinking had always been a part of her family life. "I thought it was a tradition, not a religion." They left the plaza and wandered in the thin woods toward a colonnade and gateway.

He took her hand. "Is there a difference?"

"There's a difference of faith."

"Don't you believe all the Confucian lessons you've learned all your life? Isn't that a kind of faith?"

"There's the difference of having faith in Jesus as your savior."

"Is that so different than having faith in revering your ancestors and their beliefs, and in that way keeping them alive, in heaven?"

Inja couldn't answer because his logic confused her, and also because it was true that during their twice-weekly church classes that had led to her being confirmed Christian at thirteen, she'd had many questions she couldn't formulate. She stopped and leaned against a column, and its splintered wood caught the threads of her angora sweater. The carved ceiling beams of the weathered colonnade had an elegant symmetry that repeated in a harmonious pattern growing smaller as it stretched toward the plaza. She wanted to memorize the beauty of that repetition to sketch, the beauty of her ancient background that stretched beyond where she could see, that she was just learning more about—and from which she was also on the verge of leaving.

Hyo stepped in front of her, and she found his eyes, calm and smiling, as he pressed the frown from her forehead. He neared and touched his parted lips to hers. She tasted softness and shivering. They kissed again, then broke out in laughter for the sheer joy of it. As if it were an everyday thing, they held hands and smiled at each other, America the furthest possible thought in her mind, and kissed again, once more, then turned from the colonnade to find Yuna and Junghi.

PART IV

REUNION

1963–1973

Family Meeting

A fter the dinner guests left on Palm Sunday, Calvin called a family meeting. Miran, washing dishes, knew it would be about Inja coming. For a month her parents had been talking about Inja finally being reunited with them, and now with date certain—next Friday—their excitement was palpable. Other than her old feelings of resentment and jealousy, which she recognized as being old and therefore ought to be discarded, she had no idea what to expect of a Korean sister and wanted to get a clue from this meeting. Otherwise, it'd be the usual Bible reading and singing of hymns, meaning she'd be on the piano. But she had already performed for Miss Lone and five other guests, so she hoped to be relieved of that duty, which seemed strange and pointless when it was only the three of them. Calvin sipped coffee and read the paper in the living room, while Najin boiled water in the rice pot to save the last bits stuck on the bottom.

Soon they all settled in the living room. Miran's parents had been behaving strangely, emotional and anxious in their own ways. Her mother talked on the phone for hours and stayed up late fussing with her papers. Her parents had gone clothes shopping at Ward's, something her mother rarely did. And she had Miran help organize and clean the sewing room. Miran even had to clean the basement around the washing machine and kimchi station. Her father painted the downstairs bedroom, washed the car, repaired the dripping bathtub faucet, waxed the floors, dug in the garden, mended the porch screens. She didn't find helpful clues in their behavior about what it would be like to have her Korean sister at home, except things were cleaner and in better shape than before. Apparently royalty was coming.

"How is school?" said Calvin.

"Good. Mrs. Samson is going to send one of my etchings to the Montgomery County Fair."

Najin mentioned something about there being two talented artists in the family.

Miran wondered, who was the better artist? She wanted to be the best, as she was among the best in school. She wondered if Koreans drew differently but figured that was a ridiculous idea. Drawing was drawing; it was the individual artist who made art different. She didn't like the feeling of competition that rose inside. She said to her father, "After school's out we're going camping at Swallow Falls, the second weekend in June, and I need a permission slip and ten dollars dues. Is that okay?" She knew it was queer of her to still belong to Campfire Girls, but it was one of a few places she didn't feel a self-consciousness so awkward that it was as if she were seeing herself in the third-person point of view she'd learned about in English class—from distant and critical eyes that were never her own. The only other time she could sort of relax was with her school friends. And now this.

"We'll see," he said. "Which leads me to our discussion about your sister."

Practically speaking and based on her experiences, Miran dreaded yet another Korean person who'd stay for weeks or months—and now, forever—taking the sewing room and all the attention in the house, of which there wasn't much anyhow. She'd have to cook extra and clean extra and be extra nice to the guest who didn't speak a lick of English. "Has something changed?"

"No," said Calvin. "It's still next Friday, but we should nail down some details. We'll all go to the airport to meet her, but now others will be joining us, some church people. I'll give you a note to excuse you from school."

"How's she getting here?"—a question for her dad, who loved timetables and maps.

"She'll be flying from Seoul to Tokyo, to Anchorage, Alaska, to refuel and go through customs, then land here at National Airport on Northwest Orient Airlines—an almost nonstop flight. One of these days they'll make it nonstop, I'm sure."

"Sounds like a long trip." She pulled at a run in her nylons at the knee and made it ladder up under her skirt.

"Considering it's taken more than fifteen years to bring her home, I don't think seventeen hours of flying is going to matter too much."

"Wow," and, "how old is she now?"—a mistake.

"Aigu! How can you not know?" said Najin.

"I get confused with the twin thing." But she remembered sending Inja a self-portrait on a recent birthday. "Her birthday's September 24 so she's still a year younger," Miran said, redeemed. Inja had sent back a portrait of herself, and Miran liked it, as if they were pen pals. She thought Inja looked very Korean, more than she herself did. She recognized the oddity of this thought. She didn't write her again—they couldn't read each other's letters so what was the point? She could have sent more drawings, but again, what was the point? She hadn't expected the oft-mentioned reunion to ever happen—*the boy who cried wolf, a broken record, promise the moon.*

"She was one when we left?"

"That's right," said Najin.

Miran thought a moment and discovered she and her sister were ten months apart. She had never made this gestational connection between

294

their birthdays, and it now made her squirm. She scratched her knee and made another run. "Where's she going to sleep?"

"We thought we'd let you decide," said Calvin, beaming.

My clever father, she thought. The natural location was the tidied sewing room, but her own room was freshly painted and huge. She believed her teenaged sister would prefer being farther away from her parents than the sewing room, just as she herself did. And her mother stayed up until the wee hours sometimes sewing in that room. "She can have one of the bunks. We should take them apart."

"Agreed." He looked pleased, so she knew she'd guessed right. "Take school off the week after to show her how things work at home and to get her acquainted with the neighborhood. I've already enrolled her in all your classes so you really will be like twins." He slapped his newspaper on the armrest. "Help your mother this week making the house ready. We want to make her feel completely at home, though it will be a very different sort of home for her. She's lived a hard life in Korea, and she has lots to learn from you. Be kind to her, okay?"

"Yes, sir." She washed her face and left the bathroom synthesizing memories in the new light of Inja's actual presence in the house, her brain clacking like the Jacob's ladder toy that flipped its wooden panels over in surprising ways within its bands. Inja would be a sad person because she'd lived with their grandparents her whole life, now both gone. She'd be skinny from hunger, but she'd have good clothes, and probably bad teeth from all the candy they'd sent overseas. Miran laughed at herself. In her parent's bedroom hung a hand-tinted portrait of Inja at nine or ten years old, curtseying, and she looked completely normal, though not much like a twin. She was rounder from eyes to cheeks to body shape. Who would be taller? Being the eldest, she hoped she was.

Miran was fine with the week off from school to help her sister get acclimated. She was used to this hospitality, having been asked twice by the principal to befriend the foreign exchange students and show them around. She was proud to be chosen for this task until she gleaned how the new students were considered nobodies, and her association with them added zero merit in the popularity department, which she was failing miserably anyhow.

Miran hung up her skirt and blouse, and pushed her clothes to one side in the big closet to make room for Inja, the wire hangers screeching on the wooden dowel. She reclined in her lower-bed alcove to read another chapter of Charlotte Brontë's gothic novel and fell asleep wondering if her new sister was like Mr. Rochester's mad wife,

Bertha, in the secret rooms at Thornfield Hall—a constant, but hidden, threat—the knowledge of whom would only cause unhappiness, as it had for poor Jane Eyre.

27

Departure

The morning of departure Inja woke at dawn, her eyelids like scale weights dredged in sand, her chest tight as if a dream-bear were hibernating on it. She wondered how emptiness could feel so heavy. She listened to the morning and was flooded with an intense longing for Grandmother's steady breaths shushing in the quilts. Sparrows tittered in their mad clusters in bushes, the willows trembled, a truck lumbered up the road, and its diesel exhaust stained the reassuring scent of her room. From down the hall, Uncle mumbled something about a special breakfast, and Aunt replied, sleepy, "Ara can do it."

"How can you sleep on this day?" They grumbled at each other until he shuffled off. Inja felt certain she wouldn't miss Aunt at all, though she would miss seeing her new baby, due any moment. She hoped it was another boy. She'd make Uncle swear to take pictures and send the film to her so she could develop them and have photographs for an album she'd make of her Korean family.

She focused on every inch of her body, hoping it would absorb the sensations of her bedding, the floor, the air, the room that would never again be hers. Her eyes roved the walls and corners and ceiling, to press their cracks and crags into memory. Tears crawled down her temples and into her hair, as every breath, throat raw from crying, inched the day forward toward leaving. She closed her eyes to the swirling gray of grief and touched her lips to remember Hyo's kisses. Her lungs flared with warmth, then frustration rose at the unfairness of her life.

She sat up and shivered in a lingering nighttime chill. A thin pink light seeped through the high window, and she folded her bedding, conscious that each act of her daily routine would soon be replaced, forever, and by something unknown.

Uncle would send her steamer trunk separately, and she'd get it three weeks later. She unlocked it and removed two woolen skirts and a bulky sweater to pack the old Bible storybook, sketchbooks, and the ink sticks and brushes Uncle had made for her. She wanted to bring with her all that she'd known here, which was everything she'd ever known, but she only had a steamer trunk and a heart full of pain. She locked it and slipped the key into a small suitcase she'd carry on the plane. Uncle had bought her three Hershey bars, and she packed a scarf from Yuna, the book from her English-language class, the sketchbook and pen from Hyo, a handkerchief, brush, and comb, the rose-pink lipstick Aunt had given her on her sixteenth birthday that she had yet to use, and a worn pair of Grandmother's thick cotton socks so she wouldn't forget her and the secret of her frostbitten feet.

Though Grandmother had endured far greater sacrifices than she had, for her mother and her father's sake, Inja would follow Grandmother's example of hidden pain and never tell them how devastated she was to be leaving Uncle and home. The long flight would give her a chance to mold her sad face into acceptable features of a daughter happy to be reunited with her family, though she was resentful and afraid of so much in America, so much unknown.

Ara made fresh rice, and only Inja and Seonil were served the remaining pieces of chicken from last night's farewell feast. Inja had no appetite then or now. Ara sat with them, speechless, weeping, which made Inja equally miserable. When Uncle said, "It's a long flight," she forced in a few mouthfuls and took special note of Ara's light touch with garlic and soy sauce—skills she wished she'd taken the time to learn. Too late now.

Seonil, playful as usual, made paper airplanes after he ate. "Noona, look," he said, twirling his planes, "zoom, zoom. Promise me you'll tell me everything you see and hear, and what you eat on the airplane."

"I will," she said, and his earnest and musical buzzing almost made her smile until she remembered he'd grow up without her and she'd never hear his little boy voice again. "And one day maybe you can cross the ocean on an airplane, too, and visit me."

"Can I, Appa?" He threw a whopper flight and it crashed beside the table.

Uncle reached for the crumpled plane. "We'll see. Maybe when you're grown. First finish school, then college and military service."

"When I'm grown, Noona, I'll find you in America." He plopped into Inja's lap, and she buried her nose in his shiny black hair and held him tight.

Uncle said, almost apologizing, "Hyo's father's driver will be here in thirty minutes." Inja's heart leaped to hear Hyo mentioned, then it melted into sadness. At any other time she might have been excited to ride in a sleek car, but not today. Mr. Jeon had loaned them his driver to take her to Gimpo Airport along with Uncle, the minister, and the deacon—an honor to be escorted by these distinguished gentlemen, and one she would have preferred to relinquish in trade for Hyo, Yuna, and Junghi beside her on that plush back seat.

Inja meandered through the house touching its walls and door frames that her father had built, its lacquer flooring that had kept her warm in winter and cool in summer. She wandered in the scrawny yard and said goodbye to Ara and Aunt. "I'm sorry not to meet the baby, and I hope it's a boy," Inja said. Aunt held her arms and gave the warmest smile she'd ever felt from her, and Inja meanly thought she could be warm now, knowing this burden was finally off her hands.

The car came and the deacon sat in front and chatted with the driver, while Inja sat in the middle of the back seat flanked by Uncle and Reverend Shin. They talked church business peppered with parishioner gossip, and she wished she had a window seat to take in the byways of her country, her home.

She had studied some American history in a world history curriculum, but she wouldn't know it in the way she knew her own nation's history displayed in its ancient city gates, its memorials, venerable temples, faded palaces, living historical sites such as Jongmyo Shrine, and even its blackened buildings still in need of repair from the war. She would be a grown-up newborn needing to learn how to talk and be with others in ways she couldn't imagine. Because of her grief in leaving so much behind, she felt not a whit of excitement about what might have otherwise been an adventure. She felt only misery.

Gimpo Airport had been transformed from a barren field of cracked concrete into a modern facility, with electric signage for departures and arrivals. It looked Western and ugly, a fitting portal for a dismal departure. Her papers had been previously examined and approved at the American Embassy, and they eased through the departure checkpoint. Her chaperones accompanied her to the gate, and like little boys they *ooh*ed and *aah*ed as airplanes landed and took off.

In the waiting area, an American mother of two middle-school children urged them to use the restrooms before it was time to board. Inja was relieved to see she was similarly dressed as the mother in a starched cotton shirtwaist with a sweater and scarf. She decided to take the advice given to those children and whispered to Uncle, "I don't know if there's a toilet on the plane." He whispered back, mirth in his voice, that he too would check the condition of the facilities. Her eyes filled—it was so like him to want to share in whatever she did, though it was true that they had grown a little apart after she'd met Hyo.

They waited and the conversation between the men dwindled, and Inja was neither interested nor able to contribute to their talk. The ambient noise of the airport soon surrounded them along with its smells of fuel and the drying sweat of people on a hot day with noisy fans.

Her flight was called for boarding, and she

stood and bowed to the men, hoping she properly conveyed by habit alone how honored she was for their company. Inja pressed Uncle's hand, his palm damp in hers, as he argued with a stewardess who blocked the glass door exiting onto the tarmac. "Only passengers, please, sir."

"She's just a child," said Uncle, and Inja shrank to accommodate his exaggeration, clearly not a child. The woman glanced at her and frowned at Uncle. Two wings like those on Mercury's ankles flanked the golden name badge shining on the woman's dark uniform. Inja thought if she had such wings attached to her shoulder blades, she would have no fear of flying, no fear of departure, for with such magic she could fly home whenever she wished. Leaving would be a temporary parting all the sweeter for the future reunion it promised.

In that moment she swore she would return. Though even her parents hadn't been able to come back to Korea for fifteen years, she would find a way.

Uncle said, "Of course she's not a child, but she's never been near an airplane, and certainly not a flight of such distance all alone." People in line jostled behind them, heads craned, and the stewardess peered at Inja, reading the Korean and English writing on the tag pinned to her chest, truly as if she were a child. But Uncle had insisted she wear it. *Hello. My name is Anna*

Inja Cho. I am Korean and do not speak English well. This is my first time flying. I will meet my family in Washington, DC, 44 Sherman Avenue, NE, telephone SHepherd 9-6397. Thank you. The stewardess frowned and opened her firm lips already formed into "no," but Inja gave her a hapless look and her eyes filled unwittingly with tears.

The stewardess's posture softened. "Only for a few minutes. As soon as she finds her seat, you must get off the plane."

Uncle bowed. He held her elbow and they stepped over the threshold, and it took such effort to move, she felt as if her feet were magnets bound to the earth of her homeland. A brisk wind rich with fumes flapped her skirt and scarf, and she clutched the train case. They followed the queue to a rolling metal stairway locked beside the airplane. The convex of the airplane body matched the concave open door, and a sharp memory warmed her back—of being a child sitting comfortably in Uncle's lap as if it were formed only and exactly for her. She couldn't bear prolonging their parting, and when she turned to take his hand, she saw they were now the same height. "Ajeossi, I'll go in. They'll help me find my seat."

He hugged her hard, as if he knew she had to take this step alone. "Beloved child," he murmured. "Safe journey." He trailed his finger up her cheek, gathering the tears, and she grasped his palm against her face.

"I'll come back. I will. Ajeossi, thank you—"

"I'm the one who is thankful. Go now. Good-bye."

How could such simple syllables be so heart-breaking? "Goodbye." She bowed low, turned toward the stairs, and at the top by the concave door she looked back. He seemed so small, his handkerchief held aloft. Inja waved. It was he who knew her best, who had always loved her best, who had made her brave enough to face America—and strong enough to leave him. All of her years with him could never be replaced, nor forgotten. She would keep this last image of him close to her heart, where hundreds of other images of him were forever stored. And she would return.

28

Reunion

Miran sat in the back seat of the Plymouth Fury idling in the driveway. Calvin tapped his fingers on the steering wheel, waiting for Najin. She came out dressed in hanbok, a summery fresh blue of sheer silk, marking this as a formal occasion. Miran had spent fifteen minutes the night before sprinkling that silk with Argo starch-water, pressing it to a sheen of stiff elegance, now ruined by her mother lifting the skirt to her thighs to roll up and attach her stockings to her girdle. Najin laughed and apologized for the habit. Backing out the driveway, Calvin smiled at this immodesty bred from being perennially tardy, because it didn't matter. Today was Friday, and they were going to National Airport to bring Inja home.

Miran rolled down her window, already nauseated from having focused on the front seat. The vinyl floorboards had withstood many incidents of her carsickness.

"You okay?" said her father, concerned eyes in the rearview mirror.

"Yeah, thanks." She kept her nose in the

warm current of the open window, and clicked off familiar landmarks toward their church on Sixteenth and P, then the White House some blocks down, the blur of government buildings before they crossed the river into Virginia, the park-like riverbanks flanking the Potomac.

Her parents talked quietly, wondering about Inja's flight, how had she gotten to the airport, worries about her immunizations, how the time change and long flight would affect her, what she would eat on the airplane . . .

Miran unrolled the window another inch, and the wind tufted her long hair. She would be a good sister, and maybe Inja would teach her Korean so she could really talk to her mother and be a better daughter. Fat chance. The chances were higher this sister would be a weirdo square.

Najin tugged at the starched collar of her hanbok as Calvin veered onto the exit to the airport. "What about customs?"

"The plane refuels in Alaska; they'll do it there. We'll see her as soon as they land."

Miran had sensed his buoyancy all day—he hadn't stopped smiling, but her mother couldn't stop fretting.

Najin smoothed down her skirt and took out her handkerchief. What if too many years had passed? What if her guilt impeded her love? What if her daughter resented this American family?

Surely, having always known they'd worked to bring her here, Inja would be looking forward to this day. But she was a young lady now, and writing letters was no substitute for mothering. She dabbed her throat.

In the parking lot at National Airport, she leaped out of the car, though it was still an hour before Inja's arrival. She saw a dozen church people and friends waiting under the awning in front of the beige terminal. Calvin had told her the *Washington Post* would send a reporter and photographer for a "special interest" story. Miran climbed out of the back seat, and Najin wished she'd dressed her in hanbok, too. Though properly attired in her Easter outfit, orange was not Miran's color. Her attention shifted to Calvin striding across the parking lot to greet Miss Lone, and she smiled to see he'd forgotten to close his car door. But her husband's energy was less about anxiety than it was excitement. Their differences could be summed up in that distinction.

She remembered her own difficulties with acculturation and worried that Inja would suffer more, being thrust into a new family as well. She could only guess how her brother had raised her, with his impractical sentimentality, his romantic optimism. How many mistakes of his had she witnessed, covered over or repaired afterward? She knew she should be more charitable to him since he'd raised her daughter. Time would tell

311

how well he had performed this act for them. She moved her mind to her daughter, but there resided feelings of guilt and regret—feelings so habitual she could no longer evaluate their merit. Here at the threshold of their reunion, these feelings merged with eagerness and anxiety. If at one time she had thought her husband's remorse for being in America without her the first eleven years of their marriage was something she'd never understand, now she knew differently. And it was worse. It was her child, and it was *fifteen* years of separation from someone who wouldn't know blame was warranted, who couldn't know that forgiveness would be needed.

She greeted Miss Lone with both hands wrapped around the one extended to shake, her smile warm with gratitude. "It's because of you this day has come."

"Nonsense," said Miss Lone with characteristic gruffness. "But what a beautiful day it is!"

Indeed the sun beamed with radiance, a crisp breeze dispatched spring's humidity, cumulus clouds shone glory in their billowing mounds, and anticipation filled every breath. They met their waiting friends and went inside. In the main hall of the terminal building, tall observation windows allowed full view of the runways. Calvin steered them to the Northwest Orient arrival gate.

Mrs. Kim said, "I know you must be both

excited and nervous. In fact, I can't imagine at all how it must feel to be reunited after so long. How are you doing? Never mind! Surely you can't even say what you're feeling," and she grasped Najin's elbow.

Najin appreciated this gesture, as it exactly captured her turmoil. Reigning over everything she held inside was the propriety of their behavior in such a situation, soon to be documented by newspapermen. It made a deeply private moment so public, and while she was proud and glad for the attention that augmented the occasion, she also wished it weren't such a flaunted spectacle. Her poor child, after a long flight coming to America and meeting her family amidst such fanfare! She also worried that Calvin, sometimes as sentimental as Dongsaeng, would erupt in tears.

The *Washington Post* journalists joined them and introduced themselves. The female reporter, a slim woman in a brown tweed suit with tortoiseshell eyeglasses, smoked an annoying cigarette while she asked Najin questions about the circumstances of this reunion. Miss Lone came to her rescue and clarified questions delivered too rapid-fire to grasp: Yes, it was because of the Korean War they'd been separated, then red tape, and, yes, immigration restrictions. Miss Lone intervened with a short explanation of the Johnson-Reed Act, commonly known as the

Oriental Exclusion Act, and how a special rider to a House bill allowed Anna Inja Cho and a few others to legally enter these hallowed lands.

The airline clerk ushered them and others awaiting the arrival of the plane outside behind a barrier of movable aluminum fencing. Their small crowd stood half in sunlight and half in shadow, and the photographer brought them all into the sunshine to take pictures. The photographer's camera clicked. Calvin's face gleamed. Miran seemed excited to be having her photograph taken. Najin heard only the roar of arriving airplanes.

The public address system blared Inja's flight number. "Here she comes!" said Calvin, and all eyes turned to the white and silver behemoth approaching the runway. Najin's eyes lifted, and she remembered other silver harbingers of life-changing news: B-29s that had dropped leaflets and scarves printed in many languages to announce the end of the Pacific War. How she had rejoiced then, knowing she could be reunited with her husband. And now . . . She twisted her handkerchief to ruins around her pocketbook handles.

The airplane landed and taxied to the gate at last, guided by men waving yellow flags, and it took another small forever for workers to roll the stairway up to the plane. Then the engines cut off, and in the surprising silence the door swung open. Many people got off—and a girl in a blue shirtwaist dress and a cream-colored sweater, who was clutching a beat-up train case, was guided by a stewardess onto the stairs' platform.

"Dear God," cried Calvin. He *hurdled* over the barrier and ran up the metal stairs, footsteps clanging, pushing past deplaning passengers. Najin gasped at both the glimpse of her daughter, looking tiny, tired, and sad, and her husband's leap. Calvin enveloped Inja in his arms, and Najin clutched her purse to her chest. Her heart swelled to see the pure joy in his features, and at the same time, she felt anger that she herself was too proper to jump the barrier and leap up those stairs to hold her child—shockingly a real person, a young adult, and one who looked forlorn.

Calvin was halfway down the stairs with Inja when Miran tugged her arm. "Mom, let's go! They said it's okay." The barrier had been opened, and they hurried through followed by the photographer and reporter. Calvin, tears streaming, cried out, "At last, at last, blessed child," and delivered her to Najin on the tarmac.

She grasped Inja's shoulders—so thin, so tall—and searched her face, both familiar and foreign. She thought it must be the same for Inja when their eyes caught and her daughter looked startled—or was it afraid? Then love filled her with gratitude, and she hugged her to her heart and said, "My child, my daughter. Are you well?"

All the years of anxiety melted, and she held her daughter tight until Inja stiffened and they parted. Najin's eyes filled to see Inja's features so close by, the shape of her own eyes on her daughter. But she looked sad, tired, and Najin's heart ached with love and protection.

"How was the flight?" Calvin said at the same time as Najin's greeting.

"I am well, Mother. It was good, Father," she said, head down, almost inaudible.

The sound of her daughter's voice, the melodious language of her nation spoken by her own blood—those words claiming her as belonging to them—made her eyes overflow with love, and Najin hugged her again, then hung tight to her elbow as if she'd lose her. Calvin wrapped her beneath his arm, and they stepped aside to allow other passengers to exit.

"Here is Miran," said Calvin, taking Inja's case. They were not a family who hugged easily—rather, Najin was not one who hugged often or easily—but Miran embraced Inja with sincerity, saying, "Inja dongsaeng, *hwanyeong*," welcome, little sister. Their crowd of greeters came up and each was introduced by Calvin to Inja, who bowed and kept her eyes down except to glance at Miss Lone.

"You must be tired, my daughter," said Najin.

"A little, Mother."

The reporter flapped her notebook and asked

them to line up at the bottom of the stairs, while Inja stood at the top. When they were all in place, Najin thought Inja looked so desolate alone by the airplane door, hand raised ready to wave, that she wanted to run up, as Calvin had, and scoop her into the safety of her arms.

"Can you ask her to smile?" said the photographer.

"Can you smile?" called the reporter.

Inja waved feebly.

"Make her smile for the camera," the reporter said to Calvin. Najin wanted to slap her. *Can't you see she's exhausted!*

Calvin said, "They're asking you to smile and wave."

Inja waved again, this time twisting her lips in a small smile, which gave her a strange grimace. Najin saw the effort of that smile, and she worried.

Several more pictures were posed and taken, and at last the photographer put away his equipment, goodbyes were said all around, and when the reporter asked Calvin to verify the spelling of everyone's names and for their address, Miss Lone took over and shooed them off for home.

Inja hesitated when leaving the terminal. Najin steered her to the ladies' room, and Miran followed. She restrained her desire to go into the stall with Inja, laughing at herself. Still, who could blame her. Instead she ran water in the sink, in case her daughter was modest to that degree. She doubted it though, having a good idea of what life in Seoul must have been like with her soft brother, his common wife, Inja's ailing grandparents, a toddler cousin, and a country girl all in a few simple rooms. She barely remembered those rooms now, and without her mother or daughter in them, her concern for them dropped out of her mind like a forgotten childhood toy.

When they came out, Calvin slung his arm around Inja's shoulders and led her to the car. Miran said she'd get up early to buy tomorrow's *Washington Post* from the market—they subscribed to the *Evening Star*—and he said, laughing, "Good idea. Anything to get you up early on a Saturday is a good idea." He stowed the train case in the trunk, and Najin sat Inja in the front seat between them. He explained the joke about rising early to Inja, who attempted a smile.

"She's tired, Yeobo," said Najin.

"Of course. Inja daughter," said Calvin, smiling as if uttering those words had intoxicated him. "If you feel unwell, let me know. Your unnee Miran gets carsick, so I wouldn't be surprised if you do, too."

"She'll be all right in the front seat," said Miran.

The car hummed along the parkway. Najin

asked Inja about her flight, and Inja responded, monosyllabic, though polite.

Calvin pointed out the Jefferson Memorial and the cherry blossom trees lining the Tidal Basin. Najin admired the blooms out loud and thought she saw light in her daughter's eyes for the first time since her arrival.

She remembered what she'd learned about the cherry blossom trees from the many times she and Calvin had taken visitors to see them. The Japanese had given them to America in the year Najin was born, 1910—the year in which Japan annexed Korea. The first two thousand trees were delivered that year—a gift of collusion, thought Najin, to thank America for looking the other way when the Treaty of Annexation was signed. As it turned out, those trees were all diseased and replaced two years later with three thousand healthy trees. And so, even after Pearl Harbor, while people of Japanese descent were interned in remote camps, the trees flowered and made the nation's capital uniquely gorgeous in springtime. Nature would always circumvent history.

Calvin and Najin kept up a flow of small talk, which one tended to have when the occasion was too momentous to discuss, and through it all their daughter seemed buried inside herself— from exhaustion, Najin supposed, and everything strange and new. Love and pity rushed through her. She wished again she could return to the fateful decision that had resulted in such pain for all of them.

She took Inja's hand and examined how the nails were like hers, the thumbs and palms like Calvin's, the long fingers like the artist's fingers of her father and brother. She had thought she would feel content, and at peace, to have her child home at last, but it was peculiar—she'd forgotten Inja would be a young lady, that she'd have a complete and separate history than hers, and one with its own experience of tragedy, of war and loss. She would have to learn who this daughter was, though surely she already knew— she was her Korean daughter, the one made most beloved by absence, by guilt. She was her flesh and blood.

These thoughts were not useful, especially as her other daughter sat directly behind her, the draft from the back seat's open window blowing on her neck. Inja appeared to be napping. "Did she say if she ate on the plane?" Najin murmured to Calvin. And they talked quietly about what the next few days would hold for their reunited family.

29

Arrival

To Inja, her parents and sister looked like their photographs, but different—her parents smaller and her sister taller than expected, the details of their features sharper and surprising. She imagined it must've been the same for them seeing her, especially considering the moment her mother so closely examined her after her father had dragged her down the airplane stairs. It was startling how expressive he was—like Uncle—and in comparison, how reserved her mother seemed. But Inja understood her mother's reservation when she was introduced to dozens of people and was told to pose here and there for the camera by a bossy American woman whose clothes reeked of tobacco. The woman gave unsmiling instructions to her father, who asked Inja to smile and wave by the airplane's curved door while her American family lined up below. Flash, snap, flash, snap. Inja longed for Yuna, who would laugh at her acting like a big starlet, but she couldn't smile. She was relieved to learn the cigarette lady wasn't Miss Lone, and then felt badly that amidst all the fuss she hadn't said a proper goodbye to her seat companion, whose name was similar to Miss Lone's.

In the car, overwhelmed, Inja could barely interpret the sensation of being in between her parents on a sticky vinyl seat, with Miran occasionally leaning in from the back, a smile masking her open stare. Her father started the car, told her to tell him if she began to feel ill. Miran said something and he answered in English, and in the same breath said in Korean, "—and she's worried you'll get nauseated, too. It's a beautiful spring day, so we're going to take the scenic route by the memorials."

Rather than absorbing the content of his speech, Inja's thoughts clicked to acknowledge his carefree demonstration of what it meant to be bilingual. That must be her first and most vital achievement. She battled the sensation of being among the enemy.

Her mother's questions were simple, but she felt compelled to keep things to herself and wished she could stick her head outside like Miran so the rushing winds of the scenic route would whip her hair against her cheeks.

"Were you comfortable on the plane?"

"Yes, Mother," *but not in the way you're asking.* Inja had taken comfort in knowing that every moment they flew east toward America, time would theoretically slow such that when she landed in Washington, DC, according to the calendar it would still be the same day she left—only half a day away. She didn't want to be crying the entire seventeen hours it took to cross half the world. The stewardesses had been kind, as was the lady in the next seat. She'd shown Inja how to attach the seat belt, open the tray table, and later gave her a magazine, whose pages she politely and blindly turned one by one.

Father drove out of the airport and onto a highway he said was the George Washington Parkway. To have recognized "George Washington" gave incremental relief, proving she wasn't completely ignorant of the English language and American history.

Miran leaned over and gestured. "That's the Potomac River, named for the original Indian tribe who lived here."

Inja thought she should respond despite catching only a few words, but she couldn't move, stuck as she was between her parents. The scenery was expansive and pristine—mowed riverbanks sloping toward water glimmering in the sunlight, a river unencumbered by shacks or people using its wealth of clean water, an abundance of perfect grass below tall familiar trees, everything lush and bountiful with green. "Willows," Inja said as a way to answer Miran.

"Widows?" Miran said.

Inja nodded, and when her father said, "Willows," she wondered why everyone was repeating it as if she had never uttered a word before.

He patted her knee. "They're just like at home. I planted a weeping willow in our front yard for that very reason."

She thought of the willow shoots in their yard they'd harvested for grandmother's feet—and then she put all thought aside.

They sped on the smooth black highway beside the glistening river—her father drove very fast—and he pointed out the pale snow of petals falling from the cherry blossom trees lining the river-bank. "Look there in the distance to that small domed building surrounded by columns. That's the Jefferson Memorial, a tribute to our third president. He was one of America's Founding Fathers and quite the Renaissance man. See all the cherry blossom trees in a circle there? That's the Tidal Basin." A little later they crossed a stately marble bridge flanked by statues of muscular men and horses made of what looked like solid gold, and he explained how a tidal basin worked with the Potomac River.

She understood these explanations were meant to ease her alienation, but all her muscles had turned into wood. With her mother's thigh so close to hers, her skirt pocket scratched, and she took out the ridiculous tag Uncle had pinned to her sweater. Inja ran her fingers over his writing and saw the name her seatmate had written on the back after she'd examined the tag, which had amused her. Inja wished she'd had enough English to tell her that she found the tag amusing, too, and stuck it in her pocket. During the flight she would have explained that the tag with Uncle's writing was a tiny souvenir of the special bond she shared with him.

Mother read the tag. "At least your uncle's heart is in the right place."

If Inja had been more astute to her feelings in those confusing first minutes of being in America, she might have recognized the stab of anger at her mother's assumption that she could tell her anything about the beloved man who had been both father and mother to her.

Mother turned the card over. "Who's this?"

"She sat next to me on the airplane."

"I see."

"She was very kind and gave me gum. Miss Aag-ress Ronegan."

"K'rae, Agnes Lonegan."

"I must to learn," she said in English.

Mother held her hand. "We can learn together."

Her mother's dry touch sent a shiver up her arm, and to reclaim her hand she took back the tag and slid it into her pocket. The kindly Agnes Lonegan had rummaged in her purse while rattling off a series of questions. When Inja merely stared, Miss Lonegan smiled and said,

"The universal language of giving," and offered a stick of Wrigley's Spearmint gum.

"Thank you." Inja had set it on the arm of her seat to chew later, but her seatmate took it and unwrapped it for her, so she had to chew it. "Very good. Good," she said, wishing Miss Lonegan had just given her half, to save the other half for later. Sudden yearning for Hyo filled her eyes, and she turned to the window to watch the takeoff—seeing very little through her tears until the view was white with clouds.

Miss Lonegan chatted at her occasionally, and she tried to look interested, but she felt like that lonely girl crossing the park without Yuna beside her, supremely self-conscious and struggling to look composed. When Miss Lonegan was served a cup of coffee, and the stewardess asked what she'd like, Inja gestured she didn't want any-thing—too afraid she'd have to use the bathroom, which she'd learned was at the back of the plane from the Northwest Orient brochure Miss Lonegan had taken pains to show her. She didn't want to make her seatmate get up for her or have to climb over her. Inja took out her chewing gum, wrapped it for later, and tucked it into her shirtdress pocket, but Miss Lonegan said, "Dear, let me have that. The stewardess will take it." She parked it on the edge of her tray table along with empty crumpled sugar packets. Inja must have looked at it with sadness because Miss Lonegan went through her purse and gave her the entire pack! "And there's more where that came from, dear."

In the car, Mother said, "She must have been kind—to have written down her name for you. Too bad she didn't write her telephone number or address so we could thank her for watching over you."

I am sixteen years old, Mother, and I thanked her myself. Somewhere in all her misery, she had managed to thank her as politely as she could. The remainder of that long flight she remembered as being imprisoned in the seat, exhausted from tears, afraid to drink anything, afraid of the terrible-smelling food set in front of her that Miss Lonegan had unwrapped for her, afraid to use the bathroom, afraid of what would happen when she landed, afraid of everything—and grieving — none of which she could admit to her mother.

But feeling the pack of gum in her pocket, she did feel badly about not saying goodbye to Agnes Lonegan, who, unlike her mother at that moment, had left her alone. But she was being unreasonable, melodramatic, and unfair. She would have to change her attitude or live the remainder of her life in misery.

The very thought drained her, and she closed her eyes.

Mother took her hand again and massaged the palm, and she stifled her instinct to withdraw it. She dozed, deeply enough so that when she woke, she was disoriented about where she was until reality descended and weighted down her heartache.

When they got home, it, too, looked to Inja like its photograph, but bigger, and though it was plain white stucco with turquoise trim, it seemed more colorful because of Mother's opulent gardens. Big white and fuchsia azalea bushes bordered the porch steps, and the small front yard was lined with tulips and stout green hedges. Solid, huge, and a little forbidding, the house had a twin to its left but with green trim, and woods to its hilly right. Inja climbed out of the car and involuntarily shivered. Miran touched her elbow to draw her up the stairs, chattering and gesturing. Mother told her sister to change out of her Sunday clothes. Miran took her train case and went downstairs, "to the room you'll share," Mother said. Inja had a pang of anxiety to be separated from her sole belongings, but her tongue seemed glued behind her lips.

The rooms were enormous, like in Hyo's house (but less shiny), tall and filled with big things, plentiful things, and draped with ribbons of green and pink paper. Inja tried to smile at Miran who came up and said she'd hung the streamers for her.

"It's like *saengil*, Miran Unnee, is to see year and year." Half-Korean, half-English.

"The birthday pictures?" Miran said a bunch of other things with the shy smile Inja remembered from her photographs, and again, "Hwanyeong," welcome. Miran trailed them while Mother showed Inja the living room—with the piano!—dining room, kitchen, then in the back half of the house, a hallway room that led to a huge bedroom on the left with a giant bed—her parents' room, the bathroom and sewing room to the right.

"For the first few nights, I think you'll sleep here," said Mother in the big bedroom.

At Inja's look, her mother said, "Appa will take the sewing room," which wasn't what she was questioning. The only bed she had ever shared was with Grandmother—and thinking this made her remember that her mother herself had shared Grandmother's bed, so it must have made some kind of sense to her. She wouldn't be thinking that in the year since Grandmother's death Inja had had her own room and her own bedding. But here in America, who knew what was proper?

A photographic portrait of Grandfather on the master bedroom wall surprised Inja—one that seemed familiar though she couldn't remember ever having seen it, in which he looked a little more solemn than she remembered. A similar-sized photograph of Grandmother in a lacquer and mother-of-pearl frame sat on a small table next to the bed, and its placement revealed how hard it was for her mother to not have seen her own mother for so many years. Her mother had spent her entire life until age thirty-seven with Grandmother, and Inja had always known they were close. She remembered her promise to Grandmother that she'd be a good daughter, and just then she wished Grandmother were there in color and flesh to bridge the alienation between her daughter and granddaughter. Then she recognized that these particular photographs of her grandparents had been the models for Uncle's color paintings that hung in their sitting room and had been used at each of their funerals. It gave her comfort to know these images were a constant between her two families.

Also on the improbably pink walls of that master bedroom—Miran would later tell her that Calvin had bought the paint because it was cheap, and Najin hated the color but she hated waste more—in a frame half the size of the windows on each side was her portrait from her tenth birthday. It startled her to see how happy she appeared, but she had gone downtown with Uncle that day and been treated like a queen. The frilly dress also reminded her of Aunt and the birthday soup, and of Ara who had washed and ironed it at night so Aunt wouldn't know. It had been but a single long day since Inja had left them, yet they seemed incredibly far away— far away and present at the same time. Inja was confused and tired.

She admired Miran's annual school portraits lined up in the sewing room, big versions of the ones in the *Family in America* album, and noted the many decorations throughout the house: Korean embroidery scrolls of traditional scenes—girls on swing and seesaw, grandfathers playing chess—and paintings of a falcon and a tiger, both browned by age with their wooden dowels falling off. Above the black sideboard in the dining room hung a framed reproduction of Leonardo da Vinci's *The Last Supper*, a far better depiction of the event than the one in her Bible storybook. She hoped her trunk would arrive soon. There were no photographs of Father's parents, and she remembered Mother writing they had never heard from them again after the war began. When she'd learned this news many years ago, she didn't think much of it—many families' members were separated or lost because of the war—but now she wondered if her father missed them like she missed her grandparents. Like she missed Uncle.

While Najin changed out of her hanbok and Calvin was on the telephone telling someone she had arrived safely, Miran took Inja down a wooden staircase into a dark and cool area of cement and small high windows—the first time she had ever stepped into a basement. Miran pointed out their mother's kimchi-making station and the electric washing machine, and in a wide-open peach-colored space bigger than four sitting rooms combined, she raised her hands and said, "Ta-da! Here's our room." On one of the matching beds lay Inja's train case, opened with its contents scattered about.

"Thanks for the Hershey's Bar," Miran said.

Appalled at this invasion, tears came to Inja's eyes as she put the rumpled contents back into the train case. How could she? Was there no privacy to be had in America? She didn't care about the candy, but like a magpie Miran had taken that case and everything she owned at this moment, her soul included, and strewn it about carelessly in a room in a house in a family in a country in which she was supposed to belong, but that couldn't have been more foreign—and unwanted—to her.

Inja clicked the case shut, sat on the bed, and wept. Miran stared wide-eyed a few moments, then brought her a box of tissues and crowded in beside her, awkwardly sliding an arm around her shoulders. Inja almost shrugged her off but was moved by her gesture and gathered herself. "I'm sorry," she said, forgetting Miran didn't speak Korean. "I'm very tired. So much is new here."

"*Jada*?" Sleepy? she said. To Inja she sounded like Seonil, and she blew her nose and forgave her. She stood and named some of the stars in the magazine pictures Miran had taped to a bulletin board: Bobby Vinton, Lay Chahles, Chubby Checker, the Shillels, and Elbis—and Miran laughed at her funny diction. It was the most Inja had spoken all day. Miran showed off her record collection, pulling out favorite 45s, and Inja showed her the ones she knew from having played them with Yuna. Perhaps they could be united over music.

Mother, in a cotton housedress, came in and said she would help Inja change out of her travel clothes.

Miran said, "I thought you'd like that bed, but you can choose which one is yours. I've changed the sheets so they're both clean."

Mother explained what she said, though Inja didn't understand about sheets, and she chose the obvious bed with her train case on it. "Is good, thank you. Good," she said.

Miran's smile revealed a single dimple in her left upper cheek.

Mother showed her a bureau of five drawers, as high as her neck and as wide as two steamer trunks, and said it was for clothes. Inja had known to expect a raised bed with a mattress—and by inspecting the bedding had figured out what sheets were—but the bureau flummoxed her. She had never seen such a big piece of furniture with this many drawers, even in Hyo's rich house. "Which drawers are Miran's?"

"These are all yours; that bureau is Miran's."

She indicated the set of drawers with a mirror on top on the other side of the room.

Inja grew more and more amazed as she opened each drawer packed beautifully with folded clothes, including pajamas, which her mother explained were sleepwear. No one she knew wore pajamas. Maybe Hyo did, but she wouldn't have known such an intimate thing about him. At home they'd slept in whatever they were wearing or in underwear. Pajamas! The casual presentation of this chest of drawers filled with clothing of all sorts gave substance to "mountains of gold."

Inja hung up her dress in the bare half of the massive closet that Miran said was her portion, chose a white camp blouse and pale blue capri pants with a shiny white belt—because it reminded her of Yuna—and changed into everything new including socks. Miran lay on her bed, reading, and Mother helped Inja change. Though embarrassed by this attention, she understood her mother wanted to inspect every part of her long-lost daughter, and she suppressed modesty for her sake. Her mother said they'd go bra shopping later in the week. She took her underwear and demonstrated the laundry system, and outside, the ropes strung across trees in the park-like backyard, where clothes would be hung to dry, attached by clothespins. Inja's astonishment—and vocabulary—grew with each step of introduction to this house, and the wonderment worked to numb the razor edge of grief.

Then the girls sat at the kitchen table with their parents. The sun streamed hot through the windows above the sink, and frilly white curtains stirred in an occasional breeze. Najin asked if she was hungry. Strangely she wasn't, nor did she want her mother to fuss over her with food, afraid she might actually want to spoon-feed her. Najin gave her a glass of water and also a bottle of Pepsi-Cola with two straws to share with Miran. She heated coffee for Calvin and opened a new blue tin of cookies lined in fluted paper cups. Their buttery smell turned Inja's stomach. Her features must've shown her revulsion, because after Miran ate one, Najin closed the tin. "Your father can't have any—it's not good for him."

Inja didn't know if her mother was allowing her to save face or if her father was ill. Her mouth still didn't want to volunteer much of anything, so she saved that question for another time. At the stove, Najin heated water and opened the refrigerator to take out a covered dish of kimchi and a glass container of some kind of green vegetable mixed with some kind of sliced meat, odorous of hot pepper sauce and cabbage, and though Inja's eyes widened at this casual presentation of meat, its smell reminded her of the airplane food. Miran set the kitchen table—Inja's inner clock was too disoriented to predict if it was lunch or dinner— then she and her father negotiated something

335

until Miran nodded. He translated the exchange. "She wants to go camping with her friends, but your mother doesn't like her going away for weekend trips with people we don't know, so we agreed she'd practice piano without complaining, weed the lawn, and clean the bathrooms twice a week from now on."

It all sounded too foreign for Inja to think of anything to say.

Only she and her parents sat at the table to eat, and her father apologized for Miran, but thus did she learn "It's too early for lunch."

Najin served small bowls of rice, and the steam of the plain rice opened Inja's desire to eat. "It's so tasty," she said of her mother's kimchi, which was better than Aunt's, of course, but even better than Ara's. Inja didn't tell her mother that part, wanting to spare Ara this small slight, though she'd never know about it. She lost her appetite then and put her chopsticks down. Najin didn't say anything about the wasted food.

"It might ease your mind to know what to expect in the next few days," said Calvin.

While he talked, she stole glimpses of her parents and saw that her mother and Uncle were similar in appearance—both had Grandmother's nose, while her own was more like Grandfather's. It was reassuring to see Uncle's face in her mother's, though her formal demeanor had stiffened those features somewhat. Her father handled his chopsticks in an odd way, but she could see her fingers in his. Inja wondered if her sister compared her features to their parents, or if such comparisons were discouraged. She wondered when, or if, she'd ever talk to her mother about Miran.

Her father's genial expression and deliberate articulation gave her calm; this aspect of his character likely elevating the respect he garnered as a minister. "Rest at home this weekend," he said. "I'll take your sister to church on Sunday while you stay home with your mother and get comfortable with your surroundings. You'll want to know which way to turn in this house before enlarging your comfort zone."

His manner of speech made her smile, and their quick smiles in response plus the glance they gave each other showed Inja she hadn't been terribly forthcoming with any expression at all. She would have to change her selfish behavior. How easily joy had come to their features!

"They're eager at church to meet you, but we'll spare you that ordeal until next Sunday—or later, whenever you're ready to meet that many people."

She dipped her head to express gratitude. His smile had a glint of gold around the edge of some bottom teeth, and she surreptitiously examined her mother's teeth while Najin picked at them with a toothpick; they were straight and without any gold fillings—more like Uncle's and hers; rather, her teeth were more like her mother's.

"Your mother will be at home all next week, and Miran will also stay home from school to keep you company. I've enrolled you at Blair High School with Miran. You'll both be juniors—eleventh grade, same as in Seoul."

She wanted to ask if, as Minister of Education, it was truly he who had aligned Korea's school structure to America's, something Uncle often said with pride, but hearing Uncle's prideful voice in her mind made her swallow and kept her silent.

"The principal agreed to keep you in the same classes until your English improves enough for you to be on your own. We know you want to study art, and your sister is active in that area, including an after-school art club. How does that sound?"

"Yes, thank you." She grasped only vague outlines of his plan—except that more unknowns awaited her—and that she must learn English quickly.

He reached across the table, took her hand in both of his, and his expression shifted to a tenderness that reminded her of Hyo and Uncle combined, but so intense, eyes filled with tears, that Inja looked to her lap. "We praise God and are blessed and pleased to have you home at last." Mother held her other hand while he gave a prayer of thanks, then said, "I can barely remember my first days in America, but I know they were confusing, like in a whirlpool, so I want you to take your time getting adjusted. This family's job is to make your transition as easy as possible. Okay?"

"We have many things to talk about," said her mother, "but now we have many hours ahead of us as well."

"Thank you," she said, and failed to return a genuine smile. Inja supposed his little speech was meant to ease her "transition," but that very word had the opposite effect of hammering in the permanence of this life here and of never going home again.

Najin guided her once more through the house with particular warnings about the hot-water faucets, and she took her through the back of the basement to explain about the hot-water heater and the furnace in an area crowded with a big desk, upside-down chairs, cardboard cartons, and rolled-up rugs. "We've had many Korean students coming and going, and they end up leaving things for the next person to use. It's a mess back here."

Inja liked that messy corner with its oily iron behemoth, rough and cold to the touch, the mysterious boxes and abandoned furniture lit with a single naked lightbulb, reminding her of their sitting room at home before they'd gotten a decent ceiling shade of white glass. When she knew the words, she would ask Miran if she'd like one of those rugs in their room. Only rich people did that. Even Yuna didn't have rugs on her floors (but Myeonghi probably did).

"Inja, my child, after such a long day, you probably want to rest," said Najin, and, "Miran, come help me in the kitchen." Miran made an "ugh" face to Inja without Najin seeing, a surprising first chip in her image of them as the perfect American family. Inja hoped she wouldn't have to choose sides. At least with Aunt, it was clear they did not care for each other, to put it nicely, but she knew nothing about this family's internal alliances.

Najin led her to the master bedroom and darkened it by closing the Venetian blinds, which she showed Inja how to operate, though she already knew from Hyo's house. Her mother left the door ajar and said to call her if she needed anything. Inja stood in the middle of the room, unsure in general and especially unsure about climbing onto that big bed, until the things atop the bureau and dresser called her to examine them. The mirrored bureau was messy with cosmetics and creams, books and Korean newspapers, a basket made especially for needles and threads and such, and an old Korean lacquer box and miniature chest. Inja opened the little chest and found a stack of yellowing thin papers with old-fashioned brush writing. One glance showed they were letters from Halmeoni, and the fluid brushstrokes revealed they were written before her stroke. For the first time since her arrival, Inja felt a sense of union with her mother in the love they still shared for Grandmother. A brass rice bowl overflowed with hairpins, safety pins, and rubber bands, and any remaining space was filled with a heap of nylon stockings, garter clips, and a pile of diaries and spiral-bound notebooks. Her father's dresser was orderly with an electric clock, a chipped glass holding pens and pencils, an enameled dish with collar stays and buttons, a stack of ironed and folded handkerchiefs, a Bible with a zippered cover, a Korean Bible and hymnal, and medicine bottles. These two surfaces gave Inja easy insight into their personalities, and the cluttered disorganization of her mother's bureau felt as familiar as Uncle's desktop and shelves that had a little bit of everything on them.

Inja studied the portraits of her grandparents and herself, then gingerly climbed onto her parents' bed in her new clothes. The soft mattress enveloped her, and the pillow smelled faintly of an herbal scent she would later identify as Vitalis, her father's hair tonic. In this immense strange room with its terrible pink color, its odd light and shadows and the grit that seemed to coat the inside of her eyelids, it seemed a mercy to close her eyes to this day, and she slept.

30

Writings

27 April 1963, Saturday, to Ajeossi

I arrived safely. Thank you for taking me to the airport. That day is hard to remember, it seems so long ago. The airplane flight was long. That is about all I can remember. After arriving at Father and Mother's house, I slept through more than one night. The hours were all wrong. I went to bed on a Friday afternoon and woke up Sunday before dawn. Father said I would have this problem with sleeping for a few days. "Adjusting your inner clock," he says. Did you know he was funny? He laughs often. Mother does too. They are generous and kind and gave me a good welcome, but I am lonely for home. I cannot express how much I miss my family and friends. How is everyone? Is Seonil excited about having a new dongsaeng?

I am so thankful for all those years you kept that family album for me, because I have at least a photographic history with my American family. Miran seems not to know much about me, but maybe that is because we do not talk to each other very well yet. Here is a photograph of Miran and me that Father took. Father spends a lot of time with me for English vocabulary, as does Miran Unnee. Mother gave me a spiral notebook to write down English words and meanings. She says she does the same thing. She laughs at her poor English and says we will be students learning to speak together.

It is strange with Mother. She often tells me how to behave, as if I don't have any manners. She did this at church, and it was embarrassing. She seems to want something of me I cannot give, though I cannot say what it is. For the first week I slept in her bed with her, and I suppose it was because she was missing me for so many years and wanted to make up lost time. But I cannot sleep when she is in the bed. She makes lots of noise sleeping— more than Halmeoni—and sometimes she shouts out loud in her dreams. It is uncomfortable in that big soft bed, with her so close beside me like two lost souls on a fluffy sea. After a few days of not sleeping, Father noticed how I seemed to nap when I sat down in an armchair or the couch, and then we had the talk about "the inner clock."

I know I should be a good daughter and not ask for anything for myself, but over the days Father continued to say to me, "How are you feeling? Is there anything you need?" It seemed easier to talk to him than to Mother, so I mentioned how difficult it is to sleep in that big bed. No, I did not say it was difficult to sleep with Mother.

He is wise. Later that night after dinner, I was doing homework with Unnee—it is very hard, this English language—and I heard him say to Mother that his back was hurting from sleeping in the sewing room, and did she think it was time to let me sleep downstairs in my room? It felt wrong to eavesdrop, so I went to the very back of the kitchen and clattered the dishes (they have many, many dishes— *we* have many dishes) into the cabinet so I would not hear any more. I slept in my own bed that night in the cool basement room Father had built. The bed is still too soft and Unnee also snores, but it is better now.

Miran Unnee stayed at home with me for the first week, and we walked all around the neighborhood. She is a little shy but tries hard. We do not talk very well together, but it is getting better. I teach her Korean words, and she tells me what they are in English. It is very pretty here, and everything is green and so clean. The streets are all paved with raised cement paths, and the curbs are so clear, I wonder when am I going to see the people who wash them. So much green! Everyone plants flowers in their yards. Unnee says the people with big flower gardens are not rich people. They are just like us, she says. They do not know how rich they are. We sat in the backyard and drew flowers, and then we drew each other. She is good as an artist, but she tells me that Mother and Father think she should study "something more practical." At the same time, Father says it is fine if I want to study art, so I do not understand this family.

School is very difficult. Unnee tries hard to keep me company, but her Korean is limited to "toilet" and "drink water" and "let's go" and "eat," which I suppose is all I need. Though I cannot speak enough English and do not fit in one bit, I can see that the other students shun her and that makes me sad. But I did not have many friends either. She plays piano very well and plays in the school orchestra. Because we are in all of the same classes, the teachers call us "twins," though we look nothing alike! Some of the students are kind, and she has a few friends who eat with us. They look together like United Nations delegates, they are from so many places.

Say hello to everyone. Tell them I miss them. I miss you the most.

Your daughter

Tuesday, 14 May

This is my diary. I know it's supposed to be for studying English, but if I cannot write to Uncle, then I must write to someone, and that will be you, spiral notebook. I am so sad and upset. I have been crying all day and trying to hide it. Dinner was torture. Finally I said I wasn't feeling well and was excused from washing dishes. Later I told Miran thank you for doing my housework. Mother told Father I had gotten a letter from Uncle, and it must have made me homesick. She asked to read it, but I didn't answer and when she wasn't watching, I took it in the backyard, tore it into tiny pieces and threw it in the brook in the woods. Yes, I got a letter from Uncle, and I was so happy to hear about Aunt's healthy baby, a girl they named Seonwu. But then Uncle said after he got my letter, he had to pray every day for a week to decide what to do. He said he hopes I understand that I should not write to him about my troubles because I need to bond with my family here. He said he loves me with his whole heart and prays for happiness to enter my soul, but if I continue to be attached to him, I will not give myself a chance to have a good life with my family in America.

I am heartbroken. He will not write to me anymore. He says this is very difficult for both of us, but he does it out of the great love he has for me. Could anything be more painful? I am so angry and sad! His letter makes me understand there is nothing behind me and that I am truly alone. Even it is pointless to try to keep up a friendship with Yuna or Hyo. Here comes Mother.

Wednesday, 15 May

When I got home from school, this notebook was moved from one side to the other in my bureau drawer. I think Mother wants to know what I am thinking since I do not talk so much and she sees I have been crying. So today I have begun to write in a secret code. I don't think it will make any sense to her. I will have to write the letters I transposed somewhere else, or I will never figure it out. But I'm supposed to only think forward, not back, not even to reading what I have already written, so it does not matter. I had a terrible day in school. Headache and angry. Only the math teacher is kind to me, because I know their trigonometry already. She puts me to work on the chalkboard and gives me lots of praise. This is helpful to lift me out of the miserable days of not understanding anything. Also the students look at me differently because of the math work, like I'm some kind of idiot-genius. Mrs. Samson, the art teacher, is kind too. Like Hyo said to Uncle that day, art and math do not need English. Oh, how I miss them! Miran knew I was sad, so at lunch she bought me an ice-cream sandwich in the cafeteria. That was very sweet of her. Ice-cream sandwiches are delicious.

Thursday, 16 May

It feels itchy all over to be so unhappy, and to not want to be here. There is nowhere else for me to go. I am so unhappy. I wish I were the adopted daughter, then, like Grandmother feared

when my parents left Korea, I would
have been left behind forever. Adoption
is different in America, and now in our
family, too—an adopted daughter is not a
second-class family member as she would
be in Korea. Like Uncle says, it is pointless to talk about what can't be changed,
but how am I supposed to change how I
feel about it? And yet I must.

Saturday, 18 May
I tried to not write in this notebook for
a whole day. I am trying to do what Uncle
says and bond with my family. It will
take more than one day! Miran took me
to the library this morning. She helped me
get a library card and showed me how to
use the stacks. It is a big rich library, but
Miran says it is "small town." She reads
thick books. One day I want to read like
she does. It seems her reading is like this
notebook is to me, something private
and all for herself. Then she practiced
piano, and I studied English with some
of the children's books we checked out.
Miniature books about Peter, a cute rabbit
who always gets in trouble with a farmer.
They are too easy so I feel good to move
up to the next grade level. I played piano
a little bit with Miran. Though sometimes

she is frustrated with me, especially in school, other times she is sweet. She plays with lots of emotion but also technical skill. Hyo would be impressed. But I am not thinking about Hyo anymore.

My trunk came last week right before I got Uncle's letter, and when I first opened it, I could smell my room. I never thought such a brief scent that was lost in a few seconds could bring so much pain. Even in one month's time, I can see how my things from Korea are simple and poor. I wish I did not know this. Miran and I sat on her bed and looked at that old Bible storybook. How many memories it brings! I noticed for the first time that Uncle had written a few translations in his handsome penmanship. Surely I must have seen that a hundred times and perhaps even witnessed him writing it out, but only now do I really see it. It makes me wonder what else I didn't see in all that was so familiar to me, and which is now lost forever.

No more crying. Miran has old storybooks with broken spines on her bookshelves, so we are joined in loving books from our childhood. Father belongs to a club that sends him books every month, so there are shelves and shelves of books in this house. I like that part about my family and plan to learn English well enough to read every single one of the books in this house. Maybe not the encyclopedias and theology books. Mother copies pages from those books as a way to learn English. I will do the same with my textbooks.

It never gets completely dark in this neighborhood, and I cannot see many stars. I sneak out the basement door when I cannot sleep. Miran sneaks outside too, to smoke cigarettes. When I caught her once, she acted very guilty and said, "Don't tell Mom," like a little girl. Of course I wouldn't, and I think she likes me a little better because I keep her secret. She sleeps very well and I envy her for that. I dream every night of being lost in a giant apartment building or a hotel looking for my room in Korea. I'm unsettled when I wake. I see the half-moon and feel calmed, as if I am seeing the moon at home, but then my eyes catch sight of the tree line, and I can no longer fool myself that it is home. I cried all day thinking about Uncle, and then I was so mad I could not sleep. I wish I knew how to curse in English. I would cuss at the world.

Sunday, 19 May

I couldn't help it and wrote letters to Hyo and Yuna today. I tried not to say anything bad, but I also didn't say I was happy and the streets are flooded with gems. Mother is disorganized, so busy doing things, she forgets what time it is. It seems we are always rushing when we need to get somewhere. I think I can help Mother with this, and that will make me feel useful. When Miran talks in her childish Korean, she sounds like Seonil. How I miss that little boy!

Monday, 3 June

I have made a big effort to not write in this diary and to be a good daughter. Sometimes it's easy to laugh, because Mother can be cute and funny, like with how much joy she gets from seeing our artwork, and she loves to laugh. My best place here is to be a good daughter for Mother, and it is easy to do, because Miran does not talk very much to her. I can see why she did not learn Korean, though I do fault her a little. It is hard enough to fit into school with everyone else, and who am I to judge? This is a phrase Mother uses after she has gossiped about the churchwomen. I would like to point out this irony to her, but I am not yet certain of her reaction, though I think she would laugh. School will end this week, and then it is summer break. They have a very short school session. We would still be in classes until August. I got a strange letter from Hyo today. He did not write anything personal, only about politics and organizing his classmates to join demonstrations. I wrote him back right away to tell him not to put those kinds of thoughts on paper. I have not heard from Yuna.

Thursday, 13 June

Today I received another terrible letter from Seoul. Actually it is not as bad as Uncle's letter, the very thought of which gives me such heartache I want to crawl into a deep hole. Yuna finally wrote me a short note and asked me to not be mad that she and Hyo are close friends now. My first thought was "Oh! She too knows what it's like to be kissed by him!" And then I had ugly feelings of jealousy. *Hell and damnation.* See, it does help to curse even in English. It makes sense, but I wish she hadn't told me. Like Uncle says, I must separate from my past in order to find happiness in my future. But how can

I do that when I am feeling everything right now?

Next day

I cried all day thinking about Hyo and Yuna. Then about Uncle and Seonil. Then about the baby Seonwu I will never know. Then about Ara. Then about everything. I will not write letters to anyone at home anymore. I wish Halmeoni were still alive and younger, and then I could write to her. Could anyone be so unhappy as me?

Thursday, July 4, 1963—Father's favorite holiday

Weeks of crying, anger, frustration, and sadness. I am a walking thunderstorm. It's like something I had forgotten about—the gray days when the crematorium ash covered everything. Nobody talked about it, but it was everywhere, underneath our fingernails and in our hair. The storm will always be a part of me, pervasive like that ash is surely still inside my lungs. I must put my hard feelings inside a drawer in my head. There are many drawers there, and like the bureau of drawers filled with clothes just for me, these drawers are filled with memories that are only mine with no one to share them with. Hyo and

Yuna. What happened to poor Junghi, left behind by those two? Lucky he was carefree and lighthearted. I wish I could be that way, then I wouldn't be upset by, well, everything. I will never forget my life at home and my love for Uncle, but those drawers must be shut tight. This one drawer that holds the storm will have an iron padlock and key so heavy it cannot be lifted.

On this American holiday, I pledge to work hard to make my parents happy. They suffered so much to bring me here and to live all those years worried about me. Mother tells me stories about those years, and they make me see things differently. One day in the kitchen, long after everyone was in bed, she told me the story about Miran, I think as a way to help us both to understand her decision. The way she told it was the same as Uncle and Halmeoni except for one thing—that part of her decision to leave me behind was not only because I was the true blood daughter, but that Miran needed to stay with them because she was inherently more needy, having been abandoned by her mother. The widow had sacrificed her child for a better life, knowing her own life was ruined from having birthed her. Mother did not want to erase the benefits of that sacrifice with a second abandonment. It is good to know this story from my mother's perspective; it is a generous and loving perspective. Still, though it is at the root of what I suffer today, it does little to ease my daily regrets and unbearable longing.

It is Independence Day, and I declare independence from my past. Yesterday I discussed with Father that an English tutor could help me learn faster. I believe that is one way for me to find happiness. Language is a different kind of key to a different set of drawers. I should have studied harder in Seoul, like Hyo said (I am not thinking about him), but who knew what it would really mean? There is a young man at church, thick glasses, a round head, and thin hair who is bilingual. Miran says he looks like a Korean Charlie Brown with eyeglasses. He is attending Maryland University to be an elementary school teacher, so he will know how to teach me basic English. Father said it was a good idea, and though I offered to do some job to pay for it myself, he said it is his responsibility to ensure my success. I think he understands me more than Mother, but I am not supposed to write bad things about Mother.

31

Art Class

Inja was so clearly unhappy that, at first, all Miran wanted to do was make her feel better. She tried to think of things that would lift her sister's spirits, but all the things she herself did to lift her spirits she didn't want to share—her Campfire trips, her friends and their bad habits. She guessed Inja wouldn't appreciate the luscious sense of rebellion she felt smoking cigarettes and drinking cheap wine. She was used to reading feelings when language was a barrier, but not when the person was such a strange presence in her own bedroom, and one as closed up and miserable as Inja was.

It seemed like her parents, too, were tiptoeing around Inja's feelings, speaking softly to her, solicitous about what she might like to eat, careful in how they showed her something new, such as how to use scouring powder in the sink or the vacuum cleaner on the rugs.

By summer break, Miran was fed up with the vigilance about Inja's sensitivities, which had spilled over into the summer art class they took. Her friends and the teacher were as cautious and considerate of her sister as her parents were. Mrs. Samson was more accommodating to Inja than to Miran or anyone else. Miran wasn't resentful at first; she got a secondary glow of attention from what was showered on Inja. But then Inja's artwork took center stage, from sketches to watercolors and finally to ceramics.

A week into the summer class, though Miran was in the midst of a cups and bowls project, she willingly relinquished the sole potter's wheel for her sister to learn how to throw a pot. Miran sat nearby making a coil pot, and she taught her sister the language of pottery: silica, slip, wedge, bisque, fire, kiln. Inja took to it immediately, and within a week had thrown two vases with elongated Asian profiles: a long-necked flask and an urn-shaped amphora.

"Extraordinary," said Mrs. Samson, admiring the taller vessel. "Tell your sister no one has such steady coordination, or an eye for profile like hers. That's a gorgeous vase. Everyone, come look at the balance of these curves. It's almost like yin and yang, it's so harmonious. Absolute perfection." The dozen students crowded around with exclamations that matched Mrs. Samson's in wonder—and envy.

Miran showed Inja how to look up *gorgeous, extraordinary, harmonious,* and *perfection* in her English-Korean dictionary. At each translation, Miran begrudged the growing smile on Inja's lips that, at last, erased her perennial frown. Miran's double bind couldn't last: she resented her sister's natural talent and hated herself for resenting her sister. She also begrudged the months-long frustration of caution and constraint without relief, tense even at bedtime when Inja wrote furiously in her spiral notebook, often crying silently until she had to grab tissues.

They stayed late alone in art class that afternoon and would lock up when finished—something they'd done before with Mrs. Samson's permission. Miran stuffed her coil pot with damp newspaper for support before firing, vexed at her own admiration of Inja's two vases that had garnered such praise. The urn was upside down on the wheel, and Inja carved its foot with a wire loop tool, turning the wheel slowly, applying the tool with just enough pressure for the firming clay to peel off in smooth layers. In rhythm with the creaking of the potter's wheel, Inja recited her new English words in a soft singsong: "gorgeous, perfection, extraordinary, harmonious."

"Fuck!" Miran said, and leaned over to crush Inja's vase with a swift clutch of fingers. "Fuck your damned perfection!"

"*Wae geurae*! *Michyeosseo*?" Inja cried, eyes wide. "What's wrong with you! Are you crazy?" The wheel spun her lumpen vase. She threw her wire tool at Miran, and it cut above her left eyebrow, drawing a bead of blood. "Oh! I sorry! Not meaning to hitting you."

Miran, equally surprised that she'd been struck, blotted her forehead with a rag, dusty with clay, and when she saw blood, she burst out laughing and crushed her own pot with a fist. "There, we're even!" It made no sense, but she laughed and threw a piece of her clay pot at Inja. Inja grabbed her broken pot, threw it at Miran, and it landed on her apron. They both laughed.

"Oh jeez, I'm sorry," said Miran, wiping her eyes and brow.

"See your face, all clay," said Inja, and they went to the mirror above the sink to laugh at Miran's face streaked with brown and a little bit of blood.

"I ruined your pot," said Miran, washing her face.

"You ruined your pot, too," said Inja, and they laughed again.

They cleaned up their mess, recycled the clay, and walked home in the late summer afternoon, ribbing each other and giggling now and then.

Before they went into the house, Inja touched her sister's forehead. "You okay?"

"Yeah, sorry about your vase."

"Is okay. We sisters."

"Yes, we are," said Miran, and they went inside.

32

At the Movies

Inja's seventeenth birthday present was to celebrate it however she wished and have prepared for her whatever she wanted to eat. In a rare display of selfishness, she told her mother she wanted rice, kimchi, Spam, and also the sailor hot dogs she remembered from pictures of Miran's birthdays. She wanted to spend all day at the movies and have birthday streamers hung in the dining room. Since September 24th was a school day, they celebrated on Saturday: a matinee at the Avalon Theatre downtown to see Elizabeth Taylor and Richard Burton in *Cleopatra*, and after the silly Spam and hot dog dinner, to the Thunderbird drive-in to see Alfred Hitchcock's *The Birds*. Both girls were titillated by the scandalous Taylor-Burton affair that had emerged during the making of *Cleopatra,* and Miran, who still charted stocks for Miss Lone, had bought half a dozen movie magazines with headlines like "Brazen Burton!"

In the theater during the kissing scenes, Najin clucked her tongue, making Inja uncomfortable to be watching with her mother. But Miran said she loved all the indecent innuendo. Later at the drive-in, sitting in the back with Najin, Inja easily ducked her head behind the front seat when the scary parts came.

On the way home, Inja spoke to her mother about Hitchcock's film, "I don't like how that ended. What does it mean, all those birds sitting quiet, and they drive to the hospital. Will they attack again? Are they everywhere in California and in America?"

Najin said, "You understood a lot."

"They used simple English or none at all," said Inja. She swatted her hands, mouth open and silent, like Tippi Hedren in the phone booth being attacked by birds, and they all laughed. "Mother, didn't you once live in California? Was it like in the movie?"

"No birds like that," said Najin. "How awful for that poor schoolteacher!"

Inja tried to shake the image of Suzanne Pleshette with her eyes gouged out. "Awful." They drove by the darkened storefronts on Chillum Road, and the early autumn evening blew cool through the car. Her mother rolled her window closed, and in the windless quiet of the back seat, Inja said, "It's like the newspaper photograph that started the Four-Nineteen Uprising."

"Yah," said Najin, her voice a warm response

to Inja's rare initiation of a conversation. "It makes me sad when I think how much of your childhood I missed."

"I was old enough when it happened, just a few years ago. Did the Korean newspapers here show that photograph?"

"I'm not sure. What was it?"

"I forget the boy's name, but he was a village boy visiting Masan City. He and his brother had taken high school entrance examinations, and then marched in a protest against another rigged election by President Rhee."

"How knowledgeable you are," said Najin. "I did hear about Masan. Seems there are always student protests in the Korean papers. But I remember that was a bloody uprising." She tapped Inja's knee. "Tell me you didn't join those students!"

"Ajcossi wouldn't allow me to go. I was curious though. A friend of mine went." Inja remained silent awhile, sad about Hyo.

"What was the photo?" said her mother.

"The younger brother—yes, his name was Ju-yeol—disappeared that night and was found a month later floating in waters of the Masan port. The photograph showed him with his arms halfway raised, as if he were calmly sitting up submerged in the black water, but he had a tear-gas shell in one eye coming out the back of his head."

"Aigu! That poor boy's mother! Why would they publish such an image?"

"I thought the same—to see her son like that."

"I'm sorry you had to see it."

"It had its effect. The shock of that one photograph rallied the protesters. It's like in the movie how the farmer's death and then the teacher's death made the threat of the birds real," said Inja. "None of us are going to sleep tonight." Inja heard her own voice as relaxed and unguarded, and her mother must have felt it, too.

"Are you sleeping well?" she asked. "Is it a little easier these days?"

Something slammed in Inja's mind. "Thank you, Mother, but I'm fine." She felt bad a moment for her mother's sigh but couldn't fight the urge to hold it all in.

They crossed from Prince George's into Montgomery County, and Inja caught bits of explanation that her father was giving to Miran about a displeased Julius Caesar when the Egyptians presented the head of his enemy Pompey, " . . . because an assassination isn't an honorable way to die."

"Ironic," said Miran, "considering that's how he got it himself. That head was gross."

"What is *gross*?" asked Inja.

"Disgusting, scary, ugly, nasty, repulsive, perverse, putrid," said Miran, laughing with each added synonym.

"It also means a sum that had no deductions, like 'gross wages' in a paycheck before taxes; and it means a dozen times a dozen," said Calvin, "like a 'gross of eggs.'"

"Wow." She definitely got more than she expected.

"That's the problem with English," said Najin. "Multiple meanings for a single word."

Inja sat back and after a while, her mother talked about the old days, as she often did as a way to find commonality between them. "Your grandfather joined the demonstrations for independence on Sam-il. Did you know?"

"Yes. I never asked him about it, but every Sam-il, Ajeossi told me the story of how he'd shouted in the streets and was arrested and beaten, which explained his sore back when it was damp and cold. Ajeossi said he was just a baby so doesn't remember anything." Inja startled and sat upright. "Mother—how old were you then? Do you remember it?"

"Nineteen-nineteen, so I was nine." She sighed. "I only remember my father's face when he came home, swollen yellow and purple, and his black thumbs. They'd hung him by his thumbs." She swatted the air, as if to erase the image from her mind. "We lived in Kaesong then. Mostly what I remember is my mother holding Dongsaeng as a baby high in the air, the unison chants from the marchers, and how the yellow dust from the road coated our clothes and shoes."

"One night during the Seoul protests, I did sneak outside," said Inja, "but I couldn't hear or see anything—we lived too far away."

"How is the house that your father built?"

"Probably the same. It was home." A small pain shot through her, but at least it didn't cause tears. Inja thought that was progress.

Najin said nothing for a while, and her tone softened. "My daughter, I understand that you would have a completely different attitude about moving to America. We've always wanted to bring you home, but your home was also there." Inja shifted and drew centimeters away and closer to the window. "I don't mean to pry," said Najin, "but your father worries, as do I, about how you're getting along."

Inja blew out air, then after a moment said, "It's better, thank you, Mother. It's good to be here"— the last part sounding hesitant.

"We've lost so much time together . . ." She stopped, and Inja heard the tears caught in her throat. Something shifted inside, but she couldn't yet acknowledge it.

Calvin turned off the main road and said, "We're almost home. You two ladies doing okay back there?" Miran must have sensed something, too, because she had quieted up front.

"Yes, Father. I'm not carsick at all," said Inja. She thought about everything she hadn't said since she'd arrived—five months filled with resentment, stress, and tears, the complexities of the unknown in a transition she had never wanted to make. What could she say? Only apologies, again, though it wasn't her fault. The fault that belonged to her was her unwillingness to be compassionate to her mother's needs, and though she tried in her mind to be compassionate, she wasn't ready in her heart, which was where it mattered. To give up the resentment of this unwelcome passage was to give in to something she never would have chosen—but now she was seeing it differently, and her stubborn position, ultimately unsustainable, was shifting despite herself.

In the dark Najin couldn't see Calvin's eyes in the rearview mirror, though she heard his curiosity about their quiet discussion. They had often talked about everything Inja wasn't saying since she'd come home. They had, of course, anticipated an adjustment period, but it had been glossed over in the excitement of the reunion. Considering how long Najin herself had taken to "get her sea legs" in America—including a notebook filled with colloquialisms—how could she have missed planning for such a complicated transition?

Najin thought she would adopt Calvin's compassion and protect her daughter from bad news, from concern even about herself and Calvin; she would be foolish and generous with love. "When we first came to America," Najin said to Inja, "your father gave me a checkbook that had no account balance. You have your own bank account now, but when your father gave me that blank checkbook, he said, 'Whatever you want, whatever you need.' To be honest, I thought him a little crazy to be so free with money, but his attitude actually made me more careful." She laughed a little and twisted off a gold ring, its nickel coating to mask its real value worn through at its edges. "When he came back to Korea at the end of the war, he gave me this ring with that very same sentiment, and so that I would always have something of monetary value with me—a kind of security." She touched Inja's hand and folded the ring into her palm. "My daughter, keep this to remember that we are like that blank checkbook. Will you do that? Whatever you want, whatever you need."

Inja turned, and Najin sought her daughter's eyes in the dark. In accepting the ring, Inja did not withdraw her hand. "Mother, I'm sorry I've been so— Well, I'm sorry. Thank you for understanding."

"You are my daughter." The moment Najin said this, she heard her own mother's voice speaking these words, words that hopefully Inja herself would speak one day, words that would echo through the generations. Her heart overflowed with gratitude and love for her mother, and for this gracious and fragile young lady, beside her at last.

After a pause and with laughter in her voice, Inja said, "How about I need to go to the drive-in next weekend to see *Bye Bye Birdie*?"

"I want to see that, too," Miran chimed from the front seat.

Najin said, "I don't know how you can stand that caterwauling," and they laughed.

Calvin pulled into the driveway, and they went inside for cake and ice cream. Najin saw Inja slip the circle of gold onto her right hand's ring finger. It hung loose, but Najin felt sure she'd grow into it soon.

33

Blizzard

Heavy snow in January canceled school for a week, and Calvin drove to work with chains on the tires. Miran cleaned up the sewing room to transform the catch-all space into a dressmaker's studio. At the sewing machine, Najin hummed hymns and pieced together a cropped jacket with a white rabbit-fur collar in thick pink brocade, while Miran hemmed the matching full-length sheath dress, and Inja basted a satin lining—an outfit she'd wear to her first dance. Earlier, Najin, mocking a scandalized look that made them all laugh, had deemed the pattern for the strapless dress too risqué. She added shoulder straps to the bodice and a solid inch to the décolleté.

Though Miran had only been to a few school dances, she declared the gown was perfect for the University of Maryland's Winter Ball, to which Inja had been invited by her English tutor, the Korean Charlie Brown, whose name was Sammy Jang. When Inja had asked permission to go earlier that month, Dad had approved against Mom's demurral, saying it was what American teenagers do. Miran was certain her mother's misgivings were based on Ann-Margret's bold behavior in *Bye Bye Birdie*. Further assurances came when Sammy announced that it was a double date, he didn't drink alcohol, and he would pick up and drive Inja home in his roommate's big four-door and safe sedan.

Miran tied off a line of stitches and read the Winter Ball invitation, "'Formal dance in the new ballroom at Stamp Student Union, free soda pop and cash bar.' And cool, there's a live band, the Chessmen."

"They are rock-and-roll?" said Inja. "What kind of dancing, like twist?" She spoke in English, accented but much improved, to Miran and switched to Korean with her mother.

"I don't know how you kids can stand that caterwauling," said Najin on cue, to laughter.

Dad had bought a tabletop Zenith TV the previous summer to see the national broadcast of Dr. Martin Luther King Jr.'s speech at the Lincoln Memorial. Or so he said. Based on his devotion to Westerns and his love of NASA launches, Miran was sure it was otherwise. If she watched TV when she was supposed to be practicing piano, her mother said she'd take a baseball bat to it, but since they had all witnessed the live assassination of Lee Harvey Oswald and the Kennedy funeral—her mother peering into the screen to see the cortege and Jackie's veiled face—she knew it was an empty threat. Plus,

Najin had discovered televised beauty pageants.

"Yup, rock-and-roll dancing," said Miran. "On *American Bandstand* they do the twist, the wah-watusi, and mashed potatoes." She stood up and executed a few well-practiced mashing of potatoes from hours spent in front of the mirror. Inja got up and danced hand in sleeve with her jacket lining, twist-kicking.

"Wow, that's great—you already know it!"

"I learn the mash dance at ho— in Seoul. You do it well."

"I studied the kids dancing at the mixers. Nobody danced with me except teachers."

Najin said, "I didn't know that. What an honor!"

Miran said to Inja as if her mother weren't there, "She has no idea. It puts a target on your forehead that says 'loser.'" She laid fingers shaped in an L on her brow.

"You just too shy for boys," said Inja, patting her shoulder.

"Dates are icky anyhow." She wouldn't admit that a date was exactly what she dreamed about. She'd never wear a dress like Inja's, though. She couldn't imagine who'd be attracted to her, or who she'd be attracted to, for that matter. She supposed she'd be attracted to anyone who was attracted to her, as if that would ever happen.

"Wait your turn and changing mind."

"Doubt it, but no biggie. Mom, the hem's done."

"What is *nobiggie*?" said Inja.

"Not a big deal, not a problem, nothing to worry about, who gives a hoot, I don't give a rat's ass."

Inja laughed and shushed Miran, who had lowered her voice for the last example.

"Let's see how it all fits together." Najin frowned as she inspected the hemming, and Miran sighed, seeing this prediction of criticism.

But Inja said, "Mother, she did well; brocade isn't easy to sew." She tossed off her clothes and slid on the sheath and the high heels that her mother had expertly glued with matching brocade, including perfect square bows she'd made for the toes. While their mother pinched and pinned seams, Inja showed Miran the poufy hairstyles she could copy from the models on the Butterick pattern. "We can tease up and shape like this with rollers; you can help me, okay?"

"And lots of hairspray," Miran said, grateful for her intercession. Her sister's effortlessness with her appearance and body both awed her and made her envy her perfection, as well as her growing ease with language, boys, grownups Korean or American, and her easy acceptance of being different from everyone else in school, in the entire neighborhood, and probably the entire city of Washington, DC. Maybe it was because she was *so* different, that she never knew she needed to fit in. For Miran, that yearning was nearly unbearable, unattainable as it was. There were too many hurdles: not only was she Oriental and her hair wouldn't curl; she was skinny with oily skin that she battled with Sea Breeze, and she made her own clothes—the final nail on the coffin of forever unpopular. She roamed the worn linoleum of Blair High School's hallways, hugged her textbooks to her cleavage-less chest, and kept her eyes down—a loser in every sense, and one who fit best into the books she read.

And now, with her Korean sister's easy deflection of her mother's fault-finding, Miran thought of Inja more as the best friend that she'd never before had.

On February 8, the evening of the Winter Ball, snow still covered the ground and most of the side streets, but Sammy Jang arrived promptly in a big Fairlane at seven. Miran pitied him, stiff in his rented tuxedo in the living room surrounded by her family, his round head shining with embarrassment. Najin took the corsage he offered to Inja and pinned it to the rabbit-fur collar of Inja's brocade jacket. She barraged poor Sammy with questions, instructions, and jovial warnings that teetered on the edge of being threats. Another snowstorm was predicted tomorrow, and he was made to promise to have her home by ten, but Inja pleaded with Calvin and they compromised with eleven-thirty. Somehow Inja was able to get permission from their parents that Miran never had the guts to ask for, resorting instead to lying or sneaking out the basement door to meet her friends. They'd sip on a week-old bottle of Lancers Rosé and smoke Winstons, trying different cool ways to hold the cigarettes, coughing, laughing at themselves. It was okay to feel foolish and dumb with her friends, because they all felt that way.

Miran took many photographs, and the flash-bulbs and *ooh*s and *aah*s made the occasion more festive than a birthday. As if the couple were celebrities, her family clapped when they left. The gallant Sammy offered Inja his arm when they went down the stairs, and he opened her car door. Inja waved with her evening-gloved hand and blew them a kiss, which Miran knew was meant for her. Earlier when Miran helped fix her hair, she teased her, "Is Sammy going to kiss you?"

Inja had laughed. "We friends but I don't think of him that way, but maybe he is thinking of me like that because I see he is color change when I read poetry in our lessons. I read 'She Walks in Beauty,' and he blushes. I said yes to the date because I like to get dress up and go to college dance."

Miran sprayed the heaped curls while Inja held a tissue over her made-up face. "Careful," Miran said, "it's what they mean by *leading him on.*" Together the two often read *Teen* magazine, and Miran would define words like *comb-outs, beehive, popularity,* and *kissable.* With her sharp angles and awkwardness, Miran was certain she wasn't at all kissable, but Inja was eminently kissable with soft curves and black-lined eyes on a perfect complexion with full pinkened lips.

That evening at nine o'clock, in the guise of not waiting for Inja to come home, Miran joined their father to watch his favorite show, *Gunsmoke*, while her mother, pretending to be busy in the dining room, got up every five minutes to check if they'd returned. Halfway through the show, Najin came in, arms crossed. "Yeobo, it's snowing. Should we be worried?"

He smiled and said, "You're already worried," and looked out the window. "It's not heavy and it's melting on the road. They'll be fine." Miran got up to see, and the streetlight illuminated the snow swirling like the cartoon Tasmanian Devil, sticking to the sides of trees and telephone poles. She believed they ought to be worried—she had just completed driver's education and had seen the gruesome auto-accident film *Mechanized Death*, which gave her nightmares. Inja, who said the film wasn't that bad, had to take the written part twice, but they had both obtained their learner's permits.

The snow thickened and was accumulating

when Marshal Dillon and the good citizens of Dodge got justice in the time-honored formula of what goes around, comes around. Calvin turned on the radio for the weather report, Najin paced, and Miran wished it weren't snowing so she could sneak out for a cigarette. She went downstairs to read until Inja came home.

She dozed and was woken by her mother shouting. She thought she was dreaming until she heard her father's voice, too. It was eleven-forty-five, and perhaps Inja was home and getting yelled at for being late. Her mother had been yelling a lot lately. Miran wrapped a blanket around her shoulders and crept to the top of the basement stairs to listen. She felt a kind of evil glee that finally her sister was getting yelled at, not just her.

Najin's voice faded in and out of hearing, meaning she was pacing. "Maybe they had an accident." So she wasn't home yet. Pace. "Why didn't you know about this snowstorm?" Fade and volume. "I'll get Miran to tell me what she knows about that boy. She's here when he's here."

"Yeobo, be reasonable."

"He's skidded off the road. She's lying in a ditch."

Miran heard placating murmurs from her father, and she worried that her mother had spun herself into a tizzy that wouldn't easily wind down. Last week her mom went batty because Miran left the laundry in the washing machine overnight, but her dad told her later it wasn't that serious an infraction, so not to worry.

"Dear God, where could she be?" said Najin. And a little later, "We should call the university." Her father, soothing, then, "We should call the police."

Miran crouched on the top step huddled in her blanket, glad she wasn't on the receiving end of the barrage. She dozed and woke to "How can you nap like that?" and thought for a second her mother was yelling at her. "He's taking advantage of her in some alley, or that roommate is. It's midnight, why aren't you concerned? We didn't even meet the roommate. How do we know what kind of boy he is? Does he even exist? Why haven't they found a phone booth to call? Something is wrong. Call the hospitals. Ask the Bushongs next door; they're firemen, they'd know. Call the police."

Her father grumbled a prolonged response that ended in English with "—responsible young man, driving slowly as he should in this weather."

Similar episodes of her mother's worry and her father's attempts at calm were repeated. At twelve-thirty, Calvin said he'd shovel the walk, and Miran went downstairs to get a pillow for her bottom and a pair of socks for her frigid feet. At one o'clock, her father shoveled again, returned, stomping on the front porch. At one-fifteen, she heard him on the phone, apologizing for the hour and asking for Sammy Jang. "How about his roommate? Can you tell me his name?" Pause. "Is he available? No one's there? Yes, thanks, anyway."

"Why won't you call the police?"

"I don't believe they'd be able to tell us anything. If they've been in an accident, the police would have called us already."

"What if she can't remember her phone number? What if she's been so injured, she can't talk? What if they're bleeding on the snow or dead?" She was shouting by the end.

At some point her father was on the telephone again, but Miran was too sleepy to listen. At one-fifty, a shout, and tire chains crunched in the snow. Miran went down to peek out the window near her mother's kimchi-making station. The Ford Fairlane idled at the curb, and Sammy was ushering her sister to the porch as the front door opened to her mother's cries.

"Mother, I'm fine!" said Inja.

All of the night's worries culminated in an onslaught and the door slammed.

Her father and Sammy talked outside. Miran cracked the casement window open. Sammy's back was to her so she only caught snippets, or maybe he was shivering.

"I'm so sorry, Reverend . . . swear we left the

dance . . . snow . . . chains on. I never . . . Inja told me how you'd done it."

"I'm glad you did, young man. It's quite late. Come inside; you should stay the night."

Sammy backed down the sidewalk, bowing. "I'll be fine now with the chains, sir. I should be on my way. Tell her thank you, and please tell Mrs. Cho I'm terribly sorry I got her home so late."

"Thank you for getting her home safely. We'll see you next week when the roads are clear."

The shouting escalated in the living room. Calvin stayed out by the road, hands in pockets, until Sammy drove off, chains clacking when they hit macadam where the wind had drifted the snow. Her father's shoulders rose as he heaved a sigh and went inside.

Back at the top of the stairs, she heard her mother both shouting and crying, and Inja crying, too. Miran could neither hear clearly nor understand much of what was said, but it made her fearful of her mother's wrath, which had never been so intense. Embarrassed by the hysteria in her mother's voice, Miran swore she'd never be the object of that rage. She wondered what Inja herself was so upset about that she actually yelled back—a huge breach in their ingrained respect for one's parents. Then her dad intervened with a long preachy talk and forced a prayer of reconciliation on them. Miran tiptoed downstairs and waited in the dark for her Korean sister.

Inja sniffled and blew her nose when she entered their bedroom. Mostly she felt guilty for having screamed at her mother. *You never should've left me behind, then!* But Mother had been equally unreasonable, Inja rationalized. Lots of venting about those fifteen years of worries and casting blame over the heartache she'd suffered—crazy talk, things her mother never would've said if she wasn't so worked up over nothing. None of it was Inja's fault, nor was it her mother's, though. She sighed and tossed her notebook diary on her bed.

Miran seemed asleep but was too still, meaning she was feigning sleep. Inja hung up her dress, and the hangers squeaked on their closet pole, then she turned on her bedside lamp.

Miran turned over and said, "What the hell, are you okay?"

Inja sat cross-legged atop her bed perpendicular to Miran's, her red and swollen eyes at odds with her attempt to smile. She capped her pen and closed the spiral-bound notebook. She hadn't written in it for months. "Did you hear?"

Miran sat up and coddled the blankets around her legs. "Yeah. Pretty bad."

Inja teared up, blew her nose again, and tossed

the tissue box atop her notebook. She sat like Miran, legs triangled beneath her blankets, and the lamplight struck the panes of her cheeks like moonlit wax. "I shouldn't have talked back, but I couldn't help it. She's not making sense about the whole thing."

"You mean the dance?"

Inja sighed. "That, and everything else." She put her pen and notebook away and turned off the lamp. Her eyes adjusted to the dark, and she felt her disquiet ebbing into the intimate shadows of their bedroom. Sometimes when Miran came back late after having sneaked out with her friends, they'd sit in bed like this and talk. Usually Inja would scold her a little and tell her how impossible it would be in Korea to behave that way—being deliberately bad. Other times Inja would talk about their Korean relatives. She had told Miran about their fierce aunt and loving uncle, and had described the dreams about Grandfather's watery grave, and Uncle's and their mother's letters crossing in the mail— Miran said she knew about the dream, and Dad had told her about the letters. Inja also related their grandmother's pregnancy dreams predicting the sex of Uncle and their mother, and before she thought more of it, she told Miran their mother's dream that foretold Inja would be a girl. "I know the story so well because I read that letter over and over again." She described how their mother dreamed she was at a beach and waded into the sea. The sunrise revealed the sea floor for a long distance, even through the waves. There on a bed of pebbles, she saw an abalone shell, and its mother-of-pearl bowl shone like the moon. She reached for it and the tide washed it away, but the next wave dropped it right into her hands. When she lifted it high, the outer surface was polished like water and the inside shone with the light of stars.

"That's how she knows I am girl," said Inja. She caught herself and added, "I don't know if she dreamed about you, but I'll ask her."

"That'd be cool, I'd like that," said Miran.

Inja grimaced at herself for telling that story.

"So how was the dance?"

"Fun!" she said, relieved. "Watusi and twist, but Sammy couldn't do mashing potatoes. He likes to slow dance. I learn the swim—very hard in that dress."

"Good music?"

"Loud, and everyone seems to like it. My hair doesn't stay like pouf, but the girls in the ladies' room helped teasing up, and they have hairspray in their purse. They like my dress a lot. Who thinks to bring hairspray?"

"College girls."

"They very nice to me and don't laugh at my accent. And I tried beer."

"Oh wow. Did Mom smell it on your breath?

I can teach you how to cover up beer or wine breath."

"Yes, you are expert, but I only had two sips—terrible tasting. Sammy finished my beer so I think he feels courage to slow dancing with me." Inja laughed.

"Gross."

"Do you mean like counting pay or twelve dozen?"

"Ha-ha. Do you like him more now?"

"Not that way, but maybe Mom thinks so and why she worries." She sighed, chin on knees.

They had no windows in their basement bedroom, but Inja believed she could hear the snow falling, or at least she felt a shift in the sound of a night now whitened and cloaked with snow. She checked the glowing alarm-clock dial, past three o'clock.

Miran murmured, "They were both worried because you were so late. You're the first one to go on a date, you know."

"Yes, but still it was too big upset. *Punishment does not fit crime.*"

"Yeah. Did he get stuck in the snow?"

"Only once we slide into curb. He drives slow, like turtle, and he laughing and making jokes, but his hands are white on steering wheel—is what made me nervous. It took a long time to put on chains, but I remember how Dad spread them out and drive over them. Very hard on a snowy road, so Sammy waits until we go under a bridge. He is smart and a gentleman, but his head is like a globe!"

"A worldly Korean Charlie Brown," said Miran, and they laughed.

"It was very beautiful outside—snow shining in streetlights against black sky like so many stars and remind me of home . . ."

"What made you shout back at her?"

Long silence, then rustling of blankets. Inja remembered saying to Mother, *If you had let me stay in Korea, I wouldn't be treating you like this either. Whose fault is it now?* Of course she regretted it and apologized as soon as she said it, but all her frustration had boiled over in the moment. Now she thought of how Uncle had always framed the story of her being left behind as an act of great love and sacrifice on his sister's part.

"I will tell you something you should know, but let's light a candle."

Miran fetched a candle from the basement windowsill, stashed for power outages in lightning storms. She dripped wax on a chipped saucer taken from beneath an African violet and set it upright on the night table between the foot of their beds.

Inja scooted halfway down the bed wrapped in her blankets. Miran did the same.

Inja's voice was as soft as the candlelight. "Did

you ever wonder why you go to America and not me? Why not two daughters?"

"Gosh, no, I never thought about it. It was just always that way." She paused. "I guess I was never curious because I had no cause to be curious. Also, I miss a lot—Mom's Korean and her constant frustration with me. She used to scold me about how beautiful my Korean was. I wonder if that's why I have so few memories of childhood because I understood the language back then but don't now. Weird thought. I do remember when I was little, they talked about going back."

"Yes, they think only a few years then going home." Though Inja had decided to tell her Uncle's version about their separation as infants—nothing about the adoption, of course—now, after what Miran said, she would tell her something that would bond her closer to her mother. "They take you because you almost died as a baby, and they still worry you get sick, and also you are oldest so you could know about them leaving you. I was too young to have that thinking."

"Died? Wow." Miran thought awhile. "I guess I had the usual kids' illnesses: chicken pox, measles—normal except for the scarlet fever. I have a total of two memories from before we moved here: a glimpse of a lawn in sunshine with Mom sitting on a rock, and waking up somewhere and looking for Dad—Mom said it was on the ship coming over. That's the sum of my earliest memories. How come I didn't know? What kind of sick, and how did you know about it?"

"You didn't know because you were baby, and I always knew because it is why I am staying behind with Uncle," said Inja. "You didn't eat, something wrong inside, how to say, stomach isn't working right for a long time. Mom stayed up night after night taking care of you, the sick baby, so weak and close to dying." She also said their parents never told her this because she was fine now, strong and energetic, an unspoiled and thoughtful young lady, and who wants to think about hard times?

"Hah. Maybe that's why I get carsick."

"No joking. They worry a long time about you as baby. Uncle said it proves how much Noona— that's what a boy calls his older sister—how much Noona loves him, because she took you to America and left me behind."

"That's so weird—it doesn't make sense."

Inja told her how Grandmother, in light of losing half her family, feared they would never return, and said of the decision that had determined their identities, "So they think to leave one child behind like, uh, a swearing to return."

"A guarantee."

"That's it. You're lucky this did not make changing your life, and come to America so much later like me."

"But it did," said Miran. "You would've been

390

my sister my whole life instead of only this year. I would've liked that much better."

"I know. Me too." The candle flickered with Inja's sigh. "Anyway, you can remember this, how Mother took such good care of you, how much they love you and make you stay alive in hard times." Because of the gaping language differences between their mother and Miran, she wasn't sure if she should tell Miran to keep this knowledge—a slanted truth—secret. But her revelation needed some kind of protection; she didn't want Miran asking their mother about the choice to take one daughter over another. She also remembered the sense of privilege she'd always gained in learning and then keeping secrets. "When Mother gets mad at you, you remember this as secret; how she works hard to make you stay alive."

"A tall order."

"What is *tall order?*"

"Something big and hard to do. Strenuous. Challenging. Onerous. Pain in the ass. Not really. It means 'hard.' "

"Yes, tall order, but we can do together and keep secret you know this story, okay? No need to worry them about old hard times."

"Okay."

When Miran nodded, the flame glimmered in Inja's dark eyes, and Miran felt the intimacy of kinship in a secret shared. Until this night, she hadn't consciously known how vital it was to recognize love, but the lasting power of this image of a mother's love, and herself as the needy child, struck her spirit and opened her heart to new depths layered with glimmers of self-acceptance. So striking was this knowledge that many years would pass before she was able to articulate the certainty gained this night that she was loved, that she herself could love because of it, and that she did love this Korean sister.

34

Plans

30 September 1965, to Ajeossi,

How are you? How is Aunt and Seonil, Seonwu and the new baby, Seonmi? How old is your baby girl now? Mother told me but I cannot remember her birth date, will you send it to me? How is Ara? Is she still living with you? Mother tells me only a little news from home, but she did not know Ara. I am happy to be writing to you as a college student at the University of Maryland to study art— the same kind of art that was your work, though here they call it commercial art, or graphic design. It is a very big university with a big art department, and I am living at home. Miran went away to school and is living in a dormitory. I hope you do not mind I write to you now. I am sorry you did not write many times to Mother also, and thought it must be for the same reason, which is my fault. I do understand why we could not write to each other for those years, and though it was very hard in the beginning, it must have been all the harder for you, Ajeossi, and I am as sorry it was hard for you as much as I know you are sorry it was hard here. That doesn't make much sense, but you understand me.

Actually, it is wonderful to be in America, speaking English well enough and going to university, and most of all it is especially wonderful to know my mother and father and sister as well as I know my first family in Seoul. So you were right.

I would like to send my cousins presents. I remember how much we enjoyed opening the packages from America, and I do not recall seeing Mother send you a single package since I left home.

My first goal is to study hard and finish college. Though I did not have the best grades in high school because of my language problem, I had high marks in mathematics, and made all the posters for the school plays, and paintings and drawings, many of them from memories of home. I worried at first that Miran would be jealous that all my designs got turned into posters, but she won for her abstract oil paintings, so we were both winning prizes, like you used to win prizes with your art. This makes me so happy to be like my uncle in his artwork.

I want to tell you my second goal. After college I will get a well-paying job to earn money to fly home and see my Korean family, whom I miss very much.

With love, your American
Korean daughter, Inja

After that horrible evening following her first American date with Sammy Jang, Inja's perspective about her mother shifted. She had regarded her as being the obstacle to her returning to Seoul, but that blowup made Inja see her mother less as the unwitting agent of her unhappiness, and instead someone who could be funny, a great storyteller, as creative as Uncle, as industrious and devoted as Grandmother, and at the same time flawed with impatience and temper flare-ups as sudden and violent as Aunt's, though it never happened again. No one said anything the next day, or ever after, about the shouts and tears, but Miran was unusually solicitous of their parents, and the house was subdued, as if the world had quieted under concealing veils of snow.

Inja and her mother were not quite friends, because while her mother spoke freely to her about whatever was on her mind—church, neighbors, the old days, and even Father—Inja was circumspect about what she told her. Najin was someone Inja was growing to love, and for that, and especially after the shame she felt for her own yelling that night, she would protect her mother from her own foibles and hurtful thoughts.

Miran was accepted at a small college in a tiny town in Connecticut, with scholarships and work-study stipends, but Inja chose to attend the University of Maryland as a commuter, primarily because she felt she couldn't leave her parents after a mere two years since her arrival.

They discussed it one rainy day in the final months of her senior year at Blair, driving home from a site visit to the university. "What did you think?" asked her mother in the front seat.

"They're so welcoming, and those studio classes are huge. I can easily see myself there."

"Are you certain?" her father said. "Your sister's going to be leaving, and you might feel lonely downstairs. I know a man who runs the new Asian Studies Department at Colgate, and I could call . . ."

"No, Dad, I'm sure. I doubt I'd get in with my grades. I can think about going out of state after I take some advanced English-language classes. I want to be able to read big books, like Miran. I'll have our bedroom all to myself and can put in a drafting table." Also, the in-state tuition was cheap, and she was offered a minority scholarship and work study in the Art History Department, like Miran.

Najin turned fully around to smile at Inja.

"I didn't want to influence your decision, but it makes me very happy that you'll be home. Maybe I can take English with you—but you're already more advanced than I am!" Her musical laugh blended pleasantly with the sound of rain.

"You should take a class in art," said Inja, remembering that Hyo said art didn't need English. It surprised and pleased her that thinking about Hyo brought no residual feelings of longing or resentment. "I bet you can paint just like Ajeossi."

"Maybe," said Najin. "There's a woman Mrs. Kim knows in Silver Spring who teaches Asian brush painting."

"Then it's settled," said Inja. "We're both going to school in Maryland."

"I don't know, church business . . ."

"I agree," said Calvin, pulling into their driveway. "Church demands are never going to change. We're the ones who have to change, so it's settled. I'll drive you to Silver Spring, and we'll buy a used car for Inja. If the timing works out, she can drive you sometimes on her way to classes."

By summertime, her father bought her a used beige Volkswagen Beetle, and Inja learned how to drive a stick shift and to maintain the simple engine. For two years at the University of Maryland, she drove back and forth in her reliable Bug to the sprawling campus, content to find her place in art and in industrial art classes, where she was the only female.

Inja introduced her parents to Patrick, one of the many industrial arts young men who clamored for her attention. He was a urologist's son, and a huge disappointment to his parents for choosing art over medicine. Inja's parents liked him because he pruned their hedges and was a former altar boy. Neither he nor Inja mentioned to her parents that he was now anti-religion, anti-war, and anti-establishment. He was smart, narrow-faced handsome—he kept his long locks in a ponytail around Calvin and Najin—sweet to old folks and kind to the stray cat in the neighborhood Najin fed on the mud porch. In her parents' view, his only shortcoming was his blue eyes—"Too bad he's not Korean." He and Inja were considered boyfriend-girlfriend, but she wasn't long-term serious about him. Nobody was long-term serious about anyone those days. Inja brought him home because she knew he would pass muster. Plus he was a talented craftsman— and a great kisser and lover, and believed in feminism probably more than she did.

Miran wrote despondent letters from college and came home every holiday and college break, saying she missed Inja but was happy to be away from their parents. At some point during those college years, Miran told Inja she had adopted a facade in dealing with their mother. She saw herself as an American soul in a Korean body—a state of being she called "the Great Pretender," after the song made popular by Sam Cooke, meaning she always felt as if she were acting at being either Korean or American, and as a result always acting at being anyone at all. It made Inja wonder if her being abandoned by her blood mother had this kind of lasting effect—a constant search for an identity that was both secret and forever lost to her, but somehow known in the heart. Could infant abandonment result in lifelong alienation? Pop culture had taken the biblical phrase "The truth shall set you free" and made it into psychedelic posters. Would it help if she knew the truth?

After two years at Maryland, Inja felt wings of independence itching on her shoulders, and for her junior year applied to and was accepted at the Rhode Island School of Design in Providence, a costly college made affordable by scholarships and continued work study. Since RISD was a short train ride away from Miran's college, and the trains were convenient for trips home, Inja sold her car.

By 1967, "the Summer of Love," Miran was a hippie leaning toward socialism, moratoriums, Eastern religions, and psychedelic music. She wore bell-bottom blue jeans, construction boots, a beaded headband over long flowing hair, and wire-framed glasses. She smoked marijuana, tried LSD, and Inja didn't know what else. Inja, too, had tried pot, but it gave her a headache and made her nervous, ruined for the eight-hour Painting Foundations class the next day. Almaden Chablis was her choice for an altered state, and only on weekends.

The first time Miran visited, Inja dragged her to the free clinic in Providence to get her on the pill. "If you weren't my sister," Miran said, "this would be too weird and totally gross." Inja took that to mean they were great friends with double benefits of sisterhood—the flower-child sisterhood in addition to the literal sisters they were.

Being apart from her mother allowed Inja to understand that Najin had tried to mother her as Grandmother had mothered Najin, but that model fit neither this country nor this time. Inja was one of three female students in RISD's graphic design program, and their little triumvirate had big New York design firms in their sights—not marriage.

One winter break at home, at the kitchen table over tea, her mother told her how scandalous her own marriage was at the ripened age of twenty-four. She had deferred marriage in favor of education and work—and said her father had tried to marry her off at age fourteen to a nine-year-old boy. In the style of the many conversations about Korea they shared at that Formica table, Inja told her Grandmother's version of the same story, and that Grandmother had said, "It's the first time, and maybe the only time, I openly defied your grandfather, but not only had I transferred all my dreams for education upon my child, I could see how thirsty she was to expand her mind." They had a solid cry in that sun-filled kitchen remembering and missing Grandmother in the separate yet similar ways they knew and loved her.

In that moment, Inja remembered wrapping Grandmother's feet and the smell of wet willow bark, and her desire (Uncle's too) to protect her mother from knowledge of this suffering, a secret Inja had easily agreed to keep. Her mother as well as her father had their secrets—about Miran, and Inja couldn't know what else. These were all precedents that venerated keeping secrets from her mother as being rituals of love.

On the train ride back from DC to Providence that winter, Miran napping beside her, Inja gazed at the melting snow in industrial back-lots. Her mother and grandmother had risen like dragons from the sea floor of a centuries-old, neo-Confucian culture of female oppression. She had been given a tremendous gift of two unique women whose lives—whose Korean lives— had already exemplified for her what she could learn from the burgeoning American feminist crusade.

· · ·

Upon graduating from RISD, Inja landed in New York aiming to find a good-paying job in order to go back home, to visit Seoul. Her portfolio was polished enough to impress a RISD alumnus who was the creative director of an eminent firm with significant corporate clients. She was hired for paste-up and whatnot, and became a thrilled and energetic New York City girl, riding the crosstown bus to Park Avenue, striding the streets in her camel-colored maxi coat, long hair swinging as her boot heels echoed in the windy alleys, returning home at night to a small apartment on Twenty-Eighth Street.

The rent had stabilized at $145 a month, and though the teachers' strike, then the sanitation workers' strike and the rising crime did little to endear the city to tourists—or her parents— Inja loved the crowded sidewalks at rush hour, the cheap luncheonettes, and ready access to friends from work and college. Familiarity with her neighborhood made it a home that was hers alone, and one not layered with painful memories or hindered by negotiations to prevent more pain for her parents. The city suited Inja, but two years later her low-paying job hadn't moved her any closer to flying back to Korea. She knew it was time for a change. She would never be assertive enough to advance in the cutthroat culture of the Big Firm, and for all the praise she received for overtime and dedication to her advancement as junior assistant designer, her creativity was credited to the person several rungs above her lowly position on the ladder.

In early spring of 1971 on the steamy bus after work, Inja shook the classifieds open and scanned the *A* columns for advertising artist, *C* for commercial artist, *D* for designer, *G* for graphic designer or graphic artist, and finally the scant *I* category for industrial artist, groaning at the multiple classifications of her profession. By the time she got home, the newspaper was a jumble and her fingers stained black, but she had four torn clippings folded in her checkbook and a lighter step into the elevator toward her junior one-bedroom on the sixth floor, certain it would soon be the sole "junior" in her life.

Inja took the job of marketing designer in the public affairs department of the Port Authority in April 1971 and walked the easy four blocks to work, until two years later when their offices were moved into the newly opened South Tower of the World Trade Center. Antonio from the Italian market up the street turned out to be quite a handyman on multiple levels. Free love was everywhere, adventurous and noncommittal, and the attention from this beautiful man boosted her confidence and softened the seediness of the city for three glorious seasons.

After Miran had finally graduated—she'd

grown lax with her studies and needed another semester—she'd fallen in with a guy who made sandals, belts, and leather wristbands. They took long motorcycle rides to craft fairs, took drugs at rock concerts, and he took all the money she earned as a drugstore cashier. Inja and Miran both agreed she was headed to nowheresville, and Miran came to New York. In Inja's apartment, Miran unpacked her many boxes of books onto new shelves the building super had allowed them to build, with Antonio's help, on the living room wall behind the couch. Inja bought another twin bed, and since they had shared a bedroom, each understood the necessary etiquette for close-quarters living. Miran's new job at an international art dealers' association had little to do with art and everything to do with meeting planning, but the commodity was ultimately art and soon she was in the know for the very hip and growing gallery scene in SoHo and the East Village.

At last, with Miran's help with expenses, Inja's savings account grew. Her satisfaction with work and the growing closeness with her sister renewed her yearning for Korea. They discussed it one night in late October 1972 over a bottle of Ruffino.

"If I go this winter, it should be cheaper," said Inja. "Nobody wants to travel then."

Miran lit a cigarette. "You can't possibly leave

with what we're learning from Deep Throat." She referred to the Watergate break-ins, and her tone turned gleeful. "G. Gordon Liddy's got to go to jail. I almost wish I were home."

"I can't keep track. Korean politics was always like that."

"You have to vote for McGovern before you go, promise? Don't do the Dad thing and pull the lever for Nixon." Miran and her father had become naturalized shortly before Inja arrived. He had registered Independent, though he'd leaned toward Republican ever since Eisenhower, and Miran had registered the same because she liked how it sounded. Their mother and Inja had sworn the Oath of Allegiance to the United States soon after Inja's five-year permanent residency date. They, too, followed Calvin's precedent as Independents.

"I wouldn't! But I'm thinking of going after New Year's, or in February. Do you think I should tell them?"

Miran got up and went to the window. "We have to go downstairs to watch the news with Derek." Derek was their Vietnam vet neighbor directly downstairs, whose copious marijuana aroma wafted up through their windows in summertime. Miran had gotten bold and introduced herself when she smelled it week after week, and she slept with him on occasion. She turned to her sister. "When are we going to buy a TV?"

"When you earn more than one-twenty a week. Use your own savings. So should I tell them?"

"Our parents?"

"I don't want to hurt their feelings after all they'd been through to get me here."

"I'm asking for a TV for Christmas."

"Miran, listen!" Inja cracked a window to release cigarette smoke and lit a candle in an old Chianti bottle. "Do you think I should tell them?"

"All I know is that—based on these cover-ups and conspiracies—whatever you try to hide is going to come out eventually."

"I know, but—"

"How could Dad vote for Nixon when all his cronies were spying on the Democrats?"

"Nixon said he didn't know anything about it."

"Bullshit."

"Hey, getting a little Korean in you wouldn't hurt to clean up that mouth."

"I've got more than a mouth," and Miran flipped her the bird. They laughed.

"You should come with me," Inja blurted.

"What?"

"You should come with me! You'd have until February to save up. It's cheap then to fly. Come on, it would be fun for you to meet Uncle and see the house Dad built."

"I don't know, but you'd definitely have to tell them if I went."

"I will, and I'll help pay your way." This would

cut into the amount she'd set aside for Uncle, but maybe she could work in a store for Christmas.

Miran stood and folded the newspaper. "I'll go if you come downstairs to watch the news right now."

"Outstanding! Bring the wine."

A month later when Miran was out having pizza with Derek, Inja called her father. It was the week before they'd go home for Thanksgiving, and she figured he'd be in a good mood, his man having been reelected president in the biggest landslide in history. Plus it was Wednesday and he'd be working on his Sunday sermon and near the telephone. He would know how best to tell Najin. Inja worried that her mother might feel betrayed. Her father, like Uncle, had always been supportive of her desires, so she feared his reaction less.

After the usual catching up, Inja shifted on the kitchen stool by the wall phone, looking out the window at a brick wall. "Dad, what would you think if I planned to go back to Seoul to visit Uncle?"

"Why, I think it's a fine idea. Your mother and I have often talked about sending you back."

"You have?" Her heart opened to hear this. They knew her better than she thought.

"Of course you'd want to go, and I'm sorry we haven't been able to afford it. Every time we save a few dollars, something goes wrong in the house or the church needs an influx of cash. It gets more expensive to fly every year, and you couldn't go empty-handed. It would take some planning."

She was relieved they'd be on board and touched that they'd considered it. "I've been saving now and have enough for airfare. I can stay with Uncle. This winter? February? Early March? It'll be beautiful in March."

"I see," he said in his measured way. "I'm impressed with how you've managed to save and prepare for a trip like this, but I'm afraid the climate isn't right. I can't allow you to go."

Her ears didn't register this kind of restriction coming from her father to his twenty-six-year-old daughter, and she went on. "I haven't told Uncle—I wanted to run it by you first, and Miran's been thinking about going, too, and that way I won't be traveling alone so you don't have to worry about that part."

"Inja, daughter, you are not hearing me." His pulpit formality made her sit rigid on the stool, as if she were back in a church pew working to digest his heavily theological sermons. Poor Miran hadn't understood one whit of his talks all those Sundays but had had to sit through the service all the same. She'd read through the Methodist hymnal while congregants pretended to look awed or at least engaged out of respect. Back then Inja could almost hear the distractions floating in the air: people's to-do lists, worries about their kids losing Korean language, the youth culture that drew those kids away from the church, what to make for supper, how was it that it was only two minutes into the sermon . . .

"I'm sorry, what did you say?" Inja said.

"To put it bluntly, I forbid you to go."

"Forbid?"

"Hold on. I'm impressed you've been planning so well on your own, and I do think you should go sometime, just not now. Korea still doesn't get attention from American newspapers. Earlier this week, President Park invoked martial law."

"Again?" She didn't know much about South Korean politics anymore, except that tremendous modernization occurred hand in hand with protests about fixed elections and Park Chung Hee's intransigency, including imposing martial law when it got too hot, then lifting it once the populace had been tamed.

"Yes, again." His voice shifted as he tucked the phone on his shoulder and shuffled papers. "It's not even in the Korean newspapers."

"There's always that kind of trouble there—it's been like that since I left."

"This is worse than usual. He's dissolved the National Assembly and undoubtedly plans to rewrite the constitution once more so he can be president for life. It's simply not safe for you to go at this time."

Resistance swelled in her throat. Even with the Vietnam War moratoriums downtown last summer, the terrorist attack at the Munich Olympics, and Watergate, she hadn't once considered the obstacle of political hostilities. She wanted to argue with her father, remind him she had lived through worse and came out okay, and it couldn't possibly be that dangerous for a young woman whose only interest was to visit family. What did all her work and independence mean if she couldn't pursue this principal desire?

He read her silence and said, "These things come and go. As you know, it's been like this for years, but at the moment it's dire—the last vestiges of democracy may be crumbling, and the climate is too uncertain. We think there are blackouts on news from Seoul. I'm not saying you can't go, just not right now."

Inja wiped her tears and runny nose on a tea towel and forced an even-toned response. It wouldn't do for him to know the depth of her disappointment. "Okay" was all she could manage.

"I'll be the first to tell you when it's stable over there. Perhaps next summer. That's not so much longer to wait, and we can bolster your savings by then. See if you can find Korean newspapers in Chinatown to monitor what's going on. In the meantime, I'll talk it over with your mother, so she knows it's on your mind. Agreed?"

She muffled the handset, coughed out the letdown, and blew air to clear her larynx. "Agreed, Father. The newspaper is a great idea. Okay, thanks, I'll call on Sunday as usual."

She lay in bed that night with the longing for home as heavy in her spirit as it was that first year in America, and when Miran came home and asked if she was awake and how the call went, Inja didn't answer.

35

Home Visit

Miran and Inja went home for Christmas 1972, and along with the gift of his old Zenith television to Miran, Calvin gave Inja an all-clear for springtime in Seoul. Martial law had been lifted on December 13 and the crisis had, once again, moved into a phase of relative calm.

By mid-January, Inja had convinced Miran to go with her, especially since their father would pay half her fare and they'd stay at an inn rather than at Uncle's. Miran had been reluctant because the shame amassed over the years for not speaking Korean lay inside her like an immovable boulder, but she chose to go knowing Inja wouldn't embarrass her as her mother had. In her youth if she was with her mother among Koreans, Najin would say with a joking tone and a frown, "She doesn't speak; too stupid to learn." Miran surmised, in retaliation, this was her mother's way to cover her own inability to have taught her daughter Korean, though she was a skilled language instructor. Oh, the irony. But sarcasm couldn't gloss over the blame she cast upon herself—those dining-room lessons when she was a kid were boring and pointless, and she had clamored to be outside playing; then later, she wanted to learn French like everyone else in school—and each similar decision prompted by the need to fit in added another barnacle on the boulder of the Great Pretender.

In March she and Inja went home to see their folks a month before the trip. Inja admitted to the need to visit Takoma Park on the eve of returning to her first home, to assuage feelings of guilt over her divided loyalties. Miran spent the long weekend at home sewing a few skirts, while Inja and her mother hung out in the kitchen and talked. In a quiet moment between seams, Miran overheard Inja asking something like "Mom, is it okay if I go? Don't you want to go back?"

Najin answered with a word and tone that implied "Ugh, no thanks." Their conversation continued in Korean too fast for Miran to grasp, but her mother's strange response piqued her interest.

On Saturday evening before dinner, with Inja and Mom fussing in the kitchen, she brought her father coffee in the living room and sat nearby to hem an A-line skirt, the radio tuned low to classical music.

"Dad, can I ask you something? How come you haven't ever gone back to Korea? Doesn't Mom want to see her brother or home or anything? Don't you want to go?"

"In the past few years, I've asked your mother now and then, but she always says no, her home is here. We didn't live in Seoul for very long, and it's a completely different city now." He explained that Najin had grown up in Kaesong, and he'd grown up in a fishing village and in Pyeongyang, all now in North Korea. After Najin's parents had died, her only desire to visit Korea was to see their graves. "You'll agree that's not exactly an international flight-worthy trip. But you'll visit the graves and can take pictures for her. I'm of your mother's sentiment—our home is here, and it would be difficult for me, as a federal employee who often broadcasts anti-Park views, to travel without attracting unwanted attention."

"You'd be in danger?" Was her father's news program that big a deal?

"No need to take risks when we have little interest in touring Korea at this time. We'll drive up to see some old friends in Long Island, and we'll say goodbye to you at Kennedy Airport. That's about as close as we'll come." He smiled at his silly joke.

Miran sewed awhile. "So . . . why doesn't Mom want to go? Gosh, she hasn't seen her brother for a gazillion years, and Inja says she's never met his kids."

Calvin sighed and set the paper down. "You may as well know they're like oil and water."

"No kidding."

"Nope. Completely opposite in personality. Not close like you and your sister are."

Her father was clueless about lots of sister things, but he was right that they were close, so she believed the oil-and-water thing. Plus, after Inja came, there were fewer letters to Korea and no packages, telegrams, or phone calls. The blue aerogrammes with her uncle's handwriting lay unopened on the sideboard with the junk mail for days before her mother read them.

"It's a little different now," said her father. "Your mother respects him for the fine job he did in raising your sister. But that, too, isn't reason enough to visit Korea."

There was truth to that statement about how Inja was raised. Miran knew for certain Inja was more confident and self-aware than she herself was. People would say things like "That's who I am" or "That's not who I am," and it would only reinforce Miran's alienation from herself. She had no idea what it meant to say things like that. Who was she? Who wasn't she? How was it that Inja seemed to inherently know and she did not? It may have been their different upbringings, Inja having a sentimental uncle and Miran having an anti-sentimental mother, or it may have been as simple as her sister both looking Korean and speaking Korean and therefore being Korean, while she herself only looked Korean. She felt it had more to do with her childhood of silences, the reservoir of words dammed in her throat.

"Okay," she said, gathering up the hemmed skirt and pincushion.

"Okay what?"

"Okay, I'm glad she's not upset that Inja's going back to Korea."

"I wasn't aware it was a concern. She's actually quite excited for your sister's sake. And yours, too, of course. Look here." He showed her a headline: "Nixon Orders New Watergate Probe." "You can ease your mind about the Senate hearings—they won't begin without you."

PART V

HOME

1973

36

Customs

The requirements Inja listed for their two-week journey were reasonable. Miran agreed to keep her long hair neatened into a braid or knotted in a bun, wear skirts and dresses—ergo the sewing—never to curse in any language, eat everything offered but not the entire portion, avoid blowing her nose as if it were a trumpet, avoid laughing out loud and showing all her teeth, and to not smoke cigarettes, which an hour into their flight was Miran's most difficult concession. Trying to sit primly in coach class in her skirt and scratchy sweater, shoulder to shoulder with Inja, she chewed gum with vigor to overcome the nicotine cravings.

"And don't chew gum like that," said Inja. "I can't stand you chewing without me. Give me a piece."

Miran shared her Teaberry. "Is this anything like your first flight?"

"Honestly, I barely remember. I was too miserable to know what was happening." Inja sat by the window, and leaned back to show Miran the cloudscape of wispy peaks. "Beautiful," Inja said. "I had a window seat next to a nice women who gave me gum, but don't remember seeing anything like this, though I must have. I was too nervous to eat or drink anything because I was afraid of the bathrooms on the plane. Too naive."

"And brave," said Miran. She scratched her back against the seat. "Do you know what's weird? I've never really thought about what it was like for you, but considering all the brouhaha in getting on this damned plane, you must've gone through a worse ton of crap to take an overseas flight back then." She saw Inja's lips tighten to restrain a warning and more behavioral cautions. "Oops. Christ. Jeez! Crap!" They laughed.

"What is *brouhaha*?" said Inja.

"It means 'crazy big fuss.' "

"Like Mom made when we left."

Miran sighed and kicked at a lumpy food bundle stuffed beneath the seat in front of her. "Right on."

On the day of departure, almost as if it were a reverse of Inja's arrival, their parents and the Long Island friends with whom they were visiting met them at the airport. Najin had created a brouhaha at JFK International while they waited for the call to board the 707. She insisted they take the big basket of food she'd prepared for the journey, but both were reluctant because of its impossible mass and the pungent kimchi she had surely packed in a leaky jar. Inja conceded by wrapping half of the food in the small table-cloth—a tablecloth!—Najin had tucked on top of the travel-picnic masterpiece. It didn't fully satisfy Najin—"Take fruit, apples, banana!"—but they got away with leaving the kimchi behind.

"She can't help herself," said Inja about their mother's aggressive hospitality. "She didn't think about customs, either."

"She didn't believe they'd feed us, but the stewardess said it's three times for this trip."

"Are you hungry?" Inja leaned toward the bundle under the seat.

"No way. Every time my toe touches it, I get a whiff of garlic." Miran opened her book, *The Farthest Shore* by Ursula K. Le Guin.

Inja glanced at it and said, "Appropriate title for our trip."

"Hah. It's science fiction— is that inappropriate too?"

Inja said of its lurid purple cover of a dragon, "Maybe you keep that in your suitcase while we're there."

"Christ, are we going to a nunnery? Oops." Miran acted out zipping her lips.

"Something like a cloister." Inja smiled. "I haven't been there for ten years, so I'm not sure what to expect."

Miran closed her book and turned it face-down. "Might as well get into practice. Take a guess at the worst to prepare me."

"The worst will be if the house is a wreck, but Uncle says it's all modernized and they have a refrigerator and electric stove. Dad built that house, did you know?"

"You said something about that once, or was it Mom?" She couldn't remember details of the story—more likely she couldn't understand the storyteller's tongue.

"The second worst thing is if our hotel is dirty and awful. I think Uncle booked us into a traditional inn, meaning we'll sleep on the floor."

"I wouldn't mind that, unless there's bugs."

"Right. We have a fund—what's the word—contingent money, but not much. The inn is about twelve dollars a night. Uncle wanted us to stay with them, but Seonil comes home on the weekends from university and the girls are still children. Seonwu is ten because she was born a few weeks after I left—wow, it's been so long . . ." Inja quieted awhile and gazed at the clouds. "I think the baby's six—hardly a baby. I can't wait to meet them. Your cousins!"

Miran's nervous shame surfaced at the prospect of meeting relatives—even children—with whom she couldn't communicate. She would definitely be an idiot in Korea. "If there's a youth hostel, those are a couple of bucks."

"That's actually the least of my worries, so let's make that the third worst thing. Then the second worst thing is if they fight all the time. I'd be sad to see them fight and embarrassed for you."

Miran wrapped her chewed-up gum in paper and took out a fresh piece. "No hints from his letters if they're still fighting?"

"I wish you could read his letters. Next time I'll translate. He's sweet and sentimental. After he gives me news about the family, he fills the rest with how much he loves us, his sister—Mom—especially."

"From what I've seen, she doesn't exactly reciprocate," Miran said, remembering what her father had said.

"They're like reverse yin and yang—he's the soft loving side and she's the hardworking practical side." Inja shifted to catch her eyes. "Do you remember when you told me neither of our parents ever said 'I love you' and you'd never heard them say that to each other?"

"Was that in candlelight in our bedroom or hiding out in the woods, avoiding chores? Oh, ha. That's right. You're the good one who loves washing dishes and vacuuming."

"I love that miracle machine." Inja reached up to twist open the fan. "But we were talking about love. You said you couldn't remember the last time they hugged you, and I was amazed. Uncle is the complete opposite. I can also see how it's so different here for Mom that she would stay old-fashioned—waiting for me, she once said about not being diligent with English. It's ironic to hear her say that Grandfather was the stubborn, old-fashioned one."

"She's always been grossed out by all the *love love love* shit on TV, and she acts disgusted when she sees people kissing or hugging."

"Upper-class propriety is important to her, Miran. It's pure Confucian to assume parental love without showing it."

At such moments when Inja sounded exactly like their mother, Miran felt excluded and American-ugly. But she preferred not to talk about love either. In that way, she supposed she was her mother's daughter.

The stewardess served beverages and peanuts. Inja said, "I can't believe I didn't eat or drink anything on the flight over. When I was a kid, we used to beg for a single piece of gum, and they served many entire meals for free on that plane that I was too afraid to touch."

"What do you mean you begged for gum? On the streets? You were that poor?"

From then on and in the hours between the movie, the first and second meals, nibbling on treats from Najin's food bundle and fidgety upright napping, Inja talked about her childhood and youth in Korea. Entranced by the stories and struck by the poverty and making-do of the way they lived, Miran's memory expanded when she connected the packages sent to Korea as being useful not for the generic Korean orphans for whom she cleaned her plate, but for her sister's family and their entire church community. Some of her earliest memories were about cartons going to Korea. How could she have known so little about her own family, even the names of her first cousins, and about her country of origin? The last was easier to answer: because, duh, her country was America.

37

Seoul

A delay in Tokyo made them an hour and twenty minutes late, and though Inja had told Uncle they'd take a taxi from Gimpo, she knew he'd be at the airport and probably with a small crowd of people from church. It would be similar to how they'd departed JFK with brouhaha, and how she'd arrived in America with hullabaloo ten years ago. A transpacific flight was no everyday event, and her return would be as big a reunion with her Korean family as it had been with her American family. Though the years of separation were fewer behind this reunion, the circumstances were fraught with as much emotion and expectation as was the reunion after fifteen childhood years apart from her parents. The captain announced the imminent landing, and the stewardesses roamed the aisles to check passenger protocol. Inja shook Miran's elbow to wake her.

On the 707's approach to Gimpo, the view was clear—and completely foreign. It was April, the same as the month she had left. With this thought a flash of memory surfaced from when that plane had ascended—the mountains and countryside surrounding Seoul beginning to green with trees finally reaching maturity after the devastation of war. Now the view was gray and ugly, crowded with buildings and industry, raw clusters of high-rise apartments, and as they descended, road congestion and black poles strung with criss-crossed wires.

"Wow," said Miran, leaning in to look.

"I know. Not terribly inviting."

"But I'm glad we're here," she said, being kind. "It's wild and different, and an adventure not only for me, but for you, too, after so many years."

They deplaned, and going through customs took forever since they had extra luggage filled with wrapped gifts, but it all passed muster with their American passports. Inja couldn't remember what credentials she'd traveled with to America, but in order to acquire her passport, her father had found in his filing cabinet old affidavits about her birth, and her certificate of naturalization. As the officials inspected their luggage, Miran hung by her side wide-eyed.

Inja's first shot of home warmed her—the familiarity of her own language all around her, the signage and crowded sense of space. She got a porter for their numerous bags, and at last they swung through the glass doors and into a mass of people craning their necks looking for those who belonged to them. And there was Uncle with his graying crown of hair—a little wild and exposing a balding head—his unmistakable huge grin and arms opened wide to take her in.

"That's him," Inja said. "Ajeossi!"

"It's you!" he cried.

With her nose against his cheek, she smelled home, and they both burst into tears.

"You're so grown up!" He held her apart and seemed confused when searching her face. "The same but all grown up. A real beauty."

"And you—showing all your distinguished years." He'd take this as a compliment as would any elder worth his Confucian salt. Inja introduced him to Miran, and after he hugged her, his eyes widened at her appearance, too.

"Both such women—where did the children go?"

They were soon surrounded by cousins, the inevitable church people, and the best surprise—Ara with her husband and their toddler girl in his arms. Such shouting of introductions, cries of delight, wiping of tears—such utter joy.

And confusion. Somehow they spilled out of the flat ugly terminal and got sorted into various cars—here the churchmen proved most useful—everyone counted and promises made for visits tomorrow and tomorrow. In Elder Hwang's car, Miran, Inja, and Uncle sat in the back, and her young-man cousin Seonil sat in the front passenger bucket seat.

"Inja child," said Uncle, "you're all grown up. I can't get over it! I was expecting you to be like when you left." He laughed. "How did it happen?"

Inja didn't want to bring up painful memories, though he repeated this sentiment several times on the drive home, and she changed the subject, asking about his daughters and church. Seonil, in whom she clearly saw a young version of Uncle, seemed equally aware of the pitfalls of memory and helped her divert Uncle's attention by asking about their parents, their own jobs, and what it was like to live in New York City. Seonil's fascination with both her and Miran's work made Inja understand that Korean women were still relegated to home economics and jobs in service and menial positions, or in education. Here she was, both feet firmly home in Seoul, but thoroughly altered because her footsteps had traced the hard-won paths of liberation and opportunity in America.

Conscious of Miran beside her, Inja did her best to translate and include her, and Uncle, Seonil, and even Elder Hwang were generous in asking her specific questions through Inja, such as what she'd studied at university, did she like Korean food, did they have traffic like this in New York, and soon—the work of translation performed best by the supremely patient or one able to be invisible—Inja merely answered the questions for her sister, who seemed to get the rhythm of these conversations and relaxed. Inja knew Miran understood more Korean than she admitted, especially to herself. Miran had built a wall between herself and the sounds of her childhood, sounds that had always been there for her. Inja hoped this trip would crack that barrier and that not only would Miran see her Korean background and how it had shaped her home life, but also that the experience would allow her to see herself anew.

"You sisters are much alike," said Elder Hwang, "but she stands out differently. She looks more foreign than you."

"It's because they're grown now," said Uncle.

Inja understood Elder Hwang's observation but was glad Miran couldn't understand it. Even in the tight quarters of his tiny automobile, Miran's very posture made her stand out as foreign, while her own backbone had immediately melded into the comfort of her homeland.

They rode up the street to home, and though the house was diminutive and dingier than what she remembered, Inja's spirit surged with recognition and reminiscence. She stole glances at Hyo's house across the street, but it was so dilapidated she knew his family no longer lived there. Uncle caught her glance and said, "They moved many years ago. The young man always had trouble with the police, especially when he went to university, and I think his mother took him south to protect him. His father lives in a big mansion in Pyeongchang-dong with his third wife. But he's still a friend to me. I'll always be indebted to him for the graves."

She'd forgotten that Hyo's father had regularly infused cash without strings into Uncle's life at moments of need. Uncle said the former brick magnate took advantage of President Park's generous tax benefits intended to expand core industries and had furthered his holdings with glass, ceramic, and porcelain. His mention of police trouble aroused concern and interest in Hyo's whereabouts. Perhaps Yuna still lived in the same house—unless she was also somewhere unknown with Hyo.

They climbed out of the car, and the mix of smells filled her with nostalgia—the sweet perfume of the princess tree in the tenant's front yard with its first blooms, the sharp warmth of hilltop breezes tinged with the faint dusky odor of sewers. One's nose induced memories more vivid than images even after an ocean apart.

Aunt appeared more aged than Uncle, but perhaps it was the bad permanent frizz and dye job on her hair. Inja decided she would treat her to a beauty salon. Aunt's mouth and chin retained wisps of her youthful beauty, though her eyes remained shrewd, even when they softened to fuss over Seonil. Inja recalled how having children had changed her and hoped it had benefited their cousins.

They had a simple dinner at the house, chattering madly to bridge the years, then Inja distributed gifts from America. Afterward Miran claimed sudden and thorough exhaustion. Though too excited to feel tired, sand did tug at the edges of Inja's eyes, so Seonil found a taxi to escort them to the Top Inn several blocks away, a distance walkable without luggage, and perfectly clean with modern amenities like a hot-water shower, sheets, and padding beneath the bedding rolled out on the floor.

Thursday 4.19

The minute I wrote the date Korean style, I saw it was the same as the Masan Uprising from so long ago. Being back feels like everything was so long ago, and of course it was. I'm too wound up to sleep, but Miran is snoring like a man. Good thing we aren't staying at the house! It's so small and cluttered, and though I knew I would see it differently, I'm dismayed by how they live. I don't think I could've tolerated staying there now, snobbish to say. Uncle seems to have gotten only sweeter. He keeps searching my face, as if the naive teenager he said goodbye to will resurface. I'm surprised to see him aged, but he's less changed than I am obviously, and what is it they say—resilience of youth or, in my case, resilience of memory? I don't think I should give money to Uncle because he might give it to the church like he did in Busan. I will have to find private time to get the real stories from Seonil or, god forbid, from Aunt. Wow, I just swooned with sleepiness so I see what Miran meant.

Seonil alone time
Ara alone time
cheap but good restaurants?
take girls shopping
visit graves + buy picnic so no brouhaha
   hullaballoo
church Sunday
Aunt beauty parlor
museum (?), palace, temples and sights
   Miran will like
markets?
English guidebook for Miran
Yuna?

Seonil excused himself from most of his university classes their first week in Seoul and shuffled them around town with Uncle and sometimes Aunt. The girl cousins joined the sisters in the evenings for dinner and bonded with Miran Unnee. After the first few days when Miran seem strangled with Korean words fighting to find their shape on her tongue, Inja overheard her speaking and laughing with them—simple stuff in simple language—and she was pleased to hear how much her resistance had eased.

They walked or tried to take buses, but the terrible fumes made Miran nauseated, and though taxis weren't much better, they were cheap and not too hard to find. Then Elder Hwang decided he knew Seoul better than anyone and designated himself tour guide to the two young ladies from America, and they had their chauffeur—without cost but with its own price in limiting their freedom to roam. Propriety demanded they accept his suggestions about what to see. Seoul had only gotten uglier than what Inja remembered, though she knew her memory was rosy-colored with sentimentality. Signage was everywhere, but all in Korean and frequently wrong, which added to the difficulty of following directions. The narrowest streets had the biggest store signs masking how tiny each shop was, with most of the goods displayed in layers and piles on rickety tables and mats on the street. This was Miran's favorite pastime, wandering the markets.

"But you never buy anything," Inja said one

night at dinner with the family at a restaurant near the house, by then six days in Seoul and accustomed to drinking lukewarm bottled beverages or searing hot coffee, and avoiding raw vegetables and unskinned fruit.

"I can't bargain but it doesn't matter. There's nothing I'd buy. It's just so cool to see what's on display—from salt to quilts to plucked little chickens with their heads and feet. I saw a pig being butchered when you went out with Ara yesterday."

"So that's why you didn't eat any meat last night, after she went through so much trouble and expense. You broke a rule." Inja was kidding, though. Miran was one hundred percent on board: no cussing, no smoking, no hippie behaviors. As if she'd done it all her life, she covered her mouth when she laughed or chewed something unwieldy, dressed in a skirt and good loafers, and sat erect on the floor, her legs modestly side-saddled rather than crossed.

Miran wasn't at all afraid to roam, but Inja was terrified for her alone in the city when they went separate ways. Her sister said she couldn't bear to see another university, glossy government building, or new luxury hotel, places forced upon them by their host—Elder Hwang's "price"—hoping to impress them with Park's achievements. Inja had also seen sectors of debilitating poverty, especially driving through

438

the Seongdong neighborhood by the river when she and Ara toured new medical facilities at Hanyang University, where Ara's husband was taking night classes in radiology.

The previous evening, using the palace as her compass, Miran had found her way from Geumcheongyo market back to the inn, where Ara and Inja had picked her up to have dinner at Ara's apartment. Inja was certain Ara didn't often have meat, but that night she served fish and pork. Her husband was at the university, and Miran played with the baby girl, talking a blue streak of English, the child talking back with equal enthusiasm in her own brand of jabber. Miran's disposition with children was a new and welcome discovery, and Uncle said dozens of times that she'd be a terrific wife and mother. Inja joined in the food prep at Ara's electric stove, and they stifled guilty laughter remembering Aunt's terrible cookery and her limp and bitter kimchi. "It's why everyone in her family is slim," Inja said, and Ara slapped her arm.

During that meal, morsels of pork kept appearing in Inja's bowl, a mystery solved after she caught Miran's chopsticks slipping her food when Ara was preoccupied. She'd had to eat double her share and had indigestion all night. The resistance of her stomach to home cooking surprised her, until she remembered those first weeks in Takoma Park when she had to take awful medicine and saw terrible things in the toilet afterward.

So now at this restaurant, the simple meal of fiery soups and boiled vegetables was a relief. Miran was saying, "And some of the shop owners make their displays artistic to the max, weaving fish in chains with straw ropes, scallions piled up like mermaid's hair, big shallow baskets of rice, and all kinds of grains I can't even guess at. What are those red blocks of some dried edible they tie up in neat packages? And the smells— fresh-ground red peppers and rotting produce, crisp against the pungent smells of earth."

"What's she so excited about?" said Uncle.

"She likes going to the markets." Simpler to summarize her anthropological explorations.

"Yah, she's easy to amuse—she'll make a great wife! Go to Namdaemun—show her the art supplies—and how about Gyeongdong herb market? Get some ginseng for your parents."

"Good idea." Inja turned to Miran. "Uncle says you'll make a great wife since you love the markets so much."

She laughed and didn't even roll her eyes.

"He suggests the herbal medicine market and a big commercial market by the South Gate."

"Sounds swell to me, but does it fit your agenda?" When Inja had shown her the to-do list their first morning in Seoul, Miran had ribbed her need for order and control.

440

Inja sniffed and said to Uncle, "And what can we get for you or Aunt? Do you need special medicine? You seem as strong as ever." He launched into a soliloquy about his vigor versus what the doctors were saying about osteo-arthritis—how he walked everywhere, and how his artwork was still in demand. Seonil gave Inja a look then, and she added it to her discussion list for their private talk. They'd arranged the "alone time with Seonil" for that night, using the excuse that he wanted to show them his housing at Yonsei University, where he majored in history and philosophy.

Craving drinks—and cigarettes, said Miran—the sisters took Seonil to the New Namsan, a Western-style luxury hotel, and settled at a corner table in the darkened bar. They hadn't been welcomed with much enthusiasm—the patrons were entirely men, Westerners and Korean businessmen—but when Miran ordered "Johnnie Black, neat, seltzer chaser, no ice" in English, the waiter's bearing changed from out-right rude to obsequious. Over Crown beers, Inja grilled Seonil about Uncle's finances and health. She learned that without the tenants in the front house, there'd be no income—his kinds of jobs were rare. They depended on her mother's checks, which Najin regularly sent even after her job at Fort Holabird had ended a few years ago, though she still made kimchi. Except for the increased workload for Aunt and the return to terrible cooking, they were happy when Ara got married four years ago and left them, freeing a bedroom and having one less mouth to feed.

"I have money for him," Inja told Seonil, "but I'm afraid he'll give it to the church. What needs to be done in the house? Is this something you can take care of?"

"Yes, with Mother's help. They need a new refrigerator and repairs in the bathroom. They installed a hot-water heater in the front house, but they could use one too."

"Aunt won't tell him about the money?"

He slumped and frowned but said nothing. Even after a beer, Seonil displayed not a scrap of the sunny, happy little boy Inja remembered. He was quiet and painfully pleasant. She resisted reaching out to tickle his ribs to stir him up, and now she could guess why. "I see."

He turned as if to study the diminishing number of people at the bar, and Inja said, "Miran, why don't you get cigarettes." Though she'd said it in Korean, her sister got the message and went out to the front lounge.

Inja ordered another round, and after the waiter left, she said, "Still fighting."

"They've been polite to each other since you've come. At least the girls can understand what a normal home is like, even if it's only two weeks."

He sat with hands between his knees, shoulders sloped, a practiced smile beneath intelligent but withdrawn eyes.

"And how about you? How are you getting along?"

"Fine. I stay out of trouble—I don't even join the campus protests, though I support them and I should be out there."

Miran came back. "I guess I've quit. It tastes awful. Here." She slid the Winstons to Seonil. "Maybe you know someone who'd want these."

He pocketed the cigarettes. "You should've bought cheaper Korean tobacco, but it'll impress my roommate."

Inja didn't need to translate; Miran understood—more and more each day. In ending their conversation, Inja said to Seonil, half in English, "They call that *keeping your nose clean,* at least I think that's correct." And to Miran, "What's slang for 'stay out of trouble'?"

"Keep your head down. Keep your hands clean. Take it easy. Stay cool, man."

He tried them all and they laughed—the first time he'd freely laughed since they'd arrived.

"Stay out of the doghouse," said Miran.

Inja raised her glass. "Have you met anyone special?" she said, and was rewarded with a wash of light over his features.

"Maybe." He blushed. "Too soon to tell."

"Keep to the straight and narrow," said Miran.

"Who is she? Tell me more!"

"She wants to be an educator, to get her master's degree in America. But everybody does."

"Love it or leave it," said Miran, making quarter rotations in her swivel seat.

"You too?" Inja said to Seonil about American studies. "Maybe I can help."

"I'd like to, but I'm the eldest . . ."

"I understand, but let me know if you want to study there, will you?"

"Keep the peace, baby," said Miran.

Seonil said, "I must *keep the peace baby,*" and drained his beer to their laughter. "I'm serious though," he said. "Even after my sisters are grown and married."

Miran asked what he'd said, and Inja patted her leg to say she'd tell her later. They sat quietly a few moments. "You were so young," she asked him, "do you remember our grandparents?"

"Harabeoji, not that much." He gave an odd smile. "What I remember is being afraid. He must have done something terrible with a turtle. I detest turtles—it's like a phobia."

"How strange." Inja didn't have the heart to tell him about the medicine he'd been forced to swallow—it would only validate his fears.

"He was already sick by the time I was born, wasn't he?" said Seonil. "The night he died is mostly how I remember him, unfortunately. And the years after that, Father's terrible dreams

444

about him being buried in a coffin full of water." He shivered.

"You remember that!"

"Only because when Halmeoni died and we buried her, it proved he'd been buried in an underground stream. Surely you remember—you were there. Ugh, I've got chills."

Inja told Miran what they were talking about, and Miran confessed to finding the photographs of Grandfather's funeral and being horror-struck by the gruesome images. "Mom shouted with nightmares for weeks," Miran said. "But she always had crazy dreams, like you told me she dreamed you were a girl. I've always wondered if she dreamed about me."

Inja hid an inner pang about this reference to Miran's birth and explained to Seonil what she'd said about the nightmare. His eyes grew wide. He hadn't known Uncle and Najin had shared this dream. More than all the other topics of conversation that evening, this one story about the filament of dream connecting a geographically divided family bonded them beyond the barriers of language, time, distance, and difference. When they parted that evening, Seonil's hug—though brief—felt to Inja as warm and genuine as Uncle's.

"How bad was it?" Miran asked when they were settled in their bedding at the inn.

"Cost us the same as three nights here," she said. "Worth it, though."

"That's not what I meant, you idiot."

Inja punched her and told her about Aunt and Uncle's fighting.

"Makes sense." She yawned.

"What?"

"The girls are starved for attention—it's why they like me so much."

"Are you kidding? You're the rich American cousin who swears and laughs without covering her mouth. Who wouldn't love that? Seriously, you've been great with them, almost like you understand everything they're saying."

"I don't, but I also kinda do. It's strange—like my earwax got cleaned out."

"Oh, ick."

For a time the only sound in their room was the dripping showerhead in the next-door bathroom, the loud ticks of the second hand on the electric alarm clock, and an occasional passing car outside. Miran's breath grew even, and Inja remembered what she'd wanted to tell her. It was a lie, but it was an important lie. "Miran, are you still awake?"

"Umhmm yup."

"Mom did have a dream before you were born." Inja chose her words carefully so as not to make everything she said a lie.

"She did?"

"She never told you?"

"She might've told me, but I didn't get it."

"She told me at some point—can't remember when, but it was after I'd been in America awhile." Inja closed her eyes and conjured Najin's animated storytelling voice, and almost as if Najin's spirit were supporting her lie, she heard it as clearly as if her mother were talking from the room's shadows. The tones blended with memories of Grandmother's dramatic cadence, and so the story flowed from three generations of voices. "She was in water, like with me, but not the sea. She stood in a freshwater brook, and the water was like music as it ran between her feet and the pebbles in the streambed. She was trying to catch a little silvery fish darting between her ankles, but it was slippery, fast, and elusive. She finally caught it and lifted it high from the water, and that's how she knew you were a girl."

"Oh wow." Her usual response but soft.

Inja wasn't sure where it was coming from, but something propelled her forward, a sensation that could have been like the dream connection between Uncle and her mother, or the ghostly encouragement of Grandmother. "She said the water droplets from the squirming fish scattered all around her like diamonds, and it made her so happy she laughed out loud. That's what makes our mother different from most Korean mothers— she loved having daughters. Her laughter woke her up, and when she did, Dad was also awake laughing because he'd had the very same dream."

"Wow. Double wow."

"You're that special."

"That's crazy heavy." She remained quiet for a long time.

It was a righteous lie, if there could be such a thing. Inja would alert her mother to the story, but it was entirely possible she already knew. The ceiling of their room seemed far and airy from where she lay on the floor. It was a squared-off ceiling, but the night and shadows had rounded its edges like arches in a chapel. "You're the crossover daughter," she said, "bridging together Mom and Dad, like Korean and American. Like you and me."

"Thanks for telling me."

She heard subdued tears in her voice. "And I love you, too," Inja said.

"Me too."

Toward the end of their final week in Seoul, Miran took to bed with her books and a stomach bug, and Inja roamed the neighborhood with Uncle to check out his routine haunts, pleased to find his daily bathhouse clean and a cozy gathering place for elders with whom he socialized for hours, until his fingers and toes were wrinkled soft with moisture. Later that afternoon, Inja left to find dinner for Miran and went down the hill toward the main road. Impulse made her take a turn toward her old school—and there she was in front of Yuna's house. She wasn't even sure if it was the same house, with kids' toys in the yard and differences she couldn't quite name, but she heard the Temptations singing "Just My Imagination" and stopped to listen long enough to hear it segue to the next song, meaning the *Sky's the Limit* album was playing, and loud. All things combined gave her courage to holler at the open gate, "Yeobosayo?" but no one heard. She went into the yard, called out at the kitchen door, and this time was rewarded with the music cutting off, a baby's cries protesting the sudden silence, and the sound of footsteps.

Yuna's face looked exactly the same, and her shoulder-length hair was cut like Inja's. Her eyes got big, then bigger, and she screamed Inja's name. Inja screamed hers back, and they were in each other's arms, all distance erased. Yuna drew her inside, sat her down in the main room, and plopped the crying baby in her lap, a three-month-old boy as fat and round as a ten-kilo bag of rice. She served barley tea and ddeok, sweet rice cakes, and right away showed Inja her wedding album from two years ago—to show that she had not married Hyo.

"He's handsome," Inja said of the bookish-looking fellow in the photos beside Yuna, a serious bride. "But you're as gorgeous as ever. Where'd you meet? What's his job?"

They caught each other up on the decade in the

next few hours. Yuna had met him at the temple where she went regularly to honor her grandmother, where he also was a regular, lighting incense for both his parents who'd died in the war. He was a Korean-language instructor to U.S. Army personnel and worked mostly evenings. Of Yuna's grandmother's death, Inja said, "She was so patient with us and always soft-spoken. You know I would've been at the temple. I'll never forget how you came to church both times for me."

"It's what friends do," Yuna said, and in the short awkward moment that followed, Inja asked to use her telephone to call the inn. The owners said they'd be sure to give Miran the message that she'd be late and would also serve her rice gruel. She and Yuna prepared a simple dinner from what was in her refrigerator, and Yuna nursed the baby while Inja sautéed greens and doled out rice.

Yuna put the Temptations back on the stereo. "I can only play it when he's at work—he hates my music. But the baby loves it." She patted him as he rolled on a blanket gurgling happily. "And naturally it's one of your favorite groups too, right?"

"They'd have to be, if they're your favorite." She smiled. "But I honestly do love them." Talking thus with Yuna was comforting and as ordinary as the shape and size of this familiar room with its plain lacquered floor, the particular quality of light from the alley shining through her windows, the intense rhythms of American music that Yuna had brought into Inja's life. "My mother isn't a fan of soul or rock-and-roll," Inja said, "and she suffered, though willingly, with two teenage girls. The only music she appreciates is on the piano or hymns."

"Did you ever get those piano lessons?"

"Only a few—I was too old to learn how to play well." She had a vivid memory of sitting on the bench beside Hyo, their thighs and shoulders touching.

Yuna picked at the few remaining morsels in her rice bowl. "Did it ever get better? All I remember is how miserable we all were you had to leave."

Pain jabbed Inja's heart, and she sipped hot tea to hide the surprise of tears. She had hoped returning to Korea would resolve those old hurts, but her tears proved that such bitter memories were not so easily appeased, even with time.

Yuna set her chopsticks across her bowl and touched Inja's knee. "I missed you terribly and that business with Hyo was a mistake. I think I was trying to have you back by going with him. That sounds crazy, but it's how much I missed you."

"Never mind." Inja took her hand. "Think how young we were. It means so much to see you happy and well"—the strains of reverberating laughter faded at the end of the record—"and still obsessed about music, even if it's weird music."

Yuna laughed, slung the baby to her shoulder, and showed Inja a long shelf of albums. "You pick something. At least my father still manages to find me LPs. And once when my husband's students had asked about me, he told them I liked American music, and now they give him record albums—some brand-new—which is also how we have all this equipment; the soldiers advised him on what to buy. We don't have eight-track yet."

She displayed and described the features of her stereo system, and Inja admired the turntable, amplifier, tuner, speakers, and reel-to-reel. Inja thumbed through Yuna's eclectic album collection: Carole King, Sarah Vaughan, Chick Corea—Yuna laughed that her father bought it thinking it was a French girl singing about Korea—Simon and Garfunkel, Stevie Wonder, the Beatles . . . and dozens of others. Inja chose *The Golden Hits of Lesley Gore*, since she remembered the two of them singing, "It's my party and I'll cry if I want to," as loud as they could, twirling around this very room with scarves flapping.

"I'll do the music if you burp him." Yuna handed her son over and attended to the equipment with obvious pleasure. She brushed the album grooves with a velvet anti-lint roll, and when the needle dropped, she turned various knobs for optimal sound.

"From elementary school teacher to sound engineer," Inja said. The former was Yuna's profession the few years before she was married, and like with Seonil, Yuna's unwarranted praise and admiration of Inja's and Miran's jobs exposed more about the feminist privileges the two sisters enjoyed that she'd taken for granted.

They cleaned the dishes, then Yuna fed her son once more and laid him asleep on bedding spread nearby. She cracked open a bottle of beer, they poured each other's glasses, and Inja said, "Tell me what happened to Hyo. Uncle says his father has a third wife, but he doesn't know any more than that."

"You don't know? I thought for sure you knew. He was arrested, then when he got out, he went to America."

She stifled concerned surprise—and amusement at her friend's assumption she'd know he was in America merely because she was in America. "Arrested for protesting? I hope it wasn't on suspicion of being a communist."

"It was for a protest when Park was tired of the students on the streets and sent the police to shut it down. I heard he was questioned but doubt if he was tortured. His father bought his way out the next day, then found a way to send him to America."

"He went to college in the U.S.? Where?"

"This was later, after university. He graduated in sociology at SNU."

The preeminent and prestigious Seoul National University required impossible entrance examinations that denied ninety-six percent of its applicants. "He was always more intelligent than all of us put together," Inja said.

"But he could be stupid, too, especially about his passions and politics. He's in California. He was always in trouble with some of the professors for organizing protests and writing manifestos, but after university he kept it up, always the idealist." She lowered her voice. "Then two years ago, he joined the masses and got arrested with those very same masses. He loved talking about 'joining the masses.' How could he not get in trouble? Junghi and I are still friends, and last he heard, Hyo lives with a cadre of anti-Park sympathizers in America. They admire him and consider him a leader in the movement. I think he's seeking asylum."

It had grown dark, and Yuna turned on a few lamps and played Joan Baez, the volume low.

"Are you in touch with him at all?" Inja said.

"Even if I were interested, it's impossible with a husband and baby. Do you want me to ask Junghi if he knows how to reach him?"

A quick inner assessment authenticated Inja's conviction. In this case, she could put the past behind her. She wondered if his "cadre of sympathizers" were like a cult, and he their charismatic leader. She could see him in that role. Though she felt concern for his well-being and peace of mind, he was safe and in the land of the free. "No, but please tell Junghi I'm sorry I didn't see him this time around."

It was near eight o'clock, and she said she had to go. She hadn't thought out this visit enough to have a gift for Yuna, but dearly wanted to give her something. She removed the ring she hadn't taken off since her mother had given it to her, its nickel coating mostly gone, the heavy gold worn smooth over the years. "I want you to have this," and she slipped it on Yuna's finger. Of course her friend protested, and Inja closed her fingers around the ring. "You see how it fits you perfectly, and it's important to me that you wear it. Will you?"

Yuna's eyes reddened with tears, and she hugged Inja, but being Yuna she had to refuse several more times until Inja threatened she wouldn't come see her next time if she didn't accept it. Saying there would be a next time made it real—a promise she wanted to keep more than a thinning gold ring given by her father to her mother, who by accepting it had shown forgiveness for his years apart from her. She couldn't remember exactly when or what Mother had said when she'd given her the ring, but she did remember accepting it as a way to ease her mother's concern about her "transition," though at that time she wasn't yet ready to forgive. And for years now, she'd felt no blame toward her parents for the reunion that had caused her so much pain. Without blame, there was no need for forgiveness.

In the dark walk back to the inn, Inja felt the unexpected relief of her empty finger, glad that circle of guilt-ridden gold was returned to Korea—to Yuna, with whom she'd be friends until the end of her days.

Tuesday, 5.1, Seoul

Two days before departure. Mixed feelings. Many feelings. Accomplished all my list plus more. Aunt loves her fancy hair, and Uncle teases about her revitalized beauty and makes her cheeks pink. Gave $300 to Seonil, and he accepted it like the man of the house. He's placid but there's fire in him still. The eldest and only son, it's all on him, and that matters a great deal to Uncle. I doubt if it would matter that much to our mother if she had a son, but what's she going to say having had only daughters? I don't think it matters to Father; his older brother had many sons, so the Cho line is safe. It raises the entire question of the eldest child and his or her (my?) responsibility. Being here brings up old injustices I'd forgotten about or buried. I'll talk it over with Uncle one last time tomorrow.

I saw Yuna yesterday—a perfect visit. Miran wanted to stay in bed. I stopped at a medicine shop on the way back to the inn and got advice and herbs to make goldenseal and blackberry tea, and she's better now, middle of night.

I loved spending the day with Uncle, though it'll never be like it was before. Now I'm the one making him feel like royalty, treating him to ice cream and pens, brushes and paper. Aunt mostly stays home. Seonil told me she had left home at age eight, but that's about all he knew about her early years. She must have had a hard life, and I should think more kindly about her, but it's difficult when I remember how mean she was. It made me sad to hear that she and Uncle still fight. They've been on best behavior with us.

Last Saturday Miran spent all her souvenir money buying the girls Parcheesi, Silly Putty, View-Master, Etch A Sketch, and boxed candies at Shinsegae

Department Store, which Elder Hwang insisted we visit. I didn't mind—I remembered its European exterior as housing the U.S. Army PX and was glad to see it modernized and Koreanized. Is that like me? Modernized and wanting to be Koreanized again? I don't completely know what I expected in coming back, but I hear myself calling each place home—and rather than being polarizing, it's a simple word whose definition can be shared in two countries, which makes it all easier to bear.

I have ddeok for Uncle that Yuna gave me. She and I are renewed friends, equals in a way like no other friend I know. When I think about it, I've known Yuna less years than Miran, and maybe it's because we were friends when no one else wanted to be friends with us that everything about her feels more deeply familiar to me as a sister—as Miran says of me—a real Korean sister. I'm not at all upset about Hyo. I can regard our youthful love with gratitude and respect. I only feel sad he's chosen such an angry lot in life, and hope he'll marry someone smarter than he is so he'll do what she says.

38

Protections

Miran still felt rocky, and they were both happy to hang out with Uncle at the house on their last full day. They filled a taxicab's trunk with market bounty: bundles of dried seafood, grains, mushrooms, beans and roots, fresh greens, and kimchi makings, and the sisters cooked the perishables all day and packed dishes into the freezer until the girls came home from school. "We should cook like this at home," said Miran, bottling the last of the radish kimchi.

"We're eating ramen and eggs for the rest of the year. Our budget is blown."

The cousins in their navy-blue sailor-styled school uniforms came into the kitchen, shouting, "Miran Unnee!" and Seonmi threw her arms around Miran's waist.

"Your fan club," Inja said.

"Greetings, children, here are apples," Miran said in exaggerated Korean, making them giggle. "Let's eat apples!" and she put them to work washing and slicing the fruit in the decorative way Najin had taught them, each wedge sitting on a peel cut like a leaf.

Inja and Miran had already said goodbye to Seonil, now back in his dorm to study for an examination. Uncle returned from the bathhouse, Aunt woke from her afternoon nap, and Inja sat with them in the main room nibbling on fruit and sipping lukewarm pineapple juice, while Miran taught the girls how to play Parcheesi in their bedroom. Inja had tried to dust and declutter somewhat, but without drawers and closets, straightening up was limited to folding clothes and lining up books and papers in tidy piles. She wouldn't touch Uncle's desk for fear he'd never find anything, but she did linger over the pages and pages of his fine calligraphic writing where he'd copied chapters from the Bible on the backs of old calendars. She wondered if Miran knew anyone in New York who might be interested in selling his work, and shelved this idea to research at home and discuss with him on the next visit. She would come back again, she knew.

"Don't come to the airport tomorrow," Inja said. "Too much trouble, and I don't want the girls to miss more school." She and Uncle sat beside each other on a row of cushions on the floor and leaned against pillows lining the sitting room wall. Aunt sat on the opposite side of a low table between them. The two grimy windows on the west wall had haphazard curtains that allowed weak streams of light, but it was bright enough to see Uncle's portraits of Grandfather and Grandmother, warmth exuding from their eyes and the colored paints.

"I'll come back so there's no need for prolonged goodbyes," Inja added.

"Elder Hwang already promised to drive us so I'm going, but you're right, there's no room for anyone else." He studied her face and shook his head. "You're so grown—it surprises me each time I look at you."

He had undoubtedly repeated this statement a hundred times, and it reminded her of Grandmother's repetition. "Here I am, Ajeossi, the same inside." For Inja, returning to him was more congruent with her memories. He was wrestling with their changed roles. She'd grown independent of him as a daughter, but he had missed the gradual distancing that comes from witnessing a child's maturity at home. So perhaps his ready demonstration of father-figure-to-child love could not so easily shift to her adult self.

While they talked, Inja listened for Miran and the kids: bouts of tapping—their wooden pawns counting moves, dice tosses—and shouts and laughter. They were absorbed playing in the room she had once shared with Grandmother. She hadn't noticed if the corner shelf where she'd kept special gifts from her mother's packages was still there. Would the girls display their presents from Miran on that shelf, listing each item's best features on scraps of imaginary paper as she had? But now they had plenty of real paper and pencils.

She said to Uncle, "I regret it took so long to come back."

Uncle rubbed his knees. "Never mind that. It was a hard day when you went into the plane. I could see you from the window waving, and that's when I cried—everyone cried. I came home and lay around crying for three days. Nobody could eat."

"Nobody could eat because we had no food," said Aunt. "They rationed rice sometime after you left—all we had was rice mixed with barley and red millet, and impossible to digest. Even later I managed to give Seonil and Seonwu money for the bus and made them box lunches, but only with rice and kimchi. Like wartime. They'd have breakfast and go off to school, with nothing left for us to eat until dinner."

"Yeobo, don't bring up that old business," Uncle said.

"You're telling her sad news, and it made me think of it." She frowned. "He did cry like that when you left, and I was quite alarmed. Three days of weeping and then he stopped. I think some church people came over to calm him down."

"I couldn't get out of bed and couldn't think or do anything. I had raised you from birth to sixteen years, and then I had to let you go."

462

Uncle's eyes filled and overflowed, as did Inja's.

This was what had made him so easy to love—his unreserved, expansive emotions that ran as freely and fully as a spillway in a storm—the very trait that Inja's mother had labeled simplistic, sentimental foolishness. How could two siblings be so opposite? She thought about Miran: how could two non-blood siblings be so similar?

"It's a tragedy—don't think about it, Yeobo, a true tragedy," said Aunt. "Think of it this way—because she went away that time, she's rich and successful and comes back to us like coming back home to her real parents."

"That was a hard time," said Uncle, "and painful to remember." He bowed his head and tugged a handkerchief from his back pocket. "How was it when you landed?"

"Same. I cried all the time and felt bad for my parents that I was crying so much. But I was also angry and helpless. I only wanted to return, and for two years I dreamed every night of coming back." She hadn't meant to say anything that would make him sadder, but his open love demanded confession of all she'd hidden away in hopes those forests of memory and forgetfulness would bury the pain. But it had rooted instead. Her hands were fists of sodden tissues.

"Your mother wrote that she cried because you would not eat, and instead wept all night."

"I think it was harder for her than she could show. She's so different from you in that way, Ajeossi."

"We waited and waited for your letter, and it came about a month after you left. You sent us a picture your father took, and it gave us so much happiness. Ah, but the letter was difficult."

Inja did not want either of them to remember this added pain, but Uncle couldn't help himself, as if now the wound was open and needed to run clear.

"I see you do remember," he said of her streaked cheeks.

"I shouldn't have complained about Mother, but she was treating me like a baby. It made it more difficult for you."

"Here you are all grown up and sitting beside me, but it's like that decision was made this hour." He beat his chest. "Terrible—a terrible thing to never write to you again so you would bond with them. I had to, you see that, don't you?"

"Of course I understand, and you were right. But, Ajeossi, none of this would've happened if I wasn't forced to leave."

"There's no point in thinking that. My sister gave me a great gift, and this is how I know she loves me best. Why else would she take her adopted daughter and leave the blood daughter with me?"

They were both ruined with tears.

"Yeobo, don't think about those things," said Aunt. "Like you say, here she is, come back to us."

"But how could she divide us after sixteen years?" said Inja. "My life was here, and if she gave me to you, then she shouldn't have taken me back—she was only lending, not giving." She was appalled at her disloyalty, but this malice had long festered in the locked drawers of her inner cabinet. Even that impressive bureau full of new clothes couldn't fill its emptiness.

Uncle sat back and massaged his knees, brows knit. "It may sound confusing, but it only further proves the measure of her love, her sacrifice to your grandmother and me, especially if you think about her father."

Aunt sighed. "Always the old stories," and she stood, saying she'd make a broth of the medicine they'd purchased from the herb market for his arthritis.

"What did you say?" said Inja. "Whose father?"

"Miran's father."

"Who's her father?"

"You know—surely I've told you. It's one of the three miracles of my life."

"Tell me again." She curled her legs beneath a straight back, her body winding tight in the face of a new vista of information she hadn't ever considered.

"About the miracles? Come to think of it, maybe I never told you because you were a child."

"You might've told me, but I was too young to know they were miracles."

"This was after the war ended—not the last one, the war with the Japanese."

"Before I was born."

"Yes. Your father was here, but he was often away with the big general, going all around the country. He came home some weekends—the trains were terrible then, crowded and always late or breaking down, they were so ancient."

Inja had heard the story of Miran's birth from Uncle, Grandmother, and her mother. Once she had arrived in America, Najin also described those postwar months with her father being away for extended periods of time. She had said it was one of the reasons he was endlessly patient with Miran—he felt guilty. Inja had not disagreed but believed it was simply his nature to be endlessly patient.

"A young widow was living nearby," and he explained that under Japanese rule, the city was organized into precincts and sectors for rallies and rationing as a way to monitor each neighborhood for proper behavior and quotas for metal, rubber, and paper drives. "She was vulnerable, being young and a widow, so they made her a block leader. The Japanese head of all the blocks in that sector was called a *tongjang*. The tongjang would go in and out of the widow's house for any number of reasons. At some point they had sex, and she became pregnant."

Images of Miran's features raced behind Inja's eyes—her fingernails, slim body shape, and the strong texture of her hair—all features she had carefully avoided pointing out as different than hers. She now envisioned those features as belonging to Miran's unnamed mother, the lips silent, the eyes empty beneath the faceless tongjang. "She was raped."

"Probably. It's bad enough for a widow to be pregnant, but being pregnant by a Japanese was the worst possible stigma, no matter how it happened. She took all kinds of pills to abort the baby, but everything failed. Somehow she heard about your mother, and when the baby was due, she found our house. She was too ashamed to give birth in a hospital or with a midwife in her own district. After the birth, she ran away. Nobody wanted another baby, especially not a Japanese baby, but your mother kept the baby, even without asking your father."

"Dear God."

"He felt guilty about leaving her in postwar hardship."

"Not about that—you've told me about that—about Miran's father."

"I have his name somewhere in my desk. The

mother did at least name the father, and I learned from her neighbors he was the tongjang. I lost that paper some time ago."

Avenues of possibility in Inja's mind opened for Miran's sake. Should she ask Uncle to find that name? What if that man was alive? What would happen if—

He tilted his head. "I see what you're thinking. No need to tell her. It would only bring heartache."

Aunt came in with his broth, switched the ceiling light on as the day was waning, and went to check on the others. Inja tuned in to the bedroom and heard Seonmi say to Aunt, "It's not an egg—it's clay but stretchier, look!"

"Ajeossi, your three miracles," she prompted. "I know the first one: how Miran almost died and came back to life."

"You know about that then."

"I heard it from everyone." She was having trouble concentrating, like her mind was that stretchier clay, in flux to learn about Miran's blood father.

"A dreadful, horrific time. Her eyes rolled up, she foamed in the mouth, and there was no pulse. I was so distressed and grief-stricken, I held the baby tight, weeping from my deepest soul. Then I heard a tiny bird-like sound, and the baby started to breathe."

"You never told me that part!"

"Your mother did most of the work. Still, this was my first miracle."

"How could you and my mother accept this baby, especially since the Japanese had imprisoned her?" Grandmother's portrait caught her eye. "I'm thinking about Halmeoni's feet, too, though Mother still doesn't know about that."

"It didn't matter."

"Mother won't even buy anything Japanese at home."

"None of that mattered, it was just a baby."

"How did you know?"

"What do you mean? Everyone knew about the widow."

Not everyone. "My grandparents? Mother knew? Father?"

"Everyone knew," he said, sipping broth.

Inja let this revelation settle and put her altruism away. Here was another reason for Miran to never know she was adopted. It was odd that she'd never thought about Miran's father before, but wartime, the distance of time, and the separating ocean left questions one never thought to ask, as if the secrets had draped themselves in heavy cloaks. Come no further, the secrets say, our very existence requires opacity.

Inja was glad that it had never occurred to Miran to calculate the date of her conception against their family's history. Even if she had, Miran didn't know that their father had been reunited with their mother just three months before she was born. She'd had no suspicion and thus no need to calculate. The cloaks were purposeful—self-protective and embracing.

"Yah, this broth is delicious. I feel stronger already," said Uncle, unable to fully mask his "ugh" expression. Protective.

"You don't need more than a sip," Inja said, and took it from him. "I'm not sure what to think about that story, Ajeossi."

Miran called from the bedroom, "Inja, how do you say 'comics'?" She wanted to show them how to transfer images onto Silly Putty.

"They probably don't have any—why don't you ask Aunt for newspaper?"

"Ajumeoni, *sinmuni isseumnikka*?" said Miran.

"Great!" Inja called amongst the giggles of delight from the other room. This could be another miracle—Korean words did indeed flow from Miran's American mouth, no matter how awkward or childish or incorrect. Those sounds that had always been a part of her had found an inner wind to carry them forth.

She turned back to Uncle. "The other two miracles?"

He opened his hands. "The second miracle was you, of course. That your mother would leave her firstborn with me and take the adopted daughter to America instead. It's why I know she loves me the most."

This time his declaration made her smile.

"You were there for the third miracle, but too young to remember."

Distracted, she parked away the question of Miran's father for later. "During the war? The Korean War?"

"Earlier. One night you had a high fever. In those days, babies—you were still a baby—got sick without cause and they would die. Your mother and I were spoiled by our parents for this very reason—your grandmother had six who died before us, so we were especially precious to them."

"Six! Does my mother know about those babies?"

"They weren't all babies; one reached age seven."

"Such suffering!" Her mother had told her many stories about Grandmother but had never mentioned these tragedies. Since Grandmother had successfully cloaked the fact of her frostbite, she had the capacity to hide this enormous loss from her mother as well.

"I'll show you the family register; that's how I know, but I'm not sure if your mother knows. No reason not to tell her."

"So tragic. Poor Halmeoni!"

"That's how life was those days. Hard life. But there you were—my sister had given me her true firstborn child, and you had a scalding fever. I was so afraid to lose you—how could I lose you after she'd put you in my care?"

"How old was I?"

He thought a moment. "Maybe fourteen months, the first winter after they left. What could I do? Every second your fever got worse. I raised you high up in my arms and prayed from the deepest part of my soul that you would get better, and I wept and wept, praying. Not long after that your fever went down, and everything was fine as if you'd never been sick. You never got sick like that again. That's the third miracle, praise God." He beamed with love, and Inja leaned to press her cheek to his.

"You saved both of your sister's children."

"Not me, God."

"In your hands, though," she said, taking his in hers. "Did you ever tell my mother about that?"

"I might have written to her, but she often scolded me for writing sentimental things, so I may not have. 'Wasting paper' she always said." His smile was mischievous. "I probably didn't. I wouldn't want to frighten her or make her think I couldn't take care of you."

"Ajeossi, I'm only grateful. I don't have words enough."

"Let's not have any more crying tonight, eh?"

They embraced, cleaned their faces, and went to his room. Inja scanned his desk, as if the lost paper with the tongjang's name would jump out at her. From a chest against the wall, Uncle dug out the family register, a worn thick book with a hand-sewn spine, which absurdly reminded her of her childhood Bible storybook, though it opened from the back. She had forgotten most of the Chinese characters she'd learned in middle school so could read only the numerals, but the more recent pages were in both Chinese and Hangul. The precise and elegant letterforms struck her as being the work of not only her talented uncle, but her grandfather, his father, his father's father, and on back. In itself a master-piece of calligraphy, the genealogy in its mulberry and silk-fiber pages was a stunning family chronicle.

Inja would not tell her mother all of Grand-mother's secrets, but she felt sure she'd want to know the names of the siblings who had preceded her. Learning about Miran and listening to Uncle's declarations of undying faith in his sister's love once again changed the direction of Inja's understanding and attitude toward her mother. She appreciated that growth in her knowledge of family had fostered the growth of her love for her mother as well. "Could you copy that page for me to show her?"

Uncle sat at his desk right away and inked a copy for his sister in his enduring script: the names of Inja's grandfather and grandmother, and four girls and two boys who were her mother's older siblings, and the dates of their births and deaths.

The remainder of the evening was less emotional, except for Miran and the two young cousins, who all cried in saying their goodbyes.

Their footsteps fell in unison on the quiet walk back to the inn. Inja's mind was full with Miran's parentage, but she diverted these thoughts by asking how the evening with the cousins went. At the inn, they prepared for bed in a well-worn pattern of sisterly consideration, then Miran sighed and said, "I'm going to miss those girls," and was soon asleep. Inja stared at the cathedral of shadows on the ceiling, thinking about Grandmother's losses. It seemed too devastating a tragedy, even to the extent that she wouldn't tell her own daughter about the six siblings before her who had died, and it gave Inja pause to consider Grandmother's immense strength. As a keeper of secrets and a teller of lies, Inja knew that not everything needed to be exposed, but what was right for Miran?

39

The Charity of Secrets

High above a soothing sea of clouds, the sisters flew across the Pacific. "How was it with Uncle last night?" Miran said.

"Sad to remember things, and wonderful to feel his love again."

"Damn, that word comes out of your mouth with such ease."

"And you, too."

"What? Oh, the swearing. Don't go all Mom on me now."

"I'm kidding. You were great. I don't think you swore once even at the inn with just me."

"Something shifted, like I'd grown antennae tuned to the Korean station. My tongue got loosened somehow." She laughed and flipped her braid at Inja. "But I guess as soon as we got out of Korean airspace that radio ran out of batteries." Miran closed her science fiction book, *The Farthest Shore*.

Inja wanted to give her something to unite her with a culture where it was common for parents to never say *I love you*. She wanted to give her a story that could demonstrate how the most precious commodities of love could be those that remained unspoken. She turned to her and said, "Being in that house and the yard with the willows reminded me about something I want to tell you." She told her the secret of Halmeoni's feet—of how the winter that Halmeoni had carried food in the snow and ice to their imprisoned mother had forever damaged her feet—and she knew Miran would keep this from their parents, their mother, as easily as she had, out of a love whose unlimited reach she would no longer think to measure.

Miran was thoughtful a long while, then riffled the pages of her book. "I didn't even know we had secrets until you told me we did, and every time another one pops up, I look at Mom differently. I see more of her, because I see more of where she came from."

Inja agreed. She also kept to herself her great regret that Miran never knew their steadfast grandmother. They had come from a long line of holding back, suppressing hurtful truths to clear the passageway of old burdens. And to the extent Grandmother could—even across the dividing ocean, as her mother had with the packages—she worked to line that passageway only with devotion. Grandmother never once mentioned her six lost children to Inja. And perhaps there were other secrets held by Grandmother's own mother, shrouded by necessity, and unknown yet intuited, from whom this pattern had derived to become a habit. It had become a way to live in the accumulation of a difficult family history, a way that was a profound expression of love.

"It changes how I look at myself, too," Miran said. "Based on how easily I reverted to swearing, the language affinity isn't going to last much longer." She smiled. "But everything I saw, smelled, everything I heard, and meeting our relatives—our sweet uncle who was your father for all those years, our adorable cousins—it fills a side where there used to be a vacuum." Her eyes held a clarity that smoothed her features. "Now Mom's not alone on that side where there was only the unknown. I was resentful of that unknown, but that vacuum is filling, and I don't see it as being one side or another that I have to choose."

"Exactly." Inja touched her arm. Their mother had made a choice to love an unwanted, abandoned baby. And in an act of love for Grandmother, she'd made a choice between two daughters, to bring the adopted one with them to America. It had engendered fifteen years of her parents' guilt, regret, and pain that was mentioned only once—that night of the blizzard. Her father never spoke of it. Perhaps in those years, her mother looked at Miran and saw only the consequences of her choice, and it had tainted the love between them. This choice had been forced on Inja herself, and the resulting reunion had caused grief and unending yearning, which, as proven by this trip, would always be a part of her. Just as Miran now understood she didn't have to choose between two cultures, there was no need for Inja to choose between her two families. She could never repair what was lost, but she could celebrate what was gained in the middle ground.

She said to Miran, "Perfectly phrased," and their eyes caught in a radiance of kinship.

Miran opened her book, and Inja turned her gaze to the window. Upon arrival in Seoul, after they had landed and were packed into the car with Uncle and Seonil, Elder Hwang had observed how much the same yet how different the sisters were—how different Miran was. She exuded a foreignness that went beyond her physical differences with Inja. Her features were Asian but lacked the subtle markings of Korean homogeneity in the way that Inja knew she was home the moment they stepped into the airport's busy customs area. She felt the same a little later among people crowding the airport and out on the streets—an indescribable sensibility of *Korean* not only embodied in language and sound, but in how one smiled, a mere turn of the shoulders, a particular sweep of wrist and hand, a sense of dignity, space, and carriage. Having been away and freshly returned, she could see in the sea of strangers how their entire sense of being, beyond the physical similarities, expressed a shared history and culture that was comforting—and simultaneously uncomfortable. She knew the discomfort came from having spent ten years in a nation where independence and individuality were prized, a country that invented such phrases as *personal space, do your own thing, let it all hang out,* and *it's who I am.*

The comfort of being home, her Korean home, came from fulfilling the drive to belong. But this drive also heightened the pain of division when a single small thing marked one as different, such as Inja having a mother but not having a mother; for Uncle, having her as a daughter who was not his daughter; for Miran, being Korean yet not being Korean; and for her parents, having the eldest who was not the firstborn blood child. No matter how enviable it may have been to have had a mother in America, Inja had been singled out when war had already made threadbare the things that bound the Korean people in common. Perhaps it was her legacy, but Miran had always treaded between belonging and not belonging, and it had destroyed her sense of comfort, denied her the surety of belonging and its gifts of pride and loyalty.

Inja had regarded her first months in America as being ripped from comfort, torn from the powerful homogeneity of the Korean people born of their long history and core traditions, a history and tradition preserved and adapted over centuries to reinforce itself. One of the reasons Najin had treated her as a baby when she first arrived was her mother's instinct of protection, having known how disorienting a transition it was—and one she herself had sacrificed in order to preserve her Koreanness for when Inja would be reunited with her. In recalling her first car ride in America, Inja had taken note of her father's careless and effortless switching from English to Korean and back again, as being the habit of an integrated man who successfully straddled the line, and one she'd sworn to—and did—achieve, at least in language.

Bands of orange and cobalt met at the gilded horizon of high altitude, a vista that had greeted her now three times on passages across the Pacific. The cold cabin air chilled her neck, and the pain of her first flight from Korea resurfaced. She would always have that pain no matter where inside she tried to hide it, just as her mother would always have her own scars from the decision she made that caused their years of separation, even after their reunion. But Inja had learned the charity of secrets. Grandmother's refusal to divulge the cause of her frostbite was the example she had tried to follow in hiding her misery—though she wasn't entirely successful—upon arriving in America. Her father never once expressed the grief of not knowing what had happened to his parents. And who knows what untold secrets lay between her mother and Grandfather, and her uncle and Grandfather, that had led to their sharing the dream from his grave? Above all, it would be charity to safeguard Miran from the secrets strewn behind her.

With her sister close by in proximity and heart, Inja examined the deepest recesses of her mind and soul, and confirmed her instinct that truth was not always the sole path to compassion, the way to redress criminal wrongs. For now, she would not tell Miran the secrets of her birth. But she had learned from this trip that change happens with the slip of a word—Uncle's mention of Miran's father—and one's view of the past and future were mutable. She didn't have to decide what should be secreted forever; she could be open to whatever was ahead in their sisterhood.

Uncle had altered the story of Najin's departure from Inja into an act of supreme love, and it had taught her the need to attest and affirm rather than to criticize. Najin, too, had altered the story of the widow's abandonment of Miran as one that expressed a final act of a mother's love for the betterment of her child. Inja and Miran had grown to encompass this love even as their histories were revised with the last secret revealed. The cycle of secrets and growth would expand every time Inja flew across the separating ocean to give back the love she'd been given on each farthest shore.

Miran's dozing head grazed Inja's shoulder. She shifted so the concave of Miran's neck and chin would rest against the convex curve of her shoulder. Outside the red and purple sky faded into night, and the cabin lights dimmed. In time, she would once again sit at her mother's kitchen table to hear her stories. She would join her father in his passion for space missions, rejoicing with him in the discoveries of their expanding universe. She would, in silence but through her actions, embrace her role as the eldest daughter for her parents, her uncle, aunt and cousins, her sister, for all her family.

Author's Note

When I was very young, my family gave presentations at civic clubs and to church groups to educate Americans about a little-known war, in a small unknown country, that lasted from 1950 to 1953. The presentations were intended to raise funds and receive clothing donations for refugees—and for our own family members in Korea who survived those years of carnage. Five of us children, from ages one to nine, wore Korean dress, sang Korean nursery songs, and displayed Korean dolls, baskets, and lacquer boxes. Another child remained in Korea, cared for by my maternal grandparents and uncle. My bilingual father, Jacob Siungtuk Kim, pointed to a big map and described the invasion by the communist North Korean People's Army—supported by the Russians—into democratic South Korea, supported by the United States and the young United Nations.

For many years afterward, I helped my mother, Alice Hahn Haekyung Kim, ship packages to Korea, filled with donated clothing and simple necessities made scarce by war: soap, toothbrushes and toothpaste, chicken bouillon, powdered milk, baby powder, fabric, pencils and paper, and luxuries such as hairpins, raisins, canned pineapple, DDT insect spray, air freshener, candy. Sitting on the floor surrounded by goods going to Korea, I slid gummed tape over a wet sponge in a saucer to seal the brown-paper-wrapped packages and pressed down on the twine for my mother to knot it tight.

About fifty years later, I found my father's tattered maps and my mother's diaries, where she listed everything she sent overseas. I knew my parents had come to America in 1948—two years before the North Korean invasion—but it was only while researching this novel that I fully understood my father's role in the American occupation of South Korea prior to the Korean War.

The origins of the Korean War occurred long before the conflict flamed to life on June 26, 1950. In 1910, after decades of political and military maneuverings, Korea was annexed by Japan until 1945. The unwelcome colonization grew harsher as Japan invaded Manchuria, China, then several countries in the Pacific Islands during World War II.

In 1936 my father had managed to depart from Japanese-occupied Korea to attend an American seminary, while my mother, newly married, planned to follow him in a few months to study obstetrics, once her papers were secured. But soon after my father left Korea, Japan closed its borders to and from the West, and my mother was stranded without her husband for what would become nine years. After the December 7, 1941, attack on Pearl Harbor and America's entry into World War II, my mother was imprisoned for ninety days by the Japanese, because her husband in America was suspected of being a spy. He would not learn of her suffering until they were reunited.

By 1943 America's involvement in World War II had helped to turn the tide against the Axis forces, and the Allied powers began to discuss the final settlement of the war, including the war in the Pacific. Around this period, my father worked in America for the OSS, the U.S. military intelligence services and precursor to the CIA, as a translator of Japanese, Korean, and written Chinese. The "Korea problem" was first discussed in depth at the Cairo Conference, November 22–26, 1943, attended by President Franklin D. Roosevelt, Prime Minister Winston Churchill of Britain, and Generalissimo Chiang Kai-shek of Nationalist China. These leaders declared that Japan would be stripped of all lands "which she has seized or occupied since the beginning of the first World War in 1914," including those stolen from the Chinese, and "all other territories which she has taken by violence and greed. The aforesaid three great powers, mindful of the enslavement of the people of

Korea, are determined that in due course Korea shall become free and independent." The sticking point for ultimate Korean independence was "in due course."

At subsequent summit conferences, Communist Party General Secretary Joseph Stalin of the Soviet Union joined Roosevelt (followed by Truman) and Churchill to consider possible Soviet involvement in the Pacific theater. Stalin agreed to the principles of the Cairo Declaration on the "Korea problem," and, following other negotiations, the partitioning of Korea at the thirty-eighth parallel was determined at the Potsdam Conference, July 17–August 2, 1945. The decision to draw the line at that latitude rose from the American belief that they could not militarily cover the entire peninsula of Korea, while Russia could easily advance from northern positions in Manchuria and China. By then it was inevitable that the Japanese would be defeated, though it was still a matter of when. This summit yielded an ultimatum to the empire of Japan that it would face "prompt and utter destruction" if it would not surrender. Japan refused the ultimatum, and President Truman dropped the first atomic bomb on Hiroshima on August 6. Russia entered into war with Japan on August 8 and, as outlined in the Potsdam Declaration, moved troops into the northern half of the Korean peninsula above the thirty-eighth parallel.

The substantial threat of Russian Allied involve-ment against the Japanese and the second atomic bomb at Nagasaki on August 9 prompted Japanese emperor Hirohito's unconditional sur-render on August 15, 1945. My father recalled he was with a few Korean colleagues in New York City when he heard this announcement on the radio, and everyone wept. My mother recalled seeing American B-29s flying in clear skies above Seoul. "Sweet silver birds," she called them, dropping leaflets that declared the liberation of Korea from Japanese rule.

My father was determined to return to his homeland to find his wife and joined the U.S. Army as a translator, given the rank of civilian field officer. Though the first U.S. forces landed on September 8 in the southern half of the Korean peninsula, the army's circuitous route for my father's transport got him to Korea sometime in October. The day he landed at Gimpo Airport, he was reunited through mirac-ulous coincidences with my mother in Seoul. My father was translator for General John R. Hodge, who led the American occupation of South Korea. General Hodge knew nothing about Korea and was hostile to communism. As such, he was unwilling to cooperate with Russia as originally outlined in the Potsdam Declaration. Both the American and Soviet "trusteeships" were intended to relieve the nation of thirty-five years of Japanese colonization, but the radically opposing ideologies of occupied North and South Korea came to exemplify the divisions of the burgeoning Cold War.

During the first five years of postwar reconstruction in Korea, tensions increased between the United States and USSR, along with communist China. The young United Nations, under control of the United States, focused on creating a democratic independent state in South Korea, while Stalin worked to stabilize Chinese-communist versus Soviet-communist factionalism in North Korea.

In May 1948, South Korea established the democratic Republic of Korea (ROK), and presidential elections resulted in a new constitution intended for all of Korea. The U.S.-favored presidential candidate, Syngman Rhee, who was a staunch proponent of total unification, was elected. My father's post with the military ended, and in June he and my mother, with two of their three children in tow, traveled by ship to America. They planned to stay about two years and had left the middle child behind, both as a guarantee to my maternal grandmother they'd return, and because traveling with three children was arduous. The eldest at three was old enough to know if she were to be left behind, the youngest was a newborn boy, so the middle daughter, who was one and could be weaned, was left with her grandparents and her uncle and his wife.

A month later in July, North Korea instituted the communist Democratic People's Republic of Korea (DPRK) under the leadership of anti-Japanese guerrilla hero Kim Il-Sung, who was favored by Stalin. The thirty-eighth parallel border between North and South Korea became more intractable proportionate to the increasing postwar ideological differences between the super-powers and their battle to attain supremacy in nuclear arms.

In North Korea from 1948 to 1950, factionalism and non-communists were quashed. Meanwhile, a number of bloody leftist uprisings in South Korea led Stalin to believe that further agitation south of the parallel could be encouraged and that unification under the DPRK could be achieved. Also, Truman was unwilling to commit to long-term military support of South Korea for fear that Rhee would employ those troops north-ward toward ROK unification. The ROK military remained dependent on the United States and were seen as weak and vulnerable. The charis-matic General Douglas MacArthur, who was the Supreme Commander for the Allied Powers stationed in Japan, and the British Foreign Office both stated that they believed the whole of Korea would be communist-controlled in a decade's time.

All U.S. military personnel had left Korea

by June 1949. By the first half of 1950, DPRK troops numbered 150,000–180,000 men, with 150 Soviet tanks and heavy artillery, and about 150 aircraft. The ROK army consisted of eight combat divisions of about 65,000 men, light artillery, some small sea craft, and no tanks, fighters, or bombers. Communist leaders took these numbers, along with earlier indicators of sympathy to the communist cause, to mean the time was ripe for their own unification of the Korean peninsula.

My mother had her fourth child, a girl, in July 1949 in Los Angeles. Because of their two-year plan, my parents didn't return to Korea, and they also likely didn't travel due to their growing family and the cost.

At four a.m. on Sunday, June 25, 1950, in drizzle and heavy fog, about 90,000 Soviet-trained North Korean troops invaded South Korea at several locations across the thirty-eighth parallel, surprising the ROK forces, many of whom were on leave.

My father got a job as translator and broadcaster with the new Voice of America radio's Korean service, then based in New York City, and my parents and their three children moved from Los Angeles to New York, where, during the three years of the Korean War, two more girls were born, including myself, the last of six. Though I helped send packages to my sister and Korean family in Seoul, I wasn't truly aware that I had another sister until many years after the war when she was finally able to be brought to America at age eleven, when I was five. It seemed a large family could easily absorb one more, and it was only much later in adulthood that I asked my sister how it was for her to be taken from her Korean family to be "reunited" with an American family, who were all utter strangers, in a country that was equally foreign to her.

This novel is a fiction derived from the facts of my family's life, and especially my sister's life, during and after the Korean War, the fifth deadliest war in human history, also known as "the forgotten war."

Acknowledgments

Thanks foremost to my sister Sun Kim, whose life inspired this story, and who inspires me still. Thanks also to her husband, Kee Lee, who helped vet the Korean elements of this novel.

My gratitude for the detailed work on this manuscript to Helen Atsma, editor extraordinaire, and Judith Weber, amazing agent. To the incredible team of individuals who helped bring this book to fruition, thank you.

Many remote locations were required along the way, and I give thanks to Phyllis Freedman and Tom Glass for sojourns at Woodlawn, and to Susan and Michael Gordon for the Bethany House. Thank you to Hedgebrook, Eastern Frontier Foundation, Ox-Bow School of Art, and for the following: Stanford Calderwood Fellowship at MacDowell Colony, Eli Cantor Fellowship at Corporation of Yaddo, Mid-Atlantic Arts Foundation Creative Fellowship at Millay Colony for the Arts, and a pivotal fellowship at I-Park Foundation.

Thank you, Paul and Robbie Hertneky, discerning readers and friends. Special thanks to Di Nicholas, and much gratitude to friends and family, especially Brian, Van, Jeff, and Henry, for constant support and love.

About the Author

Eugenia Kim's debut novel, *The Callig- rapher's Daughter*, won the 2009 Borders Original Voices Award, was shortlisted for the Dayton Literary Peace Prize, and was a 2009 Best Historical Novel and Critic's Pick by the *Washington Post*. Her work has appeared in *Asia Literary Review*, *Raven Chronicles*, and elsewhere. She is a DC Council on the Arts and Humanities Fellowship recipient. A Bennington College MFA graduate, Kim teaches at Fairfield University's MFA Creative Writing Program. She lives in Washington, DC.

| Books are produced in the United States using U.S.-based materials | Books are printed using a revolutionary new process called THINKtech™ that lowers energy usage by 70% and increases overall quality | Books are durable and flexible because of Smyth-sewing | Paper is sourced using environmentally responsible foresting methods and the paper is acid-free |

Center Point Large Print
600 Brooks Road / PO Box 1
Thorndike, ME 04986-0001 USA

(207) 568-3717

US & Canada:
1 800 929-9108
www.centerpointlargeprint.com

6-19